BONDED

CHRONICLES OF CILICIA
BOOK ONE

ALARA THORN

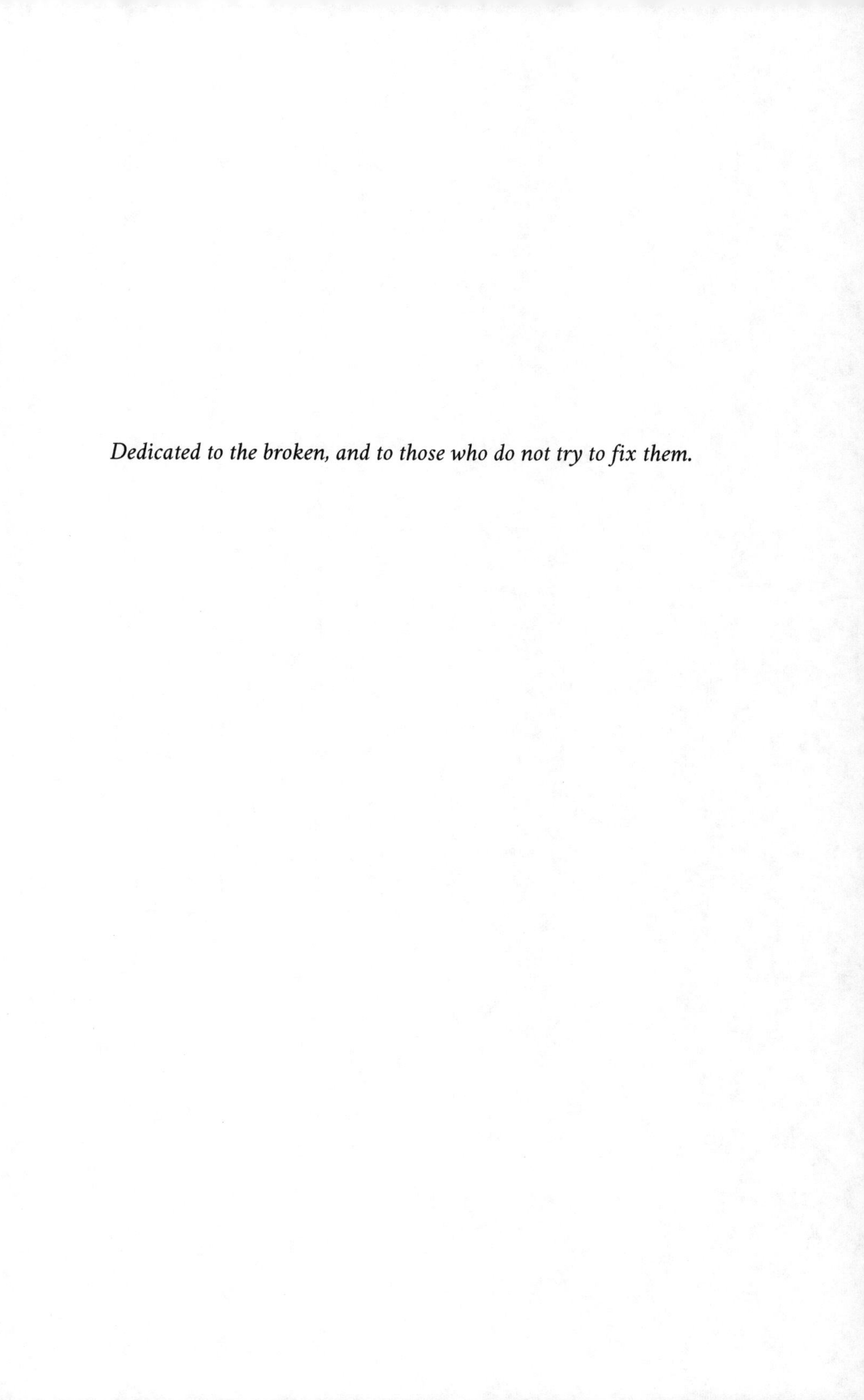

Dedicated to the broken, and to those who do not try to fix them.

TRIGGER WARNINGS

Gore and violence; mention of infant and pregnancy loss; death, including the death of a parent and of a young child; implied sexual assault of a minor; child abuse; adult content, including swearing, the consumption of alcohol, and several descriptive sex scenes between consenting adults.

Dedicated to the broken, and to those who do not try to fix them.

ALDRUIL
BERIDIAN SEA
CAPITAL
URANDUN
EDITHIEL MOUNTAINS
VALIO
NAVARRE
ELRUNE
YOREL
TARRIN
LITERRA
VITALIS
KINGDOM OF CILICIA

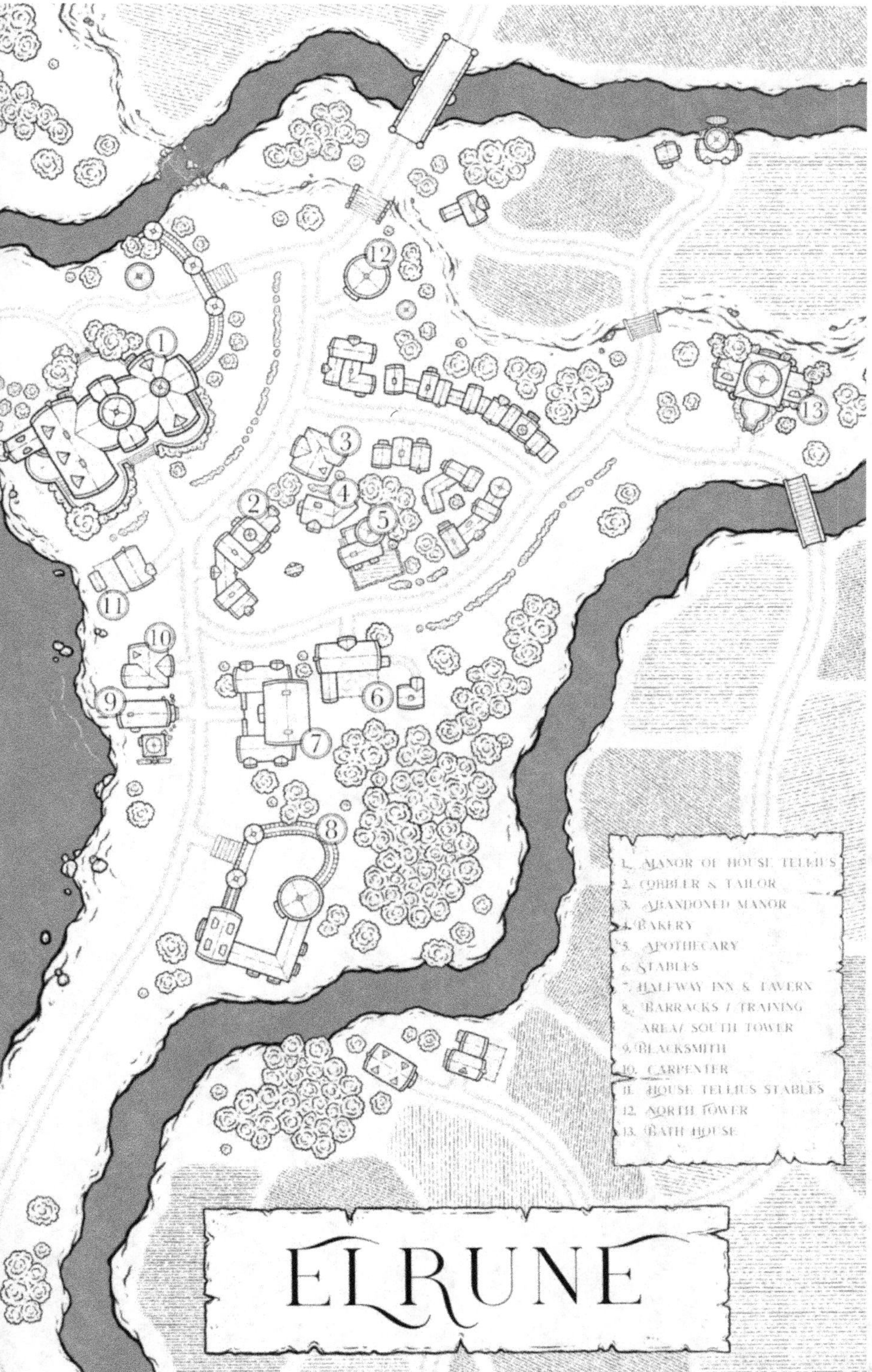

1. MANOR OF HOUSE TELLIUS
2. COBBLER & TAILOR
3. ABANDONED MANOR
4. BAKERY
5. APOTHECARY
6. STABLES
7. HALFWAY INN & TAVERN
8. BARRACKS / TRAINING AREA/ SOUTH TOWER
9. BLACKSMITH
10. CARPENTER
11. HOUSE TELLIUS STABLES
12. NORTH TOWER
13. BATH HOUSE
ELRUNE

1

NEIRIN

EYES OF PERIDOT GLEAMED, their facets reflecting the early dawn light. The pale green stones contrasted with the milky white statue in which they were embedded. But beyond their beauty, the gems held meaning.

The peridot symbolized rest and was often set in the monuments of wealthier lords and ladies when they passed. People believed the stone would ease a soul and help it find quietude in its endless sleep. The gem was a token of harmony between mind, body, and soul.

I let out a breath, considering. Each time I came to Mother's grave, the stones drew me in, yet their very existence contradicted all I was taught to believe, all I'd seen with my own eyes. As a man of the castle guard, I'd witnessed countless deaths, taken lives with my own blade. Though time had hazed the men's features, I could never forget the void in their eyes as their last breaths left them. No, there was no continual sleep. No afterlife to be perturbed by one's conscience or regrets. Death was finite, and the weight people put in beliefs of stones and legends was all folly.

Kneeling before the marble statue, I settled into the still-

"

ness of the quiet wood and fought to clear my mind. I filled my lungs with the brisk morning air, and when I exhaled, a cloud of mist formed, drawing my attention to the cold. Even in the depth of winter, I rarely noticed the temperature. Another mystery I'd long since stopped searching for answers to.

I breathed into my hands, paying attention this time to the contrast of warmth and the dampness on my nose. I returned my focus to the monument, and as I did, chided myself for visiting each year on the anniversary of Mother's death, even as I denied belief in an afterlife. Why did I come?

The statue stood amid a patch of pale, cream-colored flowers that bloomed year-round. When the wind caught, the younger, unopened buds danced, reminiscent of little bells. The monument itself was made of marble, a rare stone imported from the western lands. Expensive.

The figure carved into the shape of a fox sat with its back sloped between its shoulder blades and its chest puffed out. The tail swept across its back haunches, and its two front legs ended in intricately sculpted paws. The animal's head was raised slightly as if looking up to the sky, and both of its tipped ears were perked.

My chest ached with dull longing as memories washed over me. At five, I'd wept before the monument. At seven, I'd begged for answers. At three and twenty, I was wise enough to know asking anything of stone was futile. Yet still, I came. Still, I gazed into the riveted eyes as if they could give me some kind of guidance. I gritted my teeth, irritation prickling.

Heavy steps and the noisy disturbance of a branch drew my attention. My hand went to my waist instinctually, grasping for the familiar, worn leather hilt of my guard's sword. When my fingers found only air, they curled into an empty fist, and I hardened my jaw. I'd left the damn thing in my quarters. But this was the King's woods, heavily fortressed and guarded. Only one man aside from myself entered this quiet sanctuary, and he was no threat to me.

Brambles snapped, accompanied this time by a slur of curses. It was barely past daybreak, and already he was drunk. Not surprising, though, for what this day meant to him. What it meant to us both. I kept my attention on the statue as the King knelt beside me with all the grace of a new foal learning to walk. His head tipped, and from waves of umber hair his crown fell to the dirt.

"Damn thing." He reached again, fingers grazing the air, but he fell short.

I let out a snort of annoyance, uncaring if it was disrespectful. Though the man was often seen with a goblet of wine in one hand, he was rarely out of control. It was pitiful and disgraceful. In truth, I had no right to judge. By night's end I would likely drink twice his intake, yet I would not waver as he did. Like the cold, alcohol affected me differently than it did others.

On his second attempt, the King's searching fingers found their mark, and he adjusted the crown back on his head. We knelt in considerate silence for some time. Around us a breeze blew in, sending stray strands of silver hair in front of my eyes and rustling the quivering leaves of the aspens, their song akin to a passing shower of rain.

"Your mother loved that sound," the King said in a breath.

My heart twisted even as bitterness rose in my throat. He *so* rarely spoke about Mother.

"When she …" His words faltered. "When she passed, I buried her here amid the aspens so she could listen to them in her endless sleep. Shortly after, the blooms sprouted." He nodded to the delicate cream flowers, the feather-like tendrils at their bases fluttering on the breeze as they swayed. "As if in remembrance of her."

The King adjusted his crown resting haphazardly atop his mop of unkempt hair. Breaking my gaze from the statue to address him, I furrowed my brows, taking in the extent of his disorderliness. He was something to be seen, truly.

He wore dark breeches with laces left untied about his calves. His boots appeared to be on the wrong feet, likely accounting for his difficulties walking. About his right bicep he wore a decorative leather armlet with metal embellishments, something fit for formal wear. Yet his wrinkled long-sleeved top was nothing more than a nightshirt. Whether it was the alcohol that kept his blood warm or simply his numbness to life I couldn't be certain, but he did not shiver despite his lack of cloak or robe.

"You're a mess," I told him bluntly.

The King narrowed his eyes. With a blank expression, I met his gaze, unwavering. His title meant nothing here in the woods, and his face provided me with a looking glass to see twenty years into my future. We shared the same strong jawline, straight nose, and angled features, though the shadowing of his short beard marred some of our resemblance. Of course, the pale silver sheen of my hair set us apart as well, as did its style. My hair curled as his did, but I'd left mine long and braided back in sections, decimating the natural curl with the weight of length and braid.

Though he was a decent ruler and I honored his knowledge of our lands, the view I held of him was tainted. He made fair and thoughtful choices for the people of Cilicia, but he was detached from relationships and an inadequate father to the prince. He meant nothing more to me than what we shared once a year before Mother's grave.

His brows smoothed, and his expression softened as his eyes lowered. "What happened?"

Noting his gaze, I pulled at my tunic's dipped collar and traced my thumb over the angry, raised tissue that started at my collarbone. A slight flare of pain tingled at my touch, oddly grounding.

"Our carriage was ambushed," I replied flatly, not wanting to go into details about the attack after spending the night prior under the scrutiny and questioning of Rion, the commander of the castle guard, when we'd arrived later than expected.

The King's eyes widened. He hadn't heard, then. Likely, the commander was simply keeping quiet about things he thought the King didn't need to burden his mind with. "Lord Emeric? His daughter, Clara?"

"They are fine," I reassured him, knowing his concerns lay both in the notable silk import Lord Emeric's estate provided and the arrangements for Lady Clara's betrothal to my half-brother. I doubted the King held any care for Lord Emeric himself—a drawn and bitter man. "A few bandits. I handled it."

The King exhaled a breath of relief. "How many were there?"

Though shame tugged, I fought the instinct to look away. The east road from Urandun—so rarely traveled by anyone who might catch the eye of thieves—was considered a safe route. Yet the more often staged pass through the Edthiel Mountains would be too thick with wagons traveling to the upcoming festival to ambush successfully. With wealthy merchants heading to the capital from all regions of Cilicia, I should have suspected trouble would branch out.

"Five," I said. At first I'd only seen four. Distracted by the flood of emotions that always plagued me upon returning to the castle after a short time away, I'd let my guard down. It was my stallion—a sturdy, well-trained mount—who had detected the threat first and alerted me with nervous snorts—even outnumbered, the first three thieves fell easily, life ebbing from their eyes each the same hollow way. But as I turned my focus on the fourth at my side, I'd left my chest defenseless. A fifth man had leapt out from the brush, taking advantage of my weak spot. The fact that a thief had got the better of me—I swallowed hard, forcing down the scorn, the shame of it.

The King's eyes hazed as he turned back to the statue, and

for a moment, quiet enveloped us again. Yet there was a firm-ness in the set of his jaw that told me he wanted to say some-thing more. Fingers tapped on his thigh, lacking any semblance of rhythm or purpose. He was holding something back, but he was drunk, and that made him loose-lipped.

"Speak your mind," I pressed.

A muscle twitched at his jaw and his fingers stilled.

"That wound," he said, not meeting my eyes. "Are you like her—like your mother?"

And there it was. In three and twenty years, he'd not once asked if I was a shifter like my mother. Not *once*. Berating myself for pushing the subject, I turned my gaze back to the marble fox before us.

It shimmered as light hit its chest. Had Mother's fox been white like the statue? Or, like my own fox's form, had she been mottled shades of silver, gray, and black? The King's line of questioning suggested he knew of her healing abilities. His consideration was reasonable, for though the slash struck too high across my chest to gut me, the blood loss alone would have killed a mere human.

Had Mother's fox been a monster like my own? I pondered the question, comfortable amid the unsaid words that drew the King back to his uneasy tapping. Surely a King would not have fallen for her had she been any semblance of the nightmare I saw each time I caught my own reflection. No—whatever she was, I was nothing like my mother.

Perhaps it was rude of me not to give an answer, but it was better he didn't know. And it was none of his damn business anyway. It was too late for him to care, and he didn't. He was only curious and drunk.

The King stilled in one anxious habit and turned to another, spinning a black band on his index finger. After a moment he removed it, sighed heavily, and held it up to a sidelong ray of light. "Your mother gave me this," he said, holding it out. I hesitated, then shook my head.

"You should have it." He leaned forward, insistent, and nearly lost his balance. As he reached out to steady himself, the sleeve of his shirt pulled up revealing a band of intricate black design that wrapped his wrist. A tattoo. An unexpected risk—it was well known the chance of disease or infection was high from such a practice. It appeared fully healed—not new, then, though the starkness of it was bold against his skin.

With a sigh, I took the ring from him and he drew back, steadying the crooked crown atop his head. The ring didn't have the cool touch characteristic of metals. It could have been bone, but I'd never seen black bone. Its surface was matte and intricately sculpted. Knots and hatches made up the design, with the figure of a running fox interwoven.

I clenched my jaw and held it back out to him. "I don't want it."

"Don't be disrespectful," the King scolded. He never lectured me, never parented me. His words brought an unexpected heat to my cheeks. Then he hiccuped, reminding me he had no ground to look down on me from. Still, he wasn't wrong. If the ring was Mother's, it was impudent to renounce it before her grave.

"Astraea is in one of her moods." His words were no surprise, yet my breath hitched at the mention of the Queen's name.

"Because of the festival?" I asked. It wouldn't change anything to know, but the chill in my blood drove my responses.

The King grunted his reply.

Consider it the cruelness of fate, perhaps, that the day of my birth and Mother's death coincided with Ayrenven. Even after all these years, the King spared no expense in preparations for the festival. It was not a jump to believe the Queen saw this as a way for him to honor his late mistress and what she was. Come the time of the festival she would veil her emotions and compose herself as she always did, hiding behind the guise of the great philanthropist that she was.

"She will be the air of royalty," I said, my tone dull, edging on sarcastic.

I got to my feet, my legs stiff from the chill of the damp ground. I wasn't scheduled for duty until midday, and I wanted to visit Nyana in the kitchens to see if she needed any help preparing for the festival. Though I'd only been gone from the capital a few days, I missed her.

"Neirin, there is one more thing."

Gritting my teeth, I kept my eyes on the marble statue. "What is it?"

"Lord Raeran has requested a guard to train his sons. I'm sending you to Valio after the festival."

I curled my fingers into fists. The only purpose I had was here in the capital. "A decision you came to this morning?" I challenged. Rion hadn't mentioned it when I arrived the night prior.

As if picking up my implication, the King let out an exaggerated breath. He rose rather ungracefully. Standing before me, we came to the same height, though his crooked crown gave him another few inches on me.

"Remember your place," the King cautioned, jaw set. His eyes, however, remained hazed by the alcohol.

I straightened, rolling my shoulders back. A curling twinge of panic took root, but I forced it down and remained poised. There was no point in arguing; it would do no good.

"You should sober up, Kaius." I addressed the King by his first name, bitter emotion seeping into my tone.

The King flinched. It was disrespectful, even if I was half his blood, but I didn't give a damn. I'd long since given up caring what my father thought of me.

2

NEIRIN

I TOOK the long way to the castle kitchens, giving a wide birth to the Queen's gardens. After I left the cover of the quaking aspens, the rays of yellow light that beamed down settled a faint warmth on my back. The lick of the sun was welcoming, for it indicated the coming of spring. I drew in a breath, letting the scents of young grass and wildflowers fill my lungs.

As my feet carried me down the familiar dirt path that edged the east side of the castle, a prickle of anxiety took root, however. And with it came a tingling beneath my skin. I shuddered, eyes scanning the high-level windows reflexively. No shadows caught my attention, though, no peering eyes around drawn curtains.

Remember your place.

The King's parting words formed a knot in my throat. As much as I desired to leave the capital, to start a life far from the Queen's presence, I was bound here by the promise I had made to myself all those years ago, by the promise I'd made to my brother. It was why being sent away, even for short periods of time, was so conflicting for me.

The few assignments I'd taken over the years outside of the

capital had lent me a sense of freedom. Yet with that came the nagging concern that should any danger come to the prince, I would be unable to aid in his defense. Never before had I been absent longer than a quarter cycle of the moons. Inner turmoil twisted at my guts.

"Neirin, is that you?"

I blinked, forcing down my thoughts, and found Nyana standing in the stone doorway at the path's end, hand to her brows as she squinted into the rising sun. My apprehensions eased, if only slightly, comforted by the warmth of her voice. My steps lightened as I approached the woman who raised me.

"I've been keeping an eye out for you," she said as I stopped before her, my figure casting her in a shadow. The pale blue of her eyes gleamed, wet—from emotion or staring into the sun I was unsure. I drew her in, and she sighed contentedly against my chest. When she lifted her chin and smiled, making the fine lines around her eyes more prominent, I released a breath.

"I've not even been gone half a fortnight," I pointed out, though I'd missed her too. She was comfort, familiarity, family, as I was to her. She'd be hurt terribly by the possibility of my being sent to the western lands. But Kaius was drunk, and I could speak with Rion, tell him the importance of my place here. *Nothing is yet set in stone.*

Nyana scrunched her nose, turned her head to the side so her ear rested against my chest, and tightened her hold on me. I laughed softly, feeling a bit lighter. When she drew back, however, her eyes lowered and a breath escaped her parted lips.

She traced a finger at the base of my fresh wound, and the worry in her eyes wrenched at my gut. Damn.

"I'm okay," I reassured her. I took her smaller hand in my own and guided it down. "It wasn't a deep cut."

Her expression sharpened, and when she stepped into the kitchens, I followed. The scent of cinnamon caught my attention. I looked past Nyana to a pot hanging from one of the large stone cooking hearths.

"Rice porridge?" I asked, tempted by one of my favorite breakfasts, though I'd already eaten.

Nyana set me with a studying gaze. Right, the wound. I'd never been able to lie to her. Somehow, she always knew when I tried. She scoffed, a strand of straight gray hair falling in front of her face. She tucked it behind her ear and adjusted her white cap before gesturing with her hands to my tunic.

"Off with it," she prompted. "If it's not bad, let me see it."

I sighed, knowing well enough there was no negating her, so I unbuckled the simple leather belt that was cinched about my waist and let it drop to the stone floor. Better to get this over with. If tending to my wound gave her some comfort, it was a suffering I could endure.

I removed my long shirt, pulling it over my head, and bashful giggles erupted from the back of the kitchen. Letting the cloth drop beside my belt, I ran a hand through the long, loose strands of hair along the left side of my head and offered the girls a flirtatious smile, tightening my muscles for their reaction even as it agitated my wound. The action wasn't humble, but I liked their attention, even if I held no desire for them. Damn, I should though. Both had pretty faces, simple but pleasing to look at. Bright eyes, long lashes.

Nyana drew a sharp breath and my attention returned to her. She traced the ridge of the slash, trailing a finger just beneath it. Despite my efforts not to, I flinched when she brushed over a particularly tender spot. A bruised rib, perhaps.

"Nyana, it will heal," I said, not wanting her to worry over me. How many times in my childhood had I come to her, nails torn and bleeding, fresh marks along my back, hysterical, shaken, and every time refusing to confide in her the cause of my sufferings. But I could never tell her. If I had, she would have learned the truth of what happened to Thatcher. I gritted my teeth as the guilt of my long-kept secret weighed on me.

With a determined shake of her head, Nyana's resoluteness returned to her. She turned her back to me and paced to the cabinets. She had to stand on her toes to reach the bottles on the higher shelf. Glass clinked as she shuffled through the wine, searching for something to sanitize my wound. It would sting and be purposeless, for infection never plagued me despite my many injuries, but it would ease her troubles to feel she'd done something. She didn't know of my healing abilities.

I followed her, nearly bumping into a maid with a tray of breakfast biscuits and tea as she hurried past.

"Sorry, sir." The girl, younger than the others, dipped her head. Pale blond waves fell from her cap. She straightened, retreating a step. Brown doe eyes trailed up my bare chest until she met my gaze, and a faint squeal of a sound escaped her. Tilting my head, I drew my brows in, but she averted her eyes and brushed past me, returning to her duties.

"Leave the poor girl alone," Nyana lectured. I let my gaze linger on her, though, as she left the room, headed toward the halls and likely the stairwell beyond. The dress she wore, cinched at the waist and bunched out elegantly at the hips, indicated she was one of the girls who brought meals and refreshments to the upper levels to serve the King, his family, and those he entertained.

Nyana cleared her throat.

"Hmm?" I turned my attention back to her. Well, at least worry no longer laced her expression. She raised one thin brow in an arch, and beneath her long paisley skirts, one of her boots tapped on the stone flooring.

"You know that girl's only five and ten," she said as I approached her.

I cringed. Though it wasn't uncommon for a girl of that age to begin courting, it was a crime to lay with one. The law was firm when it came to such matters, and for good reason. Deaths among women in childbirth were high, especially in the case of younger girls. Beyond that, Nyana raised me better.

"She doesn't look that young," I defended, uncomfortable with the topic and in a sense, deflecting. I suspected Nyana knew of my affliction, though she never mentioned it. It made her lecturing feel somehow disingenuous. A cloak to cover the scar of last year's stain on my reputation after Frella, a ladies' maid desired by many men of the guard, spread the story of my inability to take her when I tried. She would have been my first, unheard of for a man my age, yet I simply held no interest in women. When Frella revealed her intentions to pursue me, it was a chance to make a show of my prowess to my brothers in arms, or so I thought. I'd been so damn nervous. And then ashamed.

Since then, I'd not attempted to take another, yet I'd learned how to please women with my fingers and with my mouth in an attempt to recover my reputation. Which I had. Since Frella had married and left for the western lands, the women I'd been intimate with spoke only highly of their experiences. I could form stories to dispel why I never took it further than pleasuring them, why I never truly took them as a man should. It was all a show, a desperate act to conceal an internal knowledge that something was wrong with me.

Nyana pulled an empty wooden crate from beneath the counter, turned it sideways, and patted it with a flattened palm. Tensed by my thoughts, I obeyed, sitting down heavily on the splintering thing as I'd done countless times before. It groaned when it took my weight, and I let out a breath, as if expelling the air in my lungs could lighten me. With knees bent, I leaned forward and rested my head in my palms, eyes falling to my worn leather boots. I could afford nicer ones, but Nyana bought me these, and they were comfortable. Similar, in fact, to the ones I'd worn as a boy when I'd sat atop this very same crate, my legs dangling, not yet reaching the floor.

"What was it this time?" Nyana asked as she popped the cork on a bottle of cheap cooking wine and held a rag to it, tipping it to wet the cloth.

"Thieves," I told her, sitting up straight so she could tend my wound.

"Thieves?" She pressed lightly with the rag and I winced, the alcohol stinging my agitated skin. She shot me a pointed look and I set my jaw. She didn't have to tell me to stop fidgeting for me to know her meaning.

"Five of them," I told her, and briefly relayed the encounter.

Nyana scrunched her nose, and remorse hit me like a wave—remorse that the life I led put me at risk, and that she was often left to see the effects of it. Remorse for the many nights of my childhood, she muffled her tears when she thought I was sleeping. Remorse for all the worry I'd brought her, all the pain. And, more than anything else, remorse for what she didn't know. For the cause of Thatch's death.

"Please don't worry over me," I coaxed, conscience heavy. I hated to see her burdened. I leaned forward to take the rag from her, but as I did, Nyana regained her composure and sniffled. With pointed purpose she pressed the soaked cloth to my ribs, a bit less careful than perhaps she could have been, and I hissed, taken by surprise.

She narrowed her eyes. "Don't fidget."

I raised my hands in mock surrender.

When my wound was cleaned and bandaged with a long strip of white cloth wrapped about my chest and over one shoulder, I slipped my tunic back on. Nyana bent to pick up my belt, and her hand went to the small of her back as she grunted. Her hair, streaked blond and silver for as long as I could remember, was of late leaning more toward the latter. Tendrils of it fell from her cap, enough this time to cause her to huff her annoyance and pull it from her head.

As she tucked the cap into the tie of her apron, solemnness weighed on me. I wanted to tell her to rest, but the words would be lost on her. As a child, I thought she was only stubborn, but life wasn't as simple as that. She was a cook, and though she was good at what she did, she was replaceable. I had the coin to provide for her, but she insisted against it whenever I broached the subject. This kitchen was her home, the girls that worked alongside her the closest thing to family she had left, aside from myself. Her work here gave her purpose. I, of all people, could understand the need for that.

"You'll give yourself wrinkles if you worry your brow like that," Nyana chided as she reached her arms around my waist and drew the leather strap of my belt back through at the front. I let her mother me because I knew it brought her comfort.

"I worry about you," I admitted.

"I know." She pulled the strap and raised her eyes to mine. "But I'm happy here, Neirin. With my girls." She nodded to one with a glint of affection.

"If it were up to me—"

"It's not up to you." She adjusted her hair and pulled it back into a tight bun. "If you want to help and have the time, wash up, and you can peel some vegetables."

"I have the time." I would always make time for her.

Along the side wall, a washing bucket sat atop a long counter. Fine slivers of ice floated at the top, broken up by whoever washed last, another reminder of the cold. Before me, and level with the countertop, an open stone archway looked out to the kitchen gardens. The yellow light of late dawn cast shadows between large clusters of herbs and berry brambles, alluding to the possibility of warmer weather as the day went on.

I took a bar of tallow soap from the worn stone bowl beside the washing bucket and lathered my hands. It had a slight herbal scent, though I couldn't name the plants. Nyana made her own soaps, had been doing so since I could remember. I smiled to myself because the scent was familiar, comfortable.

"Neir!"

The bar of soap leapt from my hands and slid across the countertop. "Dammit, Harlan," I cursed as the young prince popped his head through the archway. "What are you doing here?"

The boy beamed, even as his head dipped back out of view. The elevation outside was lower, dug out for level planting, and Harlan was too short to see through the gap without clambering his boots against the stone wall. When he rose again, pulling himself up and bracing his weight with his arms, I fought the urge to splash cold water at him. But I wasn't a child anymore, and at four and ten, he wasn't really either.

"You should be in your classes," I said pointedly.

Harlan adjusted his arms and gave a little sound of frustration, his hazel eyes squinting beneath dark lashes. He dropped to the ground, and the top of his head, a mess of umber curls, disappeared around the corner.

"Harlan's here," I warned Nyana over my shoulder.

She came through a doorway that led up from the root cellar, huffing, as she hefted a crate of carrots. I cursed under my breath and went to her side, taking the burden from her. Though she wasn't old, the years of hard work and dedication she had committed to the kitchen showed in her slightly crooked stance, stiff joints, and the dark shadows beneath her eyes. The job had aged her, as had my upbringing and Thatch's death, surely. When she looked up at me, a smile beamed across her face, and my heart warmed, ebbing the ache.

The rapping of boots on stone warned me of Harlan's approach, and I raised the crate I held just in time to be assaulted by the gangly boy. His arms wrapped around my waist, squeezing tightly. I sighed, reservations about being close to him battling with my desire to return his carefree affection.

Harlan released me, and I brought the carrots to the island counter, setting the crate beside a few others containing an assortment of root vegetables—potatoes varying in size and color, orange and violet beets, and sweet parsnips. Had Nyana brought them all up herself? A frown tugged at my lips. Hopefully, she'd asked her girls for help with the heavier items.

Beside me, Harlan backed up to the counter and hefted himself to sit atop it. "That's a lot of carrots." His voice hit the telltale highs and lows that prefaced the transformation out of boyhood, whether he was ready for the responsibilities of a man or not.

"Many people will be coming for the festival," I pointed out, having no better response to his rather obvious declaration.

Nyana wouldn't be responsible for all the cooking, of course. Vendors would erect stands. Most people would purchase their meals in the market. Nyana would cook for the King and his guests. All the kingdom's lords and their families had either arrived or were en route. They would gather in the upper levels of the castle, where they would converse and dine before the start of the night's celebrations.

Harlan aimlessly sorted through the carrots, occasionally picking one up and setting it back in the crate. "I wonder if there will be marzipan cake again this year."

"Likely," I acknowledged, selecting a wooden board to work on. All kinds of baked treats would be set out on the tables within the castle, along with chalices of wine, plates of cheeses, breads, and other snacks. Once the festivities began in the courtyard, nearly any food imaginable could be sought out and purchased.

"Have you tried it before? It's nutty, but sweet too. I asked my maid to call for some, but she told me it wasn't something made in the eastern lands, only in the west. Did you know that?"

The pang of apprehension I felt before returned at the mention of the western lands, and I swallowed. "I did not ... I put higher stock in the knowledge of politics and major trade than where nutty cakes are baked. Do you know where our carrots come from?" I nodded to the crate.

Harlan scrunched his nose, detecting my challenge at his knowledge of the kingdom, and turned the subject back to the festival, brushing past my question. "I overheard Mother's ladies' maid say a storyteller would be posted in the courtyard telling tales of the old lore and the history of Ayrenven. Isn't that interesting?" His gaze grew distant. "Mother sent her off though, before I could hear any more. She seemed upset."

No surprise there. I grunted and took the crate of multicolored carrots, halting my brother's aimless investigation of them. The boy was always doing something with his hands or fidgeting in some other way as if he were incapable of sitting still. With nothing to do, Harlan began to swing his legs, his boots kicking the lower cupboards, and leaned back on his palms.

"What happened?" Harlan asked, gaze set at the low-dipping neckline of my tunic.

"Thieves," I said with a sigh of frustration. I did not enjoy the prospect of retelling my story for the fourth time.

"An ambush?" Excitement twinkled in his eyes. "You must tell me everything, Neir."

The boy reveled in tales of bravery and adventure. In a sense, it pleased me that he held such a view of my life. Still, I was a bastard, and he was a prince. He needed to focus on his schooling. It was safer for him, too, to spend his time within the upper levels of the castles than with me.

Nyana joined us with a small basket of red berries in her arms and sat it atop the counter. She drew a rag from where she kept it tucked into the tie of her apron and swatted the boy with it. "Down. You may be a prince, but this is my kitchen, lad, and I don't need your rump on my counter."

Harlan grinned ear to ear and jumped down, giggling. Nyana's expression softened, and she tousled his hair. The gesture was simple—an older woman showing affection to a child—yet outside of the kitchen walls, she would never show such familiarity with him. It was the hierarchy of things. While on another occasion the heft of my guilt may have caused me to push Harlan to leave, the looming possibility of my departure made me hesitate; my gratitude for the moment winning over my conscience.

"Do you not have classes today?" I asked, hoping the boy had forgotten about my wound.

Harlan pouted, leaned against the counter, and rested his chin on a palm. I snapped the green foliage from the carrots and separated them. "Veritran is boring."

Veritran was the resident professor. He instructed all the children raised in the castle, including myself and the other boys of the castle guard. Harlan, with his title, was tutored in the castle library one-on-one, not in the hall where I'd been forced to sit days on end with half a dozen others listening to the man's flat tempo of a voice. He was dull—terribly so—but that didn't matter.

"It's not supposed to be exciting," I told him. "You need to learn if you want to be King one day."

Gods be good that day didn't come anytime soon. The boy wasn't ready for such an undertaking. With a prickle of guilt, I wondered if he ever would be. It wasn't his fault, really. Kaius never reprimanded him, nor did Astraea.

Despite the role the Queen took in my own discipline as a boy, she'd never once raised a hand to her son. Never scolded him or enforced any kind of boundaries. The sun rose and fell on Harlan in the Queen's eyes. She'd lost five pregnancies that I could count before the boy, and two since. He was a blessing, and I could understand that. But still, doting on him as she did would only hurt him in the long run. She had to see that.

The boy was spoiled, and because of it, he acted immaturely. His knowledge of the kingdom and the people who resided in it was lacking, to say the least. He knew nothing of which towns exported what goods, which families were to be trusted, and which to be watchful of.

By eight, I'd committed myself to the guard, killed with my first blooding, and left the comforts of the room Nyana and I shared to bed among battle-toughened guards in the barracks. Yet my brother, in all his innocence, knew only of his comfortable life within the upper levels of the castle. He cared little to learn what lay beyond the walls that separated the royal gardens and courtyards from the rest of the city, the rest of the kingdom.

"Knife," I said, tone flat, and the boy retrieved one for me. I began scraping the rough outer layer of a purple carrot, eyeing him as he picked through the basket of berries, oblivious to my scrutiny.

Perhaps I should've taken a more significant role in his life, stepped in where Kaius hadn't, and shown the boy some discipline, some guidance. But the fear that I may lose control, and may replay the horrors of the past, kept me submissive. Control was easier when I kept my emotions at bay.

"Fuck." A drop of blood came to the surface of my thumb where I'd nicked it in my distracted state. I sucked at it, tasting the metallic tang.

A rag hit the back of my neck. "I heard that," Nyana quipped.

Harlan stifled a laugh, covering his mouth with a fist. When Nyana passed, he coughed back his amusement, and I couldn't help but return his grin.

By the time I finished peeling all the vegetables at the

counter, the sun had risen above the domed opening in the wall. The morning had been enjoyable, laced with conversations of unimportant things, gossip, and festival preparations. At one point, Clara's name came up, and Harlan's cheeks reddened. Even at four and ten, my brother flushed at the thought of the young lady he was promised to. What must it be like to feel for a woman in such a way?

"You should be off, brother," I noted reluctantly, taking a basket of berries from him. It was half empty, but Nyana could send one of her girls to pick more from the garden. The small, round fruit was one of the first things to ripen each year. Seeing Harlan's lips stained red propelled me into memories of warm summers spent by the thorny bushes, of eating berries by the handful until my tummy ached. And into memories of another boy's smile—different from Harlan's, yet the same shade of red.

Harlan pouted, and I rested my hand on his shoulder, coming back to the present. "The festival's tonight. You must go prepare yourself."

Mention of the festival brought the boy's easy smile back, and he nodded eagerly. "Alright, Neir." He hugged my side. I drew my arm around him and ruffled his hair. It was thick and curled, like Kaius's, like mine was when cut short.

Harlan laughed, and when he broke the embrace, I nudged him on. He took a few steps, then turned back to me, a pensive expression on his soft features. "But you never told me about your wound. I want to know about the thieves."

"Next time." How long would that be if I was sent away?

He scrunched his face but made no further objections. "Alright."

Coming to stand beside me, Nyana too wished Harlan farewell, and the boy set off through the door that led out to the path and castle grounds. He had a short attention span, and I wondered if he would get distracted again before making his roundabout way to the upper levels and his chambers. There, a nervous maid was surely pacing, ready to tame his hair and anxious of reprimands should the boy not be made presentable in time.

"Was I ever that easy-going as a child?" I asked Nyana. Thoughts of the berry brambles returned, a faint glimpse of a memory, impossible to fully grasp, yet I could almost taste the tart sweetness of the berries, recall the pop when I bit into one, could almost hear the birdsong of early spring.

Nyana rested a hand on my arm. "Only when you were very young." Her somber tone hinted at the words that lay unsaid. *Before Thatch's death.*

The depth in her eyes dispelled the warmth of my memories, replacing them with a sobering recollection of that day.

"Is there anything else I can help with?" I asked, clearing my throat.

Nyana's hand dropped, and she straightened her apron. "No." Her voice faltered. "The girls and I can manage the rest. I suspect you need to be off."

It was true. It would be midday soon, and I still needed to return to my quarters to change into my guard's uniform and retrieve my sword. Rion was expecting me, and I didn't feel like facing his dour expression at yet another late arrival after last night's incident with the thieves. It was imperative that I return to his good graces in order to persuade him to send another to Valio in my place.

"Are you certain?"

Nyana drew a forced smile, gesturing to the other side of the kitchen where the doe-eyed girl from before made a faint squeal at the attention and dropped a metal ladle. It skittered across the floor, leaving a trace across the stone of whatever soup she'd been getting ready to dip into bowls.

"You distract my girls," Nyana pointed out.

I laughed, then immediately stifled it when the girl's cheeks flushed. She knelt to wipe the floor. A second girl, one of my own age, joined her and whispered in her ear, then looked up at me with hooded blue eyes. Age and possibly experience lent her boldness, and when she met my gaze, she nipped playfully at her bottom lip—an invitation.

I let out a breath and turned my attention back to Nyana. "Alright." I drew her into a hug. "I see you have a point."

She reached between us and cupped my cheek in her palm, her eyes sad again. My heart ached. When she looked at me like that, I couldn't help but wonder if she thought of her son.

Nyana never spoke about Thatcher, not anymore. The rippling sensation beneath my skin tensed my muscles, and I fought to level my emotions and push thoughts of the boy aside.

"Go now," Nyana said, dropping her hand and gesturing with a tip of her head.

I nodded, then pulled her back into my arms once more. Because I was selfish. Because even when her pain and the guilt of my own doings that burdened me, I still sought comfort in her embrace. "I'll return to see you before I leave again," I promised.

"You're to leave again?"

"There's word there may be another assignment for me." I simplified the truth, irritated with myself for letting my worries slip out. "We can speak of it later."

She pulled back, forced a smile, and patted my chest, avoiding the bandaged area where my wound was still tender. "Okay, be sure that you do, then."

A weight sank in my belly like a stone dropped into a riverbed. I couldn't leave; my place was here, where I could keep sentry over my brother, protect him from any outside threat. And to do so, I had to remain in the capital.

3

———

EVERA

TRAVELING BACK to our market stall from the community well with a bucket of water, I squinted up to the sun directly overhead. It was midday already. Out of the way of fellow shoppers, I sat the bucket down to flex my fingers. My brother would be growing anxious, with all that remained to be done before the festivities began. Preparing our stall was a sizable undertaking for one man. With a sigh, I dusted my hands on my skirts, the old, muted fabric lacking any patterns or embellishments.

I retrieved the bucket, which was lighter than when I'd filled it at the well, and made my way back to our wagon and the patch of dusty land Aureus had staked out for our booth. We were south of the city in the outer grounds designated for the festival's market. A line of darkened soil, the effect of the old bucket's steady leak, marked my path as I walked.

Our chestnut mare, Sorrel, nickered when I approached, tugging a smile at the corner of my lips. I set the bucket down before her, and she dipped her white-striped muzzle to investigate. She sniffed, then gave a disgruntled snort and turned her attention to the pouch that hung at my hip.

"I don't have anything for you," I said, stroking absentmindedly at her forelock, its shade a touch lighter than the copper coloring of her coat.

From the back of the wagon, my brother spoke over the noisy shifting of items as he sought something. "You've spoiled that mare," Aureus called in his typical lecturing manner. I rolled my eyes and scrunched up my nose at Sorrel, shaking my head as if the two of us shared the secret of mocking my brother.

"Spoiled," I tsked in a quiet voice, scratching the underside of her chin. "You know, she did carry us all the way from Elrune." This time, I spoke loud enough for Aureus to hear. "I do believe she's earned something for her efforts."

Coming around the side of the wagon with a table support hefted on one shoulder, Aureus grunted. "Should the market go well, she'll have less weight to carry on the way back." He laid the support beneath the tent stand next to a disorderly stack of crates and baskets.

"Did you bring the rope?" I asked. Three years ago, we left the festival with half of what we arrived with, and, with too much space to move about the wagon bed, several bottles had broken on the journey back.

Aureus wiped the perspiration from his brow with the back of his hand and sighed. "I did not." He stood in the shade of the tent to get out of the direct sunlight. Still, though, I could make out the dark circles of exhaustion beneath his deep-set blue eyes.

Twisting my lips, I patted Sorrel's neck. There was nothing to be done for it now, aside from purchasing new rope. Perhaps we would see how sales went. I thought to quip a remark about the lack of sleep and forgetfulness, but I held my tongue.

We'd traveled all night, and though I'd rested intermittently between bumps in the path that jarred me back to wakefulness, Aureus had stayed alert the entirety of the trip, steering Sorrel and keeping a watchful eye on the trees. The pass through the Edthiel Mountains was known for the thieves living in its ancient woods and the ambushes they staged on lone travelers. However, Ayrenven promised a steady flow of people making their way north to the capital, so we were never isolated. There was safety in numbers.

Aureus made another pass to the back of the wagon, returning with a stack of boards that would create the tabletop where we would display our wares. I wanted to help my brother, do something—even just hold the support beams in place—but he wouldn't let me. I curled my left hand into a fist and relaxed my fingers again to assuage my irritation. I was capable. Aureus knew it too, and perhaps that maddened me the most. Behind the veil of the back room of our shop, I was an equal. But out here, where others could see me, I was expected to know my place.

"Something is bothering you," my brother noted.

"It's nothing," I said.

"Say that to the set of your brows, Evera." He scoffed, and I shot him a pointed look, further narrowing my eyes for theatrics. He'd always said I was an easy read. The truth was, I didn't care enough to conceal my feelings or worry about what people thought of me. Or at least I hadn't before. Not until the rumors surrounding me began to put pressure on Aureus and threaten our shop. My brother had enough burdens to shoulder him without me causing more problems. So I'd been trying to behave. *To be complacent.*

"I would like to wander the stalls," I said, not wanting to fight.

Something shifted in Aureus's expression, a softening of his features, as if he could see in my eyes the way his expectations of me—society's expectations of me—were slowly beginning to chip away at my soul. Good, let him see.

Aureus didn't push. Instead, he reverted to sarcasm, a

language we shared. "Right, three silver canins enough, then?" He worked the cords of a leather pouch tied to his belt.

"That should do it," I quipped, not missing a beat. The value of a single silver canin was equivalent to fifty-four ferres, and not something Aureus would keep in his coin purse. Few were bold enough to carry around such a valued coin, let alone three.

Withdrawing two copper coins, Aureus quirked an apologetic smile and offered the roughly minted ferres. "I wish things were different." I knew he spoke true. "But you must believe I only want what's best for you."

Right. What's best for me. I sighed and took the coins. "I know."

"Chin up," he said, lightening his tone again. He touched his finger to the tip of my nose. "Go, spoil your mare."

At his touch, I fought the smile twitching at my lips. Damn him and his way of always knowing how to lighten my mood, how to counter my prickliness.

"I'm still unhappy about this." I gestured loosely to the mess of crates and unassembled sections of tables with a nod. There was still so much to be done.

Aureus ran a palm along the blond braids at the side of his head to the leather cord that kept his shoulder-length hair tied up. Though I expected him to counter with dry wit, his tone was level, somber. "It's how the world works."

I nodded. "Right."

"Go, enjoy the market." He held up a palm to display hot spots where blisters would form. "You're not missing out on much, I assure you."

"At least wrap your hands," I said with a frown. "There are cotton strips and straps of leather in my bag, and somewhere amid this mess is deer tallow. I packed several jars of it."

Aureus tsked. "Go. I am fine."

I relented, unsure how my irritation had turned to concern. "I'll be back shortly."

"Take your time, and Evera—"

"Yes, yes." I pocketed the two coins, familiar with his lecture. "Stay on the main roads where it is safe. Avoid alleys. Don't draw attention to myself."

Aureus swallowed and averted his gaze. Nodding, he turned back to his task, and I drew my brows in. Whether he was simply tired or something else was on his mind, I was unsure, but Aureus was acting off. Better not to push it, though. If he wanted to speak his thoughts, he would.

As I walked, I found myself drawn into the sights and sounds of the festival preparations. Those with stands were hurrying about, arranging their wares and hanging banners. The smell of pitch, used to waterproof stall coverings, lingered in the air, the scent reminiscent of freshly quenched coals. And amid all this was the undeniable buzz of excitement. Of all the festivals of the year, Ayrenven was the most anticipated and the only event that drew in such a vast quantity of unique goods and wares from the western lands.

A faint smile tugged at the corners of my lips as I eyed a display of carved wooden statues. I stopped momentarily to examine their intricacy. The largest was an owl roughly the size of my forearm with eyes of a strikingly clear stone.

"Crystal quartz," the merchant behind the table said, dusting wood shavings off his apron. He sat on a stool, carving a small figurine. I hadn't even noticed him.

"A symbol of the sight?" I asked, intrigued.

Standing, the man placed his newest piece—a wolverine snarling and posed in an aggressive stance—on the table. "That's right. You know more than most do of the old lore. I'm impressed."

I hummed. He was an older man, and the sparkle in his eyes gave him an air of trustworthiness. He reminded me of my mentor. "Isn't that what this festival is for?" I countered. "To celebrate the moon gods and their spirit lines?"

The man laughed. "Yes, well, to most it's just an excuse to gather, to drink, and to barter uncommon goods."

"I find the lore fascinating," I admitted. The man was easy to talk to; his candor reminded me of Leighis. My attention caught on an animalistic mask in the middle of the collection, lying flat alongside others. Absentmindedly, I traced a finger over a silver filigree brow.

"You want to see it?" the man asked.

"I haven't the money to buy anything," I said truthfully; the two coppers in my pouch would not scratch the value of any of his wares. Still, after a brief hesitation, I gave in to the allure and took it into my hands to admire the artistry. Silver ribbons at each side of the mask trailed beneath it, catching on a breeze and shimmering. "What is it?"

The carver scratched at his short beard with one hand. Without any notable features—such as ears or snout—the mask could have depicted any number of animals.

"Obscurity," he offered, though it came across as more of a question.

Amusement laced my tone as I caught a glint in the old man's eyes. "You don't know."

"Obscurity, child," he said, mock wisdom in his tone, "is the gift of being whoever you want to be. Or being no one at all."

It was poetic, despite the improvisation. Or, perhaps, because of it. I trailed my thumb over the smooth, dark surface beneath one of the eye slits. "You're incredibly skilled. Have you always been a carver?"

The old man returned to his stool and lowered slowly to sit. "When I was young, I wanted to be a blacksmith." A distant look crossed his face, and he cast his eyes down. "It wasn't an aspiration I was given the chance to follow."

"I'm sorry." I knew all too well what it felt like to be unable to pursue one's desires.

The man shrugged. "I found another method to create. Fulfillment can be found in many places."

Setting the mask back on the table carefully, I raised my eyes to him. "You've found contentment, then, in this?"

"When you approached my stand, you had a far-off look, and now you appear wistful. That has brought me happiness." He gestured with a nod to the mask. "Something about this piece speaks to you; it should be yours."

I offered him a smile but shook my head. "I haven't the coin."

He interlocked his fingers and stretched. "Take it nonetheless." There was finality in his tone. "We all need the freedom that comes with obscurity at times."

After relenting and taking the mask, I dismissed myself, musing over the carver as I walked the dust path uphill. I was grateful the old man had found happiness. Yet in the same breath, a strange bitterness befell me. I wanted to be an apothecary, to work in the shop with Aureus. Yet, as a woman, I never could be a healer, never let others see my skills. Not when such a concept caused whispers in the street. "Witch," they called me. I could only ever be someone's wife.

I let out a huff of air and brushed the thoughts away, tapping the pouch at my hip and considering how I might spend my coin. The slight weight of the mask was a comforting presence in the oversized pocket of my skirts.

After a short time, the path gave way to a cobbled road, and the hum of voices grew as people shopped in closer quarters. I stopped and raised my head, letting the awe of the city and the festival decorations settle over me.

Banners of a shimmering silver cloth that hung between buildings, some with moons painted on them, flitted in the light breeze. Though the road was narrow, stalls still lined either side, pressed in tight against townhouses and shops. In Elrune, very few buildings were taller than two floors high. Here, some reached three or four. But they were nothing in comparison to the massive castle that sat atop the hill, at the highest point of the city. With its towers, high walls, and billowing banners that must have been some thirty feet or more in length, decorated with the royal crest, the castle was a formidable and captivating sight.

A woman bumped into me, breaking me from my trance. I'd been standing in the middle of the road, completely enthralled. Yet beneath the wonder, my heart thumped with a distant sorrow. For when the sun set, the castle would stretch an impending shadow over the poorer part of the city, on the eastern side where the hill dipped down to the meadow beyond. In the alleys, the stench of decaying food and the contents of bedpans tossed from windows hung in the air. Hunger clawed at the bellies of men, women, and children alike. The path I traveled, where the higher classes lived and worked, was merely a façade.

Stepping to the side to allow people to pass by, I caught the scent of fresh bread. I let my nose lead me to a bakery with a permanent stand out front. Its awning was a stretched hide of some sort, sturdy and dyed a cobalt blue that matched the shop's door, which stood propped open. As I approached, a young boy wearing a dark apron, patted with smudged handprints of flour, appeared in the doorway, carrying a basket of rolls. The bread steamed in the brisk midday air.

"How many can I get for a single ferre?" I asked the boy, nodding to the fresh bread as he drew nearer to the stand.

"One apiece, mam," the child said. He placed the basket and adjusted the cap that sat atop his head. The cap, made of a brown fabric, matched his short, straight hair.

A ferre for a single roll. I let out a breath, and my stomach growled as if voicing my disappointment. If these were the prices in the city, I would have to head back toward the stalls in the outer grounds. I'd have better luck stretching my coppers there.

Someone brushed against my side, the touch faint, and I lowered my gaze, aware of the threat of pickpockets, though my pouch hung on my opposite hip. Beside me, a girl made a quiet noise, an apology perhaps, and sidestepped. Her shoulders slumped as if she were trying to shrink into herself, to be unseen, a shadow.

The baker's boy leaned against the table, addressing the newcomer with a hostility that took me by surprise. "If you don't have any coin, get lost."

The girl swallowed, her throat bobbing. Her clothes were simple and worn, her tawny hair greasy and dirty, indicating it had been some time since she last bathed.

"Are you daft, skell? I'll call the guards on you," the boy sneered, using the derogatory term for someone who lived on the streets. I gritted my teeth at the child's words, forgetting my vow to complacency. A fire burned in my belly.

"The fuck is your problem?" I snapped. Excellent, now I was cursing at children. Aureus would be so pleased.

The boy gawked at me, presumably never having heard a lady curse before. Well, there was a first time for everything. "She hasn't done anything wrong. Leave her be."

As if on cue, the girl at my side sucked in a breath and, with a thin arm, reached out and snatched a roll from the basket. Before I could form a word, she fled, the beige tones of her old clothing disappearing amid the crowd.

The baker's boy shot me a glare. As I had with my brother, I met the child's expression, knowing full well I'd been wrong and didn't give a damn. He was still a little prick, and the girl was just hungry. I knew all too well what that was like.

Disregarding me, the boy stood tall on the toes of his boots and scanned the crowd. I followed his gaze to a soldier, his attention rapt in the advancements of a street woman running a finger down his cuirass. The boy hollered, and I sucked in a breath. On reflex, I leaned across the table and grabbed him by the front of his shirt. The contents of a rounded bowl were knocked over as I did. The boy silenced, and a muscle twitched at his jaw.

Eyes darting back to the soldier, I released my breath, relieved to see he was still entirely distracted. The woman, some ten years older than him at least, spoke against his ear. She trailed one hand down his chest and cupped it rather blatantly between his legs. The man's lips gaped slightly; he released a moan that was silenced by the noise of the crowd. The soldier would take little notice of anything so long as that woman entertained him. So much for being a protector of the people. Huffing, I turned my attention back to the boy.

"Stop yelling," I hissed. The boy nodded, and I dropped my grasp on his shirt.

He narrowed his eyes and, without a word, pointed to my coin purse.

So that was how it would be. Fine.

I withdrew a single ferre and flicked it to him off the back of my thumb, scoffing when he missed the catch and had to drop to his knees to collect it off the ground. While he was distracted with his head beneath the table, I considered pocketing a roll for myself, but my days of stealing were in the past.

I quirked my lips, considering Aureus's number one rule. *Don't draw attention to yourself.* There was always tomorrow for a fresh start and for following the rules. At this point, the day was already spoiled. I started off in the direction the girl had taken.

As I walked, I scanned the shadows. All children raised on the street knew that the light, the open, made us vulnerable. Only in the dark recesses could we steady our breaths and wait for the passing of time, until the pounding of our hearts settled and the guards' shouts diminished. Then, and only then, could we consider our rashly stolen meal truly ours.

It took only a few minutes to find her hiding behind a cart in the narrow space between two buildings, a hiding place that would have been indiscernible except to those who knew where to look and had lived by the rules of the street. Internally, I checked off Aureus's list. *Don't draw attention to yourself,* and, as I slowly skirted the wagon so as not to startle the girl off, I mentally marked off *Stay on the main road, avoid alleys.*

Kneeling just within the shadows, some seven feet from the child, I stilled my advancement. We studied each other. She was with her back against the wall and legs drawn to her chest, eyes wide with fright. Me with the gut-wrenching remembrance of what it was like to be in her position.

"They aren't coming for you," I reassured her. I nodded to the roll. "I paid for it."

The girl's pale eyes were a watchful cornflower blue. She held tight to her meal, likely the only food she'd had in days.

"I won't take it from you. Eat. It's alright."

Hesitantly, she took a bite. Her stomach rumbled noisily, and with rapid breaths and unhinged hunger, she gave in to the need to sate the hollowness of her belly.

Sighing, I rocked back, sitting on my heels. I watched her, plagued by vague and fragmented memories of the time Aureus and I had lived on the streets. The images that came to me were fuzzy, like a fading dream.

Yet beneath that fog, there were the sensations. Those I could remember with clarity. The gnawing emptiness of my belly, the pinching ache of starvation. The press of skeletal bodies against my own, rasping with cough as the cold numbed me to my core. Counting my breaths in the dark until Mother returned for us. And through all of this, the one thing that grounded me was the reassurance of my brother's hand. And Mother's lullaby, which he would hum to me to still my fear.

When the girl was finished with her roll, I scooted closer to her, bit by bit. The rise and fall of her chest was steady, and her eyes addressed me with pointed curiosity. When I was close enough, I reached out a hand and placed it atop hers, offering a reassuring smile, for there was nothing else to offer her, and I desperately longed to offer something.

However, at my touch, the girl inhaled sharply. I withdrew, and she dug the heels of her bare feet in, scraping at the stone. She tried to back away, only to press into the solid wall behind her.

As if realizing she had nowhere to go, her breath began to hitch.

"I won't hurt you," I promised, a tightness in my chest as I witnessed the panic building within her. I worried my bottom lip, chastising myself. Each person held within them an innate response to what they perceived as danger—fight or flee. To flee was the safer option and what most chose. "I'm sorry," I said in a low voice, defeated, as I backed up to give her room.

But she didn't flee.

Statue-like, aside from the rapid rise and fall of her chest, the girl held my eyes. Like a cloud passing over the moon, shrouding the world in darkness, the blue of her irises faded. They took on an ashen tone, chimney smoke against a dusk sky. Her head dipped slightly, and her lashes fluttered; her knuckles were white where she held tight to the cloth of her pants. As if she were fighting something internal.

The healer within me fumbled over this, leaving me with a push and pull. To offer help or to stay back so as not to further frighten her. What ailment brought about the darkening of eyes?

The girl's body shook, and the air filled with an indescribable charge. My blood vibrated, accompanied by a prickling sensation that began in my fingers and spread out in static tremors. The hair rose on the back of my neck.

Releasing a breath to steady myself, recollection fell over me of the traveler's warnings. The whispers of what people believed me to be, the whispers of a dark magic. Despite my knowledge, no other possibility came to mind. The black eyes, the charge in the air. The child was an Alidian.

Aureus's last rule came to me as an echo in my mind, nearly drowned out by the steadily growing hum in my ears: stay safe.

4

EVERA

THE GIRL's chest rose and fell rapidly. My eyes held hers, drawn into the emotions that drove her. Exhaling a steadying breath, I fought to calm the racing of my own heart, to resist falling victim to panic. I searched my mind for any useful knowledge that could assist me in my current situation. The extent of what I knew of the Alidian came from legends, stories, and Leighis's teachings. Yet even my mentor spoke little of them. There was a hush to the word. When it was spoken, people averted their eyes, mumbled the word *witch*, for that title was easier to stomach.

Alidians were human by birth. They came into the world like everyone else. Until the age of five or so, there was nothing notably unique about them. Then their magic began to show. The black of their eyes was the tell of a soul consumed by dark magic, the energy in the air the forewarning of unmatchable power.

An Alidian's magic was deadly, unbiased, and unhinged. Cilician law was finite when it came to the killing of innocents. A death for a death. It was why such children rarely made it past the age of six. Unable to control their outbursts, they were executed for their crimes.

Sucking in my bottom lip, I studied the girl's charcoal eyes. Within the darkness, I detected a base drive for survival. Like an animal backed into a corner, bristling, hiding its fear behind pointed teeth and snarls of warning.

The charge in the air intensified, and through the rush of blood in my ears, I found an unexpected calm. An acceptance, a calculated cool detachment. Thoughts of Mother came to me, of her warmth, her love for the short time she was in our lives. Her lullaby hummed through me until the tune rose faintly from my throat, sweet and slow, as I closed my eyes.

Time was elusive. I couldn't say how long I carried the tune, but the charge in the air began to dissipate. Opening my eyes, I found the girl still looking back at me, her dark irises faded, returned to a cornflower blue. As the ringing in my ears subsided, she relaxed her grip on her knees and color returned to her white knuckles. I exhaled another steadying breath, grateful my first instinct to calm the girl had been successful. Grateful Mother's song had settled her, as it had so many times for me before.

"I used to live in the streets too," I said hesitantly, voice low.

The girl fidgeted, then faintly she mimicked a few notes of the lullaby. The sound from her throat was rough, as if her voice were underused.

"It was my mother's song," I offered. "It's always brought me comfort."

The child averted her eyes. What had happened to her mother? My heart wrenched.

"What's your name?" I asked, unsure if she would respond.

Tucking tawny hair, tangled and unkempt, behind an ear, the girl rocked side to side. "Kalae."

My heart leapt. "That's a pretty name," I encouraged. "I'm Evera. How old are you, Kalae?"

The girl scrunched her nose and shook her head once, frustration drawing her brows together.

"I don't know my age either. But when our mentor took my brother and I in, he gave us an age."

Her arms and legs were thin, her cheeks sunken. Malnutrition made it difficult to determine her age.

"Have you bled?" I asked.

She hesitated, then nodded. "Only once," she said, voice meek.

The loneliness of her statement harrowed me. At least when my first bleed had come, I'd been able to rely on Leighis, who'd calmly explained things and given me what I needed. To go through that alone, unknowing …

"I'm going to guess you're around five and ten," I offered, concealing the weight of my sadness for the girl. Old enough for her first bleed, but certainly she couldn't be any older than that. Not with her slight frame.

Consideration laced her expression. "How old do you believe you are?"

I smiled. "About one and twenty."

A clatter came from the street, followed by the raised voices of men arguing. One slurred his speech, the other—a merchant I suspected—riddled off a series of insults and complaints over his broken goods.

I drew a breath, but before I could comfort the girl, she was retreating down the alley, the bare soles of her feet flashing. They were raw, scratched, and agitated. Detecting such things was second nature, a part of who I was, as natural a reaction as a voyager charting the stars.

Unable to do anything more, I raised a hand to my heart and prayed to the sun goddess, Ora, that she might look after her child.

With a slow trudge, mind heavier than when I left, I made my way back to our stall. I carried four apples purchased with my last ferre from an orchardist's stand near the edge of the outer grounds.

"Are you enjoying the festival?" Aureus asked as I drew near. He'd finished assembling the tables and arranging them with our wares. Healing tinctures, salves, dried herbs, and containers of tea leaves were displayed. . Three unopened jars of deer tallow caught my attention.

My brother ran a hand across the back of his neck. At least he wore the wraps.

I tossed him an apple, which he caught with his other hand. "Apples?"

I hummed, not wanting to discuss the encounter with the baker's boy, and offered one of the remaining three apples to our mare. Sorrel flicked her tail and took it eagerly from my flattened palm. She bit it in half, and the other portion fell to the ground. Dipping her head, she snorted at the dust and wrapped her tongue around the remains of the fruit.

Aureus gaped his lips as if he were about to say more, but abandoned the conversation when a couple approached the stall. As he spoke with them, I selected an apple for myself and leaned against one of the tent's support beams.

The man, perhaps in his forties, was rambling on about his wife's frequent complaining about a rash. Both wore earth-toned clothing, simple but clean. Middle class. Perhaps shop owners from another town. Of course, if they were upper class, they wouldn't be in the outer grounds of the city anyway. I took a bite of my apple and listened.

The woman tried to explain, her voice barely more than a whisper, but her husband spoke over her. "Ever since the thing showed up," he said with an exasperated breath, "she's been whining. Constantly. It's getting in the way of her duties, and it's unsightly."

The exchange went back and forth several times. My brother attempted to gain information on the woman's ailment, but each time the man would only shake his head, interjecting with groaning complaints. All the while, the woman shrank more into herself. I rubbed the bridge of my nose, my brother's lecture already playing in my mind.

Heaving a breath, I pushed off the beam, set my half-eaten apple down, and went to my brother's side. He shot me a pointed look, but Aureus was soft-spoken, and this was going nowhere.

"Let me see your rash." I addressed the woman directly, speaking over her husband. The man visibly tensed and directed a disapproving scowl at my brother. I ignored both men.

The woman hesitated, then pulled back a sleeve, revealing patches of irritated skin. The rash was an angry, red, flaking, and localized area. Apprehension settled over me as it did Aureus, and I took a slight step back. "Have you had any muscle weakness?"

"No," the woman replied, voice low. Her husband swallowed.

"Numbness? Lesions anywhere on your body?"

She shook her head, and I sighed, relieved. Aureus, too, relaxed his posture.

"No one else has caught it," the man intercepted. "It's just a rash."

"Prickling rash," Aureus said flatly, speaking aloud the diagnosis I'd come to as well. The rash shared many characteristics of Scale, so much so that it wasn't uncommon for someone to be misdiagnosed. To be labeled with Scale was a death sentence. There was no cure, and not even the wealthy could avoid the laws in place to keep such plagues at bay. The treatment was aconitum poisoning, which brought about a quick and humane death. Then the body would be burned. Prickling rash, however, was treatable and non-contagious.

I selected a salve made of oats and a rare oil imported from the western lands, across the Beridian Sea. The lotion would cost the man, but his wife needed it. With another thought, I grabbed a sack of mineral salts. They would ease her itching if she dissolved them in a warm bath and soaked the agitated areas.

"The salve you apply directly to the rash—"

"What is this?" the man spoke up, voice hardened, now past his initial reservations.

"It's a salve," I reiterated with pointed irritation. Then I realized he was addressing my brother and no longer speaking of treatments. His tone was one I'd heard before. Accusatory.

Aureus, voice level, attempted to placate the situation, explaining the uses of the items I'd selected, but the man no longer seemed interested in his wife's ailment.

"You let your wife meddle with such things?" the man questioned with distaste.

"Sister," I corrected. The conversation was about me, but they'd left *me* out of it.

Aureus rubbed his index and pointer finger between his straight brows and shook his head.

"Sister?" The man's voice lowered. With a narrowing of his eyes, he leaned across the table. "We will not be buying anything from you, witch."

Right. Because I was unmarried, that made me detached. Uncaring. Everything people believed the stereotypical Alidian to be. Throw in potion making, and suddenly I was a witch. Indisputable logic. I huffed, and the man sneered his repulsion, breath reeking of onions and beef.

My lips turned up in a twisted grin. Though I had no magic, I did have a dagger at my thigh. Not that I knew how to use the thing, but it seemed self-explanatory, and I wasn't against learning by experimentation.

My brother took my hand in a gentle hold, a reminder to temper my emotions. To resist my quick anger at the impudence of an unintelligent, conceited man. With forced restraint, I raised my chin and set my shoulders back.

Be complacent. Know your place. Tight-lipped, I scowled.

"My sister is not a witch," Aureus stated, his tone dismissive. "And if you have no intentions of making a purchase, I'm going to ask you to leave our stall."

The man set his jaw, but it was his wife who spoke.

"I want to go," she said. Her voice was weak and edged with nerves. Was she afraid of me? The fire in my chest extinguished, and I lowered my eyes.

When they left, Aureus released a sigh.

"I only wanted to help her," I said under my breath.

"I know." Aureus dropped his hold on my hand. The absence of his touch gave an illusion of distance between us that unsettled me.

Aureus returned the bag of mineral salts to its place and gestured to the lotion I still held.

"Oh," I said, handing it to him. The woman's rash would only get worse without treatment. Just as Kalae's rough feet would only become more pained without the application of deer yarrow and the use of proper foot coverings.

The thin line of my brother's lips turned downward. He set the lotion on the table, out of place. "Evera, there's something we need to discuss."

The apprehension I felt before, the air of something being off about him, returned. This wasn't just a lecture about knowing my place; it was about keeping my practice confined to the back room of our shop, where others wouldn't know of my involvement.

My stomach turned over. "We don't need to discuss anything."

Aureus ran a hand over his short beard. "Ruairc came by the shop the other day, and when we were speaking, another man—"

"I don't want to speak about Ruairc," I said hotly. As children, we'd been close. Then he grew into a young man and started thinking with his cock. Granted, he was gentlemanly enough, but the lingering gazes were enough to put an end to our time as playmates. Over the past three years, he'd asked Aureus for my hand relentlessly.

"If you would just listen, Evera—"

"Abridged version, Aureus," I snapped. I ran a hand through my cinnamon hair, caught on a stubborn knot, and clenched a fist. Frustration made me short, and though bitterness stung at my quip, I held my ground.

"Fine." Aureus's response was cold, his jaw squared and features hard. I deserved it, but it still agitated me. "I've agreed to his request to court you."

"No." I took a step back, bumping into the table. Something fell over behind me and rolled over the wooden planks.

"If he should propose, you will accept it."

"You can't do this," I rasped. "You can't just make these kinds of choices for me." My voice cracked. The truth was, he could. We had no father, and our mentor was old. That left Aureus as the head of our household and gave him every right to force my hand. But he was my brother, and he knew where my heart lay —in our shop, helping others in the only way I could. Marriage meant leaving to live with Ruairc. It meant giving up my skill, my identity.

For a moment, we held each other's eyes. His features were harsh, rigid, while mine were soft; his eyes were cobalt, while mine held a hue of green. The only trait we seemed to share was that of our stubbornness.

I expected retaliation, but Aureus only heaved his chest with a long, drawn-out breath. No, damn him, I would not let him soften, not let him speak gently as if he could soothe me. Anger was easier, so I shoved at his chest to rile him.

Taken off guard, he retreated a step to balance his weight and narrowed his eyes. "Evera, what do you think happens if the rumors get worse?"

No one would make purchases from our shop. We'd lose our home to the tax collector, and Leighis would be on the streets with us. All because people thought I was an Alidian, because of daft assumptions based on stereotypes that held no ground. But I was beyond the point of arguing the folly of such claims. To point out that I was only assumed to be a witch because I was a woman—male healers were thought highly of—would only bring us back to the same point we'd come to many times before. It didn't matter what it was, only what people believed.

The Alidian weren't even all females; Leighis had told us as much when we were growing up. Still, men would leave that aspect out, write it off as a fluke, an anomaly. Women were expected to marry, raise children, to do as their husbands told them to do. They weren't permitted to run businesses or own property, and they certainly weren't allowed to meddle in anything related to healing or the crafting of tinctures. The only true occupation a woman could pursue for herself was as a woman of the night, a prostitute, and that was not a position anyone wanted to find themselves in.

"Are you going to say that this isn't about me? That I owe as much to Leighis for taking us in?" Despite my resolve, my voice broke. A knot formed in my throat, making it hard to breathe.

Aureus said nothing, only held my gaze.

Leighis was old now, his mind clouded more often than not. He hadn't ' only given us a home, but had also let me learn his trade and encouraged my interests. He'd made me who I was, and I owed him everything for that. I chewed on my lip and deflected. "Why Ruairc?"

"Is there someone else you'd choose, Evera?" Aureus challenged. The levelness of his tone only made me want to hit him more. "I want you to be happy, sister. You know I do. I kept hoping you would choose someone for yourself. Gods, I wouldn't have cared who he was so long as he loved and looked after you, but you're one and twenty now. Ruairc is a good man, a provider and protector." He hesitated. "He will be a good husband."

"I won't marry him."

"You will, Evera."

Shaking my head, I sidestepped the table and retreated a few paces, needing to be anywhere else. The sickening feeling of grasping for a lifeline that would not come hollowed me to my very core. What would be left of me without my work in the shop? What would be the point of my existence if the very thing that drove me was taken away?

Aureus stepped toward me and spoke in a cautioning tone. "Don't run off, Evera. I know you're upset, but this isn't the place to go off making rash choices and bad decisions—"

I took a step back, the panic in my chest funneling into rage.

Worry flashed in his eyes, and he grasped for my hand. "Evera—"

"Let me go." I enunciated each word, bitten sharply through my teeth. Aureus sucked in a breath but relented.

I shook my head and turned, disappearing into the crowd before he could see the wetness that dampened my lashes and threatened to tear.

5

NEIRIN

WITH THE COOL stone of the southern gatehouse at my back, I looked across the courtyard. The space was bordered by a formidable stone bailey where soldiers paced, keeping an eye on the ongoing festivities, all the way to the front of the castle and beyond, to the northern gatehouse. Yellow candlelight flickered from sconces along the bailey wall, casting a dance of light and shadows among the colorful gowns and formalwear of those gathered before me. The soft plucking thrum of a lute came from the stage, nearly drowned out by laughter and conversation.

From the crowd, a burly man with onyx hair and a shadow of stubble on his square jaw made his way toward me. I nodded a greeting to the guard, though agitation sent gooseflesh sweeping across my skin at his appearance.

"Neirin." He clasped a hand on my shoulder. His grip was firm, and while the gesture appeared friendly, I understood it for what it was: a show of power..

I raised my chin.

"I'm surprised to see you posted here," he stated, his dour expression a mirror of his father's. He turned, and I followed his

53

gaze to the upper-level balcony where Kaius slouched on his throne, a golden chalice in his hand.Astraea's throne beside him sat empty. My stomach churned. Though she was likely preparing for her show of philanthropy, I couldn't shake the feeling of unease at her absence.

"Being tasked to patrol the courtyard is a mark of my rank, Cyan. Your father posted me here because of my skills." Unfortunately, Rion had been too preoccupied to speak with the King about finding another to take my position in the western lands. Tomorrow I would converse with him. I pushed off the stone wall and stepped to Cyan's side, keeping my eyes on the crowd.

"You shouldn't even be a castle guard," Cyan pressed, tone flat. Positions among the guard were highly sought after and only offered to those of high standing—the sons and nephews of lords or men of the court, typically. Though the King's blood ran in my veins, I was a nameless bastard. A nameless bastard who was meant to be sent off to Valio to train the sons of a lord in swordsmanship. The irony was bitter in the back of my throat. All I wanted was to blend in, to stay where I could keep an eye on Harlan, and protect him.

Veiling my thoughts, I shrugged, letting Cyan's prodding fall flat. It would be easy to counter him, to draw attention to the reason he was stationed here—as a way for the commander to keep an eye on him and ensure his perversion caused no further issues. But there was something more satisfying in simply showing his words didn't affect me.

A moment of quiet fell as the lutanist left the stage and a bard took his place. He picked up a quick tone and bellowed loud enough to draw the attention of those farther away. Several clapped, and many stepped from the flock to dance in the moonlight, the rapping of their shoes on the marble floor adding to the rhythm of the song.

The guard beside me rolled his lip, attention focused on a group of young women gathered before the stage, their plain beige and brown skirts flowing as they spun around each other. The oldest could have been no more than four and ten. A bit young, even for Cyan. Perhaps there would be no avoiding the subject after all.

"Rion's shadow will not always protect you," I said. "Consider that before you succumb to your predilections."

Cyan sneered and spoke in a low voice. "The women I choose to wet my cock with are not of your concern."

I inhaled deeply through my nose, balancing myself. "They" —I gestured with a nod—"are girls, not women."

Cyan scoffed. "*Those girls* are using the festival as an excuse to dance in the courtyard and pretend to be something they never will be—"

"Whether they are ladies or not does not matter."

"Except it does."

I turned to Cyan, his flat tone drawing my attention to the cold depth of his eyes.

"Ever the chivalrous bastard," he said, "stepping in to protect the virtue of young girls. But their purity doesn't matter; no one cares if a commoner's ruined. I'm sure whatever farmer or farrier they get shackled to will be grateful I broke them in for him."

Clenching my jaw, I put a hand casually on the pommel of my sword. "Give me a reason, Cyan, and we will see who the stronger swordsman is." To draw a sword on the commander's son, even for good intentions, would lead to considerable consequences. There was an allure to knowing that causing a scene would soil any chances of being sent to Valio. However, if Cyan were to meet my challenge and accept the duel in the middle of a festival—

No, that would have me dismissed from the guard, if not jailed. I would be of no use to my brother in a cell.

Flexing his fist, Cyan leaned into me, lowering his voice. "Back down."

Around us, the crowd continued in their mirth, oblivious to the subtle tension between us. I held Cyan's eyes, unwavering.

"A note, sir." A familiar voice tensed my jaw as one of the castle's messengers—one of Astraea's boys—stood before us and met my gaze, offering me the letter.

Cyan huffed through his nose and intercepted, taking the scroll roughly from the boy. The child remained unfazed under Cyan's gruffness. Never did the Queen's messengers flinch or waver from a task, even the more unpleasant or dangerous ones. It was a loyalty formed from dependency and unfaltering dedication. From love, even. Without the Queen's refuge, the boy would be long dead, killed in an alley, his loss quickly forgotten.

Cyan broke the tie and opened the scroll, shaking his head once as he read, venom lacing his words. "You've been summoned, Bastard." He held the note out.

Suppressing a sigh, I took his offering. "By whom?"

"The Queen."

The familiar sickening dread of inevitability slicked over me, and though I hardened my jaw to veil my reaction to the letter, the sneer that spread across Cyan's face spoke to my momentary lapse of composure. Grinding my back teeth, I cast my eyes to the messenger and nodded. "Take me to her."

6

———

EVERA

Numb disconnect separated me from the crowd as I walked, keeping my head down. With each step, I watched my boots land, first heel then toe, knowing there should be a sound connected to the motion. That if I were alone, the stone road would echo my pathing.

Stopping, uncaring that I stood in the way of others as they parted and passed in both directions, I released a breath. I shivered, suddenly aware of the cold. It was a bone-aching frigidness, one that went beyond the chill of an early spring night.

One of the shapes moving through the street brushed against my shoulder, and I mumbled incoherent apologies, my voice meek as I stepped to the side.

The touch of daylight was long vanquished. My feet were sore from walking, my mouth dry and parched. The colorful dresses of ladies of the higher class appeared muddier in the dark; they blended in with the simple earth tones of the commoners' skirts. A blurred division.

A bitter taste tainted the back of my throat. Vile, teeth-clenching anger consumed me in a wave of heat; it left just as quickly when the breeze blew, ruffling my skirts and reminding

59

me of the cold. Tears threatened, but this time I held them back. I was every bit the healer Aureus was—less seasoned, perhaps, but no less gifted. In tinctures and the lore of healing plants, I even surpassed him. My fingers curled, restless, and I struck out at a loose stone; it leapt across the cobbles before surrendering to stillness. A sigh escaped me, heavy and hollow. To drown in my own misery, I felt selfish when others—the alidian girl, the homeless—suffered cruelties far greater than mine. Yet guilt flooded me all the same, a tide of injustice and selfishness colliding in my chest until I could scarcely breathe.

To feel bad for myself, even as I stood before a mental cliff, left me feeling vain. Stepping back from that edge meant returning to my brother, returning to the life he had set out for me, and taking it in stride. It was the correct thing to do. A young couple passed me, the woman holding to the man's arm and giggling shyly, and my gaze lingered on them.

Glancing back over my shoulder to where the road led downhill, winding with shops crammed in close together along each side, I released a shuddering breath. Aureus was right. About everything. What I wanted—to heal others, to offer a more substantial contribution than my womb to this life— wasn't a dream within reach. To accept that, to comply, would make the lives of those I loved so much easier.

Married and living with Ruairc, any rumors of me being a witch would fall away like the crumbling clay from the cliffs of Elrune. My soul would collide against the rough stone in its descent, breaking down until the last clumps that remained were devoured entirely by the murky sea.

Applause drew my attention back up the hill where light spilled from the stone archway that led into the castle's outer courtyards. Two gatehouses, one on either side, stood as sentries. Yet, on this night, when the two moons shone full overhead and people came together to celebrate Ayrenven, the harsh divides of society were hazed.

Obscurity.

My hand went to the shape of the mask beneath the flowing fabric of my skirts, and I withdrew it from my pocket. Turning it over, I traced my index finger along the silver filigree outlining the eye slits. My exhale fogged the air, and when I raised my gaze to the archway once more and the courtyards within, a flutter filled my chest.

For one night, I could be anyone. Or it could be no one. Could drink expensive liquor, dance with a stranger, lose myself to pleasure, and the rush of being alive. I could take control of my life while the moons shone overhead. Cast aside Aureus's relentless rules and the weight of all that lay ahead.

Fueled with the thrumming rush of excitement, with the draw of the unknown and new, I raised the mask to my face. It was cold over the bridge of my nose. Looking through, I blinked, and my lashes fluttered against the rim of the eye slits. I tied the silk ribbon behind my head to secure the mask and stepped toward the castle and the allure of a night of anonymity.

The hum of voices rose as I drew nearer and, passing into the courtyard, I was forced to stay still momentarily and catch my breath.

The flooring was marbled with swirls of ebony, white, and gray, with pearlescent flecks that caught the light and sparkled. To my right, a bard performed atop a platform stage, drawing the cheers and laughter of onlookers. Most were unmasked, but a handful bore festival coverings similar to my own.

Girls danced, twirling about carelessly. A few couples swayed, their dance slower, closer, more purposeful—the brush of cheeks, the trailing touch at a woman's waist. My heart leapt, and I closed my eyes, remembering the feel of a man's breath on my neck. It had been some time ago. Too long.

Beyond the dancers and the stage, an open hall of arches ran parallel to an overhead balcony. A creeping ivy of sorts, speckled with little white flowers, grew into the stone. I recognized the flower as one that clung to the manor house I had played in as a child. I used to tuck them into my hair.

Wistfulness drew me forward, and I skirted the busier areas until I stood near the edge of the courtyard before the row of arches. Humming thoughtfully, I plucked one of the flowers and brought it to my nose, breathing in the sweet, nostalgic scent.

Through the arches came a boy of perhaps eight or nine, leading a man in guard's livery. The child's seriousness was striking, so unlike the carefree children of Elrune. His hair was dark as midnight, and his long, curled lashes caught the light like spun silk. He halted before the wide double doors and spun on his heels with a precision that seemed rehearsed, addressing the guard at his back.

They exchanged words, but I was too far to hear. The guard, who kept his back to me, had hair so translucent it appeared almost white in the sconce light, long and braided in sections along one side. Perhaps older for the coloring of his hair, he stood straight and tall with the confidence and stature of a younger man.

The guard, his rigid, stark-black uniform contrasting with the light, flowing layers of the festival visitors, disappeared into the room. Curiosity tingled throughout my body, and when a group of three women entered after the man, I sucked in a breath and adjusted my mask.

Shoulders back, standing tall, I feigned belonging as I entered what appeared to be a greeting room of sorts. It was a large rectangular room; the marble floors were carried in from the courtyard. Chandeliers hung overhead, their dripping beeswax candles that lent the room warmth. Gold filigree trimmed the room along the base of the walls and met with the faintly domed ceiling in a purposeful uniformity that added to the elegance of the space.

"The castle interior is for the King's family and guests only."

Clenching my teeth, I looked over my shoulder. I'd been caught. The women ahead of me gave no notice to the exchange and disappeared down a hall. Likely the wives or daughters of a lord, then.

The dark-haired boy from before had a blank expression. Beside him, a boy a few years older—perhaps ten or twelve—with fair blond hair and round green eyes held my gaze with studying intensity. Dressed in fine clothes and clean-faced, the children were more put together than most adult men from my village.

I adjusted my mask and feigned ignorance. "I was just looking for a place away from the fray to sit for a moment. I'm feeling a bit faint."

The fair-haired boy considered a moment, then nodded to a seating area near the center of the room. "Watch her," he said to the dark-haired boy and dismissed himself into the courtyard.

Pushing past the idea of being watched by a child, I made my way to a tufted velvet upholstered chair and took a seat. *Heavenly.* The emerald fabric gave with just the right amount of cushion under my weight and, strangely, smelled almost floral. I looked around and caught sight of a bronze bowl perforated with pinprick holes atop its decorative lid. A potpourri dish.

I detected lavender and orris root, perhaps. Letting the healer's curiosity get the best of me, I leaned forward and lifted the lid from the small container to study the dried plants within.

"What are you doing?"

The boy's voice just behind my shoulder took me off guard, and I started, knocking over the brass dish and spilling the contents across the glass tabletop and onto the marble flooring. I squeaked, a terribly unladylike little sound.

"Gods, you startled me." I held a hand to my heart. *What am I doing?*

"You don't belong here," the boy observed, cocking his head as he addressed my outfit.

Little prick. I narrowed my eyes.

A door opened, drawing both of our attention. The guard from before, his silver hair tousled and his jaw set, stepped out from a side room. He was not old, as I had suspected by the coloring of his hair. Perhaps mid or late twenties. His dark uniform fit perfectly to his body, suggesting concealed muscles beneath. Gods, he was handsome.

A woman's voice stopped him, and he looked over his shoulder and adjusted the cloth of his collar as she came into view. Her gown was elegant and threaded with jewels that glistened in the chandelier's light. Her gloved hands went to the belt about the guard's waist, and he cast his eyes down as he spoke beneath his breath.

Casually, I stretched my legs out and slouched lower in my chair. Perhaps the carver was correct; obscurity could be quite the advantage. The boy beside my chair looked down at me with pinched brows and a marked look of judgment. Choosing maturity, I scrunched my nose at him.

"Calix," the woman's voice came again, calm and laced with the faintest tone of authority. Motherly, almost, with a lyrical quality.

The boy beside me raised his chin.

I slunk lower in my chair and chewed on my bottom lip.

"Fetch the commander," the woman instructed. "I must have a word with him."

Calix glanced at me out of the corner of his eyes, and a faint frown tugged at his mouth.

Approaching steps rapped along the floor, and I formed silent curses with my lips.

"A commoner," Calix said as the woman joined us. Hunched as I was, slid down in the velvet chair, I gaped my mouth to speak, then shut it again. "She was faint."

Remembering my excuse from before, I rather unceremoniously scooted my bottom back in the seat to sit higher, then straightened my skirts.

"Go, Calix," the woman said, tone level. The green hazel of her eyes stood out amid the dark curls of hair that framed her angled face. "Find the commander, bring him here."

Without another word, the boy bowed his head and made his leave, entirely too composed and polite for a child his age.

"I'm sorry," I said to the woman standing just to my side. Her eyes flicked to the mess of potpourri, then back to me.

A considering expression crossed her face. "You do not know who I am."

I shook my head.

The reservation in the woman's eyes faded, and she released a breath. It was a simple gesture, yet with it, the tension in the air fell away. Despite the woman's gown, which undoubtedly proved her to be a lady of high standing, she felt markedly human and relatable.

"Astraea," she said and smiled.

"Cordelia." I held out my hand. Why I'd given my mother's name, I was unsure.

Astraea's eyes fell to my gesture, then she laughed. It was a light, sing-song sort of sound. "Pleasure to make your acquaintance, Cordelia." She shook my hand.

"Likewise."

"How is your head, dear?" She took a seat in the chair beside mine.

"Better," I replied almost too quickly. "Thank you for asking. I should be going."

Astraea ran her thumb over her bottom lip, looking out to the courtyard behind me. "I would like to level with you, woman to woman."

Curiosity tugged at me, and despite my better sense, I indulged her. "Yes, of course."

"You saw me with that man, did you not?"

Right. Glancing past her, I found he was no longer with us. "I believe I saw you speaking with a guard." I chose the words carefully.

The corner of Astraea's lips twitched up, and again she laughed. "This is not an interrogation," she said, tone light, placing one of her gloved hands on my knee. "Did you find him handsome?"

I should be with my brother back at our wagon, pretending to be ignorant and sipping tea. "I did not get a good look at him."

The touch on my leg was light, and when the woman sighed and sat back, she removed it to straighten her elegant champagne gown. The ruby necklace that rested between her breasts caught in the light of a chandelier and glimmered. "It has been some time since I spoke with a woman outside of the court, one with whom I didn't have to keep up a façade."

Sighing, I relaxed my shoulders. "He was charming to look at," I acquiesced.

Astraea's face lit up. "Yes." She smiled. "I thought so as well. I ask, though, will you keep this discreet? My husband can be a jealous man."

"Yes, of course."

"Good." She rose from her seat and extended her hand. I accepted it, letting her draw me to my feet. "We women must keep so many things cloaked in shadow, must we not? Sometimes I fancy the thought of having been born a man, just so as not to have to sneak about for the simplest of pleasures."

Unable to resist, I scoffed. "I can empathize with that."

The clinking of metal brought a hush to our secret conversation. I peered over my shoulder to where young Calix stood with another guardsman. This one was of a higher ranking than the last, his uniform embellished with honors, glinting trinkets revealing his many acts of service to the kingdom. The commander, I suspected. The man bore a rigid, unfriendly expression and sported short black hair. Peppering stubble lined his jaw.

"Commander Rion." Astraea's easy smile faltered as she addressed the man. She gave me one last glance, apologetic almost. In a notion of casual familiarity that surprised me, she leaned in to my ear. "Enjoy the festival." A warm, gossiping tone filled her light voice. Then she regained her composure and left my side to join Calix and the commander.

Adjusting my mask, I dismissed myself, skirting the group to give them privacy. The commander caught and held my eyes for a moment as I passed. His hand went to the hilt of a dagger sheathed in a scabbard at his back. The man's uniform was similar to the guard's from before—fitted black leather with an arrangement of straps and buckles.

It wasn't until I exited the gathering room and stepped into the open hall of archways overlooking the courtyard that I relieved my lungs, drawing in a sharp breath. The confrontation in the gathering room had left my heart pounding, and though part of me knew I'd seen something I wasn't meant to, I couldn't deny the rush it had given me.

Pockets empty and a curling warmth of rebellion swelling within my chest, I headed toward the platform stage and the bar set into the wall just beyond.

7

NEIRIN

I SKIRTED the crowd and made my way to a bar set back in an alcove, out of view of the balcony. Greenery grew along the dome of the massive stone arch, beautiful in the daylight. By the dim glow of sconces, the plants appeared only as shadows, their leaves shuddering when a breeze caught them. Uncanny, almost, like the many small wings of bats.

Sitting atop a wooden stool, I worked the brass buttons of one of the stiff pockets of my guard's uniform and called to Sindri, the barkeep. He dismissed himself from whatever conversation he was having with a few men at the opposite end of the bar and raised a hand in acknowledgment.

I flipped a silver coin, waiting, watching as the bard bowed, brow gleaming with sweat in the flickering orange light. The crowd clapped, and the higher voices of the ladies called out, encouraging him. I shook my head as the young man feigned surprise at their reactions and conceded to playing one last song.

The rose hip scent of the Queen lingered on my uniform. My gut wrenched, and I subconsciously rubbed at the tender spot beneath my left ear. Another matched it just above my hipbone, but I tried to push those thoughts aside. Impatient, I placed a finger atop the coin I held and, with my other hand, flicked its edge, sending it in a spiral of circles before me.

Sindri approached and leaned against the bar, bracing himself on his forearms.

With a flat palm, I caught the coin and pushed it across the bar. "Liqueur."

Sindri took the coin and poured a small glass of amber-colored liquid. "Drinking on patrol again, are we?" The barkeep's eyes were a deep brown, yet they always held a gleam of mirth, which gave them an odd lightness, a shine.

Grunting, I took the drink and tossed it back. When I lowered my fist to the table, he filled the cup again. *I've been a fool to think I can avoid Astraea.* The second shot brought with it a burn in the back of my throat and a comforting numbness. I sighed as the scratching of the monster beneath my skin settled, then ceased. I rubbed at my temples with my left hand and inhaled deeply when the scent of my leather gloves overpowered the sickening scent of the Queen's rose perfume.

"You shouldn't let Cyan get to you," Sindri said.

I raised my head from my palm. Had he seen us talking before? My visit with Astraea had distracted me so much so that I'd forgotten about Cyan. Again, my stomach twisted, and I peered into the crowd, but the group of young girls who'd been dancing was nowhere in sight. Neither was Cyan.

I grunted in response.

"Another drink and some quiet, friend?"

I nodded, grateful, and shot back the glass so it could be filled once more, withdrawing another canin to cover my tab as I drank. "Thank you, Sindri."

The barkeep left me to my thoughts, returning to pick up the casual conversation with the men from before. Sindri had a confident air that I envied. The dance in his smile, the way people laughed when he spoke. Even as I preferred the quiet, a part of me longed to be so easily and warmly received by others.

I traced a finger around the rim of my cup.

A woman came to sit two stools down, and Sindri went to her. I gave the exchange little attention, even as the woman's voice rose, sharp and clipped as she began to argue with him. I clenched my jaw, the twinge of a headache prickling at my temples, then tossed back my drink, trying to tune them out.

"Well, I don't have any coin," the woman said pointedly.

"I'm sorry—"

"Are you?" she said.

I gritted my teeth. My glass was empty, and I couldn't hear myself think. I drew an additional silver canin from my pocket, palmed it on the counter, and slid it across the smooth surface. It stopped between the two, halting their bickering, and they turned to me in unison. Sindri raised a thin black brow, but it was the woman who captivated me. Enthralled me.

My chest thrummed. I inhaled sharply, the air crisp and new, as if I'd never drawn breath before.

The coloring of her hair was unusual. It reminded me of Nyana's spices, a mix of cinnamon, turmeric, and cayenne. A mask veiled her eyes and gave her an air of mystery. Beneath the sudden racing of my heart, I fought to determine what it was that drew my attention to her so sharply. Yet there was nothing from my training that would cause me to set her apart, no notion that she was a threat or really anyone at all. The simple coloring of her skirts suggested she was a commoner enjoying the courtyard.

The woman's lips curved up into a smile, mocking almost, as she turned back to Sindri and pointedly pushed the coin to him. Her lips were a faint peach tone, and the thought of tasting them sent a rush of heat through my body. The sensation was indescribable. Reminiscent almost of the shock that comes with diving into frigid water, yet also entirely different. I swallowed and turned my eyes back to my drink.

With a shudder, I fidgeted in my seat, face heating. The beating of my heart resonated throughout my body, throbbed even in my cock. How long had I been vexed by my inability to get a rise for a woman? Yet as I hardened, my breaches becoming increasingly too confining for the size of me, a new uneasiness filled me. One more assertive than Cyan's jibes, heavier than the lingering scent of rose hips, and more pressing, even, than the thoughts of being sent across the sea to Valio.

"Are you alright?" Sindri asked under his breath, leaning in close and refilling my cup. I stared at his presence, and he raised one brow in question.

"I'm fine," I said, tone short. I lowered my eyes back to my glass.

Sindri stretched and turned his back to the bar, leaning against it on my other side. He lowered to an elbow, feigning interest in the bard, though his eyes occasionally drifted back to the woman. "She's pretty," he said just above a whisper, "but you've turned away others just as fair. What's different about this one?"

Unable to resist, I risked another glance. The woman tapped her fingers on the bar top to the beat of the bard's song. The words choked in my throat, yet the throbbing of my need was irrefutable. Voice low, I aired the realization, more to myself than to Sindri. "I desire her."

Snorting back laughter, Sindri coughed and pounded his chest. When the woman turned to him, I quickly averted my eyes. Sindri played it off in the easy-talking way of a barkeep, then propped his forearms on the bar, leaning in close again. When he spoke, amusement laced his tone.

"Perhaps don't tell *her* that so bluntly," he advised.

Lacking a proper response, I grunted.

"Just talk to her," Sindri encouraged. With a considering

twist of his lips, he added, "And maybe slow down on the liquor."

Reminded of my drink, I eagerly consumed it, hoping it might settle my nerves. Sindri shook his head, tsked, and left me.

Talk to her.

Right. I could do that. I was confident with women, knew how to make them swoon. But where did this desire come from? Why now, after all these years? Why her?

I felt the barstool beside mine scoot sideways and turned to find the woman directly beside me. She smelled of Nyana's herbs—an earthy scent, one much more pleasant than Astraea's perfume. All natural, I suspected.

"The barkeep asked me to move over a seat," she said, "so there would be more room for people wanting to sit together as a group." The woman tipped her head, considering. "Though it really doesn't seem that busy. Everyone's dancing."

My mouth went dry. Maybe not so confident after all. "The bard plays well."

"The same one comes to our local inn sometimes," she mused, evidently much more comfortable than I was. "I recognize him."

There were certainly replies to be given, but they were all lost on me, so I pinched my lips and shifted in my seat. Though I wasn't one for anxious ticks, I began wiggling the toes of my right foot in my boot. Every muscle in my body screamed for me to stand, to not sit still. *To do something.*

"Though he says each song is his last, he keeps playing," the woman continued. "Every time he passes through, it's the same routine, yet no one seems to tire of it."

"Do you tire of it?"

The woman shrugged, brought her glass to her lips, and turned her head back. Coughing, she set the glass back down, laughter breaking up her rasps. The sound was light, melodious.

The urge to raise her mask, to gaze into her eyes, was nearly strong enough for me to reach out. But I refrained, clenching my fist in my lap instead. "Do you need water?" I queried.

"No." She waved her hand. "It's good. Remarkable, actually. Just much stronger than I'm used to." She tilted her head back, and when her gaze met mine, the light hit just right to catch beneath the eye slits of her mask. Irises of a stunning blue-green sage shone back at me with … was that mischief? She turned her attention back to the stage. "And I prefer storytellers."

"Someone will be coming to recite the old lore," I said, recalling the conversation Harlan had overheard. "The night is new, still."

She hummed, and Sindri came to refill our glasses. I laid out another two canins, having lost track of my tab, and he took them without any further comment. The woman watched the exchange but gave no reply.

The bard played on, as the woman predicted, through another four songs. When he left the stage, a woman with a harp took his place and sat atop a stool. She played with her instrument tucked at her chin, and those dancing either changed their pace or dispersed, replaced by others.

The harp's song was sweet and rich. It cast an air of romance, reflected in the hooded gazes of the women before the stage, their arms wrapped over their men's shoulders, bodies pressed close together in a gentle sway.

"Would you like to dance?" I asked the woman, emboldened by the shift in atmosphere.

Her tone soured slightly. "Have you not had enough dancing for one night already?"

Confused, I drew my brows together.

For a moment, she studied me, then turned in her seat and leaned back against the bar, her head tilted up to the sky. "I was hoping the storyteller would be next."

Unsure how to respond, I made a slight sound of acknowledgement and followed her gaze to the two moons, full on this night. They shone bright, despite the haze in the sky.

"A traveler came to our inn once," she said, "and told a story of the moon gods. He said that when Ayre and Wyn fought, their anger cast upon the world in strikes of lightning and booms of thunder. And that the rain was their sisters' tears."

Unable to resist, I snorted. "Storytellers will make up anything if they believe it will earn them coin and fund their travels."

"Perhaps. It's something to consider, though. When my brother and I fight, it sometimes feels as if a storm has broken loose within me."

The way she let her sentence fall off caught my attention. Something was bothering her, weighing her down, and though it wasn't my place to press, I couldn't stop myself. "Brothers can be …" I sighed.

"Pricks?"

Caught off guard by the woman's candor, I laughed. Again, my heart leapt against my ribs. "Yes, something like that."

"I've not heard Neirin laugh before," Sindri said, coming to check our glasses. Leaning in close to the woman, he whispered something in her ear, and she giggled.

"What has he told you?" I asked when Sindri left us again, suspicious of the barkeep.

The woman took a sip from her cup, and I resisted the urge to grin at her poor handling of the smooth drink. When she lowered the cup back to the bar, she leaned toward me. She looked up at me through her lashes, her face close enough to mine to feel her breath, to see her eyes behind the slits in the mask. I sucked in my breath, heart pounding, suddenly very aware again of the effect she had on me as she rested a hand on my thigh.

I swallowed, and she lost her composure, a smile tugging at her lips. "He said that you fancy me."

Damn the barkeep. I lowered my voice. "And if I do?" The confidence in my tone boosted my ego, if only slightly.

The woman narrowed her eyes, a challenge dancing in them, and trailed her hand higher on my thigh. Biting her lower lip, she hummed. "I don't know, Neirin, what if you do?"

Hearing my name on her tongue made my cock ache, almost painfully so. Her hand stilled in its path, and despite my efforts of restraint, I shifted my hips, instinct driving me, needing more. A look of satisfaction flashed in her eyes, glinting with mischief.

Before I could respond or find the courage to close the short gap between us and kiss her, she withdrew. The lack of her presence, and warmth, caused a knot to form in my throat.

"You were telling me of your brother," she said as if the conversation had never shifted.

"Sindri is a traitor, and you," I rumbled, letting playful amusement lace my words, "are a tease."

She laughed and shrugged.

Despite the fluster I felt in her presence, the woman was easy to talk to; her candor was light, casual, and whatever forwardness I lacked, she more than made up for. She was bold and a bit crass. Stunning.

Determined to keep her engaged in conversation, I followed her lead. "He is young, irresponsible. It lends me to worrying over him and…his future. His safety. What of your brother?"

Scoffing, she took another minuscule sip of her liquor. "My brother aims to marry me off to a shoemaker."

"Do you care for the man?" The words stung.

"Not like that, no." She set her eyes back to the night sky. "But if I do not marry— It's not about what I want."

The sorrow in her tone drew a sigh from my lungs. "Very rarely is our life what we want it to be." I ran my hand through the section of my hair left unbraided. *What we want it to be.* A muscle in my jaw flexed.

Perhaps the only thing worse than having unfulfilled desires was to not have any hopes for the future to begin with. But what future could I have? All I could do was look after my brother. That was my purpose, and that alone was all I needed. In an effort to lighten our conversation, I nudged her shoulder playfully. "Tell me then, what do you want?"

With a tilt of her head, she looked over her shoulder at me, studying. "What I want will only cause trouble for my family." She spoke faintly, defeat lacing the words. "The people in our village whisper that I am a witch."

A witch. *An Alidian.* My stomach dropped. "Are you a witch?"

"Would it matter if I were?"

"No," I said, knowing that if I hesitated in my response, it would distance her affections. Still, the lie was bitter on my tongue.

Seemingly not catching the weight her question bore on me, she resorted to rambling. It was one of the reasons I didn't take to courting a woman, the way they went on about things. Quiet was better. Yet with her, I didn't mind. Clearly, the situation with her brother burdened her, and in truth, I could listen to her voice endlessly without growing tired of it.

Half of what she told me made little sense out of context, but I listened anyway. I let her speak and enjoyed the play of light across her soft features, as well as the sharp, contrasting shadows the mask cast in curving shapes and ridges on her face.

"So yes," she finished with a breath. "He is a prick." I parted my lips to give a response, but she cut me off. "And who is he to tell me who to bed?"

If her brother was the head of their house, it was in his right to arrange a betrothal for her. But something about the woman made custom seem irrelevant. There was a fire within her, one that, if quenched, would leave a darkness in the world.

My heart leapt. Though my nerves had lessened as we spoke, they flushed through me again. But this was my chance. I recognized the signs in the way she positioned herself at the edge of her stool closer to me, and the lingering glances. Even the path of her conversation was pointed.

"Yes." I tucked a strand of her cinnamon curls behind her ear, letting my touch pause on her cheek before I drew back. "Who is he to tell you who to bed?"

Mischief danced in her eyes again, and when they lowered to my lips, I took my chance.

Leaning in until my nose brushed hers, I brought my hand back to the side of her face and stroked along her jawline with my thumb. She whimpered faintly. The sound tightened my body, and I released a heady breath. But what if, like with Frella, I was unable? If I lost my vigor? The thought made me hesitate.

"I've broken rules today," the woman said against my lips at my demurral, allure thickening her voice with sex. Her fingers tapped at my thigh.

"Your brother's rules?"

She hummed her acknowledgement.

"Are you telling me this because you plan to break another?"

She ran her nose along mine.

I sucked in a breath as she moved her hand slowly, teasingly, sending waves of throbbing need between my legs. When her touch found me, she grasped my length through the cloth of my pants, and I let my head fall back, entirely lost in the sensation of her touch. I thrust against her, and a faint sound of amusement escaped her.

Through the haze of need, remembrance of Frella's laughter came back to me. I drew back. But this woman's eyes held a different kind of teasing. Narrowing my own, I withdrew her hand, even as it went against all my desires to do so.

"Tease," I lectured.

"Are you so sure?"

"Are you implying you aren't?"

She shrugged.

On the bar top, my last drink lay untouched. I took it and gestured, using the moment to calm my racing heart. The woman made me weak, shaken, and desperate in ways I didn't know were possible.

Playing along, the woman retrieved her half-finished shot and held it up, mirroring me.

"To witches and monsters," I toasted, and she tipped her glass to mine. The clink resonated through me, a realization of the words I'd spoken. They'd come to me without thought. Peering over the rim of her cup, she took the remainder of the liquor in stride. I mimicked her, yet the weight of my toast left me conflicted, unsure.

"Are you a monster?"

The question took me off guard, sobered me. I gritted my teeth to still the tremble of my hands and pushed down the memory of Thatch's eyes, wide, as he'd backed away from me all those years ago. I shut out the memory of the hate in his eyes as he retrieved his wooden sword from his feet.

My response came in a breath. "Yes."

The woman set her glass down, and I followed her movements, surprised when her expression softened. I'd laid the most vulnerable part of myself before her, yet she didn't falter. Even if she couldn't possibly understand the extent of my words. The pounding of my heart fumbled and leapt.

"Aren't you going to ask if it matters?" she asked.

If being a monster mattered? If it scared her? If she hated me as much as I hated myself? "I—"

"It doesn't." Her words were resolute. With them, something locked into place. It terrified me, but there was no way to deny it.

My soul became hers.

"We all have monsters," she said. "I'm not afraid of yours."

Heart pounding, I offered her my hand. "Dance with me." The words came out stilted, but if she had noticed, she did not say so. Nervous excitement heated my veins. Would she turn down the invitation again?

For a brief moment, she rocked in her seat as if considering. Then she hopped down from the barstool, almost childish in her carefree mannerisms, so unlike those of the ladies of the court. Even the girls in Nyana's kitchen held themselves with more decorum; it was expected of them, working in the castle as they did.

A strange lightness fluttered in my chest. Tucking her hand in the crook of my arm, I led her to a space close to the front of the stage, though off to the side enough that we weren't crowded in by others. The harpist's tune was rich, slow, and held a note of melancholy.

"What is your name?" I asked as she turned to me, and I took her waist in my hands. My heart thundered.

"Tonight, I am no one." She hooked her arms over my shoulders.

Sighing, I pulled her body close against mine, and we swayed together to the emotive tune. "So, you are an *elusive* tease."

Resting her head against my chest, she laughed faintly. The sound made my heart flip. "Are you complaining?"

"No. Though"—I rested my chin atop her head—"I would like something to call you. You have my name. It seems only fair."

"Cordelia."

"A fake name?"

"No," she said, tilting her head up. The sparkle of her eyes caught the light, and again I found myself struck with the desire to raise her mask and gaze upon her unveiled face. "My mother's name."

I grunted, and a smile tugged at my lips. Leaning down, I spoke against her ear. "Do you truly wish for me to call you by your mother's name tonight?" My question held clear implications, and a flare of heat rose in my chest at my own boldness.

Brushing her cheek against mine, she rose to her toes, and I tightened my hold at her waist. The faintest touch of her lips brushed my neck. The remembrance of the scent of rose hips returned to me in an instant, churning my stomach and subduing my confidence.

What am I doing?

When I stood straighter, she took the hint and lowered from her toes, a frown tugging on her lips. She rolled her bottom lip with her teeth, worrying it, and an ache of need shot straight to my groin.

After all these years, why now? Why her?

We swayed in quiet, her head resting sideways against my chest and her fingers playing subtly with my hair behind my neck. Without consciousness, I lowered my head and breathed in the scent of her hair. The tightness in my pants became prevalent again, and a low groan escaped my lips. Hardly notable, but she caught it.

The tease of a woman giggled and swayed her hips against me. I sucked in a breath. "Cordelia," I mock-lectured.

She looked up at me, her smile dancing with warmth. "No," she laughed. "No, you're right; don't call me that."

"Then what can I call you?" I leaned in pointedly, closing my eyes and breathing against her lips.

The woman swallowed. For a moment, I thought she might retreat. Instead, she pressed her breasts against me, raised to her toes again, and closed the distance between us. The kiss wasn't pressing. When I sought to deepen it, she pulled back. "Tonight," she said again, the words firmer this time, "I am no one."

Disappointment tugged, even as the ghost of her kiss still lingered on my lips.

"Can you come to terms with that?" she asked.

I tucked a strand of hair behind her ear, wishing I no longer wore my gloves so that I could feel her soft skin. How could I tell her what this meant to me—this sudden attraction, the way she roused me as no one had before. That if her suggestive notions held any weight, she may very well end up being my first. Would she be my only? Would I never know her name?

"If I must," I conceded.

The mask partially veiled the softening of her features. The corners of her lips relaxed in not a frown, but not a smile either. It was as if I could somehow detect a sadness in her, a melancholy. Perhaps I was reading too much into things, or perhaps it was only my nerves.

With my index finger and thumb, I raised her chin, and again the light caught at just the right angle to illuminate her eyes between the slits of the mask. Slowly, I lowered my head to hers, and when the warmth of her lips met mine, heat coursed through my body. A tremble raced along my spine, and I fought the urgent desire to run my hands lower down her waist, cup her ass, pull her more firmly against me.

When she parted her lips, I took the offering, deepening our kiss, letting the fire between us spark, blaze. The dance of her tongue along mine spoke of the confidence of experience. She'd been with others. Of course she had. It was evident in the way she composed herself. Still, my blood heated at the thought of her with another. I growled against her mouth, and when our kiss broke, I nipped at her bottom lip.

She moaned—an involuntary noise I was certain—as her cheeks flushed, and she lowered her forehead. A rumble of amusement came from my chest, and when it did, she mumbled an incoherent rapprochement.

Stroking her cheek, I coaxed her to look up at me again, and spoke with deliberateness. "Do not be ashamed of the sounds you make."

She bit her bottom lip, and I detected a battle of nerves and longing within her. If only she knew how much she frightened me, how much all of it did. Confidence could be feigned, as could all emotions. But her bashfulness, the rapid rise and fall of her chest—those things were real, true, and raw.

"Is there somewhere we can go?" Her question was quiet, meek, nearly mute.

Leaning down to speak against her ear, I pulled her firmer against me, inconspicuous enough to not draw attention, but pressing enough that she could feel my desire for her against her belly. "Is that what you want? Are you sure?"

Her breath came in a pant. "Yes."

Excitement rushed through my veins as being with a woman —inside of a woman—became a feasible prospect. Being with *this* woman. The woman with cinnamon colored hair, mischievous grins, and knowing touches. What would it feel like to move inside of her, when the press of her body against mine alone evoked such sensations?

She twisted herself into my grasp, her back settled against my chest as if she belonged there—effortlessly. My arms wrapped at her torso, it all felt so incredibly natural. *So right.* Hesitantly, I rested my cheek on the top of her head, knowing there was an intimacy to it not accordant with what we were sharing.

When she didn't brush me off, I buried my face in her hair, taking comfort in the undertones of herbs and spices she always smelt of.

"That woman," she said in a hush, and I raised my eyes to the stage. "Who is she?"

My stomach sank. Astraea. "You do not know your Queen?" I questioned beneath my breath so only she would hear me as those around us set their attention on the stage.

She inhaled sharply but gave no further response as the Queen began her speech. It was the same show of altruism each year—warm smiles, acknowledgment of the lords and men of the court who made donations toward the benefit. Then she would parade her newest charity cases upon the stage, raising shows of approval from the crowd.

"Come," I said against the woman's ear. I had no desire to watch the kingdom fawn over Astraea and her generosity.

For a moment, the woman in my arms hesitated. There was a new tenseness in her shoulders, a stiffness to her form. Before I could question it, the Queen's eyes fell upon us in the crowd, and I held my breath. The monster beneath my skin crawled, scratched, and writhed under her gaze, and the desperate need to be anywhere else overwhelmed even my desires for the woman I held.

Then the Queen nodded faintly in acknowledgment and smiled. But not of me, of the woman with the cinnamon hair. Confusion drew my brows inward, but in the next breath, the Queen disregarded us to voice the names of the two new children that would join her under her cause. Both boys. The children she brought in off the streets were always male. Boys with the special skills she needed were much harder to come by, much rarer, but the tasks of a messenger were considered unsuitable for girls.

Someone brushed against me, and I lowered my eyes as Calix came to stand beside me. He gazed up at me with that void expression all of Astraea's messengers bore. To the Queen's credit, the boy was well-trained. His restraint in this proximity was commendable.

"Let's go," I said again to the woman in my arms, irked by the child and the power he believed he held over me. No, the power he did hold over me. Again, my stomach roiled.

This time, my unnamed companion nodded and allowed me to lead her through the gathered group and toward one of the towers that stood where the courtyard wall met the castle. It was one of the lesser-known entry points to the inner castle, one used only by soldiers and guards. It would be quiet, far enough from the fray that no one would notice our tryst.

I took one last glance over my shoulder to where Astraea knelt between the two boys on the stage, speaking to them, all broad smiles. Then I dipped my head and led the woman beneath a stone archway.

My eyes adjusted quickly to the dimness within the tower. Two soldiers stood together, posed with bows. They exchanged confused looks. I didn't know their names; castle guards rarely worked alongside soldiers. It didn't matter.

"Out," I snarled, my unnerved energy showing more than I'd anticipated. The men jumped, standing taller and abruptly dismissing themselves. Taking a sense of satisfaction from their response, I snorted my approval. The uniform had its advantages—even as a nameless bastard, I was held at a significantly higher rank than these men. They knew enough not to contradict a demand given to them by a castle guard.

Unsurprisingly, the two had gone through the doorway that led into the castle, not out to the courtyard. Soldiers posted in the towers were commonly residents of the private castle garrison. Such men were trained to defend the castle's interior first and foremost.

When the door shut, I turned back to my companion.

She stood with her back up against the wall, a playful smile tugging at her lips. "You dance with Queens and commoners alike, then?"

Danced with Queens and commoners alike? I opened my mouth to speak, but the woman grabbed me by the buckles on my uniform and pulled me toward her. She nodded to the doorway the soldiers had exited, seeming again to shift the conversation.

"Do all men cower when you speak?" she asked, a seductive depth altering her tone.

Despite the tension in my body, I laughed, surprised by her question. "No." I braced a hand against the stone above her. Quirking a smile, I let thoughts of the Queen leave me and refocused my mind on the stunning and curious stranger before me. "Only the soldiers."

The woman hummed and traced the dimple at my cheek, the one that only showed when I smiled. Something I did rarely, it seemed. Her exploratory touch made me feel vulnerable, rocked by the intimacy of a shared moment, of the connection. These sensations were balanced by more primal, pressing desires that sent a flushing heat radiating across my skin. The urgency to take her and rut her returned, pulsing between my legs. I longed for her to learn not just my body, but my soul. It was a sudden and strange realization; one I could not accept even as I knew the absolute truth of it.

Her fingers carved a slow path along my jaw, sliding down the side of my throat. When she stilled and retraced a spot, I inhaled sharply. The mark Astraea had left on me was still tender. In the light of a flickering sconce, the woman's lashes caught, the only tell in the darkness that she'd raised her eyes to mine. Again, I longed to withdraw her mask, to expel the concealment.

Her touch explored along my collarbone then stopped again. "What causes scars like this?"

The marks she indicated were nearly undetectable by sight, faintly raised and branching like tree roots. So few ever noticed them. Then again, so few ever touched me so intimately.

I lowered her hand and shook my head, a heaviness weighing me down, tainting the moment. "I do not wish to speak about my scars." I whispered, my voice weighted with regret.

The woman pouted, and I touched my thumb to her bottom lip in an attempt to redirect her attention. Again, her lashes flitted in the yellow light, and she nipped at me, catching the leather of my glove between her teeth, raising her chin. A challenge.

Slowly, I withdrew my fingers from their confines, and she

dropped the glove. It fell between us to the stone floor. The hold she had over me was as unsettling as it was intoxicating, tugging me from my duty as a guard. She was a mystery I couldn't look away from.

When I brought my thumb to her mouth again, she sucked it in, her tongue slick, warm, and wet. As she teased me, I yielded to my imagination, my aching desires. Images sparked behind my eyes as I gave into fantasies of her on her knees before me.

"Do not tease me, or you'll be left with something else in your mouth," I warned, my voice a low rumble. I withdrew my finger, letting my thumb trail down and catch her by her chin.

I studied her like that, the small frame of her face held in my hand. To have her locked against the wall as I did was possessive, yet she had pulled me to her. It was her invitation to take this role, and the spark in her eyes said that her submission was something only to be granted, not taken. Something about that made me ache, for I knew what she wanted from me was no more than a fleeting moment. A decision she had made for herself when she felt her life was being planned for her.

"Please, give me your name." The plea revealed my aching desire, and lacked my earlier gruffness. Swallowing, I reached for her mask. She turned from my touch.

"We each have our secrets," she said, coldness lacing her words. "I didn't push yours."

The weight of her statement settled over me. I dropped her chin, and as if she detected me pulling away, she brought her hand to my chest. "Give me this."

I replied with a gruff noise from my throat, not quite a scoff. "Give you concession to this disagreement, or to—"

The tightening of her grip and tug at my uniform cut me off. Her nose scrunched, and I suspected that beneath her mask, her eyes narrowed. The woman was so readable, even with her face half concealed as it was. There was something oddly endearing about that.

"Very well, Cordelia."

She exhaled sharply through her nose, a little sound of annoyance.

starting at my collar, she worked nimbly with her fingers at the brass buttons that lined the front of my jacket. Other straps crisscrossed with buckles, clips, and latches, making the top tedious to remove. It gave me a moment to think, though, and I enjoyed watching her undress me.

Even as it was distasteful to do so, I thought briefly of the other women I'd shared intimacy with over the past year. Mentally, I tried to tick them off. There was the blonde in Aldruil whom I'd lain with in the gardens and set my mouth between her legs until she shuddered with release. She'd gone by Trill, but I couldn't remember what it was short for. Then the sisters in Literra, who'd kissed each other passionately, which unsettled me more than anything, but it was a story to tell the other men of the guard. Had I even asked their names?

Perhaps it wasn't important, then, that I knew this woman's name. In time, maybe it wouldn't matter. The thought crinkled the lines in my brow.

Oblivious to my musing, the woman moved to the large buckle that belted at my waist. As she unlatched it, I tugged off my other glove with my teeth, as she had the first, and let it drop before returning my hand to the wall. The build of our shared fervor drew out a primal roughness, a possessiveness.

Exhaling headily, she freed my belt. It fell to the ground, and its metal latch clattered across the stone, echoing around the small room. The sound paused time, held it, and when quiet fell around us again, everything else fell away. Only instinct, drive, and need remained.

Eagerly, the woman opened my uniform jacket only to meet with another layer of clothing—a dark cotton undershirt.

"Dammit," she hissed.

I laughed, rumbling, amused at first, then deeply aroused to see her struggling. Desperate.

Mine.

Aiding her, I untucked the shirt from my breeches and took her hand in my own, drawing it beneath the cotton. Her fingers trailed over scars, but she moved past them without comment. Breath heady, she trailed her touch down one of the muscular grooves alongside my hip and bit her lip.

"Is this where you show me that you aren't a tease?" I asked, leaning in, caging her.

Her response was a whimper.

I kissed her chastely but denied her further advancement, eliciting another moan from her parted lips. She rocked her hips off the wall, her squirming nearly driving me to lose my constraint.

I needed more.

Growling against her mouth, I quickly worked the ties of my pants and loosened them, a silent challenge. I urged her hand back to the band. Panting, she gave in and pulled the cloth down just enough to free my length.

She wrapped her fingers around it. My cock throbbed beneath her grasp, and all conscious thought faded to a white light of pleasure. I shuddered and hung my head, breathing against her ear. Her hand stroked up then back to the base, and I groaned.

Instinct pulled at me, telling me to turn her, push her to the wall, and bunch up her skirts, to take her from behind like that, where I could grasp her hips for leverage. Clenching my jaw, I forced restraint, wanting to draw this out, to make it pleasurable not just for myself but for her as well.

And despite the haze of lust, a knowing nagged at me that this may be my only time. I couldn't rationalize it, but beyond having never risen for a woman before, it was as if I knew that my body belonged to the elusive, beautiful woman without a name.

Can you come to terms with that? She'd asked.

I ground my teeth. I could very well never see her again. Still, to deny myself the opportunity to explore this inexplicable connection … Perhaps it was my need speaking, or perhaps it was the vulnerabilities of my past, a resolution to prove myself a man. Or, perhaps it was something more, something deeper. I exhaled a long breath through my nose. It didn't matter the reason, not at this moment. Reasoning would come later, with the clarity of dawn, but I would not regret this, I knew. And that was all that mattered.

8

———————

EVERA

THE LENGTH of his cock was impressive, and with my hand wrapped around its girth, my fingers barely touched. As far as bad decisions went, I was pleased with mine.

As I moved my hand along his length, the skin velvet in my grasp, a fleeting moment of hesitation struck me. Aureus's disappointed scowl flitted before my eyes. Finding a rush in a stranger's touch was, possibly, not the healthiest coping mechanism, but it wasn't as if I was a virgin. This wouldn't change anything. It was just an escape. A chance to enjoy the frivolousness found in the dark, taken in obscurity.

Neirin moaned at my touch, drawing me from my thoughts, and I ridiculed myself for my moment of uncertainty. The man was delicious. *The consort of a Queen.* And she'd seen me with him, nodded her blessing. I would enjoy this man, would revel in knowing that a man who lay with royalty desired me, ached for me. Swearing off thoughts of the future, of what was right or wrong, and of my brother's condemnations, I put them to the side—far to the side. I returned to the present and quickened my strokes.

Neirin hung his head, and the rough stubble along his jaw

93

brushed my temple. His breathing hitched, and he suppressed a moan as he rocked his hips against me.

"If you don't slow down—" His warning ended with a guttural rasp, and he wrapped his hand over mine, stilling my motions. Beneath our grip, his cock throbbed. And fuck, there was something primal and raw about that. It sent an ache straight to my center. I raised my eyes to his, and a whimper caught in my throat.

His face was perfection, chiseled and rugged. High cheekbones complemented the oval shape and stern lines of his jaw—harsh, almost, as if set by a life spent in focused determination. The slight part of his lips as he exhaled and held my gaze was seductive and tantalizing. Then there were his eyes, set beneath drawn brows. They were a soft gray, deep and thoughtful. In the dark of the room, they reminded me of the twin moons that watched over the courtyard.

When he brushed his nose along my cheek, his silver hair fell between us. Portions of it were braided, others left loose in a manner I assumed was meant to keep it out of his face when fighting. The length of it came past his shoulders.

Without breaking my gaze, Neirin rumbled against my neck. He worked his length in our shared grasp with languid movements. "Slow," he instructed against my ear.

He withdrew his hand and returned it to the wall just above my head. There was a possessiveness in the way he pinned me between his body and the cold stone. Strength emanated from him, yet he made no move to take me. He was letting me explore him, giving me control. The way he let me touch him, let me bring him pleasure, only made me want him more.

It made me feel powerful.

I stroked up the base of his length, and a bead of liquid formed at its tip. I ran a finger over it, and he shuddered.

"Tease," he reprimanded, voice husky.

Releasing him, I tilted my head against the stone, baring my neck. The change in position arched my back and pushed my breasts out, and when he lowered his gaze, hunger flared in his eyes. His lips parted, and his exhale fogged between us, prickling my skin.

A low sound came from him as he cupped one of my breasts in his palm. The touch sent shocks of pleasure through my body, and when his fingers found my nipple beneath the fabric of my dress, I inhaled sharply. Neirin groaned his pleasure and made small circles with his thumb.

Roughly, he pulled down the top of my dress, and I rocked against him, urged on by the momentary lapse in his restraint. My nipples hardened to firm buds in the chill of the air, and when Neirin dipped his head to take one in his mouth, warmth pooled between my legs.

I arched further into him, needing this, needing him, and he rewarded me with a flick of his tongue. All my awareness focused on that one hardened point, wet and puckered by the cold as he returned his thumb to it and circled, moving the warmth of his lips to the other side where he kissed first, then sucked with a fevered need. The sensation was too much.

"Neirin, I—"

His lips stole my words, the kiss deep and full of desire. He pushed his body against mine, pressing a thigh between my legs. I rocked against it, losing myself to the need, taking what friction he would give me.

His touch left my breast, and he grasped my hand, drawing it up and pinning it above my head. His grip on me was firm but not painful. Possessive, claiming.

A soft moan escaped me, and he sucked my bottom lip into his mouth. When he released my lip, I raised my chin, and he trailed frenzied kisses along my jawline to my neck. He spread his fingers, and I mimicked his motion, my hand trapped between his and the wall. He rubbed his thigh against my center, his cock firm against my belly.

"I need you," I gasped, grinding shamelessly against him.

Neirin stilled, his lips at my neck. When I whimpered and circled my hips, he raked his teeth across my fevered skin and bit.

I gulped in a breath. Licking the tender spot to soothe the initial sting, he pinned me firmly to the wall with his body, stilling my movements. Where the sharpness of his bite lingered, tingles of pleasure shot out, sending tendrils of need through me. He found my pulse and sucked.

"Please." My skin was on fire. I needed him now.

Pulling back, he met my eyes. He was breathing heavily, his chest rising and falling beneath his dark cloth shirt. Damn the thing. I longed to see his body, to explore him with more than hastened touches beneath his clothing.

Whimpering with impatience, I squirmed, but he held me firm . t My mouth found his again, demanding, teeth grazing his lips in a sharp nip. Neirin's low growl rumbled between us, edged with frustration, and his jaw tightened as his eyes locked on mine."I've never finished inside a woman before."

"You don't have to finish inside me," I said, though that seemed obvious.

"I want to." His tone was firm as he held my gaze, and when he spoke again, sorrow laced his voice. "I have no name to give."

Oh. Neirin's admission cut through the haze. I let out a breath, empathizing. I was a bastard too, though the weight of the title lay heavier on men than it did on women. Without a name, a man held less value for marriage.

But Neirin's thoughts weren't on marriage. He didn't want to risk putting a child on me. It was something most men didn't consider, and there was a vulnerability in his admission. One which hinted at a depth beyond my understanding.

"I know how to make the tea," I told him, my tone sober. The bitter drink prevented a man's seed from taking root. It was a simple brew, one we dispersed discreetly in our shop regularly.

Neirin held my gaze as if weighing the truth of my words. Or perhaps weighing the risk that I would fulfill them. It struck me then that he was sweet, in a brooding sort of way. Quickly, I pushed away the bud of warmth that was taking root in my chest. I wasn't looking for sweet. Ruairc was sweet. I wanted fevered kisses and rough sex with a handsome stranger that spent far too much coin on liquor and drew desire from me more profoundly than any man I'd lain with before.

The searching look in his eyes softened, and he nodded faintly. When he brought his lips back to mine, his kiss was gentle. The play of his tongue around mine was slow and thick, with a depth that sent a tingling of worry to my skin. This was only a tryst, a release of tension, and a shared rush in the shadows. I broke his kiss and put an edge of sharpness in my voice. "Rougher," I commanded.

Neirin's chest vibrated with soft amusement. "Is that what you want?"

I clutched at a strap on his jacket, trembling. "Yes."

Unwrapping my fingers, he adjusted his hold and pinned both above my head in one large hand, leaving my body fully under his control. With his free hand, he bunched my skirts, and my body trembled. I was ready for him. *Gods*, I was so ready. He nuzzled into the crook of my neck, and I tilted my head, giving him access. He nipped, distracting me as his hand trailed up the inside of my thigh.

When his fingers found my center and teased at my opening, I arched off the wall.

"If you don't want me to be gentle with you," he spoke against my jaw, "then I have to make you ready." He brought his lips to my ear, his breath hot. "Because when I enter you, you're going to take all of me."

The breath I sucked in was ragged, broken, and though it filled my lungs, it gave me no relief. For there would be no relief until …

With tantalizing slowness, Neirin slid one finger inside of me. The sound that escaped me was something between a gasp and a moan, and my body quivered. My muscles tightened. He withdrew, then slowly, so fucking slowly, he slid a second finger in.

I rocked against his hand, needing more, but he used the firmness of his body to restrain my movements, holding me to the wall. I relented and closed my eyes. When I did, I understood why he wanted me to still. Gods, the man knew what he was doing. He curled his fingers as he pumped, and the spot he struck was one I'd never even found myself before. It built the tension quickly, and just as I neared the edge, as my legs quivered and threatened to go out on me, Neirin withdrew his fingers, breaking the build.

"Damn you," I cursed with a hiss as he denied me my release.

He laughed, the sound coming from deep in his chest. His hand moved over my leg, my slickness still wet on his fingers, and he cupped my ass. He released his grasp on my hands and pulled me with him, backing from the wall a step. I wrapped my arms around his neck, running my fingers through his long, silken hair, and devoured him with my mouth.

Working through the layers of my skirts, he found my thigh with his other hand and lifted me in a single movement. I gasped, breaking the kiss, and he held me, the head of his cock positioned at my entrance. Firm, pulsing.

In a single motion, he stepped, pushed me back against the wall, and thrust into the hilt. The wind rushed from my lungs on a cry as he stretched me, as I formed into him. I never had a man that felt like this before.

Panting, Neirin held me, his body rigid against mine, every muscle coiled but unmoving. The silence between us pressed heavy, broken only by the pounding of my heart. Then—a voice came from the other side of the closed door, which I suspected led into the castle's interior, and I flushed. Heat flooded my face as the realization struck: the soldiers hadn't gone far from their post. They were right there, close enough to catch every desperate sound that escaped me. I swallowed hard, whispering, "They can hear us—"

Neirin's words were a sharp growl against my lips. "Let them listen."

With my legs wrapped around his waist, Neirin began to move inside of me, and everything else fell away—the soldiers outside, my impending courtship, the rumors people spoke of me and their effects on our shop, all of it. His grip on my ass was firm, holding me in place, and the stone wall at my back grounded me as he claimed me with each thrust.

All that mattered was this moment, our ragged breaths, and the connection of our bodies.

With a gasp, Neirin adjusted my weight and moved one of his hands from beneath my skirts. He wrapped his arm around my back, and I arched into him. Pulling out to the tip, he moved his lips to the crook of my neck. His breath was hot and quick against my skin. He nipped, light and teasing. Then, all at once, he bit down hard and thrust deep. I swallowed my cry as pain and pleasure pulsed through my veins in unison.

"Mine," he rasped.

Mine? I was too gone to care; he could have said anything. Nothing mattered but the fullness of him inside of me. Any conscious thought left my mind. The coil within was tightening, building, my walls contracting. As if he could sense the change in my body, he quickened.

"Come for me," he demanded.

His command was my undoing. I bucked against him, trembling as my orgasm shook me. He didn't slow. He pushed me over the edge, rebuilding the tension in a way I hadn't thought possible.

I sucked in a breath, and as Neirin moved the arm from behind my back, my right boot dropped to the stone. Trailing his hand up, he hiked my left leg higher, altering the angle, and when he thrust in again, his cock struck me in such a way that I lost all sense of myself. I gave in to the pure ecstasy of it, uncaring of who heard my cries. A sharp prick of pain struck where he hit, so deep that my barrier was reached. The pain shattered into immense pleasure as he throbbed inside of me. His body trembled, and as he moaned his release, I came again.

The aftershocks shuddered through me, and, gasping for breath, Neirin adjusted his grip on my leg. His cock pulsed, and he trembled, resting his forehead against mine. Around us, the dark room returned.

I gave him a moment as our breaths steadied. His hand trailed over the leather strap of the scabbard that held my dagger to my thigh. In the rush, I'd forgotten about it, but the stroke of his fingers told me that he'd known it was there.

I looked up at him through my lashes. Neirin held my gaze, and in the silver depths of his eyes, I saw such sorrow that it ached in my chest. He didn't pull from me, as if remaining like this would make the moment last, if only for another breath. But what we'd shared was over.

He belongs to the Queen, and I ... I don't want to belong to anyone. At least not yet.

Bitterness rose in my throat.

"Stay for a while." Neirin's words came out thick with emotion, and my heart leapt at his vulnerability.

No.

I set my jaw and shook my head once. This was just sex. Incredible, shattering sex that had absolutely ruined me for anyone else. Nothing would ever again feel like he felt. But still ... It was just sex. I was a commoner, and he was a *castle guard.* Bastard or not, we did not walk the same path.

A muscle at his jaw twitched, and Neirin cast his gaze aside. There was the faintest moment of hesitancy, then he lowered my leg. He pulled from me, and I drew a breath; the moment of breaking that connection—when a man withdrew—was always uncomfortable. Our combined spend coated the insides of my thighs, sticky and warm.

Neirin stepped away from me and drew his breeches back up, tucking his still-firm length in and working the ties. The air was thick and choking, and I straightened my skirts for a distraction from the discomfort in the air. I turned my head to the stone doorway, needing to set my gaze somewhere other than on the man before me.

Neirin rapped on the wood of the closed door the soldiers had left through. After no response came, he pounded heavier. Apprehension trickled through my blood. As if he sensed it too, Neirin stepped backward toward me and looked over his shoulder. Indistinct chatter carried from the courtyard through the archway as the festival goers mingled. The glow from the sconces outside and the warmth and mirth of those gathered drew all the more contrast to the dark stillness of the stone tower we shared.

"Something is wrong," Neirin said, his voice low. "Return to the festival."

His command cut, and irritation overcame my unease. "No," I said on a hush. Though only moments before I'd been ready to leave the stranger, stubbornness now held my feet. He cast a sideways glance down at me, his jaw flexing. Before he could muster a response, I hitched my skirts and, with some struggle, unhooked the latch of my scabbard and drew my dagger. When my boot returned to the stone flooring, it caught on my dress, and when I stood upright, blade in hand, I lost my balance.

Neirin caught and stabilized me, his expression something between irritation and concern. I raised my chin and adjusted my grip on the worn handle.

"Just—" He released a long breath. "Stay here, then."

"Fine." In truth, I had no desire or skillset to go traipsing after him into the castle. Gods, what was I doing? Scrunching my brows, I held the guard's glare with an indignant look of persistence.

He scoffed and shook his head, reaching behind his back. Then he stilled, his throat bobbing as he swallowed.

"What is it?"

"My dagger." Remembrance came over me of the commander's uniform, and the smaller weapon sheathed at his back. Neirin's eyes lowered to my hand, and for a moment I thought he may take mine. Planting my feet, I prepared myself to be difficult for the sake of it.

The guard tugged at a part of me somewhere deep inside that told me to surrender to him, to give him my everything. But he had no claim over me. Indignation led me to stubbornness and a will to do the opposite of whatever the man told me to do.

He is a castle guard. He is trained for this. What are you doing? I flexed my fist.

"Use your sword," I hissed beneath my breath.

Neirin ran a hand over his face. "It is too large for small spaces."

The tension in the air drew up the corner of my lips, and I suppressed a nervous giggle. "Too large, is it? For a small space?"

Evidently not amused, Neirin stepped to me, forcing my back against the stone again, and placed a hand firmly beside my head. The glare he set me with sobered me, and I lowered my eyes, averting my gaze. Submitting. *Dammit.*

Cursing beneath his breath, he drew back and went to the door. When his closeness left, the chill of the night and the unease at our situation returned. I swallowed hard, fingers tightening around the handle of my dagger, slick with the sweat of my palm. Neirin's hand closed over the brass handle, steady and sure where mine trembled, and with a slow push, he opened the door.

9

NEIRIN

I SWUNG OPEN THE DOOR, spilling light into the corridor, barely beating back the void of darkness that continued in either direction into midnight ambiguity.

"Perhaps they sought to give us privacy?"

Though the woman spoke in a whisper, my body tensed at the purposeless noise. Did she not understand the seriousness of our situation? Did she not see that quiet was essential at such a time? Gritting my teeth, I looked back, finding her only a few paces behind me. She clasped her dagger with both hands, her fists held to her chest. The woman was maddening. Perplexing. And she had no sense of how to use her dagger; that much was clear.

"Stay here," I said again, voice low.

She nodded once, the cinnamon curls of her hair bouncing.

Sighing, I turned my attention forward again. At all hours of the day and night, the windowless corridors of the castle were kept lit by wall sconces. It was not just a matter of convenience, but safety. Darkness bred opportunity for scandal and wickedness. The notion that the sconces were snuffed, not just in one direction of the hall but in both, told a story—or the beginning of one, at least. It was not a coincidence. Something was at play, and my missing dagger remained a flaring warning at the back of my mind.

But who could have taken it?

Stepping over the threshold, I listened for any sign of movement, any noise. When nothing came, I crouched and strained my eyes to address the scuffed dust along the stone flooring. In the dim light from the doorway, I could make out the shapes and sizes of boots of men, women, and children. Frustrated, I stood. The corridor was used during the day hours by many of the castle staff. This told me nothing, then.

"Right," the voice behind me suggested. "When I can't make a decision, I always go right."

"Quiet," I hissed, putting command behind the word.

She scoffed.

Considering, I began to move to the left side for no reason other than my reluctance to take the strange woman's suggestion. Within a dozen paces, the darkness consumed me entirely. Leaving the woman behind evoked a knot of worry in my throat, and the monster beneath my skin scraped.

She was a civilian, a commoner. I had done exactly as I was trained to do, given the situation. It was safer for her to stay behind than to come with me. And if harm did befall her, it was simply a casualty of necessity. My duty was to the kingdom, the castle, and to my brother. Not to her. Through my reasoning, the knot in my throat thickened, and a blazing heat of panic swelled. I could not leave her. I simply couldn't.

I turned, then hissed as metal scraped my side, slashing through the leather of my uniform and grazing my skin. The woman squealed and rambled off apologies as if they were, in fact, an adequate response to her action.

To keep her from accidentally stabbing me in my chest, I clasped her combined fists; her skin was cold and clammy. "I told you to stay," I snarled. What a fool I'd been for turning back to her, for even considering it.

"Did I hurt you?"

Sarcasm flicked off my tongue as I growled my response. "Is there blood on your blade?"

"It's too dark. I can't tell."

Gods, this woman would be the death of me. I suspected she wasn't daft, just … I could not say. "Keep your dagger in one hand at your side," I instructed, painfully aware of each sound we made. "Pointy end to the floor."

"Okay."

Releasing my hold on her, I turned forward again. Letting her follow me went against Rion's rules, and for good reason. The sting at my side and the unnecessary noise were enough to attest to that. Still, my unease settled, if only slightly, knowing she was within my reach to defend. The elusive stranger—what was it about her that held me in such a way?

Farther down the corridor, one of my boots struck a solid form and nearly tripped me. I braced my right hand against the wall just as the woman collided into my back. Grunting, I suppressed the lecture that rose to my tongue. She was not some young guard in training, nor a messenger—sharp ridicule would not shape her, help her grow. But it might make her crumble, and we could not risk that. At least she'd listened and kept her blade down. With the impact of her stumble, she'd have gutted me. Gods, why had I let her follow?

Crouching, I confirmed my suspicion. Warmth came from the soldier, but his chest did not rise or fall. Someone lurked in the shadows, using the darkness to their advantage. Someone who knew the halls well, then, someone who was trusted.

The physical threat of the situation before us assuaged my monster, and although he scratched from time to time, I was able to keep him under control. Before standing, I felt about for one of the woman's legs or boots. When I found her, she jumped. At least she remained quiet. Hoping she would catch the implication, I tapped at the toe of her boot several times. *Watch your step.*

Standing, I kept a hand on the wall and felt out a path with my feet, stepping over the first soldier's body, then finding the second soldier with my next step. A chill raced down my spine. Behind me, the woman's breath quickened, but to her credit, she did not falter, testing her steps as she kept just behind me. At one point, she reached out and grasped the back of my uniform. Whether it was for stability or comfort, I was unsure, but it caused my heart to leap.

Some distance farther, a flickering light illuminated a sharp turn of the hallway. I slowed my steps and reached back with my left hand, stilling the woman. A silent command to stay put. This time, she cooperated, likely seeing now the gravity of the situation.

Hand at the pommel of my sword, I stepped to the edge of the corner. The weapon would be awkward to wield in such close quarters, but I would have to make do. Instinct told me to leave the woman with her dagger, even if it would allow me to better defend us both. For a woman to carry a blade as she did was unusual; I suspected she needed it as a comfort of some sort.

I stepped with practiced movement, my left foot first, to turn the bend, my hand at the ready. But I was greeted by only an empty corridor. Nothing appeared out of place. Ahead, the wall sconces remained lit. No. One farther down was quenched. My stomach curled. Someone was playing a game with me. It explained my missing dagger, too.

"Come," I said to the woman, needing her beside me and not in the shadows. My mind raced with implications.

Not many options left to me. If we turned back, we would be vulnerable from behind. Yet continuing forward was certainly the purpose of this message. Who knew I was in the tower with the woman? Though Cyan despised me, I did not suspect he had the forethought to stage such a thing. Nor did I suspect he would strike from the shadows. Cyan was impulsive, brash—the opposite of his father, Rion.

Rion. I swallowed. The mishap with the carriage was not reason enough to lure me to death's door. Not even enough to dismiss me. Or perhaps that was the cause; perhaps he needed a way to be rid of me. Did he want the Valio job for his son? Firming my jaw, I set a slow pace forward.

When we reached the unlit sconce, I hesitated. The feeling of being watched scraped at my consciousness, and I spoke to the woman beneath my breath. "Is anyone behind us?"

She pivoted, her boots making more noise than necessary. "No."

Having no option other than to trust her observational skills, which I was unsure she actually possessed, I kept my eyes trained ahead and began to move again. The corridor ended at a door, one I knew led into one of the castle's common rooms. Gritting my teeth, I tapped the knob with the back of my hand, suspicious of the games at play, but it was cold to the touch.

Right hand at the pommel of my sword, I opened the door with my left.

The light of chandeliers illuminated the room and spilled into the corridor, causing me to blink as my eyes adjusted. A gurgling, rasping sound came from ahead. The sound of blood filling someone's lungs. Above that, the hum of festival goers carried from a balcony overlooking the courtyard.

Swallowing, I scanned the room. Accent chairs, recently polished to a black leather, sat close together, arranged around a low table. Chairs for lounging, for conducting intimate meetings. Ahead and to our right, the King's desk sat with papers strewn atop it, but the legs were thin, impossible to hide behind. Aside from that, the room was scantily furnished. Ornate framed oil paintings hung on the walls, and a few potted plants accessorized the space. It was a room for business, not for pleasure.

Content that there was nowhere fit for a man to hide, I moved toward the seating area where the sounds of death had since diminished. A hand, pale, fingers twitching, came into sight between two of the leather chairs. The cuff of the victim's sleeve was long, stopping at the wrist. It was bunched with intricate designs of golden threading.

"Neirin," said the woman behind me, her voice shaky, as I continued to move forward.

I saw the dying man first. My breath caught; my steps stilled. My gut roiled, and I nearly lost the alcohol churning in my belly.

Coming to my side, the woman clasped my arm and sharply sucked in her breath. "Oh, gods."

10

NEIRIN

Looking down at the body of the King—of my father—a cool displacement settled over me. The sight before me was so over-powering, it numbed me and set me apart from myself. He trembled with spasms. His mouth gaped for air. Blood trickled from the corner of his lips, but I knew him to be lost to the world already. There was a haze in his eyes, wide and set on the ceiling. That look spoke of death.

The woman at my side broke from the stupor of shock first and rushed to the King. Her quick movement tore me from my displacement. As she knelt, hands quivering, my heart leapt back into rhythm.

"You must go," I said, the words coming out forced.

Shaking her head, the woman placed her hands around the dagger that protruded from Kaius's chest, applying pressure to the wound as I'd learned to do in basic field training.

"I am a healer," she said, though the statement was laced with self-doubt.

"He is already dead," I snarled, panic rising.

"No," she gasped. Tears began to roll down her cheeks from beneath the mask, and I cursed. "No, I can help him."

I grabbed her by the crook of her arm. The sickening twist of emotions that swirled within me added a sharpness to my actions. I tugged on her, harder than necessary, when she resisted. Blood pooled from the wound in the absence of pressure, and the woman cried out.

Turning her to face me, I held her firmly by her shoulders. "If you are a healer, then you know he is beyond saving."

Her lips quivered. For a moment, I despised her for making this about her, even if it was not her intention to do so. She did not know Kaius was my father. So few did. My eyes flashed beyond her to where the King lay in complete stillness. Dead. Again, my heart caught.

"Let me go." The woman writhed.

Hardening my expression, I released her shoulders and, before she had the chance to withdraw, took her by the wrists. She flinched.

"You need to leave," I told her again, sharper this time, wiping her red-stained hands on my uniform. It only smeared the blood.

Swallowing, I forced emotion down. Amid the death of a King and the loss of a father I never got the chance to truly know, it was the safety of the elusive woman that took the forefront of my attention. The King's death could not be pinned on her.

Setting her with a firm look, I released my hold on her and bent to retrieve her dagger from where it lay beside Kaius's body. As I did, the intricate design of the hilt embedded in his chest caught my attention. The sinking in my stomach intensified. It was mine.

"Lift your skirts," I bit out, turning back to the woman.

"I will not," she gasped.

The urge to wrap a hand at her neck and command her obedience drew a snarl from my throat, but I restrained myself. "Lift your *fucking* skirts."

Cowed, the woman finally nodded and worked at the layers of fabric. I knelt before her and trailed my hand up her thigh, finding the scabbard strapped there. The scent of her, of us, took me by surprise, my mind otherwise consumed. Setting my jaw, I sheathed her weapon. "No one must know you've been here."

"What—"

"They will hang you." I stood and retook her bloodied hands.

Her small figure trembled, the first sign of fright she'd shown.

Releasing a sigh, I went to the desk, my strides long, and retrieved a bottle of liquor. If I were being framed for this, someone would be sent to catch me here, in the act. Heart thundering, my thoughts went to my brother, to Harlan. This was not about me; I could be jailed for the death of someone much less important. This was treason and, very possibly, a play for the crown. But by whom? And if I'd been chosen purposely to take the blame, was someone trying to get me out of the way? Someone who knew who Harlan was to me, who the King was to me?

With the liquor, I wet the corner of a blanket that was hung over a chaise and used it to remove the stain of death from the woman's hands. At least her skirts were not tainted.

"There is a maze of passageways within the castle," I said, my words rushing out without thought. "The route we traveled is only one." The tower from which we entered the passageway, however, would likely be overrun with soldiers at this point. Agitation hardened my jaw, and the monster within me roiled as I fought for control, making it even harder to focus.

"I'm scared." She sounded so meek.

My calm returned, and I tossed the soiled blanket aside, cupping her face and resting my forehead against hers. For a moment, we drew comfort from each other, two strangers brought together first by desire and then by the hand of disaster.

"Find your courage. It is within you," I said, my voice soft. "There is a lattice along the castle wall, within reach of the balcony. It will not hold much weight, but it is the only option. Leave the courtyard immediately, before attention is drawn to what has happened here. Walk out casually. Do not show any sign of suspicion."

Footsteps sounded from the hallway leading to the main door of the study. There was no more time. With trembling hands, I worked the silver ties at the back of the woman's head. "Nothing to draw attention," I reiterated, and the mask fell between us to the floor.

Our eyes held, and an aching I'd never felt before consumed me.

"Go," I said, swallowing the knot in my throat.

The steps stopped outside the door, accompanied by the voice of a boy, one of the messengers: "The cry came from the study."

The woman's hands fell from my own, and then her back was to me as she ran to the balcony, holding her skirts up as she fled. When she was hidden from view, my eyes fell to Kaius. A trembling shudder coursed through my body, and I bit back the sting of tears as the door opened.

Rion stepped in first, the shock on his face convincing. But was it honest? I could not say for sure. Calix's eyes widened, and he stepped back into Rion's shadow.

"Neirin." Rion's tone was level as he moved toward me. It was a technique I learned from him to subdue a dangerous threat with calm, rather than rash violence, whenever possible.

I retreated a step but the backs of my legs hit the chaise. No one could be trusted, certainly not Rion, so I held my tongue.

"Father?"

No, Harlan.

He stepped into the room, and his gaze fell to the body of the fallen King. Every instinct told me to defend my case. However, doing so could pose further danger toHarlan, should Rion be to blame for this. With only the three of us in the room—aside from the messenger boy whose word, or very life, should it come to it, was unimportant enough to be noted—the situation could get messy much too quickly if Rion believed that Harlan was aware of his treason. It was better to leave Harlan in ignorance for the time being, though I hated the conclusion he would come to when I fled. If Rion were at the head of this, he would keep Harlan on his side for some time, until another opportunity arose. The commander was not a man to rush. He was a strategist. He would play the long game. He was clever enough to see that the death of both the King and the prince at once would be too much for the kingdom. Beyond that, Harlan was his only alibi for Kaius's murder.

"That is the dagger of a guard," Rion stated. "Turn."

Releasing a breath, I turned, revealing my back and the empty scabbard there.

I'm so sorry, Harlan. I will make this right. But the only way to do that was to run. To flee like a coward. It went against my training, against my every belief, but the need to protect my brother, even at the cost of my own shame, prevailed.

Without turning back to see the hurt and betrayal in my brother's eyes, I fled through the corridor. The air in my lungs burned as my feet pounded the hard ground, not from the short burst of speed but from the choking in my throat, as I pressed down my emotions.

I passed the unlit sconce and nearly slid at the corner just beyond. Behind me, Rion's voice boomed out as he called for soldiers.

Heart thundering, blood pounding in my ears, I took to the shadows, regaining speed.

Lost to the moment, I forgot about the fallen soldiers. When my boot landed too high, and ribs cracked beneath my foot, I fell forward. The stench of foul breath rushed my senses as I braced myself just above the second soldier. A shudder shook my body, and I stood, rasping.

Bracing myself against the wall, I placed a palm to my chest. Breathing became difficult, but I pushed off the wall regardless, forcing my legs to move even as they burned with the fore-telling of a shift. Not here. Not now. *I had to get to the woods.*

Shouts came from ahead, and the zing of drawn swords. Soldiers, possibly guards as well, in the tower. Stopping, I brought my hand to the pommel of my sword. The faint light from the tower illuminated the side of one of the men's faces— Cyan. He spoke to the soldiers, his voice raised, commanding silence and order.

I stepped back, keeping to the darkness. Raising a hand above my head, I felt for a ceiling but didn't find one. I drew a steadying breath and braced a hand on one side of the hallway, the stone cold and rough beneath my palms. Gritting my teeth to hold off the monster inside of me, I positioned a boot on the opposite wall and found a grip, then repeated with my other foot. Cyan stepped from the tower. Sweat beaded on my brow and dampened the back of my neck as I strained my muscles and scaled the space, walking up the corridor walls with feet on one side and hands on the opposite, until my shoulder blades pressed against the ceiling, my head craned to the side.

Closing my eyes, I focused my attention on each of my feet. The left cramped terribly, and the right was at an uncomfort-able angle. To adjust myself, though, I risked falling, so I breathed through the sensations.

I counted four men along with Cyan as they entered the corridor. Each passed under me, unaware. My body trembled with the strain of my position and the press of my monster's urgency. It wasn't until the steps faded that I let myself descend, each movement sending a shot of pain through my right ankle. Twisted, likely.

Exhaustion and the urge to surrender to it weighed each step as I continued into the endless darkness. I needed to escape, needed to get word to Harlan of the treachery somehow. I brushed wetness from my cheeks, unsure if it was due to the sweat that dripped from my brow or from silent tears.

The scent of dirt washed over me as the corridor opened up to the castle's old storerooms. Somewhere above me, Nyana worked in the kitchen, oblivious for the time being. Though dizziness hazed my movements.

Swallowing, I pushed on until I reached the ladder that led up to the woods. I climbed, the pain in my ankle no longer notable over the searing heat that burned within me. The bones in my fingers stiffened, and I snarled. With my last moments of control, I pushed at the hatch, forcing it open, even as the pressure shattered the bones of two of my fingers, fragile as they fought to reform, reshape.

Shuddering, I dragged myself over the edge, raking at leaves and dirt.

Unbridled fear choked out everything leaving the impending shift to exist. An inhuman sound escaped my lips. A cry, a keen. The monster within took control. The heat within became all-consuming, and in the next desperate breath, my ribs snapped, putting pointed pressure on my lungs.

We all have monsters. I'm not afraid of yours. If the masked woman knew of my monster, saw me in this state, would she remain true to her words? No. She'd fear me or hate me—the only logical reactions to flee … or to fight.

My skull fractured, shattered, elongated. The ringing in my ears was deafening.

Flesh tore and reformed, and my body took on a new shape. I tried to stand, but the fit of my boots was all wrong, and I stumbled forward, falling on my face. The partially remodeled bones, weakened, shattered again at the impact. Pain flared as my body tried to put itself back together. I cried out, the sound a yelp, not wholly my own.

The leather of my uniform consumed me, drawing memories of the dark cellar of my youth, and of my cage, too small to even turn around in.

My breath quickened to a pant. And then with suddenness, the pain stopped and the fire within my muscles ebbed. I needed to free myself from the dark confines that constricted me, but I couldn't move.

My body was his now.

11

NEIRIN

MY MONSTER FEARED confinement as much as I did. It was one of the few things we shared in common. Panic seeped through the bond that connected us, raw and unrestricted. He raked at the leathers. Whimpering, he backed up, claws digging in. Cool air rushed in, filling his lungs, and we were free. The creature stepped back, its ears perked, listening. In the distance, a nightingale sang. Then its melody faded, an unrequited love song.

The intake of sounds was always overwhelming in the initial moments after a shift. Each rustle of leaves and movement of small creatures in the brush could be heard with stark clarity. My monster sniffed. Nearby, a hare nested with early kits. The milky warmth of her scent made him salivate, but my monster's unease was more pressing than his hunger.

The scent of humans came on the wind, carried from the west. The creature's lips rose in a snarl, and he huffed through his nose, trying to clear the reek. They smelled not of the woods. Unnatural. Like a sickness, something to be avoided.

He turned from the castle and trotted through the trees. His steps were light as he treaded over uneven earth and leapt effortlessly over obstacles. I had no knowledge of his intentions or connection with his thoughts beyond the primal emotions that trickled through the bond. Instinct drove him, ancient wisdom untaught yet known.

In this form, I was only a passenger trapped within fur and flesh. I could feel the earth press cold beneath the pads of his paws, the damp tang of soil and bark in my nose. Yet, the body was not mine, not truly. And with every shift, he held on longer. If nothing else, the calm of the forest gave me a moment to feel, to sort through suppressed emotions and consider what lay ahead.

Kaius was dead. The knowing hollowed me out, left me with a distinct void—not grief, not really, but the ache of missing a piece of something I'd never truly had. Harlan, however, would mourn. Our father had played some role in his life. They'd had *something*.

And though he would receive counsel, Harlan was not ready to take Kaius's place. The consult of men who believed they held power could be poisonous. Harlan hadn't the wits or cunning to sort truth from persuasions and lies from ambition.

Beneath all else, there was the comprehension that something dark lurked within the castle walls. Someone who held power and the trust of the royal family planned to misuse it. Someone strategic, patient. There was a very real possibility they would turn my brother into their next target.

A breeze caught the creature's fur, and he raised his head. Moonlight dappled through the branches overhead, painting the forest in shades of gray. In this form, the leaves were a pale, muddied yellow. The contrast of between my monster's calm and the chaos likely occurring within the walls seemed almost diametric. He existed in a world outside of all I knew—outside of all that mattered with such pressing importance—in a place where everything moved more slowly, driven wholly by instinct. Nothing existed for him but base needs and awareness of the moment.

As we drew near the river, the scent of rushing water came to the forefront of our senses. The creature stopped at the river's edge, where a steep drop plummeted to the writhing black current below. My monster snorted, and I sensed his frustration through the bond. He followed the river south for some time until we came upon a spot where the earth sloped more gradually to the water's edge. His steps scattered loose dirt and small stones as he maneuvered down the bank. With a curled, lapping tongue, he scooped water into his mouth, crisp and fresh.

A breeze blew in from the east and ruffled the creature's mottled coat. He raised his head to the sky, the fur on his chin wet. Not far off, the rolling of wagons along the main road could be heard. My monster was uninterested in humans, their carts, or the creatures that pulled them. Just as he gave no care for the sack of silver coins in the pocket of my jacket, which he'd left at the hatch door. A scent, however, caught his attention. It eluded me, itching at me like a word forgotten and just out of grasp. I knew it, yet I couldn't place it.

My monster followed the sound of the wagons until he broke through the tree line. The tall grasses of the meadow rose above his head and brushed his whiskers and flanks as he pushed forward. With a short leap, he mounted a low boulder, able to see now the winding road and the several dozen carriages traveling south along it.

The creature raised his nose and pinned his ears back, drawing the scent deep into his lungs. He keened, his song sad and hollow, not entirely unlike that of a nightingale's. Wind buffeted his fur, and he squinted.

Though he feared man, with a bunching of his haunches, he leapt from the stone and prioritized urge over instinct, the draw of the unknown scent too alluring to dismiss. He cleared the distance to the wagons with hastened speed and broke through the grass, skidding to a halt in the road when a horse's hooves came too close. His paws slid out from under him, and he fell sideways in a cloud of dust. Unbridled panic and the searing need to flee pulsed through the bond. He righted himself and stepped backward into the safety of the grass, tongue lolling.

The wagon wheels rolled by, pulled by horses who nickered uneasily, aware of the creature's presence. My monster lowered to his belly, heart thundering in his chest at a rate four times that of a man's.

The scent came again, this time stronger. When it filled his lungs, it stole all my focus. In a wave of clarity, my mind flitted back to the gatehouse. Heat, need, and belonging had consumed me, my face buried in the woman's neck. I had bitten her, claimed her, and breathed her scent.

He'd found her. *Why?*

My monster shot from the shelter of the grass. Ears flattened as he dodged hooves and swiveled his head to shouts and voices, he sought the source of her scent. Stilling at the side of the path momentarily, he perked his ears and, with rapt determination, raced forward and leapt, claws scraping at the back of a wagon.

Just as he gained leverage and readied to land his paws in the back, the wagon lurched, tossing him forward. He fell heavily against the cargo. The collision knocked the wind from his lungs, and his body quivered. The rawness of fear seared through the bond.

A male voice came from the front of the wagon: "What was that?"

My monster pinned his ears. He sought to right himself but immediately fell again as the wagon bumped over the uneven road. He panted, his flanks quivering.

"*That* would be the effect of forgetting rope." The woman's response was a flat, quipped retort.

The man grunted.

My monster remained low, hidden, and breathed in their scents. All creatures had a unique mark that told of their heritage and genetics; humans were no exception to this. The two who shared the wagon were not full siblings but half. The woman smelled of me, too, from the seed I'd left in her. Beneath these markers, I detected the pleasant earthy smell of plants, like the waking of spring. All these things made up her unique scent, who she was. It ingrained itself in my mind, my soul.

Though his heart still raced, my monster was settling, his fear less potent. I wondered if she soothed him as she did me. My thoughts went to the first time I saw her at the bar, how she'd pulled me from the depths of my thoughts in a single breath. The implications were out of reach, but I knew with certainty that she meant something to us.

The woman didn't speak again, and after some time, the wagon's motions became rhythmic. The passing of time was lost on me. Whether my monster slept, I was unsure. There were fragmented memories of crossing a bridge, of horses in a pasture raising their heads and nickering as we passed, but the events were all out of place, lacking order.

The sun began to rise, painting the horizon a muted yellow, one of the few colors perceivable in this form. There was a lack of beauty to the scene before me, a dullness. My monster's head lay heavy on his paws, and his eyelids fluttered lazily. Warmth seeped over me as the first rays of the sun bathed his pelt, and my thoughts turned to the woman. How did the sunrise look through her eyes?

1 2

EVERA

THE WAGON RATTLED as we crossed over a bridge leading into town. It was late afternoon, and a chill hung in the air. I drew my hands into my cloak. The arm warmers at my wrists did little to trap heat, and my fingers tingled with numbness.

"We should talk about what happened at the festival," Aureus said, breaking the quiet.

I let out a breath, and it fogged, dampening my nose. When I'd returned to the wagon after leaving the courtyard, I'd been visibly on edge, fidgety, and had avoided Aureus's questioning of where I'd been.

"There's nothing to talk about," I told my brother, dismissing the conversation. I toyed absentmindedly with the peridot stone of my necklace. It was something I'd done since I was a child. The smooth stone comforted me.

Aureus sighed, and I watched him from my periphery. With one hand on the reins, he raised the other to rub at his temples. It was something he did when I worried him, which I did often.

I sighed. "I was with a man."

Aureus clenched his jaw and tightened his grip on the reins until his fist went white.

129

Irritation trickled in. Though Aureus knew I was not a virgin, his silent judgment was more irritating than a lecture. Of course, I could not tell him what transpired after the intimacy Neirin and I shared. That was something I could never tell a soul. Soon, word would come of the King's death. It was miraculous, really, how quiet the festival was kept.

"A castle guard," I added, putting kindling to the flame for no reason other than my own sharpness. "I don't regret it."

"I didn't ask if you regretted it," Aureus pointed out, keeping his voice level. "You brought that up on your own, Evera."

Clenching my fists, I set my gaze forward and locked my jaw. He had brought the subject up to push me, and now he chose to pretend he didn't care. To what avail? To disparage me? Tension hummed between us.

Once in town, the ride became smoother.The roads were better maintained. I turned my head away, watching but not really taking in the town as it settled in for the evening. In windows, candlelight flickered, and cast shadows on curtains. A few children chased after each other, laughing, utterly oblivious to the weights of adulthood.

The road ended, and Aureus steered Sorrel to the right and past the stables. When we reached the market square, he navigated the wagon to the front of our shop and pulled back on the reins. The supplies in the back shifted, and the old wagon wheels groaned.

Across the way, the door to the cobbler's shop opened, and Ruairc emerged into the fading light of dusk. He skirted the central well and headed pointedly toward us, his smile beaming and his cheeks faintly ruddy. I groaned.

Aureus leaned in to me. "You will be kind to him."

My pounding heart told me this was all too much. I desperately wanted a moment to myself. Instead, each and every possible thorn came forward to catch at my skirts and scratch at my skin.

When Ruairc approached, Sorrel lowered her head to him. He ran a hand down the bridge of her nose and patted her neck. The mare nickered her affections.

"I'm glad to see you back," Ruairc said, raising his eyes and holding my gaze. The depth of soulful longing in them was not lost on me.

"It's been a long ride," I said flatly. Aureus nudged me discreetly, and I set my jaw. Forcing a smile, I offered my hand for Ruairc to take. "While I would love to converse"—a lie with a pointed inflection—"I need to make some tea."

Aureus coughed his surprise beside me, and a seed of satisfaction took root.

Ruairc, oblivious to the implication, took my hand to help me down from the wagon. "Of course, you must find ways to keep warm. Spring is reluctant this year."

It was bitter and petty, but his response amused me.

"Oh, yes," I agreed with feigned innocence, stepping down from the wagon. His hand was warm and slightly calloused. "I've been finding ways to keep warm."

Behind me, Aureus spluttered, and Ruairc shot him a confused glance before turning back to me.

"I'm glad to hear it." Ruairc's smile was genuine and caring, and I almost felt a pang of guilt. Almost. He was kind, passively attractive, even, with his finger length golden blond hair and rugged beard. His eyes were a warm honey-brown, and his arms were muscled. I could do worse.

Still, I would not so easily be swooned. If I were to be married off, I would make it difficult for anyone involved. I would not conform without resentment toward those who thought my body, my soul, was something to be bartered.

A familiar sound drew my attention, and I peered around Ruairc to the door of our shop, where my friend Farren stood. The copper bell quieted as it stilled, and when Farren called a greeting, I waved, grateful for the excuse to leave Ruairc's side.

I went to her, and she pulled me into an embrace. She smelled of fresh bread, as she always did. The familiarity and warmth of her softened me and eased the turbulence of my shifting moods. I just needed time away from Aureus, away from Ruairc, away from men in general. Perhaps time with my dearest friend would, in truth, be better for me than hiding away in my room. Farren smiled, and I returned the gesture.

"You are one of the first back," Farren said, her voice melodious. If I was broken and cynical, she was the epitome of bashful innocence and lighthearted warmth. She balanced me, and I loved her for it.

"Aureus did not want to travel through the pass in the dark, so we left a little ahead of the others." *And my nervous energy put him on edge.*

I squeezed her hand. "Let's converse over tea."

Farren's smile was eager, no doubt hoping I had gossip from the capital. The concept was laughable, in truth. For what I knew—what I had witnessed—would soon be all anyone could talk about. But it would be a risk to dispense such information. Farren would have to wait to discover the death of the King as the rest of the town did.

She stepped from the door she held propped open, looking over her shoulder before leading me inside. The glance was subtle, but I caught the way her eyes sought my brother, the flush of her cheeks when he met her gaze. They were a good fit. Even if my brother acted a bit like a prick, I still loved him and I wanted them both to be happy. He was oblivious though, and she was too shy to be forward.

The shop was warm and cozy, a comforting space. After so much time spent in the wagon, I was grateful to be home. Familiarity blanketed me, and when I rolled my shoulders, the tension in my body eased.

"Leighis's gone to bed already," Farren said as I followed her into the back room.

Without Aureus to sit with him in the evenings, I wasn't terribly surprised. When our mentor's memory had begun to fade, he'd clung tighter to routine as if it grounded him somehow. It was easy enough most days. I enjoyed his company in the mornings as I prepared orders for deliveries or took note of the supplies that we were running low on. And in the evenings, when Aureus sat at the front counter going over paperwork for the shop, I knew Leighis's company was a comfort to him as well.

The scent of spices greeted me, familiar and welcoming. I crossed the room, trailing my hand over the rough wooden table that took up its center. My workspace. It was a relief to be back.

"I just built up the fire," Farren informed me as she leaned against the table. "You're running low on wood, though."

I took note of the pile; she was right. There was enough for a few more days at most. I sighed. Drying firewood was one of my least favorite chores. It was still wet outside, so the logs would need to be laid out inside to dry thoroughly before being stacked and stored. "I'll let Aureus know," I replied absent-mindedly.

I turned my back to Farren and scanned the upper shelves to the left of the stove. I'd been to an apothecary in the capital once. The jars there were clear and each was the same, meticulously kept. But we couldn't afford expensive containers; our shop ran on chaos and labels. We used what we had collected over time.

With two jars in hand, I returned to the table and placed them on its well-worn surface. Then, as a secondary thought, I clipped off a few rue branches I'd hung to dry a fortnight ago. The little yellow flowers would add sweetness to the tea and aid in the brew's strength.

"Did Leighis give you any trouble?" I asked Farren as I drew water from the barrel beside the stove, noting a puddle on the floor. The damn thing was constantly leaking.

"Leighis's never a trouble," Farren hummed. It was a lie, of course. He'd been increasingly burdensome the past few seasons, waking often in a disoriented state and wandering the shop. Occasionally, he fell and hurt himself or would set out to make tea for his aching muscles and forget the correct herbs to seep. We had to keep a close eye on him so he wouldn't build the fire too high or prepare something dangerous by accident and drink it.1

"Thank you for looking after him," I said, letting the depth of my words show in my eyes.

Farren smiled, genuine warmth giving her an air of lightness that, for a moment, I envied her. Hooking a teakettle above the fire, I reminded myself that Farren's childhood was nothing like my own. I couldn't compare us.

"Would you like some tea too?" I asked, turning to the cupboard.

"Oh yes, please," Farren chirped.

I grabbed two ceramic cups and brought them back to the table. My friend watched me with eagerness. I sighed, knowing she was waiting for me to tell her about the festival. And the guard… what had happened to him? Worrying my brow, I opened the jar labeled silphium and used a metal spoon to scoop the dried leaves and seeds into the strainer.

"Sil-phi-um," Farren read, taking the jar from me. She sniffed it, quirked her lips up, and set it back down. "What is that one?" She gestured to the second jar.

"Asafetida," I told her, scooping some of the yellow powder directly into one of the cups. It would dissolve in the heated water.

"You're just putting it in one of them?" she noted. I held the jar out to her, and with a draw of her brows, she leaned in. Her nose crinkled, and she pulled back. "Gods, Evera, whyever would you use such a thing?"

I laughed and put the lid back on the jar. "It's medicinal."

"Are you unwell?" Farren asked, concern weighing in her voice.

I shook my head and took the jars back to the shelves. "No," I said with my back to her. "It's preventative, that's all."

"Preventative?" Farren asked.

My friend was a worrier and naïve, probably to a fault. "It's a contraceptive."

Her eyes widened, and she blushed. The poor girl had never even been kissed. The entirety of her knowledge of sex and men came from myself and her elder sister, Renna, who'd married the blacksmith a year prior. The blacksmith, it turned out, was quite creative in his lovemaking, and Renna always had stories to tell when she came to visit. Ones that made my stomach coil and Farren's cheeks flush.

The teakettle hissed, and with a cloth, I took it from its hook and brought it back to the table. I poured the heated water over the strainer into the cup without the yellow powder and let it sit.

"Who was he?" Farren asked, curiosity overcoming her bashfulness.

I hummed, unable to resist the faint smile that curved at my lips. The urge to tell my friend of the tryst I had shared with the attractive stranger tugged on me. There would be no harm in sharing that much. "A castle guard." Satisfaction curled my words.

"Was he handsome?" Farren queried.

"Very." I grinned, and she returned the expression, her cheeks still flushed. I removed the strainer from the mug, placed it over the other, and handed her the brewed tea.

Farren took it in her hands and blew. "You must tell me more."

I poured water over the strainer into the second cup, and the liquid turned a muddied yellow. "He had eyes like the moons. And *gods*, his body was perfection. Scarred and rugged, muscled."

"Scarred?"

I shrugged, recalling Neirin's hesitations regarding some of the fainter marks. "The position of a guard is well paid for a reason. He bought me drinks in the castle courtyard, this excessively expensive liquor, and—" I cut myself off with a considering twist of my lips. "He was rugged and sort of gruff." Hiding something, I added ironically to myself. "He took me to a tower house, and gods"—I raised my eyes to hers and smiled, biting at my bottom lip. "He was incredible."

Farren's breath came out in a rush, and I suppressed a laugh. She was exactly what my brother needed. Sweet, innocent, and full of warmth and love. Her view of the world was untainted by hardships, and her grasp of reality was honeyed. She'd balance his soul, as her friendship balanced mine.

"Have any courters come while we were away?" I asked, changing the subject. She was of age for it and would likely be married within the year. Such things happened fast. Though I couldn't see what tempted Farren to such complacency, she was my friend, and if marriage and children were what she desired from life, that was fine. I just wanted her to be happy. We didn't have to want the same things, to see the world the same way. She supported me, even when I knew it was hard for her at times to grasp my perspective. It was the least I could do to entertain her musings of the young men who came to court her. Even if, beneath the veil, it was clear her heart belonged only to one man.

Farren's eyes fell to her tea. "Yes, one," she said, bashful. "He was kind, inquisitive, very interested in scholarly things."

I hummed. "But you turned him away, didn't you?"

"I did." She shrugged, and a faint, distant smile flitted across her face. Was she thinking of Aureus?

"How's your tea?" I asked.

She wrinkled her nose. "Better than yours, I'm sure."

We both laughed. "I missed you, Farren."

"I missed you, too," she said with a smile.

We drank our tea and spoke about unimportant things. While Farren sipped hers, I took mine in gulps, the bitter, pungent aftertaste of it rotten on my tongue. The last swig was grainy and thick, and I suppressed a gag. My forehead beaded, and heat rushed through me in a discomforting wave.

"Was it worth it?" Farren asked as I removed my cloak, folded it, and laid it on the table. She looked pointedly at my empty mug.

"Worth the bitter drink," I conceded, "certainly." Whether or not the rush was worth what transpired after, I could not be certain. Only time would tell. Though Neirin had done well in keeping my presence unknown. I was only being anxious. There was no reason I would be drawn into anything. It was in the past.

My wool arm warmers made my wrists sweat, and I pulled one off and then the other.

"Evera!" My name came on a gasp, and I studied my friend, confused.

"What?"

Her eyes lowered, and I followed her gaze.

"Is that a tattoo? Does Aureus know?"

Farren's question fell away with the breath that left my lungs. Black ink coiled around my wrist in a branded design—bold, intricate, unmistakable.. The blood in my veins turned to ice. I recognized the marking for what it was—lore, legend, the stories Leighis had told us as children. The concepts of magic that had filled my mind before sleep. What circled around my wrist was impossible.

What had Neirin said? That he was a monster.

Disregarding Farren, I took the few short steps up to Leighis's study. The room was circular, aside from the back wall, which stood as a divider. On its other side, a curved staircase led up to our shared sleeping quarters. Bookshelves lined the walls, and the platform looked over the shop's back room with an iron railing along the open portion. Two chairs sat positioned against the railing where Leighis often read, and a worktable took up the center of the room.

I pulled a wooden step ladder from beneath the table and dragged it to a shelf. As I climbed it, the old hinges creaked, but it held my weight. I trailed my fingers over muted bindings, breathing in the scent of ink and paper.

Finding the book I sought, I withdrew it and stepped awkwardly off the stool. I laid the book of lore amid the mess of papers, scrolls, and textbooks on the table and opened it to a random page. Farren came to stand beside me, quiet, apparently realizing I wasn't going to respond until I found what I was searching for. I flipped through the pages.

My heart stilled, and I drew a hand to my chest, seeking the beat of it. Slow, heavy, pounding. I held my left wrist up and compared the markings to those in the book. Some elements were different, but that was to be expected. The bonding tattoos were unique to each pair. I read the passage in my mind, and beside me, Farren leaned in, reading it too.

"Evera." Her voice was hushed. "What does this mean?"

I turned my arm. Between the thick markings, a distinct animalistic face was woven into the design, blending seamlessly. I closed my eyes, and the breath that escaped my lips came with a shudder. Farren spoke my name again, coaxing me to respond.

"You can't tell anyone about this," I said, and she stilled. "This is serious, Farren." I raised my eyes to hers, not concealing the weight of my words. She paled at my harshness, but she had to understand the importance of this.

"I won't," she promised.

I studied her, unsure if I could believe her. Though she was my dearest friend, she voiced her thoughts the instant they came to her. It was not a fault, per se, but she wasn't one to be trusted with secrets either. And this was a big secret.

"What does it mean?" Farren pressed.

I firmed my jaw and closed the book. Strewn papers left the table on a gust of wind and danced to the floor as I did.

"It means nothing," I told her, as if I could will myself to believe the statement. If my brother sought to bound me to Ruairc by obligations, this mark… it bound me by fate. Bound me to the guard who, very likely, was already dead, framed for the death of the King. To the handsome stranger I'd chosen for myself as a distraction from commitment and solidity. No, I would keep it hidden. No one else could learn of this.

Despite myself, I trailed a thumb over the markings, and hollowness weighed on me.

13

NEIRIN

THOUGH THE WOMAN'S scent lingered, I recognized her absence the moment my monster woke. It left the creature on edge. He panted, ears pinned, as two men spoke, their voices carrying from the front of the wagon. Crates and satchels of goods and wares littered the small space in disorganized chaos, most of the cargo having shifted throughout the trip from the capital.

"Her warmth is disingenuous."

"Give her time, Ruairc."

Ruairc's sigh was audible. "I will not force this on her if it's not what she wishes."

"And that is one of the reasons I gave you my blessing." The wagon rocked as the speaker stepped down from the coach's seat. "I regret I may have pushed this all on her too suddenly."

Ruairc's response sounded heavy with concern. "Have you changed your mind?"

"No." The reply came without hesitation. "No. She will come around."

Footsteps on stone sounded the approach of one of the men, and the cotton flap at the back of the wagon was drawn to the side. A rush of cold air broke the staleness, and my monster backed up, bumping into a crate of glass bottles that rattled at the impact. Lips raised and ears tucked, he snarled.

"What—" The man cut himself off, taking a step back.

"Aureus, what is it?" A second man came into view, and his eyes widened, hand going reflexively to the pommel of his sword.

My monster's heart raced, and he made a series of warning barks. Though he was a coward and would flee given the chance, he would lash out if there was no alternative. The fear scent that radiated from him was thick. Another creature would have recognized it, but humans had no sense of such things. They saw only his bared teeth.

Both men backed away from the wagon, creating a window for escape. My monster lunged forward, and the hard ground jarred his joints as he landed heavily on his front paws. Across a cobbled road, trees and brush offered cover between two buildings. My monster darted forward, but a high-pitched wail rang out, raising the fur along his spine and stopping him in his tracks. He spun, addressing the noise. By the central well stood a young boy, half-hidden behind his mother, eyes wide.

Crouched, my monster's sides heaved. Shouts came from his left, accompanied by nervous whinnies. Pelt bristling, he leapt out of the way, narrowly avoiding the hooves of a dapple-gray mare. Metal horseshoes scraped on the stone, sending a cringing shudder through my creature's shaking flanks. He inhaled briskly and turned back toward the cover of the brush, darting for their safety. Through the undergrowth, a pasture stretched to the forest beyond. He ran alongside a wooden fence, ignoring the curious nickers of a bay and her foal.

Once in the sanctuary of the woods, he slowed to a trot. The beech trees in this area grew to great heights, their gnarled trunks and twisting limbs covered in moss and cracked bark. Spring leaves shuddered in the chilled air.

The creature stopped and raised his head, scenting for

threats. Traces of humans and horses carried on the southern wind. Fainter was the scent of chickens. My monster cocked his head and swiveled his ears, listening to their distant clucks.

Through the bond came an instinctual drive to hunt, though a prickle of fear accompanied it. He'd hunted hens in this form before. On the last occasion, he was nearly skewered by a pitchfork. My creature seemed to remember this and sat back on his haunches, snorting.

I sensed it then, the subtle release of tension. It was a window, and I took it. I grasped for control, and just as I did, the creature reacted, standing with a yelp. He fought back, straining against the pull, but I had my hold on him. He bared his teeth and snarled. With each shift, he held on longer and resisted my grasp to regain power with more vigor. I feared the day his strength would overcome my own and I would be stuck in this form. Left to live a life amid the trees, imprisoned within his pelt. Forever trapped within the skin of the creature responsible for Thatch's death.

Burning heat flooded the creature's veins. He threw his head back, and anguish shot through the bond. His spine snapped with a hollow crack, and his lower half went numb. Falling sideways, he dug at the dirt, pain searing in waves of fire.

He trembled, gave in to the agony, and lay still, tongue lolling, panting as his body became mine again. The pressure in his skull was nearly unbearable. Everything was pulsing. His vision blurred, and through fluttering eyelids, I focused on one of his paws, the fur clumped and dirty.

In a motion of expanding, my fingers folded outward from the pads. The skin stretched over the gnarled bones, too tight, tearing at the knuckles. Veins pulled at the back of my hand as it flexed involuntarily. A black band stood out around my index finger—my mother's ring. It was magic, then.

Sensing the re-attainment of control, I closed my eyes and focused on the blood pounding in my ears. My left arm bent awkwardly under my weight. It ached. Wind grazed across my bare skin; the contrast to the heat that scalded my body was disconcerting, and I shuddered.

When my breath returned, I opened my eyes. Vivid green leaves danced along the branches of the beech trees, and the dying evening light cast a yellow glow against the western sides of their trunks. I breathed in, scenting only the subtle hints of dirt and dew.

My pinned arm tingled, and I rolled to sit and take the pressure off it. Head spinning with the sudden movement, I braced myself, eyes lowered as I regained my composure.

As my vision cleared, my eyes caught on black markings along my left arm. They wove from wrist to shoulder, beneath my collarbone, and ended at my chest. I ran my fingers over the design, then flattened my palm over the rapid thrum of my heart, the slick unease of a nightmare choking at my throat.

The image struck me of Kaius's tattoo bathed in the early light before Mother's monument.

Each of my scars held a memory. Those, which were plain to the eye, lines of uneven discolored flesh, were reminders of enemies whose blades had found openings in my defenses. The most recent being from a run-in with the thieves, was already fully scarred over. The faintly raised scars that branched like the many roots of a tree were repercussions of the times in my childhood that my monster took over. The subtle blade marks of Astraea's lessons—cuts along my neck and hips to draw my blood—left only the faintest of impressions.

Turning my arm over, I addressed the tattoo with a form of detachment. The concepts of magic and the cruel reminders it marked me with were not new; yet, at least in the past I had always held a remembrance. With my other scars, there was pain associated, a wound at infliction. I flexed my fist, and the muscles in my arm tightened, rippling the designs along my skin. These marks had come without pain, without notice.

A breeze rose little bumps along my skin, and I leaned against a sturdy trunk. Though I recalled waking in the wagon and brief moments after, the images were all a blur, a half-forgotten memory. I observed nothing notable around me or beyond the trees, no landmark to discern where I was. Focusing on what I knew, I pushed pointless speculations about the magical tattoo aside and assessed my situation.

My clothes were back in the forest east of the castle, along with my sword and my silver. It was dusk, which meant I was at least a day's travel from the capital. The beech trees indicated we hadn't gone as far south as the volcanic fields in the mining regions, at least. That left Urandun, Yorel, Navarre, or Elrune.

Cursing my monster, I ran a hand over the stubble at my jaw. I was stark naked in an unfamiliar wood with no coin and no way of regaining my uniform, not with half the castle guard searching the capital and surrounding farmland and forests. They were wasting their time pursuing me when the true threat walked within the castle walls. Agitation heated my blood, and I turned and struck at the tree with a closed fist. The impact bristled, and red marks scraped my knuckles where blood rushed to the surface.

Without direction, I began walking. If I found clothes to steal and a cloak to conceal my hair, I could veil myself from immediate attention while I sought out a routier or huntsman who might deliver a letter to Harlan and warn him of the treachery within the castle. A huntsman, as at odds as they were with soldiers and the guard, would be less likely to hand the note over to someone who may pass it along to Rion. Still, there was always a risk associated with putting faith in others. There was also the matter of coin, of paying a huntsman, should I find one.

The clucking of hens led me to the back gardens of a sizable building. Half a dozen free-range chickens pecked at the packed earth, searching for bugs or remnants of feed. One raised its head, dark eyes round and blinking. It clucked, and the others mimicked. The feathered creatures drew nearer, necks bobbing as they walked, and I growled my irritation.

Pushing through the flock, I made my way to a door at the back of the building and tested the handle. I cracked the door and held my breath. Nearby, coals popped, filling the room with warmth and the scent of burning cedar. Taking a chance, I stepped inside, nearly tripping over a speckled red rooster as it passed by my feet and into the room. It clucked and fled under a table. I cursed, closing the door to stop any more of the hapless creatures from following.

Kneeling to assess the dull-minded animal, I glared. Its body pressed against a small crate of wine. Dark eyes blinked beneath a sideways-flopped crown, and it ruffled its feathers. It was not of my concern—securing clothes was my priority. And coin if I were fruitful in my search.

I stood and took in my surroundings. The room was equipped with ample storage cabinets and, at the far wall, barrels and crates. The crackling fire came from a cooking hearth. Through a split door with the bottom portion left ajar, voices carried from another room. Based on the size of the building, the large kitchen, and the hum of chatter, I suspected I was in an inn. It could have been a pleasure house, but only in Valio and the capital were such places so sizable. An inn was most likely. And, at an inn, I may find a huntsman.

I took a step, and the flooring creaked as one of the wooden boards gave under my weight. The rooster beneath the table squawked at the sound, and in a ruffle of feathers fled through the gap in the split door. I gritted my teeth as the voices in the other room quieted momentarily.

Steps sounded, followed by a commotion of furniture being pushed across the floor, and glass breaking, paired with the curses of a woman. The rooster's clucks cut off sharply with the unmistakable snap of a wrung neck. I sucked in a breath.

The lower section of the split door closed, and a latch slid into place; then the two portions opened together as one. A woman stood in the narrowly opened doorway, her hazel eyes sharp. The spotted rooster hung lifeless in her grip.

Her hair was a deep brown, pulled up into a braided bun atop her head. Fine lines at the creases of her eyes told me she was likely in her early forties. Dark brows turned in, and her lips formed a thin line. The woman exuded a steadfast boldness, yet to my surprise, she made no motion to beckon for the men in the other room. When one called out, she dismissed him over her shoulder.

I suspected there were at least three others by the varying range in tones I heard during the scuffle, but they were out of view. Retreating through the back door was the logical solution, but the curiosity of the woman's unusual demeanor and the hopes that I may somehow turn the situation to my favor held me in place.

Setting the rooster down on a counter, the woman drew nearer until only the waist-high table divided us. She scanned my body unabashedly. The hunger in her eyes put me on edge, and I shifted my weight. There was a forwardness to her, and despite her being twice my age, I was coming to suspect the reason she hadn't called the others in after me. Though comfortable in my own skin, I was suddenly grateful for the tabletop between us that concealed my nakedness.

With a considering hum, the woman knelt and her head lowered beneath the tabletop. *Or not.* I sucked in a breath. Glass clanked, and she rose again with a bottle of wine and popped the cork. The upturn of her lips was approving and heady. Was she intoxicated? Could I swindle her?

The woman took a long draw of the wine, then licked the tinted drink from her upper lip. I worried my brows, considering the best way to handle her. Deception was not a strength of mine, not as it was for Rion or Astraea.

She offered the bottle, speaking with a voice youthful for her age, sharp with wit that lent me to believe she was only lascivious and not drunk. "I suspect you could use a drink."

Eyes narrowed with suspicion, I took the bottle from her and, addressing her over the rim, took a draw. The wine was sweet and light and held very little taste of alcohol. The lack of a label told me that the drink was inexpensive, its source not worth noting.

"What is your name?" the woman asked, leaning forward to rest on her elbows. The position pushed her breasts together, and the swoop of her neckline made them impossible not to notice. I allowed my eyes to linger a moment. Could I seduce her? To be taken to her room would likely give me the opportunity for clothing and coin, but I disliked the concept of taking advantage of a woman in such a way. Even if I did not lie with her—could not, for despite the events at the festival, my cock still did not stir—I couldn't bring myself to whoring my body for monetary gain. I placed the bottle on the table.

"Lark," I lied. With the festival at an end and musicians, crafters, farmers, and all manner of travelers moving south, word of the King's death would spread like wildfire. Unless it was kept veiled from the public. Regardless, discretion was the best course of action.

"I'm Maerel, and this is my inn." She offered her hand, and I shook it. Her grip was firm, as were her eyes. "Lark … is that a family name?"

I nodded. "Hadrian Lark. I'm a routier. *Your* inn?" Women couldn't own property.

"The Halfway Inn," she answered, a challenge in her eyes.

The name was unfamiliar. Not a place I'd stayed many times then, at least. *Halfway.* Perhaps I'd found myself in Elrune, the midpoint between the capital and Literra. "Because Elrune is the halfway mark from the castle to the port?"

She snorted. "Among other reasons, yes."

I narrowed my brows, not following. The innkeeper picked up the bottle and handed it over. "I enjoy a play on words." She sucked in her lips and leaned over the table, her attention going pointedly below my waist. "Though with you, half might be all I could take anyway."

"Half—" I cut myself off, catching her innuendo. I drew a sharp breath and released it. "I am in need of clothing."

Without skipping a beat, Maerel grinned. "It would appear you are, and I am now in need of a cock." When I spluttered on the wine, she laughed, and I met her gaze with a sharp expression. She gestured with her chin to the dead rooster on the counter behind her. "I only had the one."

"Then you shouldn't have wrung its neck," I retorted. Sharpness was not the answer, so despite my irritation, I drew a calming breath. If I did not aim to seduce the woman, perhaps I could play at vulnerability or offer compensation. "If you have clothing to spare, I would be grateful. I can send coin to you when I return to my stead." If I survived long enough to do so. If the castle remained under Harlan's rule. I swallowed.

"*I* didn't wring its neck," she countered. Addressing me with her gaze, she released a sigh. "Very well. Stay here and I'll get you some clothes." Maerel made for the stairs near the back of the room. "There's nothing worth stealing in here, and if you try, I will call for the soldiers in the front room," she said with her back to me.

While I waited, I took another drink of the wine. In the other room, a man roared with laughter.

"Why *haven't* you called those men in after me?" I asked when Maerel returned a few minutes later with a stack of folded clothes and a pair of boots. I knew such a question may give me insight into her intentions. Skirting the table, she came to stand directly before me. I raised my chin and took the clothing from her.

"It's not every day a handsome young man shows up naked

in my kitchen. Maybe if I keep you around a while, you'll warm to me."

I grunted and drew an off-white cotton shirt from the pile, then stepped into the pants. *Acquire clothing and coin, then get word to Harlan. Whatever it takes.*

Maerel leaned against the table. "Do they fit alright? They were my husband's."

"They fit."

"Good. Now I believe you owe me some answers. Why are you naked in my kitchen?"

I balanced on one foot, sliding on a cotton sock, then trying a boot. It was a bit tight, but would suffice. "I was with a woman. When I woke, my clothes and coin were gone." The simpler a lie, the closer it was to the truth, and the less likely I was to stumble over it.

"So, you came to steal clothes?" Maerel deduced. Blunt but fair.

"What option did I have?"

Brushing past my question, the innkeeper pressed on. "What is her name? The woman you were with?"

"That's not something for me to share," I grunted, forcing my other foot into the too-snug boot.

"Didn't think to ask?" Maerel raised a brow.

Again, I had to force down the sting of irritation. "She chose not to tell me."

The innkeeper's eyes were knowing, and her expression softened. "That bothers you."

It did. I set my jaw. This wasn't about the woman; it was about my duty to my brother, to do whatever it took to protect him and unravel the threat within the castle walls.

The last article of clothing was a worn cloak; its dark fabric was coarse between my fingers. It would give some concealment, at least, but I would need to crop my hair short or tie it back with a cord to keep the wind from stirring it out of the hood. I drew it over my head, and Maerel stepped to me.

With a familiar comfort that was out of place, she adjusted the clasp. "You're young to have gray hair."

"I am," I dismissed. "I will send coin for the clothing. And the rooster. Within a fortnight. I am grateful for your assistance."

"You speak with too much formality for a man who was standing naked before me only moments ago."

Unsure how to reply or how to dismiss myself after the first attempt was rebuked, I took another drink of the wine to cover my discomfort. Where would I acquire coin? An unsettling dread clamped down on me. "I've found in my profession that being well spoken lends me to greater positions. Now, unless you have work for me, I must be on my way."

The corner of her lips quirked up. "The days following the festival of Ayrenven bring many travelers and ruffians through my inn."

"You require protection?" It was too easy; a trickle of guilt edged at my conscience. To fake being a routier, however, was not far off from my training. "For board and coin, I can keep the drunkards from causing problems for your establishment."

The innkeeper stepped toward me and raised her chin, a cunning smile lighting her face. "There are other services I may require as well."

I firmed my jaw.

"Such as tending the bar." She tapped her index finger at my chest. "Helping me turn down the rooms, and there's a delivery due tomorrow of necessities that will need to be brought in and sorted."

"These are not jobs for a routier—they are jobs for a—" I had been about to say *commoner*, but cut myself off, finding different words. "For a lesser-trained man."

She narrowed her eyes. "As I see it, you are in my debt." The woman rocked back on her heels and turned to lean against the table again. "Now, I have no reason to believe you will send coin, as you say you will. So you will stay, work the tasks I give you, and maybe, if I am fortunate,"—she winked—"you will warm to me."

I exhaled through my nose. "I will aid with your tasks until my next job takes me away from Elrune." She was offering me what I required, yet the mischievous look in her eyes caused me to hesitate, as if the idea was not truly my own, but hers. The look she bore was that of one who was used to getting precisely what they wanted out of an arrangement.

"And what of the woman you were with?"

The innkeeper's words held me. "What of her?"

"She is here in Elrune, is she not?" Maerel raised a brow.

Through the hazed memories of my time spent in my other form, I recalled the woman's scent in the wagon. If it stopped here, it was likely she was still in town, whether she lived here or not. And, if she were only traveling through, she would be staying at the village's inn. My heart set to racing. *No. I cannot become distracted from my purpose.*

Maerel cocked her head with feigned innocence, eyes sharp as if she were watching me put the pieces together. "So you're welcome. For the clothes and for the room." She left me and paced to the split doors. "You can start with plucking the rooster. You do know how to ready a cock, don't you?"

I bit back a retort, and the corners of her lips quirked up.

"In all seriousness, I don't want you to make a mess of it."

"I know how to de-feather a bird," I answered through my teeth.

"Good." She unhinged the latch at the door, closing the bottom portion and leaving the top open. "Gut it too, if you know how." Then she left.

Growling, I paced to the countertop and grabbed the limp bird. I took a long drink from the wine bottle and began plucking. The mildly violent manner of the task was therapeutic. I mumbled, cursing my situation. I was tense with the inability to do anything for Harlan but bide my time, wait out the huntsman, and hope that my message would get to my brother discreetly and without interception. And then what? What if Harlan chose not to believe me? Or if I was too late? Clenching my jaw to restrain the emotions tugging at me, I stopped my task and rubbed the back of my neck.

I took another drink from the bottle, and the lifeless black eyes of the rooster stared back at me. For now, at least, the mindless work and cheap wine would quell my dolor. Then, in working the bar, I would acquire information on a trustworthy huntsman.

One task at a time.

14

———

EVERA

The fire burned low. Kneeling beside it, I added another log and poked at the embers with an iron rod. Flecks of orange and yellow crackled and sparked against the charred stone. I held my hands out to the flames, warming them. The room was cool, but it would heat as the fire roused back to life. Drawing my cloak snugly around my neck, I stood, letting the warmth lick at my legs, bare beneath my knee-length shift.

From where I stood, I could peer out the window in the door in Leighis's study. Not even the faintest light shone in. Dawn was still some time off. I left the hearth and crossed the room to the steps that led up to the platformed level of the study. The book of lore lay on the oversized wooden table, closed as I had left it the evening before. It was inconspicuous among the mess of scrolls and loose papers. I ran my hand over the old leather cover, opened it, and flipped through pages absentmindedly.

The parchment, tinted by age, curled at the edges. I trailed my fingers over an illustration, the scratchings indented from the artist's quill. It depicted an owl, its eyes round and flecked like the night sky. The details were beautiful, and it brought

155

back to me thoughts of the carver from the festival and our brief conversation of lore and the spirit lines of the gods.

Most of the spirit lines were considered lost or gone from the earth. When Aureus and I were children, Leighis had told us stories of their origins. The legends captivated me, but they always seemed abstract, more fantasy than reality. The only known line to still exist was that of the red deer, held by the Cervius family in the west across the Beridian Sea.

I flipped a few more pages and stopped at a scene depicting two bucks, their antlers locked in battle. Animals, and yet men too. Names, dates, and details of their lineage followed in an elegant script. How many other lines still existed, thought to be gone but only hiding in plain sight?

With a glance at the staircase, I listened. It was quiet, and outside the window, the market square remained still and empty. I let out a breath and unwrapped the fabric straps at my wrist to reveal the tattoo beneath.

I studied it. The design was clean and defined. The art of tattooing was uncommonly practiced due to the risks of the trade. The use of mallets and needles to embed ink into the skin often led to infection and scarring, and never did the designs come out as crisp or bold as my own.

I turned my arm to examine the face of a creature woven into the band. The animal had sharp features, a pointed snout, and perked ears. I flipped through the book's pages, mulling over which line the guard belonged to. Either a golden jackal or a fox, as they bore the closest resemblance to my mark.

I read quickly through both passages. The jackals were said to have once lived as a pack, having more significant numbers than most lines. Though the foxes, too, were known to have at least four families in the line at one point. I rubbed the bridge of my nose; throbbing pressure promised a headache would follow.

Closing the book, I took my face in my hands, rubbing my

eyes. They burned. I hadn't slept more than an hour or two at a time since before we left for the festival. It had been what, three nights? But I was restless. Sleep eluded me, drowned by my thoughts, and when I had finally fallen into the depths of darkness, the reoccurring nightmare of my youth stirred me back to waking. At least I hadn't cried out and woken the others.

The steps creaked, and I cursed under my breath. Leighis came around the corner, and I hurried to his side, offering my arm. He took it, and I guided him to a chair.

"I don't like you taking the stairs by yourself," I said. "Especially when it's dark."

"I'm fine, child," he replied. His tone was warm, and his eyes glowed with affection behind the rims of his rounded glasses. That's how it was with him. Either he was present, as full of life as he'd been in his youth. Or he was hazed and absent. There was no in-between. I evaluated him briefly, but he seemed alright. He'd dressed himself and pulled back his hair, black streaked by touches of white and silver. Those contrasted the nearly all light gray of his short, pointed beard.

Content, I left him to start a kettle of water over the fire. "Could you not sleep?" I called back to him.

"I heard you when you rose. Have you told your brother the nightmares have returned?"

On a typical morning, it took Aureus quite some time to wake me. Sleep was something I could never have enough of, and though my bed was simple and the blankets all old, there was such warmth and coziness to them in the cold early hours of morning that it took a fair bit of pestering to stir me. Some days, Aureus resorted to pulling the covers off me. On those days, I took to adding castor oil to his tea, hiding the taste of the laxative with a strong mix of his favorite herbs.

"It's the first I've had in some time," I replied. "I'm sorry I woke you."

When a few moments passed and Leighis gave no

response, my heart sank. I turned my eyes to him, finding his gaze set on the shelving of books, and let out a breath. Nothing could be done about it. His periods of awareness were becoming shorter and less frequent with each passing month.

When the kettle hissed, I took it from the hearth with a cloth. My mind was distracted, lost in thoughts of Neirin and the marks on my wrist. Gods, the marks. I cursed my forgetfulness and retrieved the wraps, tying them to conceal the tattoo.

By the time Aureus woke, daylight lit the study. Leighis's tea sat on the table beside him, cold and untouched. I would make him a fresh cup when he came back to himself.

"Have I slept in?" Aureus asked as he stopped by Leighis and put a hand on the old man's shoulder. The hazed look in our mentor's eyes showed he was elsewhere, lost. When he was like this, I found myself hoping he was, in his mind, walking the great library of Vitalis.

"No, we were both up early," I replied, then added, "I've caught up on our orders."

Aureus skipped a step as he came down from the platform to join me at the table. He looked over the packets, jars, and other miscellaneous containers.

The corners of his lips turned down. "This must have taken you hours."

"I didn't want us to fall behind," I said.

Aureus shook his head. "You need rest, Evera."

"I'm fine. I'm just grateful to be home and to be able to get back to work." It was a half-truth at best, but I didn't want to tell him about the nightmare. The last time I had one and brought it up, he'd been in a solemn mood for days afterward.

Aureus rubbed between his brows and sighed, but didn't push further.

"They're all pickup orders," I said as I was organizing the finished items in a basket. I made sure each container was labeled with the customer's name, dosage instructions, ingredients, price, and other essential details.

"No deliveries?" He took the basket when I pushed it across the table to him.

I shook my head. "Not today, no."

Aureus carried the basket to the front room, and I followed him, passing through the drape that separated the shop from the back room and the rest of our home. Aureus placed it behind the counter, then raised his hands above his head and clasped them, stretching. "I'm glad to be out of the wagon."

I hummed my agreement, looking past him through the rippled glass windows that overlooked our garden and the stables across the street. After I dressed, I would spend some time in the pasture with Sorrel. She needed brushing, and I wanted fresh air and some time to myself. Nature was soothing, as was the presence of animals.

"Evera?"

I blinked, having missed Aureus's question. "What?"

My brother's lips were a thin line. "I asked if you made the tea yesterday."

My fingers flexed, but I kept the bitterness from my tone. "I did."

Aureus was only looking out for me. He wanted to talk about these things as little as I did, but he would not risk me coming with child. I wondered briefly what would happen to his plans of marrying me to Ruairc if I did. Knowing my brother, he would simply rush the wedding so Ruairc could believe the child was his. The thought of lying with my childhood friend made me cringe.

"Is there anything else you need from me?" I asked, changing the subject. "I want to go to the stables and groom Sorrel. Her coat is shedding."

The shop door rattled, and Aureus and I both turned to it.

"If you must be upset with someone, be upset with me,"

Aureus said, crossing the room. "I believed there would be deliveries, and that you would enjoy the outing."

Last fall, I delivered orders myself, resulting in more than one displeased man rapping at our shop door and causing a scene. After that, I was only to deliver while in the company of a man. One of two men accompanied me, my brother or …

"Aureus," I hissed.

He opened the door. "Good morning, Ruairc."

Dammit.

I skirted the counter, making a line to the back room, but I was too slow. Ruairc called a greeting, stopping my retreat. I gritted my teeth and pulled my cloak closed in the front to conceal my slip.

"I've come to take you for your deliveries," Ruairc announced as I turned to him. His honey-brown eyes were full of warmth.

"I appreciate that, but we don't have any deliveries today," I said, forcing out the words.

"A picnic, then?"

Internally, I groaned. "That sounds lovely, but I must go to the stables and groom our mare. Her winter coat is shedding, and I don't want her to be uncomfortable."

"You spoil that mare," my brother said.

I rolled my eyes, and he shot me a pointed look. Right, ladies didn't roll their eyes either.

"I'm going," I said to Aureus.

"I will accompany you, then," Ruairc chimed in, his smile easy and honest. He was either oblivious to my denial of wanting to spend time with him or feigning daft for the chance to be alone with me. When we were children, I'd enjoyed his company, climbing trees and racing through the woods; back when he would sooner kiss a toad than consider putting his lips to mine. *Things had changed.*

I suppressed a sigh. "I'll go dress."

THE STABLE SMELLED of horses and dried fodder and dust. It was wonderful.

Though it would be better without the cobbler's voice following after me.

Friendly nickers greeted us as we entered, and Ruairc halted in whatever he was going on about when a black stallion brought his head over a stable door and snorted a welcome. Ruairc offered a hand to the animal and stroked the side of his face.

Leaving the two, I made for the back wall where tack and brushes were stored. They were communal items, free for us to use as long as we cared for and returned them. Our family couldn't afford a stall, so Sorrel was in the pasture.

"I need to grab a brush," I called over my shoulder.

I selected one, then grabbed a second, deciding Ruairc could make himself useful if he was intent on following me around. Turning back, I stumbled and tripped into him standing directly behind me.

Ruairc caught me, and I stiffened in his arms. "Are you alright?"

"I'm fine," I said sharply, gaining my feet and removing his arms from my waist.

His easy smile faded, and a muscle at his jaw twitched. I handed him one of the brushes and shouldered past him. He'd planned my future without considering my thoughts; I wouldn't feel guilty for my cold demeanor.

Ruairc walked beside me to the paddock, unusually quiet. Sorrel trotted over, nickering and tossing her head as she pranced. She was a beautiful mare, her patchy, shedding coat notwithstanding. She lowered her head when she reached us and nuzzled against my chest. I patted her neck, then stroked down the side of her face. Her thick winter hair came out in chunks between my fingers.

In the warm rays of late dawn, we brushed in silence for some time. The discomfort of the quiet was tangible, but it was better than speaking. Through hooded lashes, I glanced over Sorrel's back to study the cobbler. If he'd asked for my hand directly, rather than asking my brother, would it have changed things?

In a sense, I loved him, or at least I had at one time. In childhood, we'd been nearly as close as Aureus and I were. Though I was unsure if I could ever bring myself to desire him, if he'd come to me personally, I could have at least given his proposal consideration. It was the fact that he'd gone to my brother and never asked what I wanted that upset me the most. I saw it for what it was—a hint at what being his wife would be like. I'd belong to him, and he would make all my decisions for me. I would keep his home, tend his needs, and bear him children. I'd never be able to practice healing again. Though I knew his intentions were good and that he would never mistreat me, marrying Ruairc would stifle my soul.

"I'm trying," Ruairc said, catching my eyes. He stopped brushing. "What happened between us? Don't you remember how it was when we were young?"

I brushed along Sorrel's neck, dislodging thick clumps of fur. Her silky spring coat beneath promised the change of seasons would be upon us soon. "I grew up. We both did."

Ruairc's hand rested on mine at the top of Sorrel's back, stilling my movements, and I fought the urge to pull from his touch.

"I know." Ruairc's voice was soft, and he trailed a thumb over the back of my hand before dropping it. "I'm just a shoemaker, Evera. I'm a simple man. But I'm trying to say the right things, do the right things. For you."

I let out a breath. "What is it that you remember?" He drew his brows slightly, and I clarified. "From when we were kids."

His easy smile returned. "I remember your excitement when you first learned what wild plants could be found in the woods. I remember going with you to collect them and how your face lit when you told me of their uses. You so rarely smiled back then."

I closed my eyes. Ruairc was sweet, and he knew me for who I was; I would give him that. But he was traditional in every sense of the word, and he would expect me as his wife to fit into the image society expected of me.

Ducking under Sorrel's head, Ruairc came to stand beside me and raised a hand to my cheek. "You still so rarely do."

He was close, *too close.* Though his intentions had been clear for many years, his advancements had never surpassed lingering glances or the slight brush of his hand against the back of mine when we walked close together. Never had he touched me like this.

"I smiled yesterday," I reminded him. "When you greeted us at the wagon."

Was it the agreement he came to with my brother that emboldened him? Or was it only that he was older now, knew what he wanted, and understood how to pursue a woman? Did his confidence come from experience? Did I care if it did?

"You smiled because you've grown up. Because it was the proper thing to do." He leaned in closer. "I want to see the smile you shared with me when we were just children in the woods. When you found passion."

Oh. Gods.

His eyes hooded, and he lowered until his breath warmed my face. He wouldn't kiss me. He would wait, let me close the distance. It was the kind of man he was. But I didn't want this. And he was dreadful at reading a mood.

I put a hand on his chest and turned my head aside. "I'm sorry, Ruairc."

Quiet fell between us, even as his breath still warmed the side of my face. "Is this because of your mother?"

I took a step back, raising my guard. My tone sharpened. "Because of my mother?"

Ruairc's jaw tightened. He exhaled, retreating with carefully chosen words. "Don't be upset."

Gods, he sounded just like Aureus. Why did men always feel inclined to tell me not to be upset? Irritation stung, but I held my tongue, waiting for him to tell me what it was I wasn't supposed to be upset about.

"I know you don't like to speak of her, but you can't live your life in fear of relationships because of—"

"Because of her?" My tone was sharp. "Because she was a prostitute?"

I remembered little of Mother. I had memories of hiding with Aureus, waiting for her to return to us. Other times, of watching because the man who bought her was impatient. But I didn't resent our mother for what she was. She'd done it to keep us fed, to keep us alive.

Ruairc's eyes widened, and he sucked in a breath. He shook his head. "Evera, that's not what I meant."

I leveled my gaze, irritated that the way he said my name brought back memories of when we were children, when we were close. Ruairc's family came from the western lands, and he had a slight difference of accent, which led him to pronounce my name Ever-ah instead of Ev-air-a. It had been a while, I realized, since he'd said my name.

"When my father died," he said, "I cried. Do you remember that?"

He'd been ten. "I remember."

"You asked me why I cried. You said my mother could be free of him finally." I remembered that too. "When I told you my father was good to her, loved her, loved us both, you told me I was wrong. You were eight. And all you knew of men was what you'd seen them do to your mother."

I swallowed the knot in my throat and lowered my eyes to my boots. He raised my chin, the notion gentle, intimate. My stomach swirled.

"Not all men are like that," Ruairc said. "Don't close your heart to love without giving it a chance."

15

NEIRIN

WHEN I WOKE, the first thing I noticed in the early dawn light was a vase of freshly cut flowers on the dresser across from my bed. When Maerel had brought them in, I couldn't say. There was something uncanny about the realization she'd been in my room while I was sleeping. Something shameful, too, for guards were trained to sleep lightly, remain alert. That an innkeeper crept past me was a slight on my skills. Or a tell of my exhaustion.

Pulling back the quilts, I rose to investigate what else Maerel had brought into my room. Gods, how many trips had she taken?

Beside the vase was a washing bowl, a pitcher of still-warm water, soaps, and a rounded iron shaving razor with a curled handle. There was also a small hand towel and atop it, face down, a handheld mirror.

The corners of my lips turned down. Heaving a breath, I opened one of the top drawers of the dresser and stowed away the mirror, careful not to turn it and risk a glimpse of my own reflection. I closed the drawer, skin prickling, and gritted my teeth before turning to the razor.

I stood in my trousers, which I had slept in for lack of proper night pants, and for the first time in my life, I held a blade and pondered its possible grooming uses beyond removing the stubble on my face. In the past, I'd never revealed anything below my hips to the women I'd pursued intimately, afraid they would see my lack of vigor and mock me for it. So I'd never given the scattered hair across my body much thought. And I had been so young, I'd not had enough hair on my chest to fuss over. Yet now ... I considered it. If I were to find the woman from the festival, would she prefer—

Ridiculous ruminations. I set the blade back down and ran my fingers through my hair, wishing Maerel had provided a comb instead of a mirror. After some time working on it, most of the tangles came loose. Unbraided, my silver hair fell past my shoulders.

I would be able to conceal the unusual color more easily , though, with it short.

Loosing a breath, I gathered the hair at the base of my skull, and with the blade, sawed through. I held out the forearm's length of hair and sighed before tossing it into the waste basket beside the dresser. Running my fingers through what was left of my hair, I cut away at sections that felt too long or unruly, then lathered some soap and scraped at the slight growth of stubble at my jaw.

Despite my focus, my prior thoughts of the woman from the festival and her preferences returned. Growling my frustration and wishing I believed in gods so that I might pray I didn't cut myself, I set to making the rest of myself more presentable.

I will not go out of my way to seek her out, will not waste time needed to pursue my plan. Yet if I come upon her by happenstance... would I rise for her again? Would it be selfish of me to revel in that experience once more?

Over a quick breakfast, Maerel explained the expectations of my contributions during my stay. They mostly consisted of tending the bar, cleaning tables, carrying things that were too heavy for her, and handling drunkards should they cause issues. She also implied other ways I could repay her for the rooster and my set of clothing; I did not entertain them with a response.

After our meal, she tasked me with carrying in a delivery of new linens, soaps, and other inn necessities. The carriage driver had left the crates of supplies near the front of the inn on the side of the main road, but I was to take everything around and through the back door so as to avoid bothering guests. I didn't mind the busy work, and once I found a rhythm in which to avoid stepping on the hens that clucked at my feet each time I neared the back door, I began to enjoy the purpose the task gave me. It was simple work, peasant's work, but I was outdoors, the air was crisp, and I was being kept busy. I was earning coin, doing something useful while I awaited nightfall and, if I were lucky, the show of a huntsman.

As I made trips back and forth, I pondered over my monster's draw to the cinnamon-haired woman. I considered the effects she had on me, which inevitably led to thoughts of our encounter in the tower house. And that left me pent up, unaccustomed as I was to the new sensations of lust. Of course, such thoughts would do me no good. Yet I could not shake them from my subconscious. A yearning drew me to seek her out, to discover what was different about her, and to see if I could find need with her again. But I could not let such temptations overtake me.

I hefted another crate to my shoulder. At least in my duties as a guard, I was never placed in Elrune. The lord and his family would not be quick to recognize me, nor would the commander of the local garrison or any of the soldiers. The commoners, likely, would take no note of me at all. So long as no one saw my hair, I should be okay for some time at least. When the capital was thoroughly searched, guards would be sent to the surrounding areas. But for now, I had time to get word to Harlan and plan my next steps.

A faint humming tugged at my senses. It was more a feeling —a resonance—than a sound, similar to the sensation of the bond I shared with my monster that allowed me to detect his emotions. But it was more hazed, distant, like an attempt to make out the words of a whisper carried away by the wind.

I sat down on the crate I'd been carrying and wiped the sweat from my brow with the back of my hand. My heart thundered in my chest. It was deafening. An indescribable nervous excitement heated my body. Unable to resist the pull, I abandoned my task and moved into the shadows of the woods. The draw was irrefutable, tangible, and as I drew nearer to its source, the emotion it emanated became clear. *Distress.*

Becoming anxious, a tugging need to protect and defend was wearing on me, so I hastened my steps. The short cropping of the forest east of the inn cleared abruptly, opening to pastures and the back side of a stable.

At the forest's edge beneath the overhang of branches, I squinted, heart thrumming. Then I saw her. The woman with the cinnamon hair. A lump formed in my throat, and fire heated my blood. She stood with a russet-colored mare grazing at her side and a man looming before her.

The man stood with a straight back and squared shoulders. Confident. He held the woman's chin raised to him. The gesture was intimate, and he was much too close. Her shoulders were rolled, arms one over the other as if comforting herself. The posturing of her body screamed reservation. Did he not notice? Or did he not care? I snarled. I'd kill the man without hesitation should he try to force himself on her. In a distant way, I recognized this thought for the absurdity it was, yet somehow it was true. Irrefutably so.

With purposeful steps, I set out along the fence line, nearing them. The man's eyes rose at my advancement and narrowed.

The woman turned, brows drawn in; when she saw me, her lips parted. If any man were to brush his lips to hers, it would be me, not this brute who caged her against the mare, whose forced presence distressed her.

Without hesitation, I swung over the fence. The man, whom I recognized vaguely, though I couldn't place, stepped in front of her. His hand went to his sword. It didn't matter. He was only a commoner, or perhaps the cobbler she'd spoken of at the festival. I could disarm him.

The woman's hand covered his where it rested atop the hilt of his sword, and the man flicked his eyes to her.

"It's okay, Ruairc," she said, and gods, her voice was like spring rain. She turned her gaze to me and set her jaw. A guarded expression, the fire in her eyes a warning. *A winter rain, then.*

I stilled before them. A muscle flexed at my jaw as I resisted the urge to strike the man, sensing for some reason that it would displease the woman if I did. Something about her presence set aside all rational thought. Emotions drove me. The need to protect her, to keep her safe and … to keep her mine. *Mine.* With my heart pounding in my chest and a boiling hatred for the man who'd held her chin in his hand, my world altered.

I took a step back, drawing my brows together, and the woman exchanged words with the man. The thrum in my chest drowned out their conversation, drowned out all sound, until my name fell from her tongue. Silencing everything else. I raised my gaze to her. She stood before me, and when the sun caught her features, something much deeper than lust struck me. A knowledge befell me that I needed her, body, mind, and soul. That I could not breathe without her presence. Even as it countered all I knew to be necessary—finding a huntsman, getting word to Harlan, securing his safety before it was too late. No time for dalliances. Or anything, even, of a weightier nature. But I would make time. For her.

"Neirin." She spoke my name again, and it sounded sharp on her tongue. "How did you find me?"

I swallowed. A few paces behind her, still by the mare, the man set me with a look I knew to be a warning. Then he left, brushes in his hands.

"Is that the cobbler?" I asked, gaze locked on him as he retreated, needing to know he was far away from us.

"Ruairc. Yes."

Ruairc turned for the stables and disappeared behind a wall.

I returned my eyes to the woman, heartbeat still rapid in my chest. "Did he hurt you?"

"No, I'm fine. Neirin, you can't be here."

The weight in her eyes troubled me; her words even more so. I fought the urge to cup her cheek in my palm, suspecting she would strike me if I did. The initial physical draw I felt to her at the festival had shifted somehow to something more prominent. There was a need to touch her, yes, but something else existed, too.

"Why can I not be here?" I asked, chest constrained.

She pursed her lips. "Because—" She cut herself off, tone exasperated, and ran her hands through her curls. Sighing, she lowered her voice. "Because you're supposed to be *dead*."

"Do you want me to be dead?" I cocked my head to the side, considering, even as her statement hurt.

Sucking in the inside of one of her cheeks, she looked behind her as if making certain we were alone. "How did you escape?"

Shame bridled me. "I ran."

Huffing, she shoved at my chest weakly with one palm. I stepped back, yielding to her.

"How could you not tell me what you are?" she asked.

"Not tell you what I am?" Remembrance of her frustrating nature returned to me as her question hung in the air. A guard? The son of the King?

The woman gaped her lips to speak, then closed them again, and her expression changed. "You didn't know."

Didn't know what?

When I gave no response, she started again, tone less accusatory this time, almost defeated. "Why are you dressed like a commoner?"

"I have taken work at the inn until I can get word to—" I paused, knowing I could not give the full truth. "To the royal family, to clear my name and expose the true assassin hiding within the capital."

"Why did you come to Elrune?"

Because my fox stowed away in your wagon. "It is my hope to acquire the services of a huntsman here."

She frowned. "What are you, then?"

"What am I?"

The woman held out her wrist, covered in wraps. Not following, I pulled back my hood and ran my fingers through my hair, briefly surprised at its shortness.

The corners of the woman's lips turned up and quivered. "Your hair looks dreadful. Did you do that yourself?"

Self-conscious, I made to pull my hood back up.

She placed her hand on mine, stilling me. "I'm sorry. It's not" —she grinned and ducked her head—"*that* bad."

"You are a dreadful liar," I said, but left my hood down regardless. When her hand left mine, I sensed the absence. I looked to her wrists and the wraps that bound them. "Are you hurt?"

"Am I…?"

"I have basic field training," I told her. "Let me see it." I reached for her, and though she hesitated briefly, she let me take her left hand in mine. The delicate touch of her shot electricity through my veins and straight to my heart in the most exquisite way. I smiled at her, but her eyes were sad again.

I withdrew the wraps, careful not to agitate the wound. Yet

when the cloth fell away, I stiffened and my hands dropped. It was not a wound, but a tattoo. One nearly exactly like the one I'd seen on Kaius's wrist.

"My father had one just like this." My words were a whisper, a ghost.

"You really don't know what it means?"

I raised my cloak at my arm, a vague connection coming over me. I didn't understand it, yet I knew it meant something.

"I woke with this," I told her, revealing my own tattoo. Was it not some magical punishment, but a connection that tied me to the stunning and curious woman who stood before me?

Her eyes were knowing, soft, almost sad. "What are you?" she asked again and turned her wrist over to reveal the animal's face, intricately interwoven into the design.

I raised my eyes to her, and though the admission frightened me, I could not deny her. "A fox," I rasped. "What does it mean?"

She cast her eyes aside. "It means nothing. You should leave."

She was slipping away. My chest ached with a need for understanding. Of the marks, of why I was drawn to her. Of why she knew more about me than I knew about myself. "How do you know about the marks?"

"I read," she said. "You need to leave, Neirin."

"Wait," I said, desperate to keep her near hastening my actions, moving me without thought. I stepped after her and grabbed her wrist.

She spun on me, and I nearly ran into her. Chest to chest, I breathed in her scent. She smelled like belonging, like home.

"Let me go." She bit the words out. There was such disdain in her tone, such harshness.

I released her immediately, heart pounding, and took a step back. Bile rose in my throat, for I'd done exactly as the cobbler had—forced my touch when she did not want it. "I'm sorry, I—"

"Leave," she hissed. "Just … leave."

16

NEIRIN

THE WOMAN'S anger stayed with me long after I left her by the stables. I finished my task of bringing crates into the inn, yet no longer did I take comfort in being outdoors or in the woodsy scent that hung in the air. With each breath I drew, her words weighed down on me more. *Leave. Just leave.*

Of course, I could not. Despite the strangest sense of push and pull the woman drew from me, there were other things at play, things greater than her and me. Placing the last of the crates in the inn's kitchen beside the stairs where Maerel had instructed, I stood and let my hood fall back. Running a hand through my hair, I took note of the locks that stood up on end and frowned.

Maerel came from the split doors and placed soiled dishes on the tabletop. "Is that all of it?" She nodded to the stack of crates.

"Yes," I said, huffing the response on a breath as I dropped my hand, forfeiting my negligent attempts at flattening the stray strands atop my head. The downturned corners of my mouth deepened. "Is my hair unsightly?"

Maerel narrowed her eyes. "Flattery lands me a better chance at your—"

"Nothing lands you a chance at that," I quipped.

Maerel considered, then pulled the wine crate out from under the table and removed the last few bottles. Setting them on the table, she turned the crate upside down. "Right. Over here, then."

I shot her a questioning look.

"Before the men at the bar start calling out for more drinks," she said, impatience in her tone. Again, she gestured to the crate.

"Do you know how to trim hair?" I asked. I took the offered seat, and she leaned in, bracing an arm on the table behind my head. I narrowed my eyes, but she only winked and, searching beneath the tabletop, withdrew a dagger. "You keep a dagger strapped beneath your kitchen table?" Oddly, I wasn't entirely surprised.

"Among other places," she said.

"You did not answer my question," I pointed out. Thoughts of the willful innkeeper taking a dagger to my head further shook my nerves. I sucked in my lips. Was a tidier appearance truly worth it?

She huffed. "Well, anyone could do a better job than you've done."

I made a low, disgruntled huff but objected no further. As she worked, my thoughts swirled from my brother to the woman with the cinnamon hair, to the certain price on my head, and then back to Harlan's fate should I not discover the threat at play before it was too late.

"Do you always scowl?" Maerel asked. A clump of my hair fell to the floor.

"Just around you," I retorted, rolling my shoulders.

Maerel scoffed. "Stop fidgeting."

I stilled. And, sitting atop a crate in a kitchen and being

mothered, a pang of homesickness struck my heart. If Nyana were here, she would give me guidance. I missed her. "Maerel," I said, hesitant. "Women are—" I sighed, letting my vulnerability show was discomforting. As were the unrelenting thoughts of the woman from the festival. "They baffle me."

"All women baffle you, or one in particular?"

A clipping fell to my nose, and I huffed a breath to dislodge it. "There is only one that matters."

Pausing from her work, Maerel tilted my chin to her. "You are a difficult read, Lark."

I scoffed, and her eyes lingered on my lips just a moment before she dropped her touch.

"Perhaps you should scowl less."

Amusement drew a faint smile, pulling at the corner of my lips and lightening my sullenness.

Maerel sighed heatedly. She brushed her thumb at my cheek and faintly bit her bottom lip. "Yes," she said, voice heady. "More of that."

Though I held the half smile, it was not real. I lowered my gaze so as not to give myself away. No, Maerel was not Nyana, and her counsel, in truth, left me with little more guidance than I'd come into the conversation with. While I appreciated the gesture, my heart thrummed with a dull ache as I longed for the gentle words and comforting embrace of the woman who had raised me. I mulled over the ever-pressing swirl of unknowns— how to understand the woman from the festival, what to make of our bond, how to ease myself of her distraction, or if I should listen to the magic that connected us and pursue her. All added to the frustration in my already burdened mind.

OVERHEAD, the sun beamed in a cloudless sky. I lifted my face, drinking in its warmth. The heavy inn doors behind me shut, and I let out a breath. In my right hand, I held a list of items Maerel needed from the market. Somehow, I'd become her errand runner.

Beyond the inn's small courtyard, a wagon pulled by two black horses rolled along the main road. A moment later, a couple of children ran by, laughing joyously, entirely devoid of troubles. I envied that. Though my hood was drawn, apprehension still weighed on me at the prospect of being out in the open.

I crossed the cobbled path, stopping at the wall that bordered the inn's courtyard. Broken iron hinges set into the stone suggested the presence of a gate at one time.

Following the road, I kept to the shadows to draw less attention to myself and turned right at the corner. The market ahead was busy, bustling with men, women, and children moving about the stands and shops. Unease hummed through my veins.

I frowned, addressing Maerel's list. Where to begin? The sooner I completed my shopping, the sooner I could return to the inn. Working the bar would be my best chance at securing transport of a letter to Harlan.

It had been three days since I arrived in Elrune and two days since I last saw the woman in the pastures. Each time the front doors to the inn opened, I raised my eyes with hope despite knowing the distraction she caused, but the woman never came. Neither did a huntsman. It was time to begin devising another plan.

The nearest stall to where I stood displayed a variety of cheeses. It was as good a place to start as any. If I kept my eyes down and my hood drawn. When I approached the stand, a portly man stood to greet me. I didn't raise my eyes to see his face. He wore a beige tunic and a long red jacket with buttons. The rich color of the jacket told me his stand had done well, or perhaps that was the intention of the outerwear, and it was only a façade—he'd splurged on one piece of clothing to give an air of importance, of superiority over others who sold similar products at the market.

"That's a gruyère," the man said, gesturing. "It's one of my best sellers."

Drawing the cords of the coin purse Maerel sent me with, I read the price list laid on the table flat before me, searching for "gruyère." I didn't have the slightest knowledge of the value of cheese or whether his prices were reasonable. I'd never worried about money in the past, but now I was spending earnings that were not my own. Hesitantly, I handed the coppers over and selected one of the pale wheels. The man seemed too eager as he took the coins from my hand. Perhaps I should have bargained.

Moving through the market with my eyes trained on the stone and boots of shoppers as they passed, I worked down the list until the basket Maerel lent me was nearly full.

Leaving the bakery, a voice caught my attention, and I turned toward it. A few shops down to my right, the cobbler spoke to someone in front of his store. His eyes met mine, and he raised his chin. A challenge. I held his gaze. Would he pose a problem?

The last item on my list was an order from the apothecary next door. The doorbell chimed when I pushed through, and a man at the front counter offered an unenthusiastic greeting. The shop smelled of earth and spices, and along the walls, shelves displayed an eclectic arrangement of containers filled with different ground powders and crushed leaves or dried flowers. Plants hung behind the counter, drying. The space was cozy, homey. Light streamed in from three windows, one at my back facing the market and two along the right wall. The side windows were tucked into alcoves that looked out to a garden and beyond that, the front of the stables.

I crossed to the man at the counter. His hair was braided at the side and tied up, and when he studied me, I couldn't shake the feeling I'd seen him before. Swallowing, I set a slip on the counter that Maerel gave me with the shopping list. "I'm picking up an order."

The man knelt to pull a basket from behind the counter. He sorted through the items, reading tags. "Here." He handed me a packet as he stood. "Seven ferres."

Figuring medicine wasn't something to be bargained over, and eager to be done with my shopping and free from the unplaceable familiarity of the apothecary, I handed over the coin. He grunted his thanks.

Just as I turned to leave, the doorbell rang and the storekeeper lifted his head, frowning. "Where's Evera?" he asked.

"She hasn't returned yet?" a voice behind me replied.

I gathered my items, not wanting to be in the middle of their conversation.

"No, I thought she was with you."

I turned; in the doorway stood the cobbler. I set my jaw, and his eyes narrowed briefly before he looked past me.

"I left her some two hands ago," Ruairc said, using the common way of telling time in more rural areas where there were no bell towers rung at the head of each hour by a timekeeper.

I reached the door, and as I pushed it open, a memory fell over me. The bell above the door rang, marking my departure, and I stepped outside.

The man at the counter … I recognized him from when I awoke in my monster's form. He'd stood beside Ruairc, and he'd carried the same voice as the man who rode home with—

Evera.

My heart thundered. She'd claimed to be a healer. Even the scent of the shop was reminiscent of her. How had I not made the connection immediately? Around me, the world moved at its own pace. Her name replayed in my mind until it became too sweet not to taste on my tongue.

"Evera."

The door to the shop sounded, and I withdrew into an alcove where the shadows concealed me. The cobbler and apothecary carried a sizable empty barrel between them.

"You sure you don't have a use for this anymore?" the cobbler asked.

"I've patched it repeatedly, and it still leaks." The apothecary adjusted his grip. "It's time for a new one. If you can make use of it for your supplies, it's yours."

The pair left, walking toward the cobbler's shop. My heart thundered in my chest. It was an opportunity, a chance to learn something about the woman—about Evera—and about myself. Yet if I were discovered, it could hinder my chances of contacting Harlan discreetly. I had only moments to consider.

I will be quick.

Drawing a breath, I turned from the alcove and reentered the apothecary's shop. It was quiet, no sign of another within. A curtain at the back stood as a divider, and I pushed through it. Scanning the back room, I skipped up a few short steps to a study.

Bookshelves lined the walls. Heart in my throat, I turned in half a circle, taking in the countless books along the shelves and the mess of scrolls atop the central table. When Evera mentioned she read, I assumed the literature would be simpler to find. So few people kept books, and certainly not this many, at least not among the lower classes, where literacy was less prominent.

A side door opened, and I spun, basket of goods still held in my hands. I froze. Cinnamon hair blazed bright in the light from outside the back door, and when Evera stepped in and closed it behind her, my breath caught. She turned and saw me. Her eyes narrowed. She crossed the room and scaled the few short steps up to the study, not slowing until she stood before me.

I retreated a step, backing roughly into one of the bookshelves. My head throbbed at the impact, and a few books fell to the ground. I'd known the shelves were there, but her presence had drawn all my attention, lending me to a state of clumsiness I was unaccustomed to.

"I specifically asked you," Evera said, supporting herself with one hand on the table and bunching her skirts up, "to leave."

I cocked my head to the side, watching as she revealed the bare skin of one of her legs to me, smooth above her boot. Longing ached at my groin, accompanied by a fleeting hopefulness and excitement. Then I remembered the dagger. Struggling with the clasp, she drew it from its sheath at her calf.

"That's a bad place to keep a weapon," I told her bluntly. I could have easily overcome her in the time it took her to wield it. She stepped to me, skirts falling back around her ankles, and pressed the blade to my throat. The heat of her body met mine, and I sucked in a breath. Her closeness was intoxicating, even as she added pressure with the dulled edge. The smell of my own blood mingled with her scent.

Her eyes lowered, then rose again. It was brief, but I caught it. She hadn't meant to cut me.

"You didn't hurt me," I said to reassure her.

She adjusted her grip on the dagger, the anger in her eyes faltering. "I told you to leave," she repeated coolly.

"You did," I admitted. When I swallowed, the blade's pressure stung.

Her brows scrunched, and she scraped the dagger upward with slow and measured pressure, forcing my chin up and to the side. It scratched at my short growth of stubble, and I let out a hiss of air.

Fuck. She's intense.

"You know something you aren't telling me," I said.

Evera took in a deep breath, then released it. "It doesn't matter."

The statement was hollow, and my heart lurched at her cool indifference. "It matters to me." The words escaped my lips barely more than a whisper.

Her lashes fluttered, and she worried at her bottom lip.

Though I could have overpowered her at any moment, I held back. For some reason, I felt she needed to believe she had control over me. I would give her that. If it came to it, I would let her cut my throat if she truly wanted to. The realization was bitter in my mouth.

No, this is all wrong. How is my resolve so easily lost to her allure?

A muscle in her jaw twitched, and she stepped back, lowering the blade. Her downcast eyes were heavy with worry.

Drawing the hood of my cloak lower, I studied her. Every part of my being ached for her. Both to take her against the table and to comfort her. It didn't make any sense. But none of this did. Disregarding the reason, for it was doing me no good, I surrendered to the call of my heart.

Slowly, I reached for her left hand. Though she turned her head aside, she didn't resist me. The touch of her fingers, so slight in my grasp, seeped liquid warmth through my body. I trembled, and she raised her gaze. I offered a shy smile, remembering Maerel's brief words of guidance.

"You make me nervous," I admitted, surprised by the effortlessness with which I could voice my vulnerabilities to the woman.

She parted her lips but said nothing.

"I worry I'll say the wrong thing." I unwrapped the cloth at her wrist. "Or that I'll scare you off. I don't understand any of this, yet I know in my soul that you mean something to me. Something draws me back to you, despite the pressure of outside forces, of obligations."

The wraps fell to the ground, and I traced my thumb across

the black markings of the tattoo. "I know I'm a monster, and I don't blame you for being bitter about the situation I've placed you in, both with—" I hadn't placed her in danger, though. I had told her to return to the festival, not to follow me into the corridor that night. But the details didn't matter. What she had become a part of was not something she deserved. "What with what you witnessed in the castle, and for this, if the magic that caused it was somehow my doing." I traced my thumb over the designs of the marking.

Hesitantly, I intertwined the fingers of my left hand with hers and drew our hands between us. My cloak bunched, revealing my own markings. "Please tell me what it means."

"It is old magic." Her voice broke, and her eyes left mine to linger with a sadness at our shared designs. "If I tell you, I—"

A voice spoke out from across the room.

Fingers still interlocked, we turned our gazes in unison.

Evera gasped. "Leighis."

An old man stood from his chair. I hadn't even noticed him. Gods, was my perception truly so skewed?

He stepped forward, and though Evera flinched, she didn't move to him immediately. Something caused her to hesitate. Then I sensed it as I had in the pasture—through the connection. This time, the emotion was sharp, dark, and seeping. *Fear.*

"Do I scare you?" I asked under my breath so only she could hear.

She raised her eyes to mine and shook her head, opening her mouth to speak. She never got the chance.

The old man spoke, awe lacing his voice. "The marks of a bond. You both wear the marks of the bond."

17

—

EVERA

NEIRIN'S QUESTION HELD ME. *Do I scare you?* And it wasn't just the question, but the hurt in his eyes when he asked it.

"I'm not scared of you," I said, my voice quiet.

A breath escaped his parted lips. My heart fumbled in my chest, and I couldn't look away. There was such depth to him, such pain. I wanted to take his sadness away.

The steps creaked, and the moment broke as I realized Leighis was making his way across the room to join us. I left Neirin to rush to my mentor's side. Though I tried to coax him to a chair along the railing near to us, the old man brushed me off and stepped to the table, standing before the silver-haired guard. My mentor held his hand out, and Neirin offered his arm.

Closing my eyes, I focused on the movement of air into my lungs, letting the relaxing technique calm my unease. Why didn't I want Neirin to know what I was to him? Was it only that I feared he would suddenly feel he had a claim to me? When I opened my eyes again, I looked upon the man, and a hollowness numbed me. No, his knowing would make no difference. What did it matter if he believed he had a claim on

189

me, or if Ruairc did? I was property either way. Unexpectedly, tears fogged my vision. The scents of our family shop, the familiarity of the study, all the things I held dear to me—how quickly they could be taken away.

"The marks of a bond," Neirin said, his tone hesitant. Heavy, even.

I blinked and refocused myself. This was not the place to be emotional.

Neirin's brows drew together, and for a moment I saw in him the same expression he'd borne in the pasture. A frustration, a lack of understanding of self.

Wetting his lips, he turned his gaze to me. "What does it mean?"

Leighis ran his fingers over Neirin's markings, tracing the intricate design. "It is a bonding tattoo, rare and ancient magic. You don't know this?"

Shaking his head, Neirin frowned. "I woke with it."

The old man grinned. "You didn't wake with it," he said. "You only just discovered it when you woke. The tattoos form *during.*"

Oh gods. My face flushed.

"During ..." The corners of Neirin's lips turned down, and the crease between his already drawn brows deepened.

"I'm old, not a prude," Leighis quipped.

Despite myself, I laughed; the tension in the air that only I seemed to feel was suddenly too much. Neirin's obliviousness and my mentor's blunt candor elicited unladylike snorts as I tried to restrain myself. Both men turned to me, the lines of their faces drawn in quizzical concern.

The implication clicked into place, and Neirin's eyes widened. His gaze swung sharply to Leighis. "This is because I slept with her?"

And with that, the two men in the room were back to speaking about me, in front of me, as men seemed so keen to do.

I scoffed, any amusement from before gone, and leaned against the railing.

"The marks formed when you came together because you are true mates, a bonded pair," Leighis explained.

"You keep saying that word—bond. What does that mean?" Neirin asked.

Leighis made a faint, thoughtful noise. Knowing him as I did, I suspected he was silently brewing a lesson. I glanced over my shoulder at the curtain that divided the back room from the shop. What would happen if Aureus walked in on this conversation? If he knew about the bond Neirin and I shared, would he turn Ruairc away? Was being shackled to a man framed for treason any better? Either way, it would not be my choice but something forced upon me.

I rubbed my hand over my face. Gods, all I wanted was to be left alone in the shop to make medicines. To crack the door as spring brought with it a warm breeze. To study the different scents of plants and powders as I combined them, to memorize them, to let myself fall to the fascinations of the incredible remedies the earth provided.

"At the beginning of time," Leighis said, finally beginning his lecture, "the moon gods Ayre and Wyn created the beasts of this world. You know this, yes?" Not waiting for a response, he continued. "The brothers Ayre and Wyn were proud of their creations: beasts of land, sea, and sky. In this time, the sun goddess Ora made only one creature. The brothers scoffed at this, for they had made many. But Ora was not discouraged, for she had made man."

I studied Neirin, curious if he would interrupt. Though his body was tense, he said nothing, only held my mentor's gaze.

"Ayre and Wyn saw man, and they were jealous," Leighis said. "Their sister created a creature that could communicate and process more complex thoughts and emotions. Her creation would build civilizations, would rule over the beasts of the world. It wouldn't do, of course, so they created once more."

"With the last of their magic, the brothers created the lines of the gods. Human, yet also beast. They had the intellect and cunning of their sister's creatures, as well as the strengths and abilities of the animals whose forms they took on. Beyond that, the creatures held magic."

"I have no magic."

Leighis rested a hand on the table. I pushed off the railing and went to his side, ready to assist him if he needed it. "You do," the old man stated.

"I heal quickly," Neirin offered.

"That is not a gift. The blood of the gods runs in your veins. It is said to be something coveted, though in all my years, I never learned why. Studies proved it to be unstable, unable to heal others when used as a transfusion. Useless, except to its host." The old man's eyes sharpened in defiance.

"Curious." Neirin's jaw flexed, but he gave no further comment. If he knew something, he was choosing to keep it to himself. Though it seemed in truth that he knew very little about himself or his kind. I pitied him a bit for that.

Humming with consideration, Leighis nodded and returned to his storytelling. "The sun goddess Ora was furious. How could her brothers create something in the image of her own design? She hadn't thought to give her humans magic; it made her bitter. In her jealousy, she created the Alidian, but with this design, she was brash and thoughtless, and her anger seeped into the mold she made.

"In their feud, the siblings created beings too powerful for this world. But nature has a way of reconciling itself, forcing balance. In the image of their creator's haste and rashness, the Alidian come upon the world at random, bold and fast, and are often put out just as quickly."

Leighis sucked in a breath before continuing. "The brothers' creations were crafted to be the very best. But, in this drive for perfection, they also forced it upon their creations. The beast within each one was selective, choosing only one as its mate. Without a true mate, one with the blood of the gods could not reproduce. Slowly their lines began to die out."

And there it was. The *she's the only one who can bear a child for you* bit of the story. It wasn't that I didn't want children or wasn't fond of them, but I didn't want being a mother and a wife to be *all* I was. When Ruairc looked to me, even when my brother did, it felt as if that was the only value they assigned to me.

Turning his gaze to me, Neirin's lips parted. For someone who'd been told they'd found their true mate, he appeared devastated, entirely weighed down by the knowledge. Was it unfair of me to cast him aside but feel bitterness and rejection should he do the same to me?

"I can have children still without you," I said. "It is only you who cannot without me." The words came out as a ramble. Firming my lips, I cast my eyes aside, heat rising to my cheeks.

"I will never have children," Neirin said, and the heavy, seeping sadness in his voice drew my attention back to him.

Leighis groaned faintly, a sign he was tiring. I reached for him reflexively. He mumbled, his words making little sense.

"Come, sit," I coaxed. I guided him to a chair along the railing, then eased him down. His eyes still shone, and I held them as if I could will him to stay with me, stay present. But of course I couldn't. Even for a healer, some things were beyond reach. Fleeting awareness was perhaps one of the truest cruelties of aging.

"Is he sick?" Neirin asked from behind me.

I bit back a bitter retort, my heart aching as it always did when Leighis slipped away. When the old man's eyes grew distant, I kissed him above his brows.

Turning back to Neirin, I took a breath and braced myself

with my palms on the table. "He's absent, lost in his mind. I don't know why it happens."

The worktable between us offered a veil of separation. Eyes cast down to the strewn papers, I let the weight of everything settle over me.

"I'm sorry," Neirin said, his tone gentle.

Whatever fire I had before was extinguished. Everything was laid out now. "As am I."

"When was the last time you slept?"

I blinked, my eyes dry and weary.

"You look exhausted."

Shaking my head, I considered. "I got about a hand's worth last night." Each night since I returned from the festival, my nightmare had haunted me. The grip of fear, fingers clasped around my wrist, pulling at me. A woman's scream.

"You need rest."

Irritation firmed my jaw. "Don't do that. Don't pretend like you care."

"Why would you believe I don't care?"

Perhaps the guard was right. Perhaps I did need sleep. Everything was simply too much to make sense of, and for the time being, I was done trying. Despite cutting my outing with Ruairc short to walk alone for some time and clear my head, I felt just as lost as I had when I woke. For lack of a better way to express myself, I turned to frustration.

"I don't belong to you."

"No," he agreed.

"No?" I challenged, tone sharp.

"No, you don't belong to me. Were you not listening?"

I shook my head, exhaustion slackening my shoulders. "What do you mean?"

"If my kind is the spawn of greed, if my monster is a reflection of my own darkness, and my strength only a crutch for my inadequacies, then there is no reason you would belong to me.

You could have anyone, bear a child with anyone, as you said. If anything, it is I who belongs to you."

I was too tired to grasp the depth of his statement, my mind too heavy. I let out a breath, and Neirin came around the side of the table to stand beside me.

Caging me with his right arm on the table, he lowered his gaze to meet mine. "I've never desired a woman before you, only sought them out for their attention because, gods, I felt lacking. But with you …" His tone grew heady, and though he didn't lean in or push himself on me, his presence enveloped the space between us. "My body burns for you, Evera."

Who had given him my name? His last statement simultaneously sent a coiling warmth to my center and a trickling unease down my spine.

"You were meant to be something I chose for myself." My voice cracked. "The carver, he—" I was rambling again, but I was beyond caring. "Obscurity … that is what I wanted with you. Not this."

The bell on the shop door rang, but Neirin held my gaze.

"You have to go," I said, forcing my voice to be firm.

A muscle twitched at his jaw.

"Neirin, you have to go. I want you to go." My voice caught, betraying my emotion. Another moment under this weight, and I would be unable to breathe. I could not handle Aureus discovering this, not now.

Finding my strength, I gathered Neirin's basket and shoved it into his arms. I thought to make a comment on his trespassing, but my desire for him to leave before Aureus caught us together was greater than my irritation at his intrusion.

Above his dark brows, Neirin's hair was a tousle of thick and glorious silver waves that looked significantly better than it had the last time I saw him. I stared a moment too long, the desire to run my fingers through it nearly winning over. I stood on my tiptoes, even as I knew better than to offer any sign of affection that might lead him on, and drew his hood up, using it as an excuse to experience the brief brush of his silken hair. My heart leapt. When I dropped my hands and took a step back, neither of us broke the lock of our gazes.

The bell rang again, and my brother's voice came from the front of the shop as he greeted a customer. I let out a shaky breath.

"Go," I told Neirin. "Through the back door."

"Can I see you again?"

I shook my head, words eluding me. Was I doing as my brother always claimed I did—leaning into stubbornness when things became heavy? Was I pushing Neirin away to salvage my already-limited independence or for some other reason I could not yet articulate? Bitterness burned at my throat. Was there no situation where I could avoid marriage? Whether it be to the guard or the shoemaker.

Gritting my teeth, I found my resolve. Right now, I need to be alone. And then … I wasn't sure. If I had any sense at all, I would keep away from the wanted criminal, surely. Even if he made my stomach flip. Even if he sparked at my candor and met my energy in a way so few did. And he hadn't corrected me that night, hadn't forced me to "my place" when I followed him into the corridor. Instead of taking my dagger, he had shown me the proper way to hold it.

Without responding further, I urged him down the steps. He didn't resist me, though I suspected he could if he wanted to. The man was strong. The firm muscles of his arms flexed as I coaxed him toward the door.

The bell chimed again, announcing the customer's departure, and I looked over my shoulder to the curtain, anxious. In the doorway before me, Neirin froze, hesitating. I turned back to him and nudged him, forcing him across the threshold. He opened his mouth as if to say something, then shut it again.

Footsteps across the wood flooring neared the curtain, and I cursed under my breath. Rather unceremoniously, I closed the back door in Neirin's face and spun as Aureus entered the room.

"Evera."

I realized I hadn't rewrapped my wrist. *Dammit.* I crossed my arms behind my back. Leighis still sat in the study, dazed, and somewhere on the table, my dagger was lying amid the papers. It took a conscious effort not to glance in that direction.

The corners of Aureus's lips turned down, and his brows creased. "Are you just now getting back?"

I was horrid at lying, and my brother had an uncanny way of picking me apart, so I simply nodded.

"Ruairc came by earlier. He told me he left you some time ago."

Right … I was supposed to be out walking with Ruairc, courting.

"I told you, Aureus, I have no intentions of marrying." The words came out sharper than I anticipated. Now wasn't the time to start a fight, not when my emotions were high and my arm was unwrapped, hidden behind my back. It was a mute statement anyway. There was no situation in which my fate could be drawn by my own hand.

As he always did, Aureus fed off my energy. It reflected in his tone. "You don't have a choice."

Our gazes held, both of us bristling. I was too angry to respond, too exhausted and emotionally drained by everything that had transpired with Neirin and Leighis. Of course my, brother would come in, forcing conversation about Ruairc and marriage at this time.

My body trembled. It was all too much. Aureus's expression softened, and he stepped toward me, but I retreated, my back hitting the door. Emotion quivering my lips, I shook my head.

"Evera, I'm sorry. I shouldn't have—" Aureus ran a hand

through his beard. "You need time to think on all of this. I've pushed it on you too quickly."

I turned my head aside. I wanted him to leave, needed space to breathe. My lungs constricted.

"Please understand, I am only doing what I feel is best for you."

What is best for me?

When I didn't reply, my brother sighed. A moment later, his steps and the swoosh of the curtain announced his departure. The breath I released eased the aching in my lungs.

I slid to the floor, fighting tears. Leighis knew now, so it was only a matter of time before Aureus discovered my secret. Neirin, too, understood our connection now to an extent. And then there was Ruairc to consider.

If Aureus discovered the bond, my choice would be made for me. *Marry the shoemaker or marry the outlaw.* Leighis had raised us with a respect for lore and the histories of our people, our world, even as such concepts had seemed more like fairy tales than anything else. They seemed real enough now.

Though if Aureus learned of Neirin's involvement in the death of the King … Magical bonds or not, my brother would sooner marry me to a nameless merchant than to a criminal.

Perhaps the simplest solution was to give in to the stereotypes, disclaim myself from my family, and accept the title of a witch. Live my days out in the woods. The idea was absurd, selfish, the musings of a sleep-deprived and overwhelmed mind.

I ran my thumb over the design on my wrist, and Neirin's words replayed in my mind. *If anything, it is I who belongs to you.* Something little leapt in my chest, and I drew my wrist to my body, holding it against my heart.

18

NEIRIN

I STOOD outside in the garden, fixating on a broken board at the base of the back door of the apothecary shop. The gap would let heat escape. Although it was a little thing, I worried about it. I worried over Evera, too, over the darkness beneath her eyes and the heaviness in her steps. If she didn't rest, she would grow faint. Why did such thoughts, such cares, weigh so heavily on me?

Was it the bond the old man spoke of? Was that what drew me to her and defined this connection we shared? It made sense. My creature ached for her nearness, and the desire I experienced in her presence consumed me.

I'd never expected to care for a woman, not in such a way. And yet here I was, standing before a door so recently slammed in my face with a basket full of things that didn't matter, staring at a cracked board and worrying Evera might catch a chill. Worrying, she was tired. Sad. And that I was, at least partially, to blame for her unrest.

Inside, she exchanged heated words with her brother. It was wrong to eavesdrop, but I couldn't pull myself away. When she slid down the door, her shadow darkened the gap, and through our bond I sensed her sorrow.

At that moment, I longed for Nyana's guidance. My understanding of women was limited beyond what brought them satisfaction in a physical way. I had no idea how to comfort one, let alone how to woo one. *Is that something I want? Is it something Evera wants?*

Releasing a breath, I stepped back from the door. No, she wanted me to leave. Or maybe she just needed time to her own thoughts. I could empathize with such a need. How many times in my life had I stood outside the castle walls and considered a life beyond all that weighed on me? Beyond Astraea's lessons, Rion's scrutiny, Kaius's void of caring, the aching knowing that I didn't belong. Only Harlan kept me there, and the hollowing need to make up for the travesties of my youth.

I let my forehead fall to the wooden door. When had I begun to let my monster's desires influence my thoughts, my feelings? If what the old man said was true, the way I felt toward the woman—toward Evera—could be explained by magic. I hardly knew her, after all. Yet I *wanted* to know her. To learn the way her mind worked, what mattered to her, her dreams. To hold her in my arms, to breathe in the scent of her, to take her to my bed.

The thickness in my throat was uncomfortable. Emotions I had no reason to feel, no right to feel, choked me. Though it tore at me to walk away, like every nerve in my body was pulling me back to her, I did. I let my steps carry me back to the inn and refocus.

When I pushed through the heavy oak doors, the hum of conversation and the popping of the great central fire greeted me. Taking the items I purchased to the back, I passed Maerel at the bar. Strands of hair pulled loosely back fell about her face in the front, making her appear a bit disheveled.

"It got busy," I noted as I backed up to the split doors,

pushing them open with my shoulder and stepping into the kitchen.

"It's everyone traveling back from the capital," she called back as I sat the basket on the table. "Did you get the things on the list?"

I grunted a sound of affirmation and joined her behind the bar, self-consciously checking my hood and scanning the room. No castle guards. Some local soldiers, but mostly travelers. No lords or their families. No one should recognize me, and seemingly there is still no word of the King's death. No obvious sign of a huntsman, either.

Maerel came to stand before me and turned her chin up to meet my eyes. "Something is weighing on you." The observation made me scoff. If only she knew all that weighed on me.

"I spoke with the woman," I said, for it was plain enough talk, and I suspected it would placate the innkeeper's curiosity.

Maerel made a faint, thoughtful sound and bent to collect two small glasses from beneath the counter.

I let out a breath and continued. "She is arranged to marry another, and I am—" I raised my left hand, examining the marks of the bond. "I am making things more complicated for her." Voicing my musings lent me a lightness I hadn't anticipated. It brought, too, thoughts of Nyana. A homesickness for her and for the familiar warmth and smells of her kitchen tugged at my heart.

Selecting a bottle of whiskey, Maerel poured the two cups half full. "Give her grace, Lark. An arranged marriage is very rarely something a woman wants. I suspect there is reasoning behind the match, and the weight of her situation is surely burdening her. Men often do not stop to think about what it feels like to be put in such a position."

"You speak as if you know," I said, leaning against the bar.

Without meeting my eyes, Maerel drew out another three glasses. "I was arranged to my first husband. When my father told me the importance of my match, my soul broke. I was sent away from all I knew, and my husband … was a bad man. But had I not been sent to this town by my father to wed him, I would never have met my Tarik." The corners of her mouth turned up subtly, and a light sorrow, a longing, laced her words.

"What happened to him? To your first husband?"

Maerel shook her head. "The same thing that took Tarik. Sickness. And that's the cruelty of life. What presents itself as a blessing in one breath may shatter you in the next."

"I'm sorry," I said, meaning it.

Amid the hum of voices and singing of a bard, Maerel turned quiet, contemplative, seemingly lost in memories. She cleared her throat when she finished pouring, putting an end to the weighty conversation. She put the bottle beneath the counter. "Take these to the group in the back corner."

Five soldiers sat around the table. They wore training garb with the emblem of House Tellius, the local family, embossed on their breastplates. Nodding, I took two glasses and made my way to the table.

Though there was no reason the soldiers would recognize me, an unexpected desire to be discovered itched at me. To disarm a man, feel the weight of his sword in my own grasp. To release my tension and frustrations in the rush of adrenaline that accompanied a fight. Even to be slain, if it would release me from the weight of all that burdened me. But for my brother, I would bear the weight. I had no choice.

Keeping my head down, I maneuvered around the crowded space about the central hearth and made my way to the back table. I set the glasses down, making a comment that I would return with the others in a moment, and I took the men's orders. The Halfway Inn doubled as a tavern, and the menu was simple: whatever was cooking in the back. Today, the options were stew or roasted lamb.

Each of the men selected a dish, none meeting my eyes. The

bard picked up a faster tune, drawing the soldiers' attention. He was young, his hair tousled, and the shadow of a beard at his jaw. Strumming the strings of his lyre, he began to sing, and those gathered around raised their glasses. Encouraged, the bard braced a foot atop the edge of the hearth and upped the tempo. The lapping of the fire cast a dance of shadows across his face. Perhaps the bard would know of a huntsman. No one suspected a traveling musician, and people often spoke freely in their presence. There was value to this, value a cunning huntsman would recognize and take advantage of.

I brought the soldiers their remaining whiskeys, then their food. The bard continued to play as the afternoon wore on slowly, and as I made my rounds, taking orders and delivering drinks and meals, eyes remained trained on the young entertainer. When he finally retired from his place at the hearth and went to the bar, I followed and took my place behind the counter.

"What can I get for you?" I asked.

"Water," the bard said, voice a bit raspy.

Nodding, I filled a large glass and slid it across the bar. "You play well. Did you perform at the festival?"

The bard swallowed and lowered his glass to the counter. "It was my intention to do so, but I overindulged at a pleasure house the night before." He quirked a cunning smile. "I fancied the women who desired me for my talents when I played for them, yet when I woke, the coin I had reserved for the festival's entrance fee was all but spent."

"It would seem they placed a higher value on their own talents than yours, then."

The bard laughed. "Yes, well, not without reason."

"I'm in search of the services of a huntsman. Do you know of anyone?" No reason to prevaricate.

The young man took another drink of his water, considering. "I suspect you're willing to pay for discretion?"

"I am."

He tilted his head subtly, gesturing to a table in the corner where a man sat alone. A man who appeared no more than a traveler, who bore only one sword and boasted none of the boisterous consistencies of most huntsmen. Curious.

Nodding my thanks to the bard and pouring him a drink on the house—something I wasn't entirely sure Maerel would approve of—I dismissed myself and made my way to the huntsman.

"Pleasure to have the company," the man said as I took a seat at his table, keeping my hood drawn. There was a lack of sarcasm to the statement, as if he genuinely were pleased to have a hooded stranger come upon him unexpectedly in a dimly lit tavern.

Resting my forearms on the tabletop, I leaned in, studying the stranger. His eyes, cast to the hearth, reflected the light of the fire and shone in hues of hazel—green and amber with streaks of a dark brown. The tone of his skin was olive, and his deep umber hair was short and curly.

"You do not carry yourself like a huntsman," I said bluntly.

"Yet you know I am one." The man turned his gaze on me and held his hand out. "Nox."

"Lark." I shook his hand. "I am in need of your services for a most significant purpose."

"Tell me, Lark." The huntsman leaned back casually in his chair. "Are the intentions of your task honorable?"

Honorable? "Never have I met a huntsman who concerned himself with the concepts of honor."

Nox clasped his hands behind his head and raised a brow.

"My task is honorable," I growled, annoyed by the man and his unusual candor. "The bard tells me you carry your assignments out with discretion. I need a letter brought to the capital, delivered by hand to the prince."

"As long as intent is honorable, I am discreet, yes. If I find it is not—" His lips twisted in a considered expression. "Well, I will weigh that at such a point."

"Compelling." My patience was waning.

"So sober you are, friend." The huntsman beamed an easy smile. "The bard has played well on this night. The season is changing, outside warmth carries on the breeze. Within these walls, there is mirth and plenty of mead. Yet you are terribly dour."

Gritting my teeth, I placed my palms on the table and stood. There would be other huntsmen.

"Is it me who has put you in a foul mood?" Nox drew his brows together. When I set him with a glare, and gave no response, he smiled. "Apologies. As I said, plenty of mead." He swirled his tankard. The third, I'd brought him. Yet, he did not seem intoxicated, at least not beyond faintly so.

"I will find someone else to carry out the task," I said, turning to leave.

"Not many huntsmen have access to the castle. Though I suspect as a guard, you would know that."

The hair on the back of my neck rose, and I turned to face him. "How do you know that?"

With an expression of feigned innocence, Nox tilted his head to the side. "That most huntsmen do not have access, or …?"

I sat again, and the chair screeched across the wooden floorboards at my rough movement. "That I am a guard."

"Well," he mused, "I could claim it is the way you hold yourself or the way you speak, for in truth the hood you wear does very little to conceal that you do not come from the same place as these men and women do. But alas, such things would not be enough to draw a clear deduction. It is simply that I have seen you before. In Urandun."

"Yet I do not recall you." I narrowed my eyes.

"Nox Perdere." He dipped his head. "The youngest of

Commander Perdere's sons and his greatest disappointment. It's not difficult to overlook me, I admit."

"A huntsman, the son of a commander?" I scoffed.

"See, now you sound like my father." There was no malice, no condescension in the huntsman's tone. The man had not once lost his casual demeanor since I began our conversation. "But it is because I am his son that I have access to the castle."

"I have seen others deliver letters by hand before. You lie."

"No, friend. I do not lie, or at least, I make a great effort not to. I suppose we all lie on occasion, when there is no other choice or if it is for the benefit of preserving the feelings of those we care for." When I did not reply, he continued. "Security has been tightened since the King's death."

A flash of adrenaline heated my body. "The King's death?"

"Discretion goes more than one way, you must realize. However, what I am about to tell you is not a great secret. Word has been carried out to the commanders of Cilicia's major garrisons, and within the capital itself, the knowledge is already quite versed among the general populace. I suspect it will be here, as well, within a day or two. People do so like to talk. However, the fact that you are unaware of the heightened security, and that you are serving mead at an inn, lends me to believe you no longer serve the guard. Would you like to tell me why that is?"

"I would not."

He frowned. "Very well. What do you have as payment?"

"I will pay upon completion, whatever your price may be."

The huntsman ruffled the hair at the back of his head. "Guards. All the same. Little to no regard for coin." He nodded then to my left hand. "I will take that as insurance."

Mother's ring.

The inn's front doors swung open, and all eyes turned to the man in the doorway. Aaron, the son of the local lord, stood tall, anxious energy tightening his expression. I recognized the man immediately, though I doubted he would take any notice of me. Lords and their kin so rarely even acknowledged the guards who stood posted within the castle during their visits to speak with the King. Still, I brushed at the silver hairs that stuck out of my hood above my brows and adjusted the cloth.

Hinges creaked as Aaron stepped into the room, skirted by three soldiers. He scanned the room, then spoke to those gathered, his voice confident and coming from deep in his chest. "There is a fire in the southern fields." He raised his hands as a gesture for quiet when whispers broke out. "Report is, a group of men set it. I need all those capable to join me immediately."

At the back of the room, the five soldiers rose to their feet, one of them bumping the table and spilling a drink I would later have to clean. A few others stood too—travelers carrying swords sheathed at their hips and bearing rugged expressions.

Those able, followed him from the inn. Though it was no longer my place, my heart thrummed at the prospect of joining them. I hungered for a fight. Longed for the hum of a sword as it cut the air. Taking lives was a part of who I was, and though it chilled me, it gave me a sense of grounding. For in the moment of battle, no other thoughts could persist. Every breath belonged to movement and step, to execution.

Drawing the letter I'd written on my first night in Elrune from the band of my pants beneath my cloak, I addressed the huntsman with a low threat. "It is imperative that this gets to the prince without interception. Is that clear?"

"The King?"

I swallowed. "Yes, the King." Removing Mother's ring from my index finger, I set it atop the hardened wax seal of the note. "Beyond that, I expect you to carry back a response."

"And what if the King does not wish to offer a reply to"—he studied me—"a tavern worker?"

"He will give a response." He must. For if he did not, what

could I do for him? Stepping foot within the capital as things were was a certain death sentence. Even with the hidden passageways to the castle in the woods to the east, there was no other crossing point at the river than the single bridge, which would certainly have become a checkpoint by now. Even if I were to dye my hair, I would not make it to the castle without discovery and, likely, a hastened execution. What was the price on my head as the alleged slayer of the King?

"Very well, Lark." The huntsman stood and counted out coppers from his coin purse. Putting the rough, rounded metal pieces on the table, he tipped back the remainder of his mead. "You can expect me back within a fortnight."

"It should not take that long," I growled.

Nox only shrugged. "If it does not take that long, then I will return earlier." Briefly, he examined the ring then tossed it in the air and caught it. "Good evening to you." He dipped his head with the sort of bow that did not mock, yet did not engender respect, either. Like everything else the huntsman did, he acted with casual familiarity and a disconcerting lightness.

Without further word, the young man took the letter, tucked it into his jacket, and exited the inn. Only a few patrons remained—half a dozen older men, two women, the bard, and a portly man who appeared to never have wielded a sword a day in his life. The desire to join the group headed to the field and fight returned to me on a rush.

"You aren't going?"

The question came from behind me, and I turned to find Maerel approaching.

"You told me you're a routier. Is this sort of task not what you do?" One of her dark brows rose.

"I have no sword." The words were hardly out of my mouth before I noticed the sheathed blade and leather scabbard she carried at her side.

"It was my husband's," she said, offering it. "Go and aid the men."

Weary of the woman, I narrowed my eyes. "I won't be further in your debt."

Maerel scoffed. "I'm not giving it to you. I'm letting you borrow it. Aaron will pay those who help well. Of course, you knew that already, didn't you?" The implication was clear, and I grunted. If I were truly a routier, this would be the sort of work I'd take eagerly.

Without responding, I reached for the sword and pulled it from its sheath. It was simple in design but well-kept, its edges sharp. My reflection caught in the silver surface, and my stomach lurched. Gritting my teeth, I sheathed the blade.

If Maerel noticed my reaction, she didn't draw attention to it. Beneath my skin, my monster sought control, but I could push him down. The excitement of the battle ahead coursed through my veins. The thrill of it was wrong, I knew, but intoxicating, nonetheless.

"I'll be back shortly," I told her.

Maerel nodded and gestured with her head to the front doors. "Go. And don't get yourself killed. You're still in my debt."

19

NEIRIN

Smoke tainted the air. I turned my sights to the horizon, searching for the fire's origin. Hoofbeats sounded on the cobbled road outside the inn's courtyard, drawing my attention to the open gateway.

Aaron led the group. Beside him rode a man I'd never met; I suspected him to be the local commander by his uniform. Half a dozen soldiers took up the rear of the group, their horses all dark chestnut and of similar stock.

With a hand at the pommel of my borrowed sword, I watched the soldiers. By the time I turned the corner, they were already crossing over the bridge and heading toward the southern fields.

I slowed my steps as I neared the stables. Voices came from within, and a man hurriedly led out a bay stallion and mounted. The horse pranced and others nickered inside their stalls, the ash in the air making them uneasy.

The man pulled his reins, gained control of his mount, and took off down the path after the soldiers. A moment later, two more men exited the stable and followed suit. I would never keep up with them on foot.

Cursing, I turned to the pasture and leaned against the fence. Above the tree line in the distance, clouds of smoke rose, choking out the afternoon sky. A nicker came from the fields, and the russet mare I'd seen Evera with before approached. She stopped at the fence line and tossed her head over, nuzzling at my pockets.

Pushing the creature's head aside, I paced down the fence line and found the gate latched with a metal lock. I jiggled it, but the iron held strong. The mare followed, searching again at my waist. It was an irritating trait.

I gave a thoughtful grunt, studying the creature. Despite her pestering, the mare looked capable. I hopped the fence, and she let me approach her side. Though I suspected the horse belonged to Evera, the mare could just as easily be the cobbler's. It didn't matter; it was unlikely anyone would notice if I borrowed her for a short time. The itch to fight, to be a part of the fray, was too strong to resist.

With trained familiarity, I mounted the mare bareback, and her flanks quivered. I patted her neck to calm her. Riding bareback was something all men of the castle guard were taught. Becoming comfortable with a horse and learning to control one without tack were among the first things we learned as boys. The horses of the guard, however, were highly trained. This mare, at least, had a halter and lead to aid in directing her.

With a click of my tongue, I pressed my heel back to guide the mare. She obeyed, easing into a steady walk. At the far end of the small pasture, I applied slight pressure with my inside leg and a firm tug on the stiff leather reins, turning her cleanly before setting her back on course.

Many horses fear jumps, especially when a rider is on their back. There was no guarantee the mare wouldn't halt at the fence line, barreling me over her head. I set my jaw and took a clump of mane in my fist, balancing my weight and gripping with just the right amount of pressure with my thighs.

The creature took to a trot with a firm push of my heels. I let off the pressure and squeezed again, coaxing her to quicken, and she did. The muscles that moved along her sides and the pace of her gait became an extension of myself, and I encouraged her on. When the fence line approached, she didn't falter. I braced as she cleared the jump.

The mare's hooves raked the cobbled road, and her ears flicked as she gained footing and slowed her gait. I turned her toward the bridge and urged her on at a trot.

Nearing the river, I relaxed and leaned back, signaling her to slow to a walk as we crossed the stone bridge. The mare nickered and obliged. Without the forest obscuring my view, I could take in the extent of the fire's damage. Several buildings were up in flames, sending columns of angry black smoke to the sky.

I squeezed with my heels, and my mount picked up speed. Drawing nearer, I heard the shouts of men and the metal hum of swords rising over the crackle of embers. The mare's flanks quivered, and her steps became agitated. I slowed her, wishing for a post or tree to secure her by her lead.

"Stay put," I said, gesturing with my palms after I dismounted. The mare lowered her head to my side and nuzzled under my cloak. With an edge of force, I pushed her head away, and she took a step back with an irritated snort. In the worst-case scenario, she would return to the stables. Even daft horses knew their way home, and I could walk back and find her later if need be.

With my heart thundering in my chest, I set off on foot toward the commotion. Already, a clarity had come over me. Focus. My palms itched, ready for a fight, and I flexed my hands at my sides.

Ash carried on the breeze, sending paper-thin flakes of black soot into the air. One caught on my cheek, and I brushed it off, smearing a line of charcoal on the back of my hand. By the time I reached the fray and drew my sword, my eyes stung. I suppressed a cough and addressed the situation as I'd been trained to do.

The burning buildings were not essential to the livelihood of the town as a whole. Homes for the workers, a few shacks. The fields were all intact, untouched by the flames. The wind was low, which was more effective in controlling the fire than the peasants who carried buckets of water. Their efforts would do little good, in truth. The structures would be burned to ruins. The starting points of the fires were too thoughtful, as if the men who set them held an interest in preserving the land and the stores of grain kept in the silos.

Men ran by me, swords drawn, shouting at one another. Others stood still, looking around with expressions of confusion. The heat of the lapping flames consuming a nearby home warmed my right side to an uncomfortable level, and the subsequent smoke charred my lungs.

Squinting my eyes in the haze, I made out several of the local soldiers. They each wore the same black uniform with an emblem of a raven embossed on their breasts. The routiers and commoners who had come to aid for a share of the coin wore an eclectic collection of armor plates, chainmail, and everyday clothing. I could not determine the location of the commander, nor of Aaron, amid the chaos. Nor could I detect anyone who appeared to be a true threat. Though I could understand why reports came of raiders, as it was difficult in the fray to make sense of each man's intent and position, there was no doubt that the homes were set on fire intentionally.

Agitation struck alongside a wave of disappointment, followed immediately by shame. Coming here had been an unnecessary risk, a mistake. How quickly my reasoning quelled the desire for the calming release of battle. Had there been a fight, had my hood been tossed back, and had someone noticed me by chance …

My conversation with the huntsman came back to me as I

adjusted my cloak and took in the chaos. He had mentioned that word of the King's death had been sent to the commanders of each of Cilicia's garrisons. Snarling, I cursed under my breath. It was very possible the man who accompanied Aaron knew of me already and was keeping his gaze steady, searching for the silver-haired bastard who had killed the King.

Kicking at loose pebbles, I walked back to where I'd left the mare, ridiculing my recklessness. My monster roiled beneath my skin, a faint reminder of his presence.

If there was no raid, what was the reasoning behind setting buildings afire? Typically, such strategies were used as a distraction or to cause chaos so that outlier buildings could be robbed, so that fear could be instilled among a group of people. Raising my gaze to the hillside, I scanned for thieves or raiders, for the possibility that this was a warning or retaliation. Retribution for something. But I found nothing more than the quiet tree line.

The mare nickered where I left her, yet as I approached, I stilled. An energy hung in the air. Familiar, blood-chilling.

"Show yourself," I snarled.

Wind rolled the tall grass, and for a moment, all was still. Then the shadow of a sitting figure appeared—a boy with a head of dark curls—hidden in the field, waiting for my return.

I found breath enough to say a single word. "Calix."

20

NEIRIN

"Wʜᴀᴛ ᴀʀᴇ ʏᴏᴜ ᴅᴏɪɴɢ ʜᴇʀᴇ?" I stepped forward, closing the short distance between us, and grasped the messenger by the collar of his shirt.

Calix's body shuddered, his eyes flickered, and the charge in the air intensified. *Dammit.*

Releasing my hold on him, I let him fall to the ground and turned my back. The child made a faint sound as he fell, and the charge held. Nothing I was not accustomed to. Gazing up and down the nearby path to assure no one was coming or going, I huffed a breath and drew back my hood, letting the smoke-tainted breeze ruffle my hair.

At the dip of the valley along the river's edge, the buildings continued to burn. The routiers and soldiers who had come with intentions of fighting off raiders had since turned to aiding the farmers with their buckets of water, having found no enemy to wield their swords against.

"Why did you start the fires?" I asked, tone level, as I turned back to the boy.

Calix stood and shuddered again. The cobalt of his eyes flickered black, and static crackled, but it was clear the boy was restraining himself. And, in truth, he was doing a fairly decent job of it for a child of his age who had likely not been fed in nearly a fortnight. It was harder the younger they were. They needed the blood more frequently to sustain control.

"It was meant to draw you out," Calix replied, his tone listless. Though usually composed, the boy made no attempt to straighten his shirt or dust the debris of dirt and dried grasses from his pants. Dark shadows beneath his eyes told of his state. He would not last much longer.

"The others, do they fare worse than you?"

"The two new boys are probably both dead, taken out into the woods. We have not seen them since. They were unstable." Calix spoke with his typical trained detachment.

It was not a surprise. Their control was weak, and their need was high and frequent. The newest of the children could sometimes feed as often as twice a day in the early weeks, as they adjusted.

"The others?" I asked.

Sucking in one of his cheeks and chewing it, Calix cast his eyes down. "Astraea has us contained in the cellar room where we will not be of danger to anyone aside from each other. Two days after the festival, she selected those of us who were faring the best and sent us out to find you."

"Why did you think a fire would draw me out?"

He raised his eyes again, and the displaced coolness returned to them. The boy looked beyond me to the burning farmsteads. "It was the Queen's orders. Create a scene without causing lasting damage to anything vital. She believed your training as a guard would be too strong to allow you to resist engaging on some level."

Pinching the bridge of my nose, I released a breath. Through my worries over Harlan and the threat that lay within the castle walls, I'd given little thought to Astraea or her messengers, to the effects my absence would have on them. "Does Rion know of the Queen's actions?"

Furrowing his brows faintly, Calix shook his head. "I do not believe so."

"She needs me to return," I stated, my mind beginning to work around how I could use this to my advantage. "What does she offer?"

Without further response, Calix held out a package wrapped with thick paper and tied. The lack of a wax seal was a statement. The faith Astraea held in her messengers was absolute, for they relied on her, and she used this as a method to control them.

Untying the bindings, I opened the package. Within I found a letter and two silver canins. The letter, written in rich black ink, bore the Queen's signature at the bottom. As I read, Calix sat again, and I eyed him briefly over the paper. The boy's dark lashes fluttered as he struggled to keep his eyes open; he was using all his energy to control his magic. I swallowed and returned my attention to the note.

"I will not return for this," I said, pocketing the coins and tossing the letter back to Calix.

Despite his apparent weariness, the boy caught and folded it. Tucking it into his shirt, he sighed, the sound heavy. A muscle at his jaw flexed. Shaking my head, I turned my attention to the mare and drew up my hood.

"What did the letter say?"

Looking over my shoulder to the boy, I narrowed my eyes. "Aren't you supposed to keep your questions to yourself?"

"My friends will die," he said, voice meeker than before.

Of course, the runt would choose this moment to show he had a soul. Huffing an exhale, I turned back to him. "She proposes safe passage to her country house and a life lived out there where I can continue to offer—"

The boy's eyes flickered with hunger.

"This is not a life," I said. "It is cushioned imprisonment."

"Please." Desperation crackled in the air alongside the static of barely restrained magic.

"I have a task I must fulfill." I turned back to the mare and mounted.

The boy stood on wobbling legs, then fell once more. The mare stepped in place, clearly sensing the charge in the air as well. Despite her unsettled state, she didn't spook or flee to the stables. I found myself surprised by her courage—or foolishness. The boy looked up at me from his hands and knees, the colors of his eyes shifting, his chest heaving.

A knot formed in my throat to see him struggling, fighting to control the magic that swirled within him. Though he and I were not the same, I empathized with his pain. He had not asked for this life. A quick death when he first showed signs would have been more a gift than what the Queen offered—the false hope for a life impossible to sustain forever. She had to see that. Even before I left. What was such a life truly worth when it came with the expectation of fulfilling any task, delivering any message, without question? When rebellion or the slip of control led to repercussions, led to her thrice-cursed *lessons*?

"Your hand." I held my own out to the child, and he quivered at my closeness, teeth rolling his bottom lip. "Do not make me regret this," I warned on a snarl.

His eyes flickered again, and he pushed himself to his feet and took my hand. Effortlessly, I pulled him to sit in front of me. The child was light, perhaps lighter than a boy his age should be. Whether that was due to this stress on his body from not feeding for so long and his fight to suppress his magic, or simply a lack of nutrition, I was uncertain.

As the charge grew, the mare stepped in place again, her ears pinning back.

Drawing my borrowed sword somewhat awkwardly with the

boy in front of me, I held it before us a moment. To slice his throat, to release him from this life, would in truth be a kindness. I could free him from his inevitable suffering should Astraea learn he'd failed in his task to deliver me to her. Yet as he trembled in my grasp, my heart betrayed me. Cursing, I used the sword to create a shallow slit on the inside of my arm. Not at the wrist, for even with my hastened healing, I could not expect the child to restrain himself in this state. A slower, more controlled bleed was safer.

The body in my arms jerked, but I restrained him long enough to sheathe my blade. That done, I released my hold on him, and he took my left arm greedily with both hands, drawing the wound to his lips.

Cool ice spanned from his clasp through my body, but I resisted the shudder. The boy's thirst was desperate, lacking any semblance of control he previously showed. I could not fault him for that, though.

"Easy," I said, and the pull lessened, if only slightly.

The static in the air settled, and the mare settled, though her ears remained back.

While the boy fed on my blood, I watched the road, assuring no one was coming. The fire still held the attention of those in the field, and we were far enough from the fray that should anyone glance in our direction, they would suspect nothing out of place.

Thoughts of the old man, Evera's mentor, came to me. Though he knew much about me that I did not know about myself, I did not believe he knew the full extent of my blood's capabilities. It was an ancient and well-kept secret that the Alidian fed on us, that the blood of the gods sated them, gave them control over their magic.

Witches, blood drainers, the soulless. The Alidian had several names, or condemnations—slurs cast as a way to conceal the insecurities of those who feared them or didn't understand them. It was ironic, for the blood of the general public held no value to the Alidian

Tales were told around hearths of a time when corpses were found in the streets, drained of their blood. The bodies of my kind. Though that part of the story had been either forgotten to time or never known by those who were not a part of the fragile system to begin with.

The boy in my lap settled, his muscles relaxing, his eager draining settling into the sleepy tug of a babe close to dozing off. The mare, too, had settled.

Why was it that people presumed only women could be Alidian, could be witches? Was it only because male Alidian were so uncommon? In all my years, I'd come across many females in the streets of the capital. Once every fortnight or two, a girl would lose control, and guards or soldiers would be sent to handle the situation. To put an end to the threat.

Calix's lips broke from my arm, and he mumbled incoherently, his head swaying. There was no use musing on such things. It did not matter what was true, only what people perceived as the truth. Still, it pulled the corners of my lips down. Evera suffered from such rumors when she had done nothing wrong, when she had no connection to the Alidian and wanted only to practice her trade, her skills, and to aid others.

In my grasp, Calix swayed. The wait to feed had been too much for him, and now that he was sated, his body would need time to recover. Tightening my grip around him with my right arm so that when he fainted, he did not fall from the back of the mare, I examined the cut. It still bled, but not seriously enough to draw attention.

Clicking, I urged the mare down the hillside and to the path that would lead us back to the stables, unsure how to handle the new burden I bore. I knew the boy would not leave me to return to the Queen—that was nothing short of a death sentence for him. He was my responsibility now.

21

———

EVERA

THE SMOKE in the air enhanced the vibrancy of the sunset, painting the sky a deep blood-red hue. The sun, dipping near the horizon, appeared a blinding white beneath the black cloud of ash carrying west from the fields.

Though the day was warmer, the earth held a chill, and the bones in my fingers ached as I worked weeds from our garden. My pile was growing impressively, but there was still much work to be done. As there always was this time of year. Weeds to pull, dirt to till. The ground needed to be prepared before seeds could be planted.

Wiggling a particularly stubborn weed with fine, splintering hairs along its base, I cursed under my breath. It snapped at the root, and I stood, throwing its upper half to the pile. Cursing again, my eyes turned to the stable as they had several dozen times in the past hour.

I'd been crouched down, working, when Neirin had mounted Sorrel and taken her from the pasture. Though I suspected his use of her was related to the fire, it was still unacceptable.

With a hiss, I returned to my task. Scraping dirt aside with

227

my fingers, I took hold of the stubborn root and yanked—only to hear the sickening snap as the stem broke in my hand again.

"Fucking—" I stood and kicked loose soil over the remains of the root. *Good enough.* My eyes rose to the double stable doors, and I brushed my hands on my skirts, dirtying the fabric.

Making up my mind, I crossed the garden and unhinged the simple wooden gate.

The stable was just across the cobbled road, and as I entered the building, I lowered the hood of my cloak. The usual greetings I received were lacking; the horse's soft nickers were replaced with stepping and snorting. It was the smoke, their instinctual fear of fire.

Leaning against one of the stable doors, I held a hand out and clicked. The black stallion at the back of the stall tossed his head, and a fog of warmth clouded from his flaring nostrils.

"It's alright," I said.

The creature's ears twitched, listening to my words, and after a moment of hesitation, he crossed to me. With slow movements, I stroked the side of his face, and the muscles at his neck quivered.

Hooves on the stone outside drew my gaze, and I caught sight of Neirin's back as he rode past the double doors.

"You brought her back," I spoke loudly to draw his attention. Neirin looked over his shoulder, and Sorrel stopped. His eyes met mine as I paced to stand in the doorframe. "You stole my mare."

Neirin grunted, and for the first time, I noticed the figure of a child in front of him. Lying the lifeless form over Sorrel's withers, he dismounted, then hefted the body over his shoulder.

"Borrowed," he countered, hooking his free arm over Sorrel's neck and guiding her past me into the stable.

"What—" I cut myself off as Neirin passed me; the dark curls of the child strung over his shoulder bounced as he walked. "Is that child ... dead?"

Turning back to me, Neirin stopped and frowned. Sorrel, the headstrong mare she was, made her way to where hay littered the floor in small piles, fallen from the overhead attic space where it was kept.

"If he were," Neirin said coolly, "things would be much easier for him and I both." Then, as if the situation I'd somehow become drawn into was commonplace, he nodded behind himself to where Sorrel pushed her nose amid the hay on the ground. "Your mare is disobedient."

"She's fine," I said, the words sharp as disbelief held me in a state of shock. A lack of what to say numbed my tongue.

Neirin ran his hand back through his hair, causing his hood to fall. He sighed. "It was suspected that raiders had set fire to the farmland to the west. I went to lend my aid." He peered around me to the stable doors. "You do not need to whisper. It is unlikely anyone will return to the stables for some time. The fire has all free hands occupied."

Abandoning my whisper because it was easier than arguing a moot point, I returned to the topic of importance. "You went to lend aid, yet you returned with an unconscious child?" As I spoke, my mind cleared enough to address the most pressing of issues. "Lay him down, let me look at him."

Neirin obliged, lowering the boy unceremoniously to the dirty stable floor. When I knelt before them and shot Neirin a pointed look, he drew his brows further in and retorted dryly. "Where did you want me to lay him, Evera?"

Because there was no good answer, as there was no better place to put the boy, I huffed my frustration. "You did not answer my question." I lowered my head and rested my ear on the child's chest. It rose and fell steadily.

"It is not a simple question to answer." Crouching, Neirin propped his arms on his knees, his gaze watchful.

Checking the boy's pulse and finding it steady, I turned my attention to his head, searching for any obvious lumps. "Try."

"There is nothing wrong with him. He will wake in a few hours," Neirin stated calmly. "And I know the boy. He is a messenger from the castle."

I stilled in my task. "I recognize him."

"You do?" Confusion laced his expression, his silver eyes slits.

"I saw him at the festival." It was unimportant, though, so I moved past it. "What happened to him?"

"He is exhausted, that is all."

Nothing about the lifeless child before me implied a simple state of deep sleep, but I couldn't find anything obviously wrong with him. Sitting back on my heels, I rubbed my eyes. Emotion, pressed down in the initial moments of shock at seeing the listless boy, returned to the surface. I drew in a steadying breath to keep my voice level. "Why are you staying in Elrune?"

Neirin's expression softened. "Until I hear back from the huntsman I've sent to the capital, I have nowhere else to go. For now, I must just"—his eyes cast to the child—"avoid drawing unnecessary attention to myself."

I offered a faint, sarcastic noise.

"Admittedly, taking the child in further complicates things."

"What will you do with him?"

Neirin sat back, leaning against a post. With the dying sunlight coming into the barn at an angle, his profile cast a stretched shadow along the dirt flooring. "I do not know," he admitted. "There was a vulnerability to the boy tonight that softened me. If I cast him out, he will die." His final word hung solemnity around us. There was something about the boy Neirin wasn't disclosing, yet the weariness that darkened the skin beneath his eyes told me that was a question for another time.

"You care for the boy?"

Neirin turned to me, and the light fell evenly across his face, painting him in a glowing warmth. The length of his lashes caught, dark like his brows, despite the pale silver of his hair. They framed his eyes in such a way that my heart thumped against my ribs. "No," he said, and turned his attention back to the child. "No, I just empathize with him."

The response took me by surprise, and hesitantly, I reached out a hand and placed it gently atop Neirin's arm.

For a long moment, the stillness of the stables held us. The boy's chest continued in its steady rise and fall. The horses in their stalls snorted occasionally or shifted their hooves in place. When Neirin finally spoke, his voice was distant.

"Boys like him and I, we never got the chance to be children." A muscle at Neirin's jaw flexed. "We live our lives fully for the purpose of devotion to another. Him by necessity, me by … By the regrets of my past and an obligation to my brother."

With each statement Neirin made, he somehow became more elusive. More shadowed. I'd come to the stables to await his return, to confront him, to curse him for his insolence. Yet sitting beside him, his arm beneath my touch and the marks of his bond, *our bond,* stark and undeniable, I could do nothing but remain still. Quiet, listening, and wishing I could understand him better.

"The first time I killed, I was nine." He kept his eyes cast away, and the muscles beneath my touch tensed. "Before joining the guard, all boys are expected to perform a blooding. A first kill to show they have the stomach for such a life. I was … weak as a child."

It was hard to imagine the man beside me as anything but powerful, confident in his abilities. Yet the heaviness of the moment we shared hinted at a more fragile part of him. An aching desire to learn this side of him, to unravel the depths of his past, tugged at me.

"As the trial drew near, I became frantic. It was Astraea who … reminded me of the importance of it all."

"What of your brother?" I asked, hesitant to break his trail of thoughts, but unable to connect the brother he'd hardly spoken of, to taking a role in the guard. Or why a Queen would worry herself with the fate of two boys. Perhaps Neirin and his brother were orphans who were taken in by her. "Is your brother a messenger?"

Despite the weight in the air, the corners of Neirin's lips turned up, and he laughed. A quiet, almost hesitant sound, but there was amusement in it, and when he turned to face me, the dimple at his right cheek showed. "He is not a messenger, no."

I held his gaze; the striking silver of his eyes was all-encompassing. Warmth flooded my body. Not as it did when I felt desire, nor even as it did when I felt deep care for Aureus or Farren or Renna. It was as if I could feel the depth of his eyes in my soul.

Before I could find my breath, regain my composure, and voice another question, Neirin brought his right hand to my cheek and stroked once with his thumb, the touch so incredibly light. My eyes fell to his lips, and my heart caught, but he withdrew his hand, resting his arm atop his knee again.

A heavy sigh left him, and his chest fell with the exhale. "On the day of the trial, the charges against the man I was meant to kill were listed to the crowd. He—" Neirin shook his head once. "He had a perversion toward young girls. Children. The accusations were brought forward by more than one witness."

Something within my chest constricted, and I drew my knees up and hugged them.

"He was a bad man." There was no note of uncertainty in Neirin's tone, no need to be understood, nor a desire for forgiveness or justification for his actions, only a deep, solidified certainty.

When I remained quiet, he continued. "I came before the execution platform, pointed metal rod in hand. When I think of that day, I can remember my palms sweating and the sickening way the man's smile curled at his lips. My monster writhed; it took all I had to hold him back." Neirin's eyes went back to the boy. "Resisting magic is …" He sighed and let the sentence fall away.

Lowering his gaze, Neirin plucked a strand of hay from his trousers and let it fall to the stable floor. He swallowed hard. "Of all the forms of execution, impalement is the most horrific. Set aside only for those such as that man with an inclination for —" Neirin shook his head. There was no need to repeat the words. "When I finally went to stand before him, my monster settled. I felt a release from all of the thoughts in my mind. Clarity in the moment, on ending the life of the evil man before me. When I plunged the rod into his chest, blood seeped." He held his hands out and turned them palms up, as if he could still see the effects of the action staining his hands. "In that moment, nothing and no one else existed. I experienced complete freedom from my monster, from my thoughts."

I tucked my chin between my knees. *Nine years old. Gods.*

"Don't," Neirin said, catching my movement. He ran a hand through my hair and to the back of my neck, gently coaxing me to look at him. "Don't pity me."

"Then why?" I asked. "Why tell me this if you don't wish me to pity you?"

A muscle flinched at his jaw. "Because I've told no one else. Because I can speak to you in a way I've never been able to with another. My soul calls for yours, trusts it in a way I can't begin to comprehend." He broke my gaze and turned his eyes back to the boy. "And because he is …"

"He is like you?"

A faint laugh, and Neirin's thumb stroked beneath my ear casually. "No, not like me. Calix and I, we are different kinds of monsters." The smile that crooked his lips was sad, the creases at his forehead telling. "Before today, I'd not seen it but"—his jaw flexed—"we are similar in ways, too."

My heart twisted, and even as I knew everything about the

guard to be dangerous, edged with risk, I could not make myself pull away.

"This bonding." Neirin looked back at me and, with his hand still at the back of my neck, gently brought me closer to him and rested his forehead to mine. "I don't understand it. But you do. You seem to know more about me than I know about myself." A glint of mischief danced in his eyes. "Though you withhold the information from me, I cannot deny this feeling." He sucked in a breath. "Do you feel it too? The draw?"

"It is magic," I said, more to remind myself than to inform him. "These feelings aren't real."

Neirin dropped his gaze, then, with a hesitant glance up at me through his lashes, he unwrapped the bindings at my wrist, revealing the heavy black markings of the bonding tattoo. "Magic has always taken great humor in meddling with my life." Though he smiled softly, the slick sadness behind the expression was tangible.

As he touched his forehead to mine again, the hair that fell from the top of his head brushed my brow. I fought to control the betrayal of my heart, beating with a rapid thrum beneath my breasts.

"Whatever this is, it pulls me to you," he said. "I don't understand it. Yet maybe it's not meant to be understood."

My heart hitched, and I fought to keep my resolve even as his breath on my cheek and the brush of his nose pulled at something deep inside. Forcing down the urge to press my lips to his, to taste him, to give in to the yearning, I took a steadying breath.

"What you speak of is fate," I said. "I don't believe in fate. There's always a choice."

Neirin withdrew, though he kept his arm over my shoulder. The gesture, its familiar comfort out of place, altered the mood. Giving in to the longing for security and closeness, I leaned into him and rested my head on his shoulder.

"What of the cobbler? Is he your choice or your brother's?" Neirin's tone was level; the question held no bitterness.

I scoffed. "It's not that simple."

He nuzzled into my hair and spoke against my ear. "Is it not?"

Firming my jaw, I cast my eyes to the boy, still deep in his unusual slumber, and lowered my voice. "I won't be the reason my brother is on the streets again."

"Again?" Sorrow laced the question.

Instead of delving into my past, I sighed, letting my breath fog in the air. "I must marry for the sake of Aureus and our mentor. I owe them that much."

With his right hand, Neirin took my chin between his thumb and forefinger and raised my gaze to his. "Though admittedly this is not the most opportune time to ask ..." He laughed faintly, and despite myself I chuckled too. Nothing about the situations we found ourselves in together was ever opportune.

"What do you wish to ask me?"

"You will think me too forward," he warned, a lightness in his tone.

"Likely," I quipped. "Ask anyway."

His breath left his parted lips on a shudder, and any semblance of banter disappeared. "If you believe you need to marry for the sake of your family, let me court you."

Swallowing, I hesitated. The scent of smoke clung to his cloak, and as I cupped his face in my palm, I could feel the anxious flexing of his jaw as he awaited my response.

How have we come to this?

"Evera." My name on his lips drew me back from my thoughts as he took my hand in his and brought it between us. "If you do not feel this, then tell me; why do you look at me like you do?" He spread his fingers, and I mimicked the action reflexively until our palms mirrored each other.

My breath caught, and I closed my eyes. "You don't even

know me." The wavering of my voice betrayed my emotion. The man was wanted for the death of the King. And now he bore the responsibility of one of the Queen's messengers. Trouble followed him. To be drawn into it for the sake of my racing heart—

"Then give me a chance to get to know you." His words were husky and thick, and it took every ounce of restraint I had not to lean in and press my mouth to his.

As the moment hung between us, Neirin's breath quickened. His body was tight, strung, restrained. And gods, I reveled in the rush of power it gave me to hold his body under my control.

I am so tired of overthinking everything.

"If," I said, "I told you to kiss me—"

"Then I would steal your breath and kiss you until you moan against my lips." His response came without hesitation, thick with need. Brushing his nose along mine, he brought his lips close, so that the faintest movement would bring us together.

I lowered my head just enough to put more space between us and deny the kiss. Heat rushed through my veins, and a coiling need bloomed within me. When I spoke, my breaths came short and rapid. "And if I told you to take me here? Now?"

He growled, and something inside of me tightened. Wetting my lips, I tried to still the racing of my heart. The tension was building, and as much as I wanted to lose myself in his touch, his kiss, and whatever would follow, I knew that giving in to impulse would only bring us back to the same place we found ourselves before.

"And what if," I said, "I told you to earn my name, instead of stealing it as you did my mare?"

Neirin sighed, and the rising intensity between us shifted. Though my heart still raced, my question had altered the direction things were going. I sensed the change, and when he rested his forehead against mine, I knew he felt it too.

"At the festival, you were something I chose for myself." I

drew a stabilizing breath and spoke from my heart, even as the words came out rambling and without a clear path. "I did not give you my name because I needed to be someone else that night, to remove myself from this life and all that weighs on me. What I wanted, what I needed from you, was anonymity. I made that clear to you, and it was not your place to take that from me. If you truly want to explore whatever *this* is,"—I swallowed my uncertainties—"then you must earn my name."

A stillness hung in the space between our quickened hearts. Finally, Neirin raised his head and pressed a faint kiss to my forehead. "Then I will earn your name."

22

NEIRIN

With Evera in my arms, all outer threats fell away. The moment would not last. The time I had to embrace her was fleeting, and soon I would have to sort out what to do with Calix and return my thoughts to my brother. For now, though, I could simply enjoy her presence.

Though she'd tempered the heat, it pleased me that she felt it too—the rush, the desire, the need. Her scent frenzied my beast, and I had to fight the urge to lower my head to her neck, where it was at its strongest, and breathe her in. To find the pulse there and bite. To claim her.

No, I will do things right this time. Will not kiss her until I earn her name.

While the concept of putting such importance on a name seemed trivial to me, I could tell by her words that it meant very much to her. If she were willing to let me try to earn her heart, despite the precarious situation I found myself in—that I'd put her in—it was not asking much that I court her traditionally.

In the quiet of the stables, disrupted only by the occasional sounds of the horses, I closed my eyes and kissed her forehead once more. The touch was simple yet intimate, and it filled me with warmth. "You will let me court you, then?"

She hummed thoughtfully and drew back enough to meet my eyes. Something flickered in the blue-green hue of her irises, and from her I detected the flutter of wistfulness. "You are asking me?"

Thoughts of my prior conversation with Maerel returned to me, and in Evera's eyes I saw the heaviness the innkeeper spoke of.

"It's not your brother's blessing I want." I raised a hand to stroke her cheek. "It's yours."

With an exaggerated huff, Evera leaned into my hand and grumbled.

Amused by her expressiveness, a smile tugged at the corners of my lips. "Have I said something wrong?"

"No," she mumbled, "you've said something right, and it's irritating."

I laughed. "Should I apologize?"

"No." She rested her head back on my shoulder. "It is only that it was my intent coming out here to lecture you, and you're making that very difficult."

"I will take that as a small victory," I replied, smiling into her hair.

She scoffed. "My brother won't like you."

"All things considered, I would have to agree with him." I raised a brow, then added with more seriousness, "I must ask something of you. It is not something I wish to burden you with, but it is of great importance."

The only response I received was a faint, muffled sound of acknowledgment.

"It is very possible that my brother's life is at stake," I said, and Evera looked up at me, pursing her lips. "If I am caught before I've had the chance to clear my name, I will not be able to protect him."

"You are asking me to lie to my brother about who you are?"

Sighing, I tucked a strand of hair behind her ear. "I am."

"Very well," she said, resting her head at my shoulder again. "Then what do I call you?"

I attempted, in vain, to muffle my laughter. "I'll admit, I've become quite taken with Cordelia."

"I will not call you by my mother's name." Feigned irritation laced her tone.

Letting my soft laughter fade, I stroked her arm with my thumb. The casual way in which we fit together like this was indescribable. Courting a woman should be the last thing occupying my thoughts, but I was lost in a surge of gratefulness for my quick-tongued companion. Whatever we were to each other, it felt remarkably *right.*

"The innkeeper calls me Lark," I said.

"Lark?"

"Yes, it's the family name I'm going by."

"You have a family name now?" Evera pushed off my chest and sat. "Well, that is more than I have." I drew a breath, but before I could speak, she smiled, showing me there were no ill feelings. "If you are courting me, I should have your given name."

"Hadrian."

She quirked her lips. "Lark is better."

The woman was impossible. I released a breath and let my head fall back to the post behind me.

Evera stood and dusted her skirts. The absence of her warmth in my arms was tangible and left me with a sense of longing.

"Aureus requires a man to accompany me on deliveries. You can come by the shop in the morning." She offered me a hand.

Raising a brow at her gesture, I took her hand. With my other, I pushed off the post and stood. Evera's gaze fell to the cut at the inside of my arm; I'd forgotten about it. "You're wounded."

"Are you worried about me?"

"Hardly." She looked up at me through her lashes. *Gods, she is stunning.*

The way she countered me and quipped with teasing venom only made me want her all the more. A stir of desire pushed me to drop her hand and cast my eyes aside lest I look at her a moment longer and the state of my need become apparent to her. Heat flushed my cheeks.

"I should get him back to the inn," I said, turning my focus to the sleeping boy.

"Maerel will be pleased."

I huffed at Evera's sarcasm and knelt before Calix, hefting him back over my shoulder. The snort of Evera's mare drew my attention.

"I will return Sorrel to the pasture," Evera said, grabbing the mare's lead.

Catching sight of Evera's wrap abandoned and forgotten amid the hay on the floor, I set my jaw and crouched down to pick it up, the boy's weight making the simple task more difficult. When I stood, I offered it to her, and our eyes held.

For a moment, I wondered if she would ask me to wrap her wrist back up for her. I wouldn't. She could hide her mark if she wanted to. It was her right. But I would not conceal the very thing that bound us.

Taking the wrap, she turned from me, leading her mare at her side. With one last glance over her shoulder, she stilled, uncertainty tugging faintly at her brows. "Goodnight, Neirin."

"Goodnight." *Goodnight, Evera.*

When I was with her, it was *so* easy to distance myself from the outside forces that weighed on me. Even as I held one of the Queen's messengers over my shoulder, the impending threats felt less daunting, somehow. As if there were a possible outcome where not only Harlan's safety was secured, but where I could, perhaps, find happiness for myself. With her, with Evera.

But no. I hardened my expression and hefted the limp weight of the unconscious boy higher. The Queen would never let me have happiness. She would not allow me to escape her grasp. I huffed a breath, clearing my mind. There was no use worrying over it. It would do nothing but rile my monster.

23

EVERA

"Isn't he just the cutest, Evera!" Farren cooed over her new nephew. It was still early, but the sun had risen in a clear blue sky, bringing with it, warmth, the promise of spring, and a hum of excitement and eagerness to start the day. The day's promise was clear on the faces of the townsfolk as they shopped among the market stalls in front of our family's shop.

My waking, however, had not come with the rise of the sun but by the jarring of my reoccurring nightmare some few hours before dawn. I'd hoped working in the garden might rid my mind of the shadows that had haunted my sleep, of the faceless man who'd loomed over me, of Mother's scream. And in a sense, it had, if only because the task kept me occupied. Though, as always, the feeling of unease remained. Deeper thoughts would creep back when a breeze caught and rose the hairs on the back of my neck. Then my mind would wander to the cause of the nightmares and why Aureus always shielded his expression when I brought them up, cast his eyes aside, and dismissed them.

Renna made a hushing sound, drawing me back from my

dark musings. She gently cupped a hand over her infant's ear. "You'll wake him," she chided her younger sister.

Her son, born just before the last snow, slept soundly, secured against his mother's chest in a cloth sling. From the east, the sun glowed golden on the boy's face, lighting his fine blond hair and pouting lips.

"He's adorable," I said. "And it looks like he's a good sleeper." Despite the noise from the market, the child hardly stirred, even as two boys ran by chasing after a small dog, its tail wagging and tongue lolling. For midweek, the market was busy. The effects, no doubt, of the festival's end brought a steady trickle of travelers through town as they made their way back to their homes in the south.

"Oh, he is," Renna said, pride dancing in her eyes. A silly thing to be proud of, but she was a new mother, and she was positively glowing with the effects of it.

"Don't you want one too?" Farren gushed, her eyes dreamy as she braced herself against the outside railing of our shop's garden fence. "Gods, I do."

I leaned back against the stone wall of the shop in the corner of the fence's enclosure, eyes on the sleeping bundle. "It's not something I've thought much about." It was a half-truth. Children were something I'd thought of often when I was younger. Back when I imagined a life for myself. Before I grew older and came to learn that my life would be decided for me, including whether and when I bore children and who to.

"You could be carrying one now." Farren's remark was spoken without consideration, as every other word out of her mouth seemed to be. It wasn't that she was intentionally loose-lipped, only that her rambling often came before thoughtfulness.

I huffed a breath, but with the sun warming my side and the fresh scents of spring in the air, it was easy to dismiss bitterness. Farren spoke nothing of the markings beneath the wraps on my wrist, at least, and now that she'd caught her blunder, she was more likely to use reservation when speaking.

Renna cast a sidelong glance at her sister, lips a tight line.

"Sorry," Farren amended, casting her eyes down.

"I'm not pregnant." The contraceptive I'd drunk would be effective. And, even if it wasn't, it didn't matter much. I'd only made it as a precaution. When I became a woman, Leighis explained the windows of fertility, and I made a point only to take a man when I was confident I couldn't come with child.

Quiet hung between us, fractured only by the chatter coming from the market.

Renna shifted her weight, and when she broke the quiet, her voice held a note of hesitation. "Evera, do you think—" She licked her lips, then tried again. "Has it been long enough since Cas's birth?"

The corner of my lips rose as I caught her implication. Though Aureus would dissuade me from speaking of anything related to healing in public, those in the market were a distance off, and no one took note of us. Farren and Renna were my oldest friends, aside from Ruairc, with who I'd not been close in some years. There was a comfort in the way my friends came to me for advice on medicinal things with such casualness, with such trust in my abilities. It felt like acceptance, and it warmed me.

"She named him Castien," Farren said. "Isn't that a strapping name? A strong one, too. He'll be a charmer one day for certain." She'd obviously missed her sister's underlying question.

I exchanged a knowing look of amusement with Renna, and Farren pouted and looked between us as if aware she was missing something, but unsure of what.

"Are you still bleeding?" I asked Renna.

She shook her head. "The bleeding stopped about a fortnight ago."

"And do you have any pain?"

Eyes falling to her infant, Renna shook her head. "No, not like that. Some discomfort with nursing, but that's not really relevant. I'm not sure why I brought it up."

"Because it's on your mind."

Renna's joy in looking upon her child caught my heart. She stroked the blond waves atop his head with her thumb. Her own hair, loose and tossed over her shoulders, matched perfectly with the boy's. But his hair could darken with time, should he take after his father.

"He appears to be growing well, but I can stop by and check your latch later if you would like. It can be uncomfortable when you're getting used to it, but it shouldn't hurt." Of course, these were all the only things I knew from my teachings. When Neirin drew my nipple into his mouth and suckled—

"Is everything okay?" Renna asked.

My cheeks flushed. I parted my lips and blinked to dismiss my distracted gaze, but Farren broke in first.

"Oh, it's because of what I said, isn't it?" Her shoulders sank.

I let out a breath and shook my head. "No, Farren, it's fine, truly. My mind was elsewhere. It doesn't matter. You should be fine, Renna. Just make sure your husband knows to ease into things. It's still a bit early. Nothing too—"

"Rough?" Renna grinned.

I laughed. Being older than Farren, Renna was more thoughtful in her words, typically. More aware of the social standards she was expected to adhere to. But marriage had brought out another side of her, or rather her, blacksmith husband had.

"Yes," I said, "nothing too rough."

With a sigh, Renna conceded. "Better than nothing, I suppose."

Farren, catching on, blushed. Her eyes darted to the market square, and she sucked in her bottom lip. "Oh, not more of your stories, Renna." She glanced around nervously. "Certainly not here."

Crossing my arms, I grinned.

A wicked gleam sparkled in Renna's eyes, and she leaned in toward her sister. "You don't like my stories?" Exaggerated feigned innocence laced her tone, and the flush of Farren's cheeks deepened. Though I hadn't a sister of my own, the connection the three of us shared was as close as one could come to siblings.

There was a simple joy in flustering Farren, and those in the market were too busy with their shopping to worry themselves with overhearing our conversation.

"*I* enjoy your stories," I assured her.

Quick-thinking Renna turned the implication back on me. "It sounds like you have stories to tell of your own?"

Pushing from the wall, I retrieved the hoe and worked at the ground with halfhearted effort, using the action to appear busy. "It was nothing."

"You're no fun," Renna complained. There it was, that side she concealed beneath the veil of social expectations. The childish pouting I knew only too well.

I huffed. "Fine." I leaned against the hoe's handle. Despite my better judgment, the thought of speaking about what Neirin and I shared gave me a thrill. But it was strange, too. Because the guard who took me at the festival felt like an entirely different man than the one who had sat beside me in the stables the night before.

I took a moment to consider my words. Farren already knew Neirin was a castle guard, but I hoped she would keep that to herself, what with the precarious state of things as they were now.

"The sex was good," I said rather lamely, deciding to go with blunt and to the point. "The best I've had."

The corners of Renna's lips curled up. "More details."

Mirroring her expression, I acquiesced, despite Farren's flushed cheeks. Drawing nearer to them, I propped the hoe on the fence and sought somewhere to begin. "He took me against a wall in one of the castle towers." Emboldened, I added, "Soldiers stood outside, and when I cried out, he said, 'Let them listen.'"

A vibration of adrenaline tingled in my fingers and up my arms as I held myself at the edge of a very dangerous conversation. The rush flooded me, even as I knew it was wrong. Pushing thoughts of what came of the soldiers and all else that followed aside, I mentally forgave myself. Nothing of what happened was my fault; I should not feel guilty for it.

"Oh." Covering her son's ear, Renna released a heady breath.

Farren, devoid of words, only gasped.

"Was he—" Renna held her hands out with a generous spacing between them.

"Renna!" Farren squealed, and I grinned wickedly.

Holding my own hands out, I considered and added a few inches of space between my own palms. It was boasting, I knew, but the man was well endowed, and that was fair ground for gossip and bragging among friends.

Giddy, Renna encouraged me. "Tell us more?"

I lowered my hands to my hips. "Before we ..."

"Did it against the wall," Renna added when my words failed me.

"Yes, before that." I quirked a smile. "He touched me, or rather"—I lowered my voice to a whisper—"he put his fingers inside of me." No man had done that to me before. Sex was always about the man's climb to a quick release, but Neirin had sought to pleasure me. *And gods, had he.* Renna had spoken of such an act before. It was the only reason it hadn't entirely taken me unawares when he did it.

Covering her son's ears again as if the infant had any understanding of her words, Renna leaned in over the fence. "It's even better when they put their mouth on you."

"I know what kissing is," I retorted dully, a bit louder than necessary. My eyes darted past my friends to the market, but no one looked our way.

Renna shook her head. "Like a kiss, but better, and not on your mouth."

It was my turn to flush. Did she mean …

My brother's slate blue jerkin, one of the more colorful pieces of clothing he owned, caught my attention. He approached from the stalls carrying a basket of produce purchased from the market, his face stoic as ever.

"Where would a man kiss if not on your mouth?" Farren asked, flustered.

Aureus stilled a few steps back, having clearly overheard, and his face reddened slightly.

Because I was cruel, I sucked in my lips to hold back my amusement and leaned over the fence to whisper to Farren, to tell her exactly where a man might kiss a woman. It didn't matter if this was news to me, too. I wasn't about to pass up this opportunity.

"There? Gods, what would it be like to be kissed by a man there?" She shook her head and stepped back, bumping into the basket Aureus held in his arms.

A smile twitched at my lips; it could not have been better.

Her face nearly crimson, Farren turned and raised her gaze to my brother's. Aureus, usually devoid of any expression aside from focused disinterest or mild disappointment, paled. The gape of his mouth clearly portrayed his discomfort. It was wonderful.

"I …" Farren fumbled.

Beside her, Renna suppressed a laugh.

With his eyes locked on Farren's, my brother swallowed, his throat bobbing. For a moment, I looked past my amusement, my heart hitching at the evident attraction neither would admit to. Farren, because she was Farren. And Aureus, because he was too preoccupied worrying over me and the shop and Leighis, not giving any time even to the thought of his feelings, where Farren was involved.

Raising his eyes, he looked past Farren and addressed me. The firm line of his lips returned. "Is this the effect you have on her?"

I scoffed, but it was Farren who spoke, her voice breaking. "Please don't think less of me."

Setting my jaw, I cursed myself mentally for causing her worry. And then I mentally cursed my brother for his stupidity.

"Farren," Aureus sighed, lowering his gaze back to her. "Nothing you say could make me think less of you."

Much better.

At that moment, Castien woke, the scrunch of his face a precursor to the wail that followed. Ever the natural mother, Renna stuck a finger in her son's mouth, and he sucked, momentarily soothed. "Hungry again?" Frustration edged her tone.

"I need to bring these things in," Aureus said, dismissing himself. Farren made a slight sound of acknowledgment, and I suppressed a cringe at the unspoken words between the two. He turned his back and headed for the shop door.

I returned my attention to Renna and her squalling child. "Would you like help with his latch?" At least where breasts and feeding babies was concerned, no one seemed to care if a woman gave guidance or insight. After all, that was all we were good for, was it not? Bearing and raising children. I suppressed the frustration that rose to the surface and focused on my friend.

Without drawing the infant from the sling, Renna lowered the shoulder of her dress, and the boy rooted for her exposed nipple. When he found it, he sucked greedily, and Renna scrunched her face.

FROM OUTSIDE MY PERIPHERAL, a man cleared his throat. The three of us shifted our attention in unison as Neirin turned around the side of a tree just outside the fencing that lined the main road. He leaned against the railing a short distance away, Calix in his shadow.

"How long have you been hiding there?" Accusation laced my words, and Neirin laughed, the sound low, rumbling, and delicious. *No, not delicious. Irritating.*

"Adequate time to overhear your exaggerations." It was the boy who spoke, a bit under his breath. "No man is that big."

Neirin shot Calix a look of scrutiny, and the boy cast his eyes to the stables with bored disinterest.

"What would you know?" Neirin cuffed the boy, then ruffled his hair to soften the gentle reprimand and sighed. "Go, stay out of trouble, boy."

Calix glanced back up at him, twisted his lips in a thoughtful expression, then set off toward the market without further note. Neirin watched after him for a moment, his brows drawn with a look of subtle concern.

I watched the boy disappear into the crowd, then Renna's suppressed laughter drew my attention back. Farren's amusement followed as she choked back shy giggles. I scoffed in a vain attempt to conceal the heat that rose to my cheeks.

"Are you ready to go on your deliveries?" Neirin tilted his head back casually, seemingly unfazed by their bashful amusement at his expense.

"Not yet." The blush at my cheeks deepened. *I need to help Renna first.* Resorting to quips to hide my discomfort, I narrowed my eyes at my courter. "Go back to hiding behind the tree."

Neirin grunted and hefted off the railing. "I'll go inside and speak with your brother."

Right, there was that, too. My heart thundered. Agreeing to this the evening before was one thing. But now that Neirin stood before me in the daylight, all casual confidence and rugged appeal, apprehension gripped me like a vice.

Gods, what will Aureus say? My mouth went dry.

"Go," Renna said, drawing my attention. "Come by later. I'll be more comfortable at home anyway."

"Are you certain?"

"Positive." Though I suspected it was a gesture more than a truth, I appreciated her for it.

I released a breath. "Thank you."

"Yes, thank you," Neirin said, his strides having brought him to Renna's side. He leaned and spoke against her ear, loud enough that I could hear his words. "For the ideas. About kissing."

Oh, gods. "Neirin," I hissed.

He raised his gaze to mine, and his eyes darkened. I swallowed, catching note of my own blunder at speaking his true name.

"Let's go get your things," Neirin said. He hopped the fence effortlessly and crossed to me in a few short paces before offering his hand, a challenge in his eyes. The playfulness of it wrinkled my nose and planted within me the seed of stubbornness.

On the other side of the fence, Renna leaned in toward her sister, peering around Neirin at me. The two beamed, giddy as children, no doubt waiting for me to take the hand of the handsome stranger and allow him to chaperone me out of the garden and to the front of my family's shop.

Huffing my irritation, I brushed past Neirin with pointed intention and hitched my skirts above my ankles.

I can climb a damned fence.

There was a perfectly good gate just some distance down, but this was a matter of proving a point.

Neirin followed alongside me the few short strides back to my friends, his arm brushing mine as we walked. On it, the mark of our bond stood out in contrast to his fair complexion. Not hidden like mine was.

His hand came to my waist unexpectedly, and I turned to him, readying a few choice curses. But my words were stolen from me on a rather undignified squeal. Effortlessly, Neirin lifted me, and the back of the railing hit my thighs. He sat me down atop the fence, and I wobbled. Trying to steady myself, I clutched his cloak, and he grinned, triumph glinting in his eyes.

Last night, he'd been vulnerable, so I'd chosen to give him a chance. Today, he was being a cocky prick.

"Do you mind?" I demanded.

"Not at all."

Renna and Farren suppressed their amusement. Scoffing, I lowered my hands from his chest, steadying myself atop the fence instead. I swung my legs over and dropped rather unceremoniously to the other side. In an annoyingly graceful movement, Neirin joined me.

"I like him," Renna said under her breath, leaning toward me.

Ignoring her remark, I asked her when I could come by to help her with her son's latch. After a few brief exchanges, she and Farren walked back through the market.

"What's gotten into you?" I hissed, turning my eyes back to the smirking guard beside me. And damn him, his dimple made my stomach flip.

Neirin brushed his shoulder against mine. "Have I upset you?" Faint amusement undermined his feigned innocence.

"Yes," I retorted, trying to push down the unexpected rush of desire that clutched me. His skin was almost golden in the yellow light of the sun.

Gods, he has perfect cheekbones.

Neirin drew in his lips, trying and failing to suppress a knowing grin. My cheeks heated, but I brushed the embarrassment aside. It wasn't like he knew what I was thinking.

"I'm sorry. It wasn't my intention," he said.

"You were listening to us."

"I was." His eyes danced.

Scoffing, I paced to the shop's front door and opened it. The bell dinged. Neirin's hand braced higher up, holding the wooden door open, and I walked in.

Aureus straightened, his gaze rising, eyes narrowing and sharpening as he turned his attention from the work that occupied him at the back of the shop. "Evera."

"Where are today's deliveries?" I asked, my tone short. They would be behind the counter, just as they always were.

Aureus rose a brow, surely catching my mood but choosing not to bring attention to it. He gathered the day's orders and an oversized satchel. Taking the goods from him somewhat gruffly, I stuffed them in the sack.

"Is Ruairc going with you?" my brother asked.

"No," I retorted and left the men in order to gather the book of lore from the study table in the back room. Adding it to my bag and taking a breath to temper the mood the guard had put me in, I returned to the front of the shop to find the two men scaling each other up in a bluntly male way. I rolled my eyes.

"We spoke about this, Evera." Aureus lowered his voice as he turned his gaze back to me. "You know the rule—"

"Yes," I snapped. "It must be a man who hands the orders over. That's what Lark is for." I grabbed him by the cloak and pulled. At first, my tug did nothing, but he stepped forward when he recognized my intentions.

Raising his chin, my brother narrowed his eyes.

Neirin offered his hand and held it for a moment, but when

it was apparent that Aureus had no intention of shaking it, he lowered it. "I aim to court your sister."

Not, *can I court your sister?* Not, *I would like your permission to court your sister.* My chest fell heavily as I let out a breath.

"No." Aureus's lips were a thin line.

The prick.

"No?" I released my grip on Neirin's cloak and stepped to the counter, coming face-to-face with my brother. "What happened to 'I want you to be happy'? What happened to 'Is there someone you would rather have?'"

"I make you happy?" Amusement laced Neirin's casual intrusion.

"No," I snapped back to him, hitting the countertop with a flat palm. The action was childish and caused little prickles of pain.

"Are you hurt?" Neirin reached for my hand, any trace of amusement gone from his tone.

With calculated coldness, I raised my gaze to him, and he sucked his lips in, retreating half a step.

In the way of men, Aureus turned his attention to the other man in the room. To talk about me. In front of me. "You cannot court her without permission."

Though Neirin stood straight, his composure was casual. "I have permission." He dipped his gaze to me and smiled, but it didn't reach his eyes. Looking closer, I noted a tenseness I hadn't seen before.

"This isn't her decision." Aureus's words came on a snarl.

"Isn't my—" The words turned into a growl as hot fury rushed through my veins.

The back of Neirin's hand brushed against mine. Subtle, but enough to draw my attention and interrupt my trail of what would have inevitably been hurtful words. Had he put an arm around my waist, I'd have kneed him in the balls.

"This is her decision." Neirin's words were calm but assertive. "Do you have everything you need?"

It took me a moment to realize Neirin's question was directed at me. "Oh, yes." I swung the satchel over one shoulder. The book of lore made it heavy.

Though my brother stood at his full height and held Neirin's gaze, he made no further challenge. Something about that unsettled me. This was what I had wanted, wasn't it? Unease flittered in my chest like the ghost of a dream.

"Let's go," I said, and Neirin's eyes fell on me in an instant as if he could pick up the distress I veiled with my sharp tone. The back of his hand was a reassuring presence against mine, and acting on a need for stability that disarmed me, I intertwined my fingers with his. Neirin drew his brows inward, but he nodded, and together we walked to the door.

The bell rang as he pushed it open, and we stepped out hand in hand.

At the bottom of the steps, he turned to me, voice somber and thick with concern. "What's wrong?"

"You shouldn't have been so blunt," I said, a sharpness still in my tone. Gritting my teeth, I cast my eyes down.

Neirin dropped my hand. "Should I not have defended you?"

"No, I—" I sighed and looked up at his silver eyes set beneath brows drawn in an expression of concern. "Thank you for defending me."

He smiled faintly, but the gentle worrying in his eyes remained the same. A quiet lay between us for a moment, and I retook his hand—an offering, an apology. The creases in his forehead softened, although they did not entirely smooth out. He ran his thumb over the back of my hand. "I will always defend you."

24

NEIRIN

I KEPT PACE WITH EVERA, though she walked with a stiff, vigorous step. Lowering my eyes to her, I pondered her shift in mood as we cleared the busy hum of the market and stopped before the cobbled road. A wagon passed by, but there was nothing remarkable about it that gave cause for concern.

As the huntsman had predicted, word of the King's death had reached Elrune, and with that knowledge, I found myself more on edge. The first rumors I had detected from a group of travelers dining at the inn just before leaving to meet with Evera. A second telling I overheard along my way. It was then that I instructed Calix to spend the day observing, listening. It was my hope, however, that he would stay out of trouble beyond that. I did not trust the sleight of his hand.

When the wagon cleared, Evera set forward again, and I fell in step beside her. I couldn't shake the feeling that something was bothering her beyond her brother's disapproval. When we were in the shop and she reached for my hand, I sensed her distress through the bond. The concept of detecting someone else's emotions was new and strange. But nothing about magic was logical, so I didn't waste time worrying over it.

I longed to voice her name, but I held it back and instead stilled my steps when we neared the fence line branching out from the stables, keeping gentle hold of her hand so that she stopped and looked back at me.

"Will you tell me what made you fearful back in your shop?" I asked.

"How—" She shook her head.

"I can sense your emotions."

She shook her head again, clearly disbelieving. It was a strange confession, admittedly.

"I don't understand how it works," I said. "But I want to know what frightened you when you reached for my hand."

Evera cast her gaze aside but allowed me to continue holding her hand in my own. "Honestly, I don't know." The faintness of her voice tugged at my heart. "Can we not discuss it?"

I relented, despite the worry I held for her. Perhaps I could fluster her again, as I had in the garden, and shift her mood at least.

"Would you rather discuss kisses?" I asked, leaning down to her ear.

She inhaled sharply and dropped my hand to shove at my chest. "I do not want to talk about—" She huffed.

"Kisses," I suggested, grinning. "The kind *not* on your mouth." A reminder for the sake of adding kindling to the fire.

She flushed, her cheeks taking on a rosy tone beneath the dappling of freckles. If she did not wish to speak of what weighed on her, at least I could lighten the burden with distraction. Retaking her hand, I led her through the door and into the stables. Inside, the air was warmer and held the familiar scents of animals and dried grass.

"What are we doing?" she asked, stopping.

A smile tugged at the corners of my lips, and I braced an arm on the wooden beam of the door just above her head, taking advantage of the opportunity. The heat in her cheeks deepened, and she narrowed her eyes. Her pupils dilated as they adjusted to the dim light until hardly any color remained in their outer rings.

"It will be more enjoyable to ride than to walk." I leaned in.

"We don't ride Sorrel," she said, though this time her words came on a breath, quieter, her sharpness tempered by my proximity.

"What is the point in having a mare you don't ride?"

Not waiting for a response, I released Evera and paced to the wall where bridles, brushes, and other miscellaneous items hung or sat on rudimentary shelves.

"She pulls our wagon," Evera explained, remaining in the doorway. "Aureus travels south to the port of Literra once every three or four fortnights to replenish supplies for our shop."

"Which bridle is hers?"

"Second from the left," she said with a shake of her head. "But we don't have a saddle."

Withdrawing the tack, I passed Evera and turned left to her mare's pasture. "We don't need a saddle. Do you know how to ride?"

"Not really." She fell into step beside me, withdrew a key from a pocket in her skirts, and fit it in the lock at the gate. "Leighis used to set me on Sorrel's back when I was a child and lead me around the pasture." There was an edge of wistfulness to her tone, and when the gate swung open and she looked up at me, I held her gaze.

"That is why you care so deeply for the mare."

"Maybe so." A smile tugged at her lips, and she stepped past me.

Each time she did so, the absence of her presence left me feeling … not whole. I followed her, leaving the gate ajar as Evera crossed a short distance to greet her mare.

"Sorrel is a companion," she said, brushing the mare's forelock to the side. The animal snorted and nuzzled at Evera's neck, making her giggle.

An animal couldn't be a companion. Animals were unintelligent beasts that cared only for self-preservation, incapable of feelings or caring for others . But Evera was happy now, smiling, and that was all that mattered.

When I reached her, I held up the bridle, and the mare dipped her head obediently. Fitting it over the animal's ears, I secured the buckle beneath her jaw and gathered the reins in one hand.

"Why did you say back in the shop that you would never have children?"

The question surprised me, though perhaps it shouldn't have. It was logical that such topics would arise during the courting process. Still, it put me on edge. The concept of creating another monster like myself was not an option. I drew the reins over Sorrel's head to rest on her withers.

"As I said before, I have no name to give." A thought came to me then. "You did make the tea, did you not?" The beat of my heart quickened. I braced my hands on her shoulders, demanding her full attention. A knot twisted in my stomach as I awaited her response.

Evera only frowned. "Tea?"

"In the tower house, you promised me—" My words came quickly, but I caught them, swallowed them. Beneath my skin, the familiar crawling of my monster reminded me of his presence and of my own lack of control over my emotions. "You swore."

Realization dawned across her face. "I made the tea. Neirin, I'm not ..." She frowned. "I only wanted to know why. Seeing you with Calix ..."

I released a heavy breath, relief easing my muscles as I released her shoulders too. "Calix is not like other children, and the situation is complicated." I sighed, rubbing the bridge of my nose. I would relent to Evera's pressing questions, not wanting to keep things from her, even as answering her unsettled me. "My mother was like me. If I inherited this bloodline from her, I could pass it on to my own children. Is that not how it works?"

A sadness clouded Evera's eyes, and she took one of my hands in hers. There was no need for her to respond; I knew the answer, and by the set of her jaw, I could tell she was equally aware.

I cast my eyes aside. "I will not create another monster."

For a moment, stillness fell around us. In the neighboring pasture, a foal burst into a run, legs flashing like quicksilver beneath the sun, while its mothers warning snort rippled through the air. The breeze that followed, curled around us like a whisper, heavy with the green-sweet perfume of budding leaves and the promise of new grass, as though even the season itself leaned closer to listen. .

"Neirin." She squeezed my hand. "Why do you think you're a monster?"

The fox's claws dug in, raking beneath my skin. Heat pooled through my veins, and my breath quickened. The creature was growing stronger, reacting faster to my lapses in control, latching on to the moments when emotions overcame me and using them as a pathway toward overpowering me.

Evera sighed. "You don't have to answer …"

Why do you think you're a monster?

"My brother," I said, the words a low rasp. If not by blood, then by heart, Thatcher would always be remembered as a brother in my eyes. "Thatch, he—" Flexing my right hand into a fist, I fought to steady my heart rate. The image of his last labored breaths and of the metallic reek of his blood returned to me in a rush.

Steadying my shaking hands, I stepped to Evera and drew her reflexively to my chest, burying my nose in her curls and inhaling the scent of her. She tensed at first but quickly relaxed, then her arms came around my waist. *Safe. She was safe.*

"Please, let me hold you for just a moment longer," I pleaded, the words coming broken, weak, desperate. Although that weakness should have further unsettled me, further fed my monster, my tension only eased when Evera was in my arms.

All outward thoughts fell away, not unlike the way they did when I fought. Yet this clarity came not from a rush of adrenaline or an ingrained response to the prospects of life and death. It came with a comfort, a soothing sort of warmth. One that eased my body and lent my thoughts to a contented quiet. Reminiscent almost of the sensations that came just before slipping into sleep. As I held her, nothing else existed beyond the scent of my mate and the warmth of her body. She fit in my embrace as if we were crafted for each other.

Mate. I hated that word. It was a term used to describe the pairing of animals. Yet that was what the old man had called us. True mates. And damned if the urge to think of her that way came from my creature; I didn't care. She was mine. *No, I am hers.*

When my body settled, I drew back, and she raised her chin to meet my eyes. "I shouldn't have pressed."

"No," I countered. "My monster—" No use speaking. I knew what her response would be. "My *fox* … He seeks control when I'm unsettled. It's growing harder for me to push him down."

Her brows turned in, and her mouth formed a thin line. Silently, I pleaded she would not press further. I was not ready to revisit the darkest of my memories or voice the truth of what happened that day. After all these years, I'd not spoken it, not since Astraea had knelt before me and told me the penalty of what I'd done, the repercussions. And, beyond those, the effects such knowledge would have on Nyana. It would shatter her to know I was responsible for her son's death. A tremble coursed down my spine even as I held Evera in my arms.

"Neirin." Evera's soft coaxing drew my mind back. She reached a hand up and brushed the hair above my brows to the side, not unlike she'd done with her mare.

The trail of her touch unleashed within me a longing for the kind of companionship I'd never held faith in or even had desire for in the past. For all the cruelties magic had played on me in my life, just this once, perhaps fate had smiled upon me.

"Thank you," I said, my voice thick with emotion.

Dragging her fingers down the length of my jawline, Evera hummed. "For what?" Her palm cupped my cheek, and her thumb swept once over my bottom lip before she raised her eyes, the coloring of them even more stunning somehow in the light of late dawn.

For giving me a chance. For not pushing me away, though I would understand if you do. For this bonding that neither of us can control, yet which resonates with me to my very being. For not balking in the castle corridors or before the King's body, or any time since.

"I am just grateful for you," I said, for there seemed no way to describe the swirl of emotions holding me in place.

She smiled and sighed. Withdrawing her hand and placing it on my chest, she stood on her tiptoes and brushed her nose along mine. When I shuddered a breath, she lowered back to the heels of her boots.

"Tease," I lectured.

Grinning, she laughed, and the sound was more beautiful than birdsong or the thrum of a harp or even the crashing of the waves.

On an impulse, I took her hips in my hands and spoke against her ear. "Swing your leg over."

"What?"

In a single motion, I hefted her up, and she squealed, wrapping her legs around my hips and nearly causing me to fumble as I redirected my weight. The layers of her dress bunched awkwardly.

"That was not my intention." I laughed as she drew back to meet my eyes and set me with a false glare, the corners of her lips twitching up. To have her body wrapped around mine in this way brought back thoughts of the tower house and stirred my desire.

"And how am I to know your intentions are not impure?" She wrinkled her nose.

"Who is to say they are not?" I met her challenge, mirroring her expression. "No response to that?"

Sucking in her lips, she shook her head.

"As I said before." I adjusted my hold on her. "Swing your leg over."

This time, when I gripped her waist, she loosened her hold with her legs and let me heft her atop the mare. She landed somewhat awkwardly. Sorrel's flanks quivered, and in response to the animal's reaction, I held Evera a moment longer until I was certain the mare wouldn't spook.

"Your mare is jumpy today," I pointed out, considering how well she'd reacted to the situation with Calix the night of the fire.

"She's fine," Evera clipped, rolling her eyes.

Amusement rumbled in my chest.

Right, the animal is special to you. Very well.

Leading Sorrel by her harness, I brought her to the fence line. Mounting without someone in front of me was second nature. But with Evera on the mare's back, I was unsure I could, and I wasn't about to risk unsettling the jumpy creature. Using the fence would be easier. "Scoot forward," I instructed, a hand at Evera's waist.

She did as I coaxed. I climbed the fence and eased my weight onto the mare's back slowly, testing her. Once I was confident she wouldn't buck, I settled Evera with her back to my chest and wrapped an arm around her torso. The sight of her ass against my lap was admittedly distracting.

"Reins," I said, the word coming out thicker than I intended.

Evera lifted the leather strap off Sorrel's withers, and I drew my other arm around to take it. If she noticed the stir of my cock against her backside, she did not voice it. I swallowed, trying to calm myself. Though the newfound sensations were intoxicating, I was finding that the effects could be hindering at times.

Checking my breathing, I squeezed the mare gently with my heels and clicked, encouraging her toward the gate. Evera's body tensed, and she braced herself with both hands. The animal's ears pinned, and I pulled back on the reins, stopping her.

"Relax," I instructed, placing a hand on Evera's inner thigh.

She drew a sharp breath, and desire seeped through the bond. I cursed myself mentally for the placement of my hand, even as the racing of my heart and Evera's eagerness in response encouraged boldness.

Knowing she desired me as much as I longed for her, I allowed my touch to wander. I stroked trailing fingers lazily at her leg. The rushing warmth through the bond intensified, and I leaned in and spoke against Evera's ear. "I can sense that emotion, too."

She raised her chin, the indigence in her tone underlined with teasing inflection. "Your senses betray you, Lark."

Rumbling with my amusement, I wrapped my free arm around her torso. "I won't let you fall, but if you keep squeezing the mare's sides like that, she might take off. You need to relax. Trust me."

Though I expected a retort, Evera only grumbled. "Fine."

The tension in her body relaxed through a breath, and she wiggled, settling against me. The movement made my cock throb; I had to resist the urge to rock against her. In the tower, she'd been fully clothed aside from the slip of her top. Now I envisioned her like this, in front of me, naked, with the firmness of my length against her ass.

No, not until I earn her name. I traced my thumb beneath the dip of her ribs, and when she leaned back into me, I rumbled against her ear, "Good girl."

25

NEIRIN

As we neared the main road, the noise from the market tapered off, replaced by the steady crashing of waves at the base of the cliffside. Sorrel snorted, and her flanks twitched, then settled as she became accustomed to the riders atop her back. With a like sigh, Evera relaxed against my body. Amid the scents of brine from the sea and burning elmwood from the great hearth of the smithy shop, the faint floral and herbal scent of Evera's hair washed over me. I had to resist the desire to fall into the precious peace of the moment, to draw her firm against my chest and breathe her in deeply. It was not what she needed, not what she wanted or was ready for, so I turned to conversation instead.

"On my count," I said, "you have asked me three questions just since we entered the paddock."

The concept of courting was, admittedly, something I understood more in concept than in act. It mattered little, though, to me at least. And I sensed it did so for Evera as well. Nothing about this process thus far had been done "correctly." I only wanted to get to know her and for her to start trusting me. It was clear from her hesitation after leaving her shop that something weighed on her. And, though I'd altered her mood and she no longer seemed burdened by whatever had caused her distress, I would have preferred to soothe her worries by discussing them rather than by brushing them aside. Trust, though, would take time. I could be patient. I could earn her trust, just as I would work toward earning her name.

Resting against my chest, Evera hummed. "You have been keeping count?"

"I have, and I believe it is only fair I am allowed three in return."

"Two," she countered. "You asked me if I knew how to ride—that counts as one."

With a soft laugh, I nuzzled against her ear. "Very well. Two questions, then."

Taking my time to consider, I stroked my thumb at her belly. The warmth of the sun on my back and the carrying scent of saltwater on the breeze made me put this moment to memory. For ones like it could very well be fleeting.

"Before, you claimed to be a healer."

"Is that a question?" There was a hint of bitterness to her tone.

"I am only curious about the extent of your knowledge in the craft." Though it did not surprise me that she might respond with reservations, given the accusations placed on women who worked in medicine, it stung that she assumed so little of me that I might mock her for her skills.

"You do not believe me to be a witch?"

As we reached the crossroads, I stilled Sorrel and spoke against Evera's ear. "You are not a witch." If she were, she would have detected what I was instantly, in the same way Calix was affected by my presence. My blood called to him, and when it had been too long since his last feed, it did so with a need fiercer than any other. "Which direction?"

"Right," Evera answered. "How do you know I am not a witch? Is that not what people say about female healers?"

Using the reins to steer the mare, I started us to the north along the cliffside. Waves crashed against the stone far below, and in the distance, seabirds called to each other.

"You told me you were not," I said simply, feeling unsure about disclosing the effects of my blood. Why did I feel the need to keep that from her? Was it an innate fear of being used? But Evera wouldn't … I drew my brows in, considering. Despite my feelings for her, I'd not known her long. Still, the deep-rooted reaction to reserve information for self-preservation was disheartening.

Evera turned her head sideways against me, toward the sea. The ocean stretched out to the west nearly as far as the eye could see; at the horizon, the western lands stood as a silhouette, a dark line of jagged mountains.

"When Leighis took us in," Evera began, "he taught Aureus and me both his craft. Throughout my life, he has been the only one who has not treated me differently because I'm a woman. The only one who's made me feel capable." She hesitated a moment. "But things have changed since he became—"

"I know," I said, so she wouldn't have to voice what burdened her. I'd seen enough times the effects of old age and the slipping of memories and awareness. Though I did not know the cause, I knew it to be untreatable. Part of aging, part of life, all too likely to come to many of us in time.

I resumed the casual stroke of my thumb against her torso, and her shoulders rolled with her breath. "Now there is no one to stand up for me. Aureus will marry me off, and I'll be just another wife, bearing children and keeping a home."

I will stand up for you. Always.

My thoughts went to Nyana, to the ache she carried since Thatch's passing. To the countless nights she had cried when she thought I was sleeping, her grief spilling into the silence like a hymn only the moon could hear. To the way a sadness hovered over her, even all these years later. To be a mother could be a great hardship. "And you don't want a family of your own?"

"It's not that I don't want children. Or that I dislike"—she swallowed—"being with a man. I just…"

"Don't want to lose yourself in belonging to another?"

She raised her chin, and though she faced away from me, I could turn my head to the side and glance down to meet her eyes.

Studying her slight frown, I explained. "Before, in your shop, you said you don't belong to me."

"Oh." She set her eyes forward again, and I settled my cheek on top of her head.

Ahead, the manor of House Tellius sat at the corner of the cliff, where a river dumped into the sea. I recognized it, though I'd only passed through Elrune briefly before. Banners with the house emblem—ravens of a stark black atop a cobalt background with accents of golden threads that caught the dawn light—hung from the manor's formidable stone towers.

"If—" Evera snapped her mouth shut, rolled her lips between her teeth, then tried again. "*When* I marry, I will cease to be anything but a man's wife. Someone to bed, to put children on. To scrub and hang clothes to dry. To be complacent." She was quiet for a moment, then with a distant sorrow to her voice, added, "Working in the shop, using my skills to help others and to make a difference, even in small ways …" She sighed. "That will cease to exist."

The heaviness in her words weighed on me. Maerel had been right, then. Not just about a great burden being cast on Evera's shoulders, but that she would be the one to open up and speak to me about her troubles when she was ready. If I told her the last thing on this earth I wanted was to quell her flame, would she believe me?

Before I could find the confidence to voice a reply, Evera nodded to a smaller manor just ahead and to our right. Fair-sized for a home, certainly, though unimpressive in the shadow of the Tellius manor. A home for a nephew or brother of a lord, perhaps, or even a castle guard or commander. Many of the men I'd bunked with in the guard's quarters through the years had long since retired from their duties and purchased similar homes to raise their families in.

"When I was a girl, I would climb into that house through a broken window in the back," Evera stated.

A crooked smile tugged at my lips. "Why does that not surprise me?"

She turned her head so that her cheek rested against my chest as we passed the smaller manor. It was worn down and needed repairs, abandoned without a doubt, but it held the promise of potential.

"You're the only person I've told. Not even Aureus knows," she confessed. "I would pretend it was my home. A place of my own. Though Leighis gave us a home, I've always known it would be temporary, that when I grew up, I'd be—" She left her future unsaid. "It was a place I could imagine a life for myself that was my own.

"And there's a study," she added, a youthful longing in her tone. "With full-length windows that let such beautiful light in, I used to sit in that room with charcoal and paper for hours just sketching out where I would put bookshelves, where I would hang plants to dry, place a table to work at …"

My heart hitched, but before I could ask more, she raised her head and gestured to a side road ahead. "Here, this is the first delivery."

For a moment, I held her closer, wishing I could give her the life she'd dreamed of as a girl. *If things were different.*

"Neirin?" Evera said, drawing me from my thoughts.

"Yes, sorry." I steered Sorrel to a section of homes on the

corner where the main road intersected a smaller one and dismounted. The buildings here were constructed of stone at their base, with thick wooden pillars supporting an upper level that jutted out slightly. The second stories, hatched with criss-crossing beams, were a chalky beige.

Fishing in her sack, Evera withdrew a paper package sealed with wax and stamped with the shop's mark. Swirling penmanship labeled a tag secured by a tie.

"You can just hand it over," she said. "Aureus has already spoken with them about the dosage."

BY MIDDAY, Maerel's inevitable complaints at my longer-than-expected absence whispered in the back of my mind. Evera's stomach, however, spoke louder. And her company was preferable. So, breaking one of my silvers, I bought two small tarts filled with meat and a bottle of inexpensive wine.

"Where are we going?" Evera asked, sitting atop the mare with our wrapped tarts in her satchel and a bottle of wine hugged to her chest. We weren't traveling far, so I walked alongside them.

"Not much farther," I promised and veered off the path. Sorrel pinned her ears as I coaxed her into the undergrowth, but she didn't halt or spook, and when we were out of view of the road, I tied her to a tree. "Here." I offered Evera my hand to help her down.

Studying me, she narrowed her eyes, drew her satchel over her head, and held it out.

"What's in this?" I asked, taking it from her. It was bulky and weighed much more than I suspected it would.

Evera scoffed. Hiding my amusement, I complied with her

stubbornness. She threw her leg over Sorrel's back and slid off, her back to me; I was close enough that her backside brushed me. Whatever her intention, I doubted it had been to grind against me.

Feeling bold, I wrapped an arm at her waist and drew her to my chest. She squealed, and I nuzzled her ear, breathing on her neck. She melted into me, pressing her ass against me. Her body betrayed her, as did the warmth that coursed through the bond.

Remembering herself, Evera wiggled out of my grasp and turned back, shooting me a pointed glare. I laughed, and she huffed her frustration.

"You're insufferable," she said.

I shrugged. "Is this the place?" I asked, nodding to the backside of the abandoned home behind her.

Confusion pinched her brows, and when Evera looked back, she gasped. "Neirin, what are we doing here?"

I brushed past her, the overstuffed satchel a notable weight on my shoulder.

"Where is the window you used to climb through?" I asked, examining the building. It truly was in a state of disarray. "There isn't broken glass, is there?"

Evera ran to catch up with me. "I'm not a child anymore, Neirin. I can't just climb up walls and through windows of abandoned houses. I know better now." She stopped at my side and looked toward the old manor with wistful longing. "It would not be respectable."

"Then let us not get caught," I said, ignoring her hapless attempts at talking me out of what may have been the only romantic idea I'd had in my entire life. I stepped up to a crumbled well, resting my hand on the cold stone surface. Like the manor, it was a faded earth tone.

"Why is this house abandoned?" I asked, raising my eyes to the ruins. Ivy grew up the bricks of the manor, beautiful but unkept. "Do you know?"

Evera frowned. "House Tellius owns it. Farren told me that at one time they had a use for it, but it's been for sale for as long as I've lived here. The price is outrageous."

I left the well with a faint, thoughtful noise and made my way toward a low window, its panes long gone. Examining the opening for shards of glass, rusted nails, or anything else that may put Evera in harm's way, I didn't notice her standing beside me. When she nudged me, I stepped back—I'd come to learn it seemed to displease her when I didn't move out of her way when she pushed me.

With a grunt of determination, she braced her arms on the windowsill and heaved herself up, scraping and scrambling at the stone with her boots. I unabashedly watched her futile attempts.

"Have we moved past worrying over things that are respectable, then?" I asked, humor lacing my tone.

Her skirts bunched up to her knees as she dug the toe of her boot into a crack in the stone, but it slipped. With a defeated huff, Evera stopped her struggle and lay half in the building and half outside it.

"Are you stuck?" I bit back a laugh.

"This was easier when I was a child," she retorted.

For a moment, my smile faltered. Harlan loved climbing up into the window of Nyana's kitchen. Had the huntsman delivered my letter? How many more days would it be until I received his reply?

"Are you going to help me or just keep staring at my ass?"

Unable to resist, I laughed, and the responding sound that came from her was the essence of annoyance. I placed my hands at her waist and lifted her weight, helping her the rest of the way into the building. As she cleared the ledge, she kicked at my shoulder with her boot, rather pointedly, I suspected.

My cloak caught when I braced my hands to pull myself up. I pulled it off, and when Evera's head came to peer through the window, I tossed her the satchel first, and then the cloak, handing over the wine more carefully.

Evera bundled the cloak in her arms and sucked in her bottom lip, her gaze pointedly on my biceps. Desire seeped through the bond again, and I ran a hand through my hair, looking up at her. *Gods, I want to kiss you.* But I wouldn't, not yet.

I made an extra effort to show off a bit, flexing my arms as I easily lifted myself. Face-to-face with her, I balanced on my boots in the windowsill and held her eyes. Evera exhaled roughly, and I grinned.

Scrunching up her face with the cutest damned look of determination, she shoved the satchel back to me, nearly pushing me backward.

I braced myself with an arm on the right side of the window frame, catching the bag with the other. "Do you want me dead?" I asked, doing my best to feign injury to my pride.

"No," she mumbled, and the lack of a quip surprised me.

I studied her, and when she looked up at me through her lashes, my heart stilled.

"Am I permitted to eat now?" she demanded.

The return of her sarcastic wit curled my lips into a smile. "Not quite yet." I dropped down from the windowsill and into what appeared to be a large entry room.

Evera glowered.

"Show me your home."

"Neirin—"

"Show me what you pretended when you were a child. Amuse me with this, and I'll reward you"—I leaned down to her flushing cheeks—"with a tart." Heat trickled through the bond, and with a grin, I turned from her to take in the expansive room.

The walls were high—two stories with a railed balcony along the upper level, broken in sections. Beneath my feet, the wood flooring creaked, old but sturdy. It was clear that in its time, the manor was built without concern for cost. I rested my hand on an intricately carved support column, pondering the structural stability of the home I'd brought my mate into.

"Are you coming?" Evera called from the base of a staircase.

Worry for her well-being clenched my chest. "Let me go first."

She scoffed and ran up the stairs with hapless abandon.

I followed her, gritting my teeth when I took in the state of the upper-level flooring. "This place isn't safe."

"You worry too much."

Only over you. The realization was sobering. For I did worry over her, desperately so. My very existence seemed inextricably linked to hers; her safety was imperative. Equal it seemed, though in a different sense, to the protectiveness I felt over Harlan.

Evera continued, a lightness to her step and a glint of childish wonder in her eyes when she looked back at me.

Sighing, I allowed myself a soft smile. To see her spirit lightened, her walls down … This was a good idea. *Unless she steps on a rotten board and falls through.* The corners of my lips turned down.

"There are three rooms up here; our home only has one room we all share," Evera rambled as she led me down a hall. "What could anyone possibly need so many rooms for?"

I shrugged, considering the countless rooms in the castle. Though admittedly, most of them wouldn't be needed for a single family.

"A study," I offered, peering into one of them. A large window at its back let in ample light. "The castle has a separate nursery for the children."

Scrunching up her face, Evera shook her head. "I would want my children in my bed. At least until they're older."

"That sounds horrible," I retorted, my thoughts going to Calix. As I followed Evera into the largest of the rooms, I envisioned rolling over in the morning to meet the wide, honed eyes of the messenger boy and shuddered.

"Why's that?" She looked up at me.

I raised my brows and leaned into a lighter response. "In your imaginary world, you can sleep with your children. In mine, I'm using the bed for other activities." I nodded to the side of the room. "And that wall."

Evera flushed. "I thought you didn't want children."

A somber weight fell over us, and her smile faltered.

"No," I said. I'd only been teasing her, but now an air of discomfort disconnected us. I would never have children, not even for her. "What's downstairs?"

Evera nodded, eyes cast aside, and brushed past me, leaving me alone in the room. I sighed. She was just starting to open up, to relax, to be comfortable in my presence.

Double windows let sidelong light into the room. And though there was no furniture, I could envision a canopy bed between them. The view looked out to the broken well and what could be restored to a quaint garden. There truly was such potential here.

Leaving the room, I determined to lighten the mood, and I found Evera at the bottom of the steps. As she showed me the lower rooms of the manor and spoke of her childhood imaginings, her energy began to return. By the end of her tour, the lightness of her smile had come back to her.

Sitting before an empty hearth, I pulled the cork from the wine bottle and tested the drink. It was a red, which was not my preference, but the faint smoky flavor to its undertones was a nice surprise.

Evera stifled a giggle, and I handed it over with a challenge in my eyes.

She took the bottle and turned it up, mimicking me. It was a sweet drink, low in spirits, but if she thought herself impressive for drinking it with vigor, I would not be the one to contend her beliefs.

Drawing breath dramatically, Evera set the wine on the wood floor, pride dancing in her eyes. *Gods, she is incredible.*

"Have I earned a tart?" she asked, sarcasm lacing her words.

Acquiescing, I opened the satchel in search of the two tarts, but my attention caught on the thick-bound book shoved in with the deliveries.

"You brought the book of lore," I observed.

Evera sobered. "I thought you might want to learn more about yourself. You can borrow it if you would like."

The caring gesture tugged at my heart.

"Will you read it to me?" I asked, handing it to her. Raised in the castle, I was taught to read and write, but Evera didn't know that. I would tell her later. But for now, I wanted the excuse to listen to her soothing voice.

Scrunching her brows, Evera ran her hand over the book in her lap, then offered out her empty palm with pointed purpose. I resisted rolling my eyes and handed over a tart. She unwrapped it eagerly. When she bit into the crust, she moaned her satisfaction, and her stomach gurgled in response.

I shook my head and unwrapped the second tart for myself. This was good for her, though, to take the time to eat and relax. Even if the hearth was not lit, and the place we found ourselves in lacked basic comforts. It was still an escape, a reprieve, from the outside pressures of life, if nothing else.

Though Evera started her meal with fervency, she was only halfway through the tart when she set it back on its wrapping and, with a groan, leaned back and propped herself up with her palms. "I'm so full."

I studied her as I took a bite out of what remained of her tart. Though she appeared undoubtedly more relaxed than she had this morning, I still worried. "You need sleep, too."

Evera rolled her head to the side and scowled at me. "I sleep."

"More than an hour or two."

"I'm fine."

She wasn't, but at least she'd eaten. "Will you read to me, then?"

With a stretch and a yawn, Evera pushed herself back up and retook the book from where it lay beside her. She opened it and flipped through the pages. Landing on one, she pointed to a scramble of text beneath the title and read it out loud. The words were entirely incomprehensible, yet she voiced them with a feigned accent that hinted toward elegance. "It's the language of the old world. It means 'the line of the fox,' but it sounds better the other way, doesn't it?"

"You speak the old language?"

She shook her head. "No, I just remember Leighis telling me that."

And the translation is scripted above it in a bold scroll.

I suppressed the smile that tugged at my lips.

"It does sound better that way," I offered, failing to entirely withhold the amusement in my voice.

She regarded me with suspicion.

"What else does it say?" I queried, keeping my tone level this time in an attempt to turn her focus back to the book.

With a slight crook to her lips, Evera broke my gaze and repositioned herself, bending her knees and turning both legs to the left, toward the hearth. Though she wasn't touching me, the shift gave her an air of leaning in, and I welcomed the closeness.

Evera traced the elegant handwritten script with her finger as she read, trailing over listed family lines, names of relatives long deceased in a bloodline I held no knowledge of. Not even my mother's name had been included.

"Line lost," Evera read.

"What does that mean?"

With a sympathetic draw of her brows, she traced an inked

illustration of a fox with three kits, then trailed her finger along the delicate curves of the white flowers sketched beside them. "It means you might be the last."

"The book is old. There is no way to know. It does not list my mother's name." I resisted the urge to add that if I were the last of my kind, it would be no misfortune, knowing that such a statement would dispirit her. "What else does it say?"

"Perception is heightened among those of this line," she read on. "They obtain and remember information easily, notice the finer details of expression and posturing, and can come to conclusions based on slight signs picked up in their sphere that others would likely miss."

"Such things are not magic; all men of the guard have those skills. It's how we are trained."

"And all of them have skills as honed as yours?"

I frowned, and she raised a brow pointedly.

Brushing off her question, I posed one of my own. "Your mentor spoke of gifts. Does it mention anything on that note?"

She made a little thoughtful noise as she scanned the page. Though I could have read over her shoulder, I didn't want to look away from her profile—the way her lashes curled, the slight upturn of the tip of her nose, the pillowing of her lips.

"Their gift is the ability to perceive magic," she said as she found the section she searched for. "In the tangible form of light." She paused, and her lips twisted. "And to manipulate that magic. What does that mean?" She turned to look at me; her cheeks reddened when she caught me staring.

"I do not know," I said on a breath, finding it difficult to focus on the information despite its importance. "I have no such ability." Swallowing, I broke our heated gaze and nodded to the book. "When do the gifts develop?"

"Between the ages of five and seven," she said without having to search for the answer. "It is the same with all of the lines of the gods."

A somberness fell over me. Though I held no love for my monster—I despised the existence he bound me to and the horrors he'd brought upon my life, the pain he caused—a strange feeling of disappointment swelled.

"Perhaps there is some reason your gift hasn't presented itself yet. It may still—"

"It's alright." I didn't want her pity. I offered my hand, and when she gave me the book, I set it beside the satchel. "Thank you. For doing this for me." *For even the thought of bringing the book. And, perhaps for the pitying, too. For caring.*

Evera's smile was faint. This time, when her eyes met mine, our gazes held. The sunlight filtering through the windows lit her hair, illuminating her curls with a halo of white light. The side of her face that lay in shadow contrasted with the other boldly, yet everything about her in that moment spoke of a softness. A gentleness.

To lighten the thickness that hung between us, I nudged her. "And thank you for reading to me. Veritran always lectured me for my reading voice. He said my tone was too flat. He would be impressed with yours, though."

"You—" Evera pinched her face into a glower and shoved me. I rumbled my amusement, and when she grinned at me, I leaned in, unable to resist her. She arched up to me. Her soft exhale on my lips sent a shudder down my spine and made my stomach leap.

No, not until I earn her name. With restraint, I raised my head to kiss the tip of her nose and drew back. "Rest," I told her, even as a look of disappointment flashed across her face.

"I don't need to rest," she countered, her retort lacking its usual sharpness.

"You do." I rolled my cloak up and lay it on the floor, making a pillow of sorts. I patted it. "It's only midday. We have time." When she did not concede, I added, "I could read to you if you would like. As I said, my reading voice is terribly dull—it may help put you to sleep."

Sighing, Evera lay back and rested her head on my cloak. "Very well, a short rest." She turned to her side, curling her knees to her chest, and set her green-blue eyes on me before fluttering them and then closing them with a yawn.

My chest warmed, and I reached for the book. By the time I found a page that held my interest, Evera was asleep, relaxed breaths escaping her parted lips. Contentedness held me, and for a moment, I just watched her while she rested. It would take time to earn her name, to earn her heart. Time, I knew with a great bitterness, that I may not have. When the huntsman returned with word from Harlan, I would have no choice but to leave Elrune. Leave Evera, should she not desire to come with me.

A curious thought then arose from my subconscious. For the first time since I joined the guard, I was considering my duties to protect the prince—*the King*—as something that stood in the way of ... What? A desire? Something I wanted for myself. It was bittersweet, for I was deeply grateful for Evera and the unexpected gift of her presence, of our bond and its implications, the possibilities. But my duty still lay first to my brother. It must.

Sighing, I pushed thoughts of Harlan aside. Such things were concerns for another time. In this moment, in this breath, I could enjoy Evera's presence, the scents of spring in the air, and the budding warmth within my chest. I could take simple pleasure in seeing her restfulness, her comfort, and in knowing that for all the hurt I'd caused in my life, that at least on this day I'd done something right in lightening her spirit and soothing her weariness.

26

NEIRIN

"She won't move," Evera hissed, kicking the mare's sides.

With one delivery left and the calm of the afternoon settling over Elrune, I'd chosen to walk beside the mare and encouraged Evera to try handling her on her own. It was a skill she should know, should she ever need to ride alone. But despite her stubborn persistence and her eagerness to try, the signals she gave only confused the animal.

Calix, who to my surprise had thus far been more of a help than a nuisance, laughed under his breath, and Evera shot him a pointed look.

The boy shrugged and resumed his absent, dazed look. It was a hoax, of course, just a part of his training; no one suspected a dull-eyed child, so they spoke freely around them. Though disconcerting, it was a useful skill, one that had proven fruitful today; he'd found us some half hour ago and relayed what knowledge he'd gained.

Guards were coming from the castle, expected by sun fall, to speak with the local commander and lord. His pursuit of me within the capitals borders exhausted, the King turned to the outlying towns.

I suspected Harlan was not aware of Astraea's involvement in sending out her messengers some few days prior. She would be losing her composure soon, though. Without my blood, her messengers would destroy each other. I chewed the inside of my cheek and glanced back at Calix, the weight of the impending events settling on my shoulders. But there was nothing I could do for his friends, not without enslaving myself to the Queen—more so than before—and abandoning my brother to the hands of the assassin that walked the castle.

Beside me, Evera huffed, and Sorrel stepped in place, ears pinned.

I moved to take the reins. "Stop," I instructed Evera, resting my free hand on her calf.

Exasperation and stubborn indignation lined her face. "That's how you make a horse move. You kick their sides." The sharpness in her tone made my lips turn up. Looking at me through the corners of her eyes, she narrowed her brows. "What?"

"You amuse me," I admitted, not withholding the warmth from my tone.

A curl fell in front of Evera's eyes, and it caught in the yellow light of the afternoon sun. She blew at it and grunted when it tickled across her nose. With a faint laugh, I moved my hand from her calf and tucked the strand of hair behind her ear. She turned into my touch, though her pout remained, and I stroked her cheek with my thumb.

"I'm trying," she said, a quiet uncertainty to her voice.

"I know." I offered an encouraging smile and handed the reins back. I trailed my touch to the small of her back and pushed slightly, encouraging her to straighten. "Leaning back will make her stop. Instead—"

"I wasn't leaning back."

"Yes," I said, casually trailing my hand lower to still just above the curve of her bottom. "You were."

She gave me a pointed look but argued no further, the press of her lips a clear sign she was attempting to restrain the sharpness of her tongue.

"Sit upright," I instructed. "Back straight. Then squeeze a bit with your heels."

Huffing, Evera set her eyes forward again and raised her chin. She wiggled and straightened her back more. The change in posture pushed her breasts out, and my eyes drew to the swell of them.

"Is this better?" Despite her apparent efforts, the touch of a sarcastic quip still laced her question.

I laughed. "Yes, now squeeze with your heels, just a bit, then let the pressure off. If you want her to stop, pull on the reins and lean back."

Evera followed my instruction, and after a fair bit of frustration on her part, the mare finally began to walk forward at a steady pace.

"I'm doing it!" Her exultation came almost as a squeal. Gone was the reserve to her voice and the snark she shielded herself with. The words encompassed the innocence and joy of a perfect moment. When she looked back over her shoulder, waves of copper hair flowed about her face, and the warmth of her smile fell upon me. My heart ached with the strangest form of longing. Not lust, not desire, something different. Something that was entirely consuming.

"That you are." The words came out softer than I intended, struck as I was by the moment.

"She is your mate, isn't she?"

I lowered my gaze to Calix. He watched after Evera and spoke beneath his breath so she couldn't overhear his question. The way his empty gaze followed her and the coolness to his question set an unease in my belly. Although Calix was just a boy, he held incredible power and was not to be underestimated.

I put a hand on one of his shoulders, holding him firmly. "She is."

A moment of quiet, then the subtle pulse of electric energy tingled in my hand and shot up my arm. It was not his intention to cause pain, for if that was his goal , he could have done so easily. It was more a reminder of his abilities, a warning response to the firmness of my grip.

As quick as the sensation came, it ebbed. "You do not need to try and intimidate me." Calix kept his eyes forward. "I will protect her."

I firmed my jaw. The boy's short curls remained unmoving in the breeze, and he wet his lips briefly before looking up at me. The depth in his cobalt eyes stood so starkly out of place amid his youthful features.

"Why?" I asked, choosing to speak to him with the regard I would show a grown man, despite his age. As I'd told Evera, boys like him and I did not have the opportunity to be children.

Calix turned his gaze back to Evera atop the mare, a steady way ahead. "Because she is good."

The response took me by surprise. Calix's loyalty to me, I knew, would be one of self-preservation. He needed my blood to maintain his composure and keep control over his magic for any prolonged period. This was fortunate, as such commitment could not easily be out-bought, for what would an orphan boy tossed out by his family value more than his own life?

"How do I make her go faster?" Evera's call drew my gaze and my thoughts back to her.

"You do not," I said, jogging to join her.

Calix muffled a chuckle, and again I found myself puzzled by the boy. There was a very human side to him I'd not expected. The concept compelled me to reconsider my beliefs, and made me question my understanding of his kind.

"Do you not think I am capable?" Evera asked as I reached

her side. Gone was the beaming smile, replaced with a faint pout of her lips.

I would not lie to her. Even if she resented me for it, I would not risk her safety. "It took me many lessons before I learned to trot."

Evera's face sank. "Oh."

I sighed. It was so easy to discourage her. "Where is our last delivery?" I asked, trying to distract her from her disappointment.

She gestured with a tilt of her chin. The road we followed paralleled a short cliff that came no higher than Sorrel's withers. Still, the bank was steep, its edge crumbling away in a mess of stone and clumped earth.

Ahead, a ramp sloped up steeply, leading to the elevated farmland. I reached for the reins instinctually to guide the mare.

"Neirin," Evera said, her tone a sharp warning.

"Yes?"

"You don't need to hold on to me." Her brows creased, and at that moment, I empathized with her brother. The woman was headstrong. And while her fire was intoxicating, it was equally frustrating. And worrisome.

"Neirin is overprotective of you because of what you are to him," Calix said, skirting past us and taking the ramp at a quickened pace. His boots, substantially nicer than my own, made a tapping sound as he hopped atop a stone beside the path and looked down at us, that childlike aspect of him showing itself again.

"Would you let Calix take the ramp alone?" Evera posed her question to me.

"I would," I admitted. I had no idea if the boy knew how to ride, but the concept of him falling from the mare's back and tumbling down the short hillside gave me little concern. If he wanted to be spoken to as a man, he would be treated as one—equally. "I do not care if he falls."

"Neirin." My name on Evera's tongue was lecturing, and a bit astonished. "He is a child."

Calix snorted in amusement but sobered when I shot him a glare. He took a seat atop the large rock.

"He is hardly a normal child," I said, but that was a conversation for another time. I suspected Evera knew there was more to Calix than I'd let on, but she'd yet to press. Still, she had handled well enough learning what I was. She could take the knowledge of Calix's affliction, I was sure. I would tell her later.

Sighing, Evera cast her gaze to the side, irritation and disappointment evident in her posture.

I set my jaw. "Fine." I dropped my hand from her back and stepped to the side as we reached the ramp, even as I knew it was a poor decision to relent. "Lean forward a bit. Otherwise, you'll fall. She's going to change her gait."

But it was too late. Evera was already coaxing the mare up the wood panels. Sorrel's flanks quivered, and she took the slope quickly, as I knew she would. Horses were daft, predictable things. As all animals were. Evera leaned forward, though too late for effectiveness. She jolted forward, off balance, and grasped for a hold around the mare's neck.

I rushed to her side and took Sorrel's harness at the top of the slope. I absentmindedly stroked the mare's flank to soothe her. Calix, to my relief, remained silent. Damn the two for their consorting.

I narrowed my eyes at my foolish mate, her head sideways and her cheek pressed to Sorrel's mane.

"You are stubborn," I told her.

"I know." Her remark was small and apologetic.

I huffed a breath. "Being capable doesn't mean trying things before you're ready. It means you have the willingness and intellect to learn something properly, even if it takes time."

Evera groaned and braced herself, balancing despite the slope so that she sat straight again. I shook my head, defeated, yet when she glanced at me once more, her expression had softened.

"Thank you," she said, the words genuine. "For letting me try."

Grunting, I tugged Sorrel forward by the reins until the mare stood on solid ground. "No more ramps."

"No more ramps," Evera agreed. "Today."

Shaking my head, I returned the reins to her, and when she urged Sorrel on, I fell in step alongside them, Calix following just behind.

Fields lined the side of the dirt path, and peasants tilled the earth, preparing it for a crop. Across the river, a group on horseback rode into town, the stallions all a dark chestnut color. The men atop them wore black.

Quickening his steps, Calix came to walk beside me and gestured subtly with a nod of his head. "A guard, at the front."

The lead stallion bore a saddle blanket embellished with silver; it dipped around its neck with decorative tassels. Only mounts owned by men of the castle guard were decorated with such garb. At this distance, I couldn't make out the rider's face, but unease sent gooseflesh sweeping across my skin all the same.

"They will not come this way," I reasoned to myself aloud. "They will check into the inn and get drunk. They'll start their rounds in the morning."

"Should I return to the inn and listen in?"

"No." I caught Evera's sideways glance at us. "The guard may recognize you."

"This is the last stop," Evera said, tone flat, offering out a small burlap sack secured with a leather cord. Tied into the bow, a paper hung with details of the order, the scribbling elegant, curled almost.

"I will answer any questions you may have," I promised, tucking the package under my arm and taking her hand. "It is not my intention nor my plan to be evasive with you." I would not make excuses to myself anymore for withholding information from her, not when the bond that connected us held me to her so irrefutably. Not when the dejection on her face betrayed the effects of how many in her past had kept things from her.

My heart pounded in my chest, and my mouth went dry as I resisted saying things that I knew were much too soon to say. To tell her I trusted her, that despite the newness of this, I resonated with her. My thoughts went to the huntsman and the unknown of what may follow upon his return. The uncertainty of all that hung around us. No, it was too soon to admit how deeply I cared for her, not when it held such potential for hurting us both. Not when I'd yet to even earn her name.

A child's scream broke the calm of the countryside. Evera and I turned our heads in unison. One of the farm children, a girl of five or so, lay on the ground clutching her arm. Tears streamed down the girl's cheeks, and from the nearest farmhouse a woman ran to her side.

Without hesitation, Evera leaned forward and swung her leg over Sorrel's rump. I reflexively placed a hand at her waist to help ease her down, though the dismount was anything but graceful. The moment her boots hit the ground, she left my side, bunching her skirts to raise them off the ground and hurrying to the child.

"Neirin." Calix's steady voice bore a warning.

"I know," I said, handing him the reins. "Stay with the mare."

Kneeling beside Evera, I sucked in a breath and scanned the surrounding area. Several men in the fields had stopped their tasks and were watching, but none made any immediate move to interfere, even as Evera began evaluating the child. Biting back a curse at the attention drawn to us, I held my ground, my heart catching, my emotions conflicted with instinct and knowledge. Every muscle bunched, strained. Instinct told me to defend my mate, to take her away from here before conflict arose. Yet in doing so, I knew I would shatter her trust and her soul.

A young girl spoke frantically, explaining the child's fall. "I swear, Mama, she tripped. I didn't push her."

"Run and get the healer, Lenna," the woman responded.

The girl nodded, eyes wide, and left us.

"It's dislocated," Evera announced, her voice ringing with calm confidence. "I'm going to set it."

The child's mother opened her mouth as if to object, but shut it again. Her gaze rose, and I followed it. A man dressed in a worker's clothing set toward us with long strides. Just behind him, three young men followed, exchanging uneasy expressions.

"Whatever you are going to do, do it quickly." Urgency laced my voice. Capable as I believed Evera to be, the world claimed this was not her place. My hand went to the pommel of my borrowed sword and trembled. If this were to lead to my capture, what would happen to Harlan? And what of Evera? She could not be jailed for accusations alone, yet the men's expressions told me that imprisonment was not the height of my concerns. The men's quick reactions told me Evera had already created a reputation for herself, and that brought with it a level of danger I could not calculate. The steadfast sister of the town's apothecary who meddled with tinctures and medicine, who refused to marry, who stood out because of her candor and beliefs—she'd unintentionally painted herself a target and turned what would have otherwise been mere gossip into weighty, believable fact.

"Hold her still," Evera instructed.

The child lay flat on her back, squirming and screaming, her waves of fair blond hair tangled with clumps of dirt and plant debris.

"Hold her." This time, a firm command hardened Evera's words. Desperation. She needed to do this. Could not leave the child suffering, even as it put us both in peril, put her family at risk for the gossip that would follow. This was impulse, emotion, purer than reasoning. Even as it held such bitterness and peril, I admired her for it. It was as Calix said: *She is good.*

Heart pounding, monster scratching beneath my skin, heat flooding my veins, I restrained the child. With my left hand, I held her down by her good arm, and with my knee, I braced her legs to keep her still. My breaths came in rasps.

Evera drew the child's arm straight against her side, then out. The girl writhed, but I held her still. In a quick motion, Evera raised the arm up, and the bone popped as it slipped back into place. When it did, the child screamed, then fainted, and for the briefest of moments, everything was entirely still.

Then the quiet broke.

One of the men was upon us, disdain written in the curl of his lip. In my hesitation, my need to support Evera, I'd made a mistake.

He grasped her before I could react, yanking her up and toward him by the wrist. In the same instant, my right arm was seized by one of the remaining three men.

Evera screamed. The sound overpowered all else—the muffled sobs of the child's mother, my monster's gripping claws, fear of capture, and even thoughts of my brother. Every part of me focused on the vile man pulling my mate by her wrist, dragging her away from me.

A snarl escaped my chest from a place so deep inside, it was more beast than man. Bile rose in my throat, and I pulled against the hands that restrained me, freeing myself only briefly before the other two men closed in, blocking off my path to Evera and grasping for me, keeping me from my blade. The blade I would take to their throats in an instant, given the chance.

2 7

—

EVERA

MY SCREAM SOUNDED like one from my nightmares. A sinking horror threatened to pull me beneath its slick, dark surface, and the rush of fear quickened my heart. Memories just out of reach —lost, buried—called to me.

I began to fall, but the man dragged me. The calluses of his fingers were rough on my wrist, and something inside of me clicked open—a will to fight. Gritting my teeth, I pushed panic down and dug the heels of my boots into the earth. Dirt churned up, but still the man pulled me, his strength greater than my own.

"Bastard!" I cried out, wrenching my arm back even as the motion strained my joints.

His grasp gave, slackened by my efforts, and I fell back. But I didn't catch myself fast enough, and my head struck the dirt. A ringing filled my head. Blinking the fog from my eyes, I saw my brother approach from up the ramp. He froze, fear rounding his eyes, face pale. It brought the flash of a memory—I saw him as a boy, cowering behind a wooden dresser.

A shadow leaned over me, and in the next breath, the farmer was pulling me up to my knees by my hair. The tugging pain

303

surpassed that of the pounding in my head. I reached up and grabbed his wrist. I dug my nails into his skin. Hissing a curse, he released his grip.

I braced myself on my knees and palms before him as he looked down at me with a snarl. I met his gaze and faced his anger. He struck me. A prickling sting radiated at my cheek, immediately followed by a burning soreness. Somewhere behind me, Neirin roared, but his words were lost to me. Wetness threatened at my eyes, but a fierce determination not to cower beat back the tears.

"How dare you put your hands on my daughter?" the farmer snarled down at me. Another time, I may have tried to force logic upon the brute, told him what he was about to accuse me of, and what he believed me to be, but it held no basis in fact. If I were a witch, an Alidian, I would strike him down where he stood, not fight back tooth and nail. If I aimed to bring harm to his child, I would not have set her arm. But he could not see reasoning beyond his rage. He saw only his daughter unconscious and the rumored witch of Elrune before him. I was sick of offering logic that went unheard, sick of being pushed down and told my place. Rage fueled me, funneled my pain. The man before me stood for everything I despised, and I refused to heed my place and allow him to beat me, scorn me, without retaliating with all the force I possessed.

My dagger was impossible to reach while I knelt, so I grasped one of the man's legs and pulled hard, sending him off balance. He fumbled back, but as he fell, one of his boots caught my jaw. The force was enough to jar me, disorient me, and before I could come back to my senses, the man was upon me again, shoving me fully to the ground.

I fell sideways. A boot struck my side, and I gasped; the wind rushed from my lungs. I curled into the pain, drawing my knees to my chest. Through the pounding of my head and my wavering vision, I saw Neirin, being held back by three men.

Though he lashed out, they restrained him. For a brief moment, his gaze met mine. With shaking arms, I willed myself to rise, but the farmer's boot struck again.

I flinched and shut my eyes, gasping for air. The fight left me, and I lay, bracing myself for the next blow, but it didn't come. A strange sensation heated my chest. A burning and a slick blackness.

"You," Neirin snarled. I opened my eyes.

He stood above me, a formidable form shielding me. The light hit his sword, sleek and silver, and in a distant place, my mind noted the lack of blood on it. How had he broken free of the men who held him?

My attention moved past him to where the three lay on the ground, unmoving. A static energy crackled in the air, and the panic that gripped me struck harder than the farmer's boots had. My eyes found Calix standing in the shadow of my mare, his eyes black pools fading back to cobalt.

The farmer took a step back, and Neirin matched him. He reached out and grasped the man by the front of his shirt. The growl that came from him was low, animalistic, and powerful.

"How dare you touch her, how—" His seething, the extent of his anger, was clearly too fierce to put into words.

The farmer swallowed, a knot bobbing in his throat. Fine beads of sweat formed at his temples.

"You will repent for what you've done." Neirin brought his sword level to the fist that clasped the man's shirt. One motion, one quick slit, and the man's throat would be severed.

"Stop," I called out, voice rasping.

A muscle at Neirin's jaw flexed, and he held his stance. The farmer's chest rose and fell in rapid succession. A faint wind blew, ruffling Neirin's hair. It gave a strange air of stillness to the moment.

Pushing to my knees, I wet my lips. "Let him go. He's not worth it. Please, I want to leave."

The sensation in my chest altered. Heat and spiraling rage settled into a trickle, like the steady rainfall of spring. Clouded, like the darkened sky. Thick and almost bitter. They were emotions, but they were not my own. They belonged to Neirin.

Was it possible this rashness was a reaction to the bond as well? Like the instinct of a creature to defend what was theirs at the cost of any rationale? If Neirin's reaction drew from his fox or from the magic of the bond, perhaps my own unease would pull him back.

"Take me away from here, please," I repeated.

Neirin growled, the sound coming from deep in his chest. Primal, raw. Despite the soreness in my cheek, the ache at my sides, and the severity of the situation at hand, something inside of me coiled at the noise; at the firm set of his jaw, the toned muscles of his arms where his cloak had fallen back, at the marks of the bonds on his body that said he was mine.

The coiling heat within deepened, and I released a breath, grounding myself. This was not the time to admire the firmness of his build, the way the light caught his features, the strength in his stance.

Entirely out of place for the situation, Neirin huffed a low sound of amusement.

Seriousness returning, he leaned in toward the man. "If you touch her again," he warned, his words a promise, "I will not hesitate to end you."

The farmer swallowed, turning his chin up to release the pressure of the deadly blade at his throat. Neirin held his gaze. A power emanated from him, intense and pulsing, extending over everything and everyone.

Releasing a breath, Neirin sheathed his sword and roughly shoved the man back.

"Evera." My brother's voice stirred me, and I turned to find him standing beside me. Gods, my heart was racing. I exhaled, steadying myself, and stood up. Though my ribs ached, I was confident that nothing was broken.

"Are you okay?" Aureus asked, raising a hand to my cheek.

I brushed his touch away, looking past him to where Ruairc knelt before the three men, his chest heaving as if he'd been running. My breath stilled as he held his fingers to their pulse. Quiet gripped those who'd come closer, abandoning their tasks in the field. Though he made no sound as he approached, I could sense Neirin's presence at my side. I could almost sense his nerves at the situation we found ourselves in, even as I knew he would not show it visibly.

"They're alive," Ruairc said. He stood, and his gaze met mine. *What happened?* My mind reeled.

"Evera, what happened?" Aureus's hands came to my shoulders. He turned me to face him, tearing my scanning gaze from where I sought out Calix; the boy had vanished.

Unable to form words, I shook my head and sucked in a breath. Through the rush of emotions, my brother's touch was too much. Rage flooded my veins, and I took a step back, roughly shouldering out of his grasp.

"We need to go," Neirin said as the back of his hand brushed mine. I raised my eyes to meet his. There was a strange understanding in them, a solemnness. It tempered my rage, drew me back.

Awareness of those watching us sent a shiver down my spine, and I nodded, taking Neirin's hand in silent acceptance, in the space of words that would not come.

The warmth of his hand grounded me. "Can you ride?" he asked.

"Yes." The word came on a rasp. And as the last of my fight left me, as the turbulence of my emotions shattered, I shuddered. Hesitating only briefly, I gave in to the need for comfort, for stability, and curled against Neirin's chest.

His breath caught with a heavy rise of his chest, and with the faintest of touches, he wrapped his arm around me, embracing me. The action spoke louder than any words he could have voiced. It resonated deep in my soul. With my head sideways, I blinked and met Ruairc's gaze. He lowered his chin in a subtle half nod.

"Thank you for protecting my sister, Lark," Aureus said, his voice low, deflated.

I turned my head to the other side to view my brother; his eyes were cast aside.

"I will always protect her." There was no hesitation in Neirin's response. No pridefulness or boastful edge either. It was a statement. A promise. He pressed a soft kiss to the crown of my head. The faint trailing of his thumb at my side was a comfort.

Aureus raised his gaze, and a flash—some indiscernible emotion—flickered there. "Go back to the shop, Evera. Ruairc and I will settle things here."

And there it was, just as it had always been—my brother had come to clean up my mess, to patch our family's reputation. My stomach sank. No, this was not as every other time had been. This was not the empty threat of a merchant or the idle gossip of women. Had any of the others seen Calix's eyes darken? Or when the onlookers spoke of the scene, would they claim me the source of the magic? Would this day become a convenient anecdote to pad their speculations?

I let out a breath and hooded my eyes. Though I yearned to scan the fields for Calix, I knew the boy would be long gone, hidden beyond my line of sight, and that was for the best. Neirin would likely know where the boy would go or how to meet up with him again. What else did Neirin know? Did he know what Calix was? Surely, he did.

Neirin helped me mount Sorrel, and she started forward. Her initial steps jolted me just enough to tug at a dull ache at my side. Sucking in my lips and hardening my resolve, I lifted my chin, training my eyes beyond those gathered and to the roofs and upper story windows of the homes that lined the edge of town just beyond the farmland. It was time for answers. If Neirin truly cared for me, truly sought to win my trust, my heart, there would be no more lies or secrecy between us.

28

EVERA

As we rode back into town, Neirin held me close, his touch light, as though he were afraid to both break me and lose me. When he trailed his nose along my cheek–faintly, he released a heavy sigh.

"Did you know? About Calix?" I asked.

"I did."

This time it was my breath that left in a heavy exhale. "What else are you keeping from me?"

Neirin hesitated. On our left, the river rushed, gurgling over stones and lapping at its banks. Voices carried from a side street —the soft hush of women speaking and the giggling echo of playing children.

"Many things," Neirin said finally.

Swallowing, I waited for him to continue.

"I meant what I said when I told you I would answer your questions. You have to know I had every intention to—" He snapped his mouth shut, swallowed. "But I understand if you would rather I take you home. I'm sure your brother will worry if you're not there when he returns."

"No," I said quickly. "No, I want to talk."

At my back, Neirin relaxed through a breath. "I do not deserve your patience," he said wistfully, "but I am so very grateful for it."

Unsaid words lay heavy between us as Sorrel carried us past the market square, empty at this hour, and toward the cliffside where the main road ran parallel. Neirin turned us to the south. I wet my lips, tasting the salt in the air. The setting sun cast tangerine light on the well-packed dirt road before us and warmed the right side of my body.

Neirin rested his cheek against my head. When he spoke, his tone was lighter than before, an effort to lessen the tension. "Would you still like to try going faster?"

Tilting my head to the side to look up at him, I dislodged his resting place, and he met my eyes. I found an apologetic half-smile pulling at his lips.

A flicker of adrenaline sparked in my chest, and I returned his smile. "I would."

His arm around my waist tightened, holding me securely. "You will tell me if anything hurts?"

There was a dull ache at my sides. The farmer's kicks would leave bruises if they were not already forming, but there would be no lasting damage. "My pain tolerance is high."

"That is not what I asked."

Sighing, I said, "I will tell you if anything hurts too badly."

Neirin tensed, and though I suspected my response worried or displeased him, the feel of his muscles at my back and encircling me caused my belly to do a little flip.

"I'm okay, Neir," I coaxed, letting the unexpected warmth flutter within me.

From the cliffside, a gallon of petrels took flight, the small dark birds appearing as silhouettes against the vibrant sky, save for the broad white bands that wrapped their rumps. Sorrel snorted at the commotion, and Neirin's hand left my waist momentarily to stroke her withers before he returned his hold on me and tightened it.

"Are you ready?"

The warmth in my belly fluttered like the wings of the petrels, and I nodded, a childish excitement coming over me.

"I will not let you fall," Neirin spoke against my ear, and when his chest rose against my back and he clicked twice with his tongue, Sorrel responded. She nickered, her muscles bunched, and she pushed to a trot. As we picked up speed, I gripped her mane, teeth chattering from the roughness of her gait. The excitement within me twisted as a very real trickle of fear took its place.

"I'm going to push her to go faster," Neirin said, his voice raised so I could hear him.

I clenched my jaw.

"It will be smoother, trust me."

Trust him.

He clicked again, and as if anticipating the command, Sorrel's strides lengthened. I lurched forward with the movement, but Neirin's arm around my waist braced me. Sorrel's withers were hard against my backside, uncomfortable with the rough motion. Spots of trees came upon us and passed in a blur. The only constant was the coastline. Body tensed, I gripped tighter on Sorrel's mane, and each time her gait launched me from my seat, I tensed.

"Stop fighting it," Neirin said, curling in so he could speak against my ear, his words nearly lost on the air as it cut around us. "Relax and move with her. Move with me."

My breath left on a shudder. I gritted my teeth and shut my eyes to the blur of movements. Though it went against all instinct, I forced the tension from my muscles. *Trust him.*

With my eyes closed, I became more aware of Sorrel's

motion. And Neirin was right—though we were moving faster, it was less jarring than the trot. Fluid, really. I relaxed against Neirin's chest, all my awareness focusing on him. On the warmth of him, the security of his firm body and steady hold on me, on his movements, so naturally in tune with Sorrel's. Rolling, almost.

Letting the fear ebb away, I gave in to the movement and found the flow. Once I discovered it, I opened my eyes, and my breath caught. The wind pushed my hair from my face as the world around us passed in a blur. Joy swelled as the sensation of absolute freedom overtook me. Like the petrels overhead, I was weightless, carried with the wind.

The festival and coming upon the King as we had, the magic that marked Neirin and I from our binding, the absolute madness of it all—gods, this moment was worth it.

How long had I believed I would be nothing more than someone's property, bound to a home and expectations? But Neirin... he'd treated me differently from the beginning. The ease of our conversations, the way he never corrected my candor or told me how a lady ought to speak. Showing me how to hold my dagger the night of the festival instead of taking it from me. Teaching me to ride. Being at my side when I set the girl's arm. Despite what followed, he'd put faith in me. He accepted me for who I was, without trying to change or fix me, as everyone else did.

We rode until the sun neared the horizon, the western lands a jagged black silhouette across the sea. Neirin leaned back and pulled slightly on the reins, slowing Sorrel to a walk. My mare's head hung and her breath came heavy, heaving her sides. Neirin steered us off the path to a grassy patch a few yards from the cliffside.

After dismounting, he placed a hand on my thigh. "Toward me this time," he instructed.

I looked down at him. The hood of his cloak had fallen back

during the ride, and sidelong rays of light bathed the right side of his face with warmth. The bridge of his nose and the strong lines of his profile cast shadows across his jaw. The contrast of his contours made him all the more handsome.

Again, a coiling tightened beneath my navel, and without a moment of hesitation, Neirin grinned wickedly at me.

"Damn you and your ability to read my emotions," I lectured, narrowing my eyes playfully as I swung my right leg over Sorrel's neck so that I sat facing Neirin.

He matched my expression, though the corner of his lips rose, tugging at his dimple as he suppressed laughter. Gods, he was handsome. I truly could not fault myself for wanting him. Softening, I let the revelations from our ride warm me with a different form of desire. Something deeper, something of the soul.

"What is that emotion?" he asked, and in his silver eyes I found the same yearning for connection, for comfort, for the intimacy of foreheads resting against each other, and the faint brush of noses. For stillness. For belonging. For acceptance.

Shaking my head, I smiled and took his offered hands. "It is my turn to ask questions," I reminded him.

He stepped closer, dropping my hands. With the gentle brush of his fingers, he drew my hair over one shoulder, baring my neck, while the touch of his other hand trailed along my inner thigh, coaxing. I reacted to his touch, parting my legs, allowing him closer. Sideways atop Sorrel's back, my legs wrapped his chest. My heart fumbled, and when he lifted me effortlessly, a smile broadened across my face.

"I suppose it is," he replied with a faint sound of amusement as he stepped back and adjusted his hold on me, supporting me with one hand beneath my bottom. The other he wrapped at my waist, and I arched at the touch until our chests pressed together. The rapid beating of his heart mimicked mine.

This moment … it was mine, ours. Something we chose. Something we shared.

"Neir." I trailed my nose up his. "Kiss me."

Though his breath left him on a shudder, he raised his lips and pressed a kiss to my temple. "Not now. Not until I've earned your name."

Oh, gods. Realization dawned over me. He'd not called me by my name once since our discussion in the stable. I sucked in a breath, searching for the right words, but as I did, Neirin started toward the cliff edge. I giggled, distracted, holding tighter to his neck.

"You'll drop me," I squealed.

Amusement vibrated his chest. "I will not drop you."

The waves rolled in and out with the tide, crashing against the cliffside. Neirin crouched down, keeping his hold on me even as I squirmed and protested amid giggles.

"Though you seem to be insistent, I do," he said through soft, broken laughs as he fell back onto the grass and braced one arm behind him to keep us from falling back, the other still wrapped at my waist.

Grass tickled my legs where my skirts hitched up above my boots. A breeze blew in from the sea, catching the waves of my hair and holding us in a cocoon.

Neirin tucked a strand behind my ear. "You're stunning."

Heat rose to my cheeks, and I was overtaken by bashfulness, forcing me to break his gaze.

"Come now," he coaxed, lifting my chin, a soberness lacing his expression. "Ask the questions that weigh on you. No more secrets."

"No more secrets," I repeated.

Neirin dipped his chin in a subtle nod.

Twisting my lips, I considered for a moment. "What of Calix? Is there something more you aren't telling me about him? And are there others who know what he is?" As I began asking the questions, more came to me. I drew my brows together, frustrated by the onslaught of complicated implications. "I've only ever heard of female Alidian. And—" Too many questions bombarded me at once, too many ideas; I could barely speak. "How has he learned to control his magic? What he did was targeted and purposeful, and it didn't kill those men. Neirin, his magic should have killed them, shouldn't it have?"

"That is a lot of questions." Neirin dropped his other hand from my waist, using it to support himself as well. He leaned back slightly and held my gaze.

"I know," I confessed.

"I do not know why people only speak of women being Alidian." Neirin frowned. "But I suspect there may be a simple explanation—more Alidian are women than are men. On the rare occasion a male is discovered, Astraea sends to have him collected, even if he comes from one of the cities in the west. Females are much more commonly discovered, and when their magic overtakes them and they become a threat, they are—" His frown deepened.

Handled. Taken care of. Killed.

Sorrow lodged in my throat, but I nodded and redirected the conversation. "What does the Queen have to do with the Alidian?"

"Your questions are becoming difficult to keep up with," Neirin mock scolded. "Astraea's messengers are all like Calix. She selects them, offering them the allure of a life in trade for their loyalty. The children are trained by the castle commander in stealth and discipline. Astraea instills them with cunning, and they study among the boys of the guard to learn literature and politics. They are used for their skills and their discretion. The magic, however, to my knowledge, is not supposed to used by the children. I did not know Astraea was teaching the children to control their abilities. Or it could be that Calix learned on his own. His restraint is impressive."

Sighing, I scrunched my brows. There were still missing pieces, things that did not add up, but it was altogether too much to absorb at once. A single thought returned to me, turning over in my mind even as it held itself on my tongue.

"If your name is cleared," I said, hesitating slightly, "do you believe the Queen may let me assist in her cause? I want to help those children, Neirin. I want to do good, as she does."

"No." Neirin's tone was firm. "I will support you in all your endeavors, but for this one. I will not let Astraea poison your heart." Sitting up straight, he cupped my cheek with one of his palms. "It was not in cruelty that I stated Calix would have been better had I taken his life than bring him under my care."

"How can you say that?" I drew his hand down, hurt, confused.

Swallowing, Neirin lowered his gaze. A heat trickled from him through the invisible cords of our bond. It was not a warmth this time, though—not affection or desire. It was a fire. Something that burned, that caused pain. It drew me to hesitate as I recalled his admission in the pasture of how he feared losing control to his fox, how his own distress could rile it.

Neirin drew the dark cloth of his cloak over his head and let it fall to the grass beside us.

"Restraint," he said, "and control. They come at a great price. Whether there is kindness behind Astraea's lessons, I cannot say. A part of me believes that in her mind, she sees herself as helping those children. In a way, I suspect similar to how she was 'helped' when she was young."

"Neirin, what are you saying?" I shook my head. "I don't understand."

"She is like Calix."

My mouth gaped. I shut it, dismissing each question as it rushed over me before I could voice it. What I needed was for Neirin to finish his explanation, so I remained quiet, still, even as the breeze caught my hair and sent a chill down my spine.

A muscle at his jaw flexed before he crossed his arms and grasped the hem of his shirt. Arms above his head as he withdrew the linen garment, the muscles of his torso bunched, and I swallowed, taking him in. His body was taut, his skin stretched over muscles formed by years of training. Despite the weight of our conversation, the sight of his bare chest distracted me, if only for a moment.

"I'm trying to be serious," Neirin said as he tossed the top aside.

Reluctantly, I raised my eyes from his waist, where a distinct V shape led to the band of his pants. I found his gaze set on me, one dark, teasing brow raised.

My cheeks heated. "Yes, I know." Huffing a breath, I regained my composure. "Go on."

The corners of his lips twitched in the faintest of smiles before fading to a more somber expression. "At the festival, you asked me about my scars. Do you remember?"

I nodded.

Neirin took one of my hands in his. He brought it to the chiseled ridges of his body. The set of his jaw was a firm reminder, and I swallowed, forcing my mind to focus even as the coiling in my belly tugged at my consciousness.

Steadying my breath, I lowered my gaze to where my hands rested on him. The white line of a rough scar traced from his collarbone to beneath his ribs, and another ran above his navel. Other smaller scars left pale lines and uneven ridges. They marked the brutality of his occupation. They spoke of his strength.

"Not those," Neirin said, his voice soft, vulnerable.

I continued my exploration. As I did, I sobered, desiring to memorize his body so I could know him by touch alone. Closing my eyes, I trailed my index finger from his chest to his navel, then stopped. Brows drawn, I traced up again.

I opened my eyes and studied a faint raised line. The scarring was so subtle it was nearly undetectable. Yet, when I became aware of them, I found them to be everywhere. Like the branching roots of a plant, splitting again and again until the lines dissipated and a new section began.

"The marks of Astraea's lessons."

My heart caught, and I shook my head. "I don't understand—"

"All magic, Evera, is dangerous. The Alidian's and my own. Magic brings death, pain, and suffering. Astraea has learned how to temper that innate danger. I suspect she is mirroring her own upbringing, but I have no way to be certain.

"The connection between my kind and the Alidian is a secret held by only those who possess such magic. The Alidian feed on my blood and the blood of others like myself. And while it doesn't cure them of their affliction, it tempers it, in a way. For some time, they can control themselves with less effort. Still, it takes discipline to learn restraint. When one of Astraea's messengers slips up, begins to lose control, she *corrects* them."

"Corrects them?"

"Yes." Neirin released a long breath. "The scars are a mark of her magic, of the static pain she strikes upon us to render us useless, unable to do anything but fall to our knees. She is strong, and she knows how to harness and control the output of the power she generates. Knows how to give just enough to make us submit, to remind us of the necessity of control and obedience without killing us. And though I do not need to feed on blood like the Alidian do to control my magic, learning that restraint took the same lessons, the same reminders."

Sucking in my bottom lip, I shook my head and raised my eyes to his. "Neirin, how many times did she do this to you?"

The heat that radiated from him—that coursed through our bond—intensified, and when he spoke, his voice broke. "Many. The pain,"—he swallowed—"it is indescribable. Yet when that power courses through my body, my fox submits without fault.

Just as the Alidian's magic submits to Astraea's. She has incredible power, and though I cannot explain how it works, we sense it. We learn control through suffering."

"That's horrid …" Blinking, I cleared the blur of tears from my eyes. My heart pounded in my chest.

"It is necessary," Neirin said, wiping the wetness from my cheek with his thumb. "It has taught me to restrain my monster, or at least it has aided me in doing so. Sometimes, when my turmoil is too much, he is impossible to push down." He lowered his eyes. "It is why, I think, that I crave violence at times. Yearn for a fight. When facing death, he quiets. All thoughts quiet. Nothing else exists."

Words eluded me, so I took his hand in mine.

A tremble shuddered through him, and the fire built. He touched absentmindedly a spot on his neck, one I'd noticed the night of the festival but thought little of at the time. "Even Astraea, with her age and power, cannot control the chaos the magic gives her. Only the blood of the gods can do that."

Following his touch, I evaluated his neck and found dozens of small slits that had healed over, although time had not fully concealed them. Cuts from a blade. "Your arm." My memory flashed to the stable, to Neirin's wound when he'd returned from the fire with Calix. Turning my attention to the spot, I found countless others, some overlapping.

"The children feed there. They do not have the restraint Astraea has not to drain my blood."

It was madness. Impossible. How could such a world exist outside of what was known?

The children feed there.

"And Astraea, she—"

Neirin took my fingers delicately, keeping them at his arm. "First, here, when I was young." He swallowed and put my fingers to the marks on his neck. "When I became a man, she took to me. Did not—" He swallowed hard. "Could not force me to bed her. But she took power, pleasure, from the places she drained my blood. Perhaps she wanted me, perhaps there was an attraction, or perhaps it was only in her mind, another way to control me, belittle me. Maybe it was a way to look past my father's betrayal."

My heart sank, and I sucked in a breath to regain myself. "Your father?"

Neirin nodded and closed his eyes, brows scrunching. He shuddered as he inhaled sharply. With unbearable force, the fire within him branched through the bond. The burning, searing, inescapable suffering was tangible. It could not only be felt, but tasted, heard.

I choked on a sob. A pounding filled my head and shook my body. Through the searing heat, Neirin's hand clutched the back of my neck. A connection, a tether. Without thought, I let him pull me into his embrace.

He buried his head in my neck and breathed in my scent, his breath ragged. In that instant, I became starkly aware of the smells of tilled earth, of pine trees, and of the brisk air before rainfall. His scent. My mate's scent. Through the shudders, I held on to that, let it fill me, and as it did, the heat began to subside.

He held me like that until the pain fell away, until the sounds of the crashing waves and the calls of the petrels returned. Until I felt the breeze on my skin and the world returned around us. And even then, he continued to hold me, needing this as much as I did.

With his vulnerability bare before me as he sought comfort in my scent and touch, I accepted our bond. There would be no forgetting him, no way to move on in my life without aching for this connection. This was raw, honest, and unbreakable.

One of his hands wrapped my waist, and the other wove through my hair. His lips brushed my neck, and his exhale heated my skin. His chest thrummed, and our hearts matched pace.

The intimacy of this moment was so much more than we shared in the tower. So much more than anything I'd ever shared with someone else. My soul called to him. Spoke that he was mine, and I was his, and this ... this was everything.

29

NEIRIN

Evera's embrace was sheltering, like a cloak from the cold; the scent of her soothing, like the burn of whiskey. And more than these things was the harmony of our heartbeats. The way she settled my body and my soul.

When she drew back, I held her gaze. How could I tell her she was everything to me when I was sure she still had questions? At dawn, I'd sought to earn her trust, yet as I studied the flecks of many colors in her eyes, I knew this went beyond that. Whether or not she trusted me, I could not say. But in this moment, there was a connection between us. Would she repute that if I voiced my feelings? Or did she sense it too?

"Are you alright?" Evera cupped my cheek, her touch light, caressing, and so incredibly intimate.

"I—" The words held in my throat. A fear gripped me. If I pushed myself on her before she was ready, it could very well overwhelm her. Yet time was something I did not have. Not when my brother's life hung in the midst of it all. When the huntsman returned, I would have to leave Elrune. Whether Harlan accepted my word as truth or not, my duty to him, my love for him, would compel me.

Before Evera, I had accepted this freely. For what value did I put on my own life? I existed to protect Harlan, to ensure Nyana had all she needed, to give every moment of my existence in pursuit of repenting for Thatch's death. And while those things still drove me, Evera had shattered the numbness. There was a selfishness to it, one that brought a bitterness to my mouth, but I could not deny the longing. The aching desire to exist beyond all I was, to hold on to moments like this one—the salt on the breeze and the way it tightened Evera's curls, the warmth of her body, the resonance of her heartbeat—for the remainder of my days.

This was not living for a purpose. It was living for a feeling. And it was shattering and equally enthralling.

"Neirin." Evera stroked her thumb across the stubble of a beard growing in.

"I desire you," I said without thought. Though as soon as the words escaped me, I knew they were ill-voiced.

To my surprise, Evera laughed. "That is very forward of you."

"That is what Sindri said as well." I shook my head, recalling the barkeep's words the night of the festival. Shifting my tone back to a more serious one so she understood that my longing for her went beyond what her body could give, I placed my hand atop hers. "This, though, is a different form of longing."

Releasing a breath, Evera smiled. "It is."

"Do you have more questions to ask of me?" Keeping her hand in mine, I lowered it to my chest, to where my heart beat in rhythm to hers.

She sighed. "Yes, for each question you answer, I have three more. But that is enough heavy conversation for one night. It is, admittedly, exhausting."

"It is," I agreed, "but I believe I have earned one question for you."

"Have you, now?"

"I've been very forthcoming, Cordelia," I teased.

Shoving at my chest, Evera grinned. "Very well, Hadrian, a single question."

I considered this for a moment, enjoying the warmth of her smile and the lighter tone our conversation had taken on. It was true what she said. Though there would be many questions for us both as we learned from each other and uncovered our pasts and tribulations, there was a heaviness to such talks. One that needed to be balanced.

Evera shifted her weight, and the hilt of her blade, strapped at her inner thigh, pressed to my leg.

"Your dagger," I said decisively. "Where did you get it?"

"I don't remember," she replied with an easy comfort. "I've always had it."

"Can I see it?"

A wicked grin crossed her face, reaching her eyes. She pressed against my chest, encouraging me to fall back. I obliged and leaned back, supporting myself with my forearms. Raising to her knees, Evera bunched her skirts and withdrew the blade.

With a glint of a challenge in her eyes, she held the dagger out to me.

I supported my weight with one arm and took it from her. My muscles bunched with the effort, and I caught Evera's brief glance across my body before she returned her gaze to the blade. A slight reddening flushed her cheeks.

Stifling my amusement and my satisfaction at the effects I had on her, I held the pointed blade up to the dying light of the setting sun.

It was old, but the craftsmanship was of decent quality. Rough leather wrapped its hilt, and accents of embossed metal decorated its pommel and cross guard. The edges, however, were markedly dull.

"When is the last time you sharpened it?" I asked.

"Sharpened it?"

I scoffed and ran my finger across one of the blade's edges. "I will sharpen it for you. You should keep it on your hip, though. Where you have it now is impractical." I considered for a moment, then added, "Though, unless it was your intention to cut me the night of the festival, I suspect you need lessons on wielding it properly as well?"

One of her brows rose as I handed the weapon back, handle first. She took it and set it beside us on the grass.

The guard in me cringed at the action. "A blade should always be sheathed when not in use," I pointed out.

Huffing, Evera ignored my lecture. "I could not carry it on my hip."

"Yes," I told her with stern seriousness, dissatisfied by the bitterness in her tone. "You can, and you should." To regain the lightness, I offered a crooked smile, knowing as I did that it would reveal my dimple; I knew she favored it. "Fuck what others think of it."

"Fuck what others think of it?" she repeated on a laugh.

I drew a curl from in front of her eyes and tucked it behind her ear. My gaze fell to the faint bruising at her cheek. I released a breath, the moment stifled by remembrance of what had led us here. "You should be able to defend yourself. That is worth more than the opinions of strangers."

Evera held my eyes. Again, the emotion from before swelled from her. It was an emotion that my monster never communicated to me. Something warm, thick … I was unsure of the feeling.

She held out a hand and, with drawn brows, I took it.

"I am Evera," she said. "I have no family name, no crest or sigil, and I have a despairingly meager dowry. But now you have my name. I choose to give it to you. I hope it is enough."

"It is everything."

The amusement in her eyes fell away at my vehemence. As if she expected me to laugh at her gesture. But this was what I'd been waiting for. For her name. For her to give it willingly. A flutter filled my chest. Exciting, terrifying, weightless. I rose so that our chests met, and I threaded my fingers through her hair.

A slight gasp escaped her before I stole the sound with my kiss. The touch was light, intimate. When she gaped her lips, offering an invitation, I took it—slowly, though, not wanting to rush this moment. She melted against me, matching my pace, and when the kiss broke, she rested her forehead on mine.

"Evera," I said her name and cupped her cheek, pressing a chaste kiss to her lips once more before drawing back to study her with the need to memorize every detail; the dappling of freckles across her nose, nearly undetectable in the shadow of the setting sun; the curl of her lashes, a shade darker than her hair. "*You* are everything."

When she spoke, her voice was quiet. "How? How, Neirin, when we've known each other less than a fortnight? How can I be everything to you?"

"I do not know," I admitted, guilt stinging. The words had come to me before I could consider them, weigh them. They were spoken from my heart. "In truth, it terrifies me. But I cannot deny it."

Evera returned her forehead to mine and made a small, contented sound. All the response I would get, I suspected.

"We should return," I told her after a moment.

"Must we?" There was a sadness to her words that ached at my heart. But we could not stay here, not without the necessities to make a fire or some form of shelter. And not along the main road, in sight of any travelers who passed in the night.

"We must," I told her and brushed a kiss to her nose.

She giggled at the gesture. When her amusement shifted into a broad yawn, she fell against my chest in an exaggerated manner and nuzzled at my neck, humming.

I wrapped my arms around her, cupped the back of her head with one hand, and rubbed her back with the other. "Are you sleepy, Evera?"

"Are you going to overuse my name now that you have it?" Her voice was muffled against my neck. The brush of her lips sent a sudden jolt of desire through my body, and I breathed in deeply to settle the stirring. It was not the time. Her body needed to heal from the day. And, in truth, I did not want to cheapen this night; something told me that taking her so soon would do just that.

"I am," I teased. "Come now, let's get you back. You need rest."

THE RIDE back into town was quiet, late enough in the day that the petrels had retired to their nests, yet early enough that the crickets had yet to begin their chirping. A chill had set in with the coming night, and I held Evera close to me, wrapped in my arms. Against her neck, I sighed, and she giggled. "That tickles."

I laughed and repeated the action, this time with a breath that fogged her skin. She squirmed, a slight whimper escaping her lips. "I thought it tickled," I chided, resting my chin on her shoulder to keep the moment light.

She hummed contentedly, and quiet befell us again. Alongside the road, the cliff's edge was nearly indiscernible as the night darkened; the colors of the sunset were long faded.

Despite Evera's warmth against me and the moment's intimacy, a twinge of unease itched at my subconscious, a nagging reminder of how fleeting this all was. With it came a tugging at my heart, a hope that the huntsman would return sooner than he'd anticipated so that I might return to the castle, assure my brother's safety, and unravel the deceptions. Yet, in the same breath, I longed for moments just as this one, as many as time may grant me.

Evera leaned her head back, and I brushed my cheek up the side of her face, letting it rest atop her brow. Though this was all so new and held no logic, I could not deny I was falling hard for her—for her smile and the way it lit her eyes, for the depth of her caring when she let her guard down, for her fire, her cunning, and her sharp wit. For the way she drew me from my burdens.

Waves crashed against the cliffs below, and ahead, light illuminated the windows of shops and homes as we drew nearer to town. I nuzzled into Evera's hair, breathing in her scent. I'd said no more secrets, yet she still did not know the truth of who I was, who my brother was. It wasn't that I sought to keep the information from her. It was more than the day had already carried such heaviness.

"Evera," I started, my chest constricting as I settled on honesty, on having no more deceptions between us. "There's something you must know."

She tilted her head back, and I met her eyes. Even in the shadows of dusk, they sparkled with light. The image of her on the ground before the farmhouse ached at my gut.

"What is it?" she asked, tone languid, relaxed, as she melted against me.

I set my eyes on the horizon. Fear of her response quickened my heart. "My brother, he—"

"Evera!" A man's call interrupted me, and I shifted my attention to find Aureus standing before the inn.

Evera tensed in my arms, and I brushed my lips against her temple.

"Are you safe with him?" I asked as we drew nearer. I knew very little about her brother, and the angry set of his brows concerned me. Or perhaps it was only as Calix had said, that I was being overprotective of my new mate.

Thoughts of the boy turned my lips down. Would he be at

the inn? Why did his well-being concern me? Was it because I owed him for aiding me in protecting Evera?

"Of course," Evera said. "He is my brother. Aureus is just—" She sighed. "He worries about me."

I could empathize with his worrying, even if I did not approve of his use of sternness and reprimands. Not when simply speaking to his sister would accomplish more. Making a sound of acknowledgment, I steered Sorrel and stopped before the man. I held Evera firmly against me, needing to judge the situation for myself before I released her to him.

For a moment, Aureus only held his beard, eyes flitting between the two of us. Finally, he addressed his sister, his tone low and flat. "I told you to return to the shop."

I gave Evera a moment to respond for herself, but she only breathed deeply and placed one of her hands over mine.

"We went for a ride," I replied.

Scoffing, Aureus clenched his fists at his side. "I'm sure that's all it was."

The derisive tone and the insinuation of his words heated my blood. Through the bond, I sensed Evera's discomfort.

"Consider your words," I snarled.

In the flicker of lanterns set atop the stone fence of the inn's garden, I noted the flush to Aureus's cheeks. *Good. Be ashamed.*

When I dismounted, Aureus flinched, and I narrowed my eyes at him. Not all men were fighters; I understood this. Still, weakness irritated me. Especially when it was the brother of my mate who showed it to me. It pained me to leave her with him.

"Show your sister more respect," I warned, standing face-to-face with the apothecary.

Aureus set his jaw and, dismissing me, reached to draw the reins over Sorrel's ears so he could lead Evera back to the stable. On the mare's back, Evera sat with eyes cast down, the flame within her flickering.

No.

"Evera can steer her mare on her own," I said, intercepting Aureus's reach. Looking up to her, I placed the reins in her hands and nodded, letting a smile of encouragement settle on my face. There were words to be said, but they weren't needed. Not when the corner of her lips turned up and a sensation of weightlessness flitted through the bond. Though the world held many dangers for her, and I only added to them, she was strong of mind and body and heart. I could not let my need to protect her overshadow that.

"Can I come for you tomorrow?" I asked.

Evera nodded, and I brushed my thumb lightly over the bruising at her jawline. She held my hand in hers then lowered it, her smile soft and sad. Tomorrow I would bring her lightness, perhaps bake with her as I had so often as a boy with Nyana.

Aureus voiced Evera's name, and she squeezed Sorrel's sides, urging the mare on. Pride filled me as I watched them set down the road, and when they turned right at the corner and left my sight, an emptiness came over me. How I longed to keep her at my side, to carry her to bed with me, to lay her down. Though I ached to be inside of her again, the desire to simply be in her presence was stronger. To hold her in my arms, to watch her breath, heavy as she slept.

Skirting the fence with my hood concealing my hair, I made my way to the back door of the inn, my thoughts turning to the presence of castle soldiers and a guard. Who, very likely, would be sleeping under the same roof as Calix and I on this night. If, I reminded myself, Calix had returned. But what else could he do? Without my blood, his control would not last, and if his magic killed—if he was caught for it—a swift execution would befall him.

The hens greeted me as I reached the garden, clucking and pecking at my boots. The new rooster, a proud and aggressive creature, studied me and kicked at the earth. I scoffed, nudging the hens aside as I walked. Reaching the back door, I entered through a crack, careful not to let any of the daft creatures inside.

A pot of fresh soup bubbled over the fire, filling the room with the smell of onions and rosemary. I drifted to it without thinking, giving the creamy broth a slow stir as my stomach rumbled in response. On the table, a loaf of bakery bread sat on the table with a serrated knife beside it. I carved a slice free– the crust crisp beneath the blade, the inside was soft and pillowy– and tore off a bite. Warm. Comforting. Delicious.

The split doors swung open, and Maerel's eyes narrowed the instant they found me. With a sharp flick, she tossed a rag over her shoulder and strode to the table, snatching the bread from my hand as though it were contraband.

"Some help you are," she scolded. "This place has been packed since sun fall. Remind me what you're doing to earn that free room of yours."

Rearranging barrels of beer, washing countless dishes, dispersing drunkards, cleaning their vomit when they drink too much ...

"I'm sorry, Maerel."

"Yes. Well, you're here now." She turned her back to me and drew plates and bowls from a shelf. Returning to the table, she placed them beside the bread. "Soup tonight. There's a group of soldiers from the capital over by the hearth. Start by bringing them each a bowl."

A tightness constrained my chest. "I cannot."

Maerel slapped the rag from her shoulder onto the table and met me with a firm stare. "And why is that?"

Working my jaw, I sought the words. Then a deep laugh came from the bar, and the familiarity of it chilled my blood. I froze, listening. The quiet complaints of a young woman rose and were cut off.

Maerel hissed a breath. "That guard is a problem."

"How so?" I asked. My tone was gravelly, and my hand

itched to reach for my sword and uphold the threat I made back at the festival. Maerel gestured with her chin, and I went to the split doors and peered through a crack in the upper section.

Cyan leaned into the bar, propped up on one arm, boxing in a young woman. Her hair fell in loose waves, and when he tucked the strands behind her ear, the softness of her face revealed her youth. Barely more than a girl. Still, older than he usually went for. Bitterness stung at the back of my throat. He spoke boisterously over his shoulder, and the soldiers at the table exchanged uneasy glances.

The woman turned her head aside, and Cyan grabbed her roughly by the chin, forcing her to meet his eyes. I gritted my teeth. He reached down with his other hand as if he were working at her skirts with a cruel twisting grin, bunching them. The girl squinted.

"Go upstairs," I instructed Maerel.

"Lark—"

"Now," I commanded. The firmness in my tone gave no room for discussion, and this time her footsteps sounded her assent as she obeyed my order. Hand at the hilt of my sword, I lowered my hood and shouldered the door, pushing it open just enough to draw Cyan's attention. His hand stilled beneath the woman's skirts, and his eyes narrowed on me. I raised my chin, knowing even as I did that it was a risk. I could justify the need to separate Cyan and deal with him privately while the other soldiers were distracted. Though they surely had my description, none of them had worked alongside me, so they would not so easily take note of me in a crowd if I did not stand out. Eliminating Cyan greatly lowered the threat of my capture and bought me time to wait for the huntsman's return. Questioning him, too, could draw valuable insight. But the fire in my blood, the clench of my fist, told me this would be an act of rawness too, not one my training would prepare me for. In a primal sense, he was a threat to the fragile life I was forming here in

Elrune and a threat to Evera, my mate. That, along with the violence he was forcing on the woman he'd cornered, was enough to move me to action, even without thoughtful reasoning.

Withdrawing his hand, Cyan turned his eyes back to the girl and forced his fingers into her mouth. She choked back her fear, and his grin of satisfaction deepened. Though it took every ounce of restraint I had, I held back in the doorway. I knew what he was doing, and I would not allow myself to be drawn out into the open where he could so easily attack me.

I retreated to the table in the kitchen and braced my hands on the wood. Knuckles white, I snarled, waiting. I needed Cyan to come to me. If he were wise, he would raise the attention of the soldiers so that they could detain me as a group. But Cyan was greedy and believed too highly of himself. It was a gamble to try to draw Cyan out alone, one born of recklessness. My own frustration only further fueled my anger, further heated my blood.

When the split doors behind me creaked on their hinges, I turned to him. "A duel," I said, forcing my voice to stay firm. "In the woods behind the inn." Rash, thoughtless. I drew a long breath, regaining myself. I needed to remain level-headed, to regain my composure, and to work with the situation I'd put myself in. I could not let Cyan see how he riled me or how desperate I was for a fight.

Cyan sneered. "Fine, Bastard. A duel."

30

NEIRIN

The night seemed darker, somehow, as though hours had passed and not mere minutes since I first encountered Cyan in the inn. The hens, too, had quieted, their incessant clucking hushed after one of the guard's heavy boots made contact with one of them as he followed me out to the secluded section of woods beside Maerel's garden.

Moonlight cast shadows through the trees and across Cyan's brow; his eyes were dark beneath their ridges. He stepped sideways, and as he did, I mirrored him. A circling, a dance. A foretaste of what was to come, the reflection of years of mock fights played out in the castle's training yards. But Cyan and I were no longer boys trying to prove ourselves to the commander, no longer young men clashing blunt training swords to hone our skills, to prove strength or position. Now, we stood not as childhood rivals but as opponents with honed blades and sharp eyes.

"You're posing as a peasant," Cyan sneered.

With our gazes locked, I studied him. And when he stepped again, I did so as well. If he was intoxicated, he was masking it well. Though I had no doubt I could take the man, the fight would be dangerous. Despite the fool I believed him to be, Cyan was still a castle guard. And, not only that, but the son of a commander. Trained from the age he could hold a sword. If it were not for his arrogance and tendencies to lead with emotion, he could very well be as skilled a fighter as his father.

"No retort?" Cyan snorted.

Standing my ground, I drew my sword. "Save your condescension, Cyan. There's no one here to listen to you. No one who cares."

The burly man curled his lip, and his hand went to the hilt of his weapon. "The King will have my head if I slay you, Bastard. And you know it."

The edge of my lips turned up. Harlan wanted me captured alive. There was a part of him, then, that doubted the recounting of the events the night of Kaius's death. Despite my dagger in the King's chest and my hands stained with his blood, there was a hesitance from Harlan. That alone could be enough to secure my safe passage back to the capital.

The realization dawned on me. Would it be so simple, then, to return to the castle and speak to my brother? To defend my innocence and work alongside him to unravel the truth?

It was possible too that Cyan was lying. It would not be against his nature to do so, to feign a ruse in hopes I might surrender and return with him of my own accord. Or perhaps he aimed to put the weight of honor on me so I might hold my blows if I believed he would.

And what of Rion? The timing of his arrival when he came upon me over Kaius's body the night of the festival was convenient—too much so to dismiss. If he were not the assassin, he was at least a pawn in the game, whether he was aware of it or not. It gave only further reason to distrust his son.

Though I longed for information, for answers, I could not put any faith in Cyan's word. Nor would I allow him the satisfaction of believing he held influence over me.

When I didn't reply, irritation creased Cyan's brows. Flexing his fist, he wrapped his fingers around the hilt of his sword and drew it with a hum that rang through the woods.

"I will not hold back," I told him, because honor drove me to say as much.

Cyan raised his chin, challenging me with his gaze. The black of his hair and uniform lent him to the shadows of the wood, the moonlight on his face a contrast. His complexion was fairer even than his father's, though their rigid features were the same.

His resistance to making the first move was a strategic move. He'd learned my technique in the years we spent training alongside each other. The consideration showed more intellect and more forethought than I gave the man credit for, and it spoke to his sobriety.

To leer or to rile him would be too easy, too distasteful. Retorts stung in the back of my throat, but I held them back. If I played this carefully, there was a chance I could gain honest information from him, if only by the slip of his tongue. But not if I drew out his temper, not if I pushed him too far. I needed him to boast or to make a statement that stood outside the constructs of what I knew to be true.

Stepping to Cyan, I feigned a strike at his left, and when he countered, I swiped at his feet. But he predicted my move, not to my surprise. Our training, skills, and the very nature of our movements were shared and ingrained. A part of who we were since we joined the guard as boys, since our first bloodings. He stepped back, avoiding my gaze, and the counter leveled us. Each taking a step back, we circled, eyes intent.

Searching for a way to draw information from the guard, I considered my own blooding. The face of the man I killed, the cruel twist of his smile. He and Cyan were the same. Both arrogant, perverse, twisted men drawn to girls too young to be taken. *The girls at the festival.* "The night of the festival, I lost sight of you," I said with a step to my right. "What came of those girls you had your sights on?"

"There is no place for the claiming of honor among King killers, Bastard," he sneered.

King killer. I allowed myself only a moment to process his choice of words, the narrowing of his eyes, and the posturing of his stance. His body language spoke of a man who believed his own words. He likely knew nothing of the true events that had transpired the night of Kaius's death. It was a hunch, an instinct, but very rarely did my intuitions lead me astray.

To keep the brute distracted, off my trail of thoughts, I tugged the corners of my lips up in a mocking smile. "So, your intentions did not come to fruition, then," I stated flatly. "With those girls?"

Cyan opened his mouth to speak, but I intercepted his words, whatever they would have been.

"You've always been an easy read, Cyan. Had you taken one of the girls from the festival, you'd have boasted about it, not deflected with a quip about my honor."

His chest puffed. "What do you play at?"

Dipping my head faintly in a pose of ease, I discreetly adjusted my hold on my sword. Better he believe I did not see him as a threat in the slightest. "It pleases me to know they escaped your forced presence," I said. "That is all."

"Of what importance does this hold?" The guard stopped circling, and I mimicked him. It was clear his patience was wavering, but he'd yet to reveal any information of use—I needed to know about Rion's involvement in Kaius's death.

"Did your father catch you again, Cyan? Did he step in before you took what you thought was owed to you?"

The brute's nose scrunched, and he bared his teeth beneath the curl of his upper lip.

If Rion's night had been occupied with keeping his son in line, it was unlikely he'd killed my father. The time I'd spent with Evera in the tower, the window of opportunity, was not substantial.

"I suppose you were incorrect, then." I laughed, low and dismissive. "Perhaps you can't wet your cock where you like, not as long as your father is there to scour over your every move."

Eyes widening, Cyan lunged, lashing out with the effects of his emotion.

I countered, dodging, and he withdrew with a fine red line on his cheek. He raised his hand to the fresh cut, and blood smeared the side of his face. He snarled.

"You've told me all I need to know," I stated, voice low.

Cyan's eyes narrowed, the flicker of a thought crossing his face. He'd been outsmarted, and he knew it. Even as the draw of his brows suggested he was unsure of the manner of information I'd gained from him.

"You will die on this night." I lowered my chin. "And your death will be a mark of the life you lived, of your predilections."

The time for conversing had ended. Even Cyan, in his boisterousness, knew when to hold his tongue and when to fight. This was the time for fighting.

Beneath the moon, in the small clearing of the wood behind the inn, our movements mimicked the sway of the branches. Our breaths became an extension of the wind that moved around and through our lungs. Despite the impulse that had led me to draw Cyan out into the night, I realized that I had always known, in some part of my mind, that he and I were meant to wage this battle. We'd circled one another always, and taking his life seemed like my fate. My first blooding had set me on this path, and my honor demanded I see this through.

With precise movements and quick reactions, we parried until everything beyond the pressed circle of grass and clay earth we flattened ceased to exist. The glint of metal sparked as swords clashed. The strikes that narrowly missed their mark sent blood pounding in my ears, reminding me that I was alive in this moment, and that any breath could be my last. Whether moments or hours had passed, I could not say. The passage of time eluded me, as I suspected it did for Cyan as well. This was how we were trained—to be present in the moment of battle. Honed attention and a stillness of mind.

Though I was tiring, hatred urged me on. Disgust for who he was and for the things he'd done gave me purpose. I lashed out and, sides heaving, Cyan responded too slowly. The blade ripped through leather and cloth, eliciting a curse from him as he hugged his side.

Breathing fogging, we held each other's eyes.

Though he was wounded, I was as well. We both bore marks to show our exchanges, and we grew weaker from loss of blood and drain of energy. I withdrew several steps, and a wicked grin twisted Cyan's face.

If he believed me to be surrendering, he was about to be disappointed.

I sheathed my sword, but before Cyan could advance, I withdrew a metal rod from behind my back where it stuck out of a mound of dirt in the garden. Some unfinished project of Maerel's. It wasn't the honed spear used in bloodings at the capital, but it would suffice and would communicate the same message.

Cyan blanched, eyes widening as he saw my new weapon. Re-centering himself, he set his jaw and adjusted his grip on his sword.

I moved to him. This would need to be finished quickly. Even if my swordsmanship outmatched his, I was at a great disadvantage with nothing but an old rod to mark the shame of his actions.

I lunged, aiming for the dip beneath his ribs. When I did, Cyan leaned back and to the side. In my eagerness to end the fight, I misjudged his next move. The rod missed its mark, and Cyan slashed at my exposed torso.

The cut was deep. I perceived that instantly, in a detached sort of way. Vision blurring white at the edges, I stepped backward, the movement unsteady. I braced myself with the rod to keep from falling. Cyan snickered, the sound cruel and dark and victorious. My wound was fatal; I could see it in the glint in his eyes.

Swallowing a knot in my throat, I brought a hand to my side. The slash was horizontal, from above my hip to just beneath my navel. The cloth of my cloak stuck to my body, and the sickly-sweet iron smell of blood filled the air.

I leaned forward, caught in a wave of dizziness. Blood flowed from the wound and splattered the packed dirt. I vomited, and the bitter, foul taste of it lingered in my mouth.

Raising my eyes, I looked at Cyan through the haze of my vision. The puff of his chest spoke of his confidence. The man was a stain on this earth. A disgrace. And if I were to die, I would take him with me. He'd hurt no one else, never again force himself and his seed upon another girl.

Waiting for Cyan to begin his speech, I watched him through hooded eyes.

Just as the edge of unconsciousness threatened, Cyan sheathed his sword. He opened his mouth, boastful arrogance written in the set of his brows and the curve of his lips. *So fucking predictable.*

Before he could speak, I lunged forward and drove the rod into his chest and up through his heart. The muscles in my arms jerked, strained, and I crumpled at the effort of the movement as my legs gave beneath me. On my knees, I braced the rod up at an angle despite my clouded vision.

Impaled, Cyan grasped the rough metal; his lips worked at wordless gurgles. His blood splattered my face as gravity propelled him toward me, further embedding the rod. I blinked the burning red from my eyes.

My arms shook as I released the rod, pushing it to the side.

Using the last of my strength, I rolled to avoid his form falling atop me. The motion sent heat searing through my veins even as the wound itself had gone numb.

I stared into Cyan's eyes as we lay side by side. Two men of the guard, brothers in that right, dying at each other's hands. My breath came in rasps, and even the clawing of my beast weakened within me. My right eye burned, and red smeared my vision. Blinking, I tried to clear Cyan's blood from it, needing to watch him die.

When the rise and fall of his chest ceased, I lay encompassed by the moment. In his empty eyes, I saw the man I killed all those years ago for my first blooding. I'd wiped the crooked grin from him as well. Such men had no honor, no values, and were worse than my monster.

I rolled to my back. Stars speckled white and silver in the endless inky darkness above me. There was such a vastness to the sky. It made me feel small in that moment, somehow insignificant. It was a horrid, sinking feeling to experience death's calling, its promise a hiss on the wind.

Though weariness tugged at me, I held to that hopeless emptiness. "I'm sorry, brother," I rasped to the solitude. To Harlan and to Thatch. "I'm—"

"Neirin!"

The call of my name grounded me, brought me back from the verge of relenting to the endless sleep. With great effort, I turned my head. The cool caked clay beneath my cheek lent a chilling and a belonging. The inevitability of returning to the earth.

Through hazed, delayed vision, I made out the form of Calix some thirty paces away, barely detectable among the shadows of the trees. The boy held his gloved hand to his face, covering his nose, though even then, I was certain the pull would be intense for him. Had he been near all along, waiting for me to return to the inn? Or had he distanced himself and returned only at the irresistible scent of my blood?

The following moments came in fractured clips and sensations. My feet prickled in my boots. Numbness consumed me. Even my lips tingled. There was a dizzying rush of movement, and then the world no longer lay horizontal.

Maerel held me up, bracing herself under one of my arms, struggling to manage my weight, slurring curses into the night.

From a distant place, I drew strength and forced my legs to hold my weight, even as I relied heavily on the innkeeper's offered support.

In the next moment of recollection, my eyes focused on the crimson splatter of blood on the steps that led up from the kitchen to my room at the inn. Another curse, a rush of dizziness. Then I was alone in my room, sprawled out on the bed. The flickering light of the lantern cast shadows on the ceiling and walls. Stretched, elongated, lacking any computable form.

"Harlan—"

A woman's voice responded, though I could not make sense of the words. They held no importance.

The crackling life of a fire in the hearth dispelled the shadows across the ceiling, and I contemplated the concept of death. Though I knew I was not immortal, my quick healing had spared me more than once. This was beyond that. Where was the stillness of death's approach I'd heard so much about? The release of worries, of burdens? Without sound, I choked on the emotion, on the weight of all I was leaving behind. Would Harlan's fate mirror my own? Had I failed him just as I had failed Thatcher? It was almost too much, more painful than the wound that drained my life with each breath. Evera, at least, would be safer without me. Wed to a man she held no desire to marry, yes, but safe at least. Bitterness soured my throat, and I pushed the thought aside, for it too was too painful, in a different sense.

Vaguely, I was aware of the door closing and of the hollowing aloneness.

I lay on a quilt, its pillowed surface beneath the prickle of my fingers too sensitizing. Gasping for breath, I drew a hand under my cloak and shirt. Slick and sticky blood pasted the cloth to my skin. My fingers found my wound, a cavity of broken flesh, and I shuddered. Each beat of my heart pulsed in my ears, and a slippery, heated sack of flesh protruded from the crevasse. At the touch of it, my head spun, and panic choked at my throat.

Withdrawing my hand, I squeezed my eyes closed as tears welled. My body trembled as I cried. There was no physical pain, at least. Though the clutch of regrets, of failures, of remorse harbored greater suffering than anything of touch or sensation.

Wheezing, I lay in the darkness, terrified of the unknown. And from a deep, distant place, I detected my monster's presence. Not a clawing, for he had no fight left either. It came as a quiet voice. A goodbye.

With no reason left to fear him, I released my power to him on a breath. And when the shift came, the heat was liquid warmth. My bones didn't crack or shatter; they swelled and shifted with a strange fluidity. And then everything went white.

31

—————

EVERA

"THANK YOU, CHILD." A warm smile graced Leighis's lips as I handed him a mug of fresh tea. "Lemongrass?"

Nodding, I returned his warmth, though it didn't reach my eyes. The contentment I'd felt in Neirin's presence was soured by the tension that hung in the room.

Behind the shop's counter, Aureus sat with a stern set to his jaw, going over the day's sales. An old brass lantern illuminated the papers before him and cast shadows across his face. Creases lined his brow, and when he flipped through the pages, he sighed from time to time or pinched the bridge of his nose between two fingers.

After leaving Neirin at the inn, I'd ridden Sorrel a few paces behind Aureus back to the shop where he'd sent me in to make tea for Leighis while he returned our mare to the pasture. He'd wanted space to clear his head, and I understood that. Aureus had always been thoughtful, nearly to a fault. Always in his mind, worrying, thinking six steps ahead. The problem was that he could never see what was right in front of him. And when faced with suddenness, he struggled to make decisions.

Now, settled into the normalcy of routine, an air of unsaid words hung around us like a thick fog.

Leighis's touch drew my attention, and I lowered my gaze to meet his searching eyes. His thumb trailed the wraps at my wrist, and when he spoke, he did so on a hush so only I would hear. "Tell him."

If I told Aureus of the bond Neirin and I shared, would it change his stand? Was I ready for that conversation? Was I ready to choose a path and commit to it? In Neirin's arms, the decision seemed so simple. But nothing about the situation we were in was simple. Though we'd not discussed it beyond Neirin's statement in the pasture, I knew the time would come when he would need to leave, compelled to protect the brother he hardly spoke of. There were still many questions that needed to be addressed.

Unease trickled down my spine and, not for the first time tonight, a dark murkiness hazed the edges of my mind.

The doorknob rattled, jolting me. A fist followed—hard, insistent— and the old wood creaked beneath the blows. Aureus set his jaw but made no move to respond, so I went to the door. Premonition hollowed me as I crossed the room, each step weighted heavier than the last.

"Evera," Aureus hissed.

Did he sense it too? Or was it only the day's events that put him on edge? The image of him standing silhouetted against the fields and the dying sun, unmoving, came back to me. The same fear shone in his eyes now. Pulling my brows, I turned back to the door.

"Evera." The voice that called my name this time was youthful, familiar, and hastened.

My heart leapt. *Calix.* The foreboding intensified and settled over me like a heavy woolen blanket. Without hesitation, I unlatched the door. The panic in the boy's eyes justified the thundering of my heart.

Swallowing, I braced myself. "What happened?"

"Neirin is dying." His voice cracked, sounding small, frail, frightened.

For a moment, I felt nothing but the clench of fear. It consumed me.

Arms wrapped around my shoulders, and I succumbed to the familiarity of my brother's embrace.

Regaining myself with a choked breath, I wiped a tear with the back of my hand and pushed from Aureus's arms.

I was distantly aware of Aureus questioning Calix while I gathered the bag of emergency medical supplies from beneath the counter. My body flushed with heat, a knot formed in my throat, and my vision blurred as tears threatened, but I held to the necessity of composure. All I had were my abilities, and they were useless if I allowed myself to crumble. Calix was only a boy. Perhaps it was not as bad as he—

"Evera, stop." Aureus reached for my hand. "I will go."

"No, Aureus." I spun on him, my teeth gritted to keep them from chattering. "No." The word cracked in my throat and came out broken, splintering with the weight of everything I couldn't hold back, and my brother's eyes gentled.

"Let her go," Leighis said.

Aureus turned his attention to our mentor, but Leighis's permission meant nothing to me in this moment. Using my brother's distraction, I broke from his grasp and rushed to the doorway. I took Calix's hand in mine and tugged him after me as we broke into the chill of the night.

The brisk air hit me with a start, and I gasped, trembling. It held me in place as the shop's bell rang and the door closed behind me, the cusp between emotion and reaction a looming presence.

The small hand in mine tightened its grip and pulled, encouraging me forward, forcing me from my stupor.

"This way," the boy said, leading me at a quickened pace

between a short cropping of forest that backed up to the inn. With each step, the slick darkness within my chest thickened until it grew overwhelming. It was not a premonition, but the distant call of Neirin's bond. Of his pain.

A figure lay in a clearing beyond the garden, a formidable staff jutting from its form. I brought a hand to my chest, heart thundering, and choked on my panic. The only thing that kept me from falling to my knees was the presence of the bond, the rush of sensations, the promise that, for now at least, Neirin still drew breath.

"That's not him," Calix said.

"I know," I replied, the words broken, too soft.

Tearing my eyes away, I went with Calix to the back entrance of the inn. The thick knot in my throat made breathing difficult, and when the boy opened the door to reveal the scene within the inn's kitchen, my head spun. Clutching tight to the bag with one hand, I held the boy's hand with the other and steadied myself. Crimson pooled and streaked the floor. No one could survive so much blood loss.

As the thought came to me, a pulse of energy filled the air. The hand in mine grew sweaty, and Calix panted.

The boy's lapse caught my attention, and I squeezed his hand. "Where is he?"

Calix trembled. The current of magic ebbed and flowed around us as we followed the crimson path through the kitchen that led to the steps. Splattering droplets and smears where a boot had dragged marked the way.

I managed a brisk inhale and ascended the stairs, keeping Calix's hand in mine. His grip was slack now, as his small body fought itself. Was it Neirin's blood that affected him in this way?

At the top of the steps, I stilled.

Maerel sat atop a chaise at the end of the hall, her eyes brimming and her hand cupped to her mouth. The healer in me recognized the signs of shock instantly, and I turned my gaze from her to Calix, the weight of my responsibility settling over me.

Leading Calix to the chaise, I instructed him to sit. Time was running out, and the awareness of it stole across my skin like the breath of death itself. Digging through my bag, I withdrew a vile of dwale.

"Drink." I pressed it to Calix, whose eyes still flickered. If Maerel noticed, she made no indication of it.

Turning to her, I braced my hands on her shoulders. "Can I trust you?"

The woman blinked and met my gaze. There was no way to know if she would run to the garrison or if she would otherwise betray the situation. But there was nothing that could be done for it, and time was slipping away. She nodded.

"This is not the time to succumb to shock," I told her. "You are stronger than that. We must be stronger than that."

A clarity came over her, and as she firmed her features and nodded again, she took my hand and stood. Wiping at her eyes with the back of her hand, she sucked in a breath. Was it only seeing death that brought such emotion for her, or did the innkeeper care for Neirin?

"You need to clean the kitchen," I told her. "Can you do that?"

"Yes," she rasped, and brushed past me.

I set my eyes to Calix. He was already yawning as the anesthetic began to take effect.

"Rest," I told the boy, though it was an unnecessary order. He would be unconscious in minutes and sleep deeply through the night.

Drawing a steadying breath, I left the chaise and paced to a solid oak door, the smeared red of a handprint just above the knob. The emotions coursing through the bond were now tangible, physical things, like thick smoke choking out the air or like drowning in the sea. I gripped the handle and turned.

The tang of iron hit me as I stepped into the room. I closed the door quickly behind me, my concerns briefly flitting to Calix and the problems that could arise should the tincture I gave him not be strong enough, should he lose control.

My eyes went to the bed, empty and stained, and again fear threatened to hold me in place.

A snarl from the corner of the room sent a shudder down my spine. I whipped around. The rumble was inhuman.

A trembling breath left my lips as I met the silver eyes of a creature. The figure was curled in the shadows, its teeth pointed and bared. When the warning sound came again, I slowly lowered to my knees.

The fox's ears perked, and its black nose raised, scenting the air.

"It's okay." My tone was gentle, though my heart pounded in my chest.

Cautiously, I shifted forward. This time, the animal gave no defensive reaction. His gaze fell watchful on me, though the lids of his eyes fluttered as if they were too heavy to keep open. With a whimper, his head wavered. Reservations cast aside, I rushed to the animal, catching his head in my lap as he fainted.

I stared down at the silver fox. My hands hovered above his pelt, and in the dim light, I noted the labored rise and fall of his flank.

Whatever I'd been expecting of Neirin's other form, this wasn't it. The animal was nearly double the size of any fox I'd seen before. This was a creature that could kill, one that could rip a man's throat out with its teeth. But Neirin wouldn't hurt me, and neither would his fox. Not with the connection we shared.

With the fox's head in my lap, I lay an arm across him and

ran my fingers through his thick double coat. The outer layer was coarse, but beneath that, his fur was silken and soft. With my other hand, I traced between the ridge of his brows and down his pointed snout, stopping just before his black beaded nose. The creature was remarkable, fierce, stunning, his coat silver and mottled like a full moon, with areas of darker gray and black tipping at his ears, paws, and muzzle.

And he was dying.

Sucking in my bottom lip, I set my eyes to the sack of medical supplies I'd dropped across the room.

"You're going to be okay," I said to the unconscious creature, more as a reassurance to myself than anything else. I needed to push my emotions aside and examine the wound. Carefully, I lowered the fox's head to the floor and retrieved the bag.

When I returned, I lay my palm on the animal's side, and his eyes opened. The humming in my chest was a resonance, a claim. This creature… it was mine. Strong, beautiful, and soulful, somehow, too. If Neirin truly believed the animal to be a monster, I would spend the rest of my days disproving him.

I set my mind to my task, heart clenched. In the light of the hearth, I addressed the wound. Or tried to. Though the pooling blood originated from the animal's torso, I couldn't examine it beneath the thick pelt, matted, slick, and sticky against my fingers.

Choking back my fear, I sat back. My hands shook. I blinked away tears and cupped the animal's face in my palms, stroking the stunning silver fur on his cheeks.

"I need you to give him back to me," I pleaded with the fox, even as I knew asking something of the animal may very well be futile. What else could I do? "I need *him*." The words came on a rasp.

The animal closed his eyes, and I lowered my forehead to his, squinting against my sobs. Heat pooled through my veins, and I held my breath. The blood-streaked fur in my palms shortened until only stubble remained. In my grasp, the structure of the animal's face reformed, bone shifting beneath taut skin. My lungs ached to release, but breathing was impossible. Not until I sensed the shift was complete and I opened my eyes to find Neirin looking back at me through hooded lashes did I let out a gust of air.

"Evera." My name on his tongue was full of emotion, and I trembled through my silent sobs.

"I'm here," I reassured him and kissed his brow. His messy hair stuck to his forehead, and sweat beaded on his skin, leaving it damp and chilled.

"I need—" His words were weak, broken. "My head is faint."

Drawing back enough to address him, my lips quivered. His skin was too pale. He was lying on his side, propped up on one shoulder with his head tilted to me, held in my grasp. I coaxed him down until he rested his head on the floor, then I retrieved a pillow from the bed to make him more comfortable. The gash of his wound was seeping blood faster in this form. It puddled on the wooden boards.

I reached for the medical bag, but Neirin's hand stopped me.

"Evera." His tone was heavy with sorrow. "Just lie with me. Please."

The knot in my throat thickened. I shook my head. "No, I'm going to stitch your wound. You'll be okay."

His thumb trailed the wraps at my wrist, and sickening hatred and remorse boiled within me. I drew from his grasp and ripped the wrappings off, revealing the marks beneath. Tears rolled down my cheeks freely then, and when I met Neirin's eyes, they held such a heavy sadness.

"No healer could fix this, love."

I knew what this was. This was him telling me not to feel guilty for his death. That it was out of my hands.

"No." The word broke. He reached for me, but I brushed him off, returning my attention to the sack and forcing concentration despite the turmoil that clenched down on my heart.

Neirin didn't fight me as I examined the wound. My hands shook as I traced along the gash. The skin gaped, and when his breath shuddered, blood gushed. Withdrawing a sanitized needle from my bag, I snapped a thread between my teeth and attempted to poke the frayed end through the eyelet. The broken edge trembled in my grasp, and tears slid down my jaw, wetting my neck.

"Evera." Neirin's coaxing was weak, his voice tired.

Sucking in a breath, I stilled my sobs and focused all my attention on the thread. I wet the end between my lips and tried again, and when the string threaded, I released the air from my lungs with a shudder.

The amount of blood made it nearly impossible to discern where to begin, so I pulled a quilt from the bed to dab at the wound. Neirin flinched at the touch, and the blood pooled faster. My heart raced.

"Love, please," he gritted out.

Love. I scrunched my nose. I wouldn't let him die. I wouldn't.

Starting at his side above his hip, where the skin parted, I began stitching as Leighis had taught me, as I'd seen him and Aureus do many times. Once the trembling of my hands steadied, I became more confident. Neirin never flinched, his gaze watchful as I worked. Seven stitches in, the wound was wider. I sucked in my lips.

As I tried to pull the skin together, something slipped. With the gush of blood, a slick, swollen knot protruded from his wound, and I dropped the needle, shaking uncontrollably. Leighis had spoken of men in the capital who cut open the bodies of the dead to learn how they worked, who could discern the organs, knew their names, their functions, and where they belonged. Whether something was too swollen, off-colored, or otherwise wrong. But *everything* about this was wrong, and I was no surgeon.

When Neirin offered no remark, I turned my eyes to his face, but he was unconscious. His head lay on the pillow, eyes closed.

"No," I rasped. "No, no, no."

Choking back my tears, I set my jaw and retook the needle. The slickness of the mass slipped between my fingers, but I would not let him die. He could. *Not.* Die.

Fighting the nausea and panic roiling in my gut, I forced the wound shut, pushing back in what shouldn't be out. Everything I was doing was wrong. I was wrong. I couldn't save him.

Blinking through vision blurred by tears, I made the final stitch and secured it as I'd practiced time and again on scraps of cloth. The sharp scent of Neirin's blood filled my nose. It became a tangible taste in the back of my throat as I drew my dagger and cut the thread from the needle. I re-sheathed it, choking on a sob as a fresh wave of emotion coursed over me. Neirin's gentle reprimands had taught me better how to treat my blade. How had that only been hours ago?

I sat back and took in the rough stitching, the messiness of my work. I should have just lain with him as he'd asked. If he never woke again … I sucked in a sharp breath, though that did little to quell my panic. Had I caused his last moments to be miserable when he'd needed comfort most?

Tugging at the blanket beside me, I balled up the blood-soaked portion and tossed that corner over and away from Neirin so that what lay across him was clean and dry.

Checking that the quilt wasn't too close to the fireplace, I curled under it beside Neirin's unconscious form and cradled his head against my breasts. I ran my fingers through his hair and hummed to him, a tune from my childhood that brought back a faint image of my mother.

The quilt draped below his shoulder, revealing the top of his tattoo along his chest and at the base of his neck. I trailed my fingers along the bold black marks to his shoulder. Our bond. He was mine, and I was his. And he was going to die in my arms.

32

———

EVERA

I STOOD IN A FOREST. Pale moonlight cast the wood in monochrome shades of gray, black, and silver. Snow was falling, flecking the frozen dirt and chilling the air. The flakes glittered as they slowly descended.

I wore a thick winter cloak lined with fur that tickled my face, and when I exhaled, my breath fogged. Barefoot, I moved through the trees. They towered around me, their trunks dark and ominous. Drawing nearer to one, I placed my hand on its bark.

Beneath my fingers, a sticky liquid caused me to draw back. Crimson stained my hand, the only color in a world of gray. The tang of iron filled my senses, and I stepped back, vision faltering as the tree before me became the only one left in the woods. Its surface dripped, the substance thick and choking. Blood. Where it met the earth, the snow steamed and began to melt, creating little holes and ravines of red in the otherwise flawless white.

The tree itself was dying, melting into itself, branches warping. Swallowing, I retreated another step and then another, needing to create distance between myself and the formidable sight. Calix's echoing words came back to me, ringing in my ears. *Neirin is dying.*

My back hit something firm, and arms wrapped around my shoulders. Panic flooded me, but the voice in my ear was reassuring, familiar. I turned in Neirin's embrace and gazed into his watchful eyes. They shone like the moon, silver-flecked with stardust.

Alive. He is alive. Isn't he?

Vaguely, I was aware that the scenes before me were unreal, not true, contrived by my imagination.

"Quiet, love." His words were a warning, hushed, and one of his hands cupped my mouth. Blood coated his bare skin, and warmth emanated from him.

My body trembled. When I looked past him, I found us on a hillside with nothing but blanketing snow and hazy skies. His palm over my lips was firm but gentle. In his presence, a formidable sense of security befell me, even as the ominous nature of our surroundings and the intensity of his eyes set my heart racing. Even as I swallowed the knowledge that none of this was real.

Keeping his brace over my mouth, Neirin's other hand lowered. It bunched the cloth of my cloak and drew it up. As he had the night of the festival, he trailed along the scabbard at my thigh. Warmth flooded me, both from his touch and from his acceptance. Pressing my forehead to his chest, I hooded my eyes. I parted my lips to speak, to apologize for not giving him the comfort he'd asked for, for letting myself believe I could fix something that I clearly could not, for causing him more pain. But the warmth of Neirin's hand held my words back.

"Quiet." The command was firmer this time.

A knock on the door stirred me from my dream. My eyes shot open, and I muffled a gasp against the hand clasped over my mouth. Uprooted, I squirmed, but the steady weight above me held me firm to the floor.

Neirin's sharp eyes met mine, and I stilled. Despite the paleness of his complexion, the warmth of life emanated from him. The strength with which he held himself above me alone should not have been possible, yet ... there was magic within him, within his blood. My heart caught and fumbled over itself, and the events of the past hours rushed back to me with more clarity as the haze of my sleep left. The restraint of emotion, the fight for strength, the sureness of loss. I shuddered, wanting nothing more than to be held, to be comforted by him, even though he had been the one to face death and prevail, not I.

His trailing touch at my thigh drew my thoughts briefly back to my dream. One word remained, an echo in my mind. *Quiet.*

The rapping at the door came again, and Neirin withdrew my dagger and rose to his knees, one between my thighs, and the other at my side. When he addressed me with his eyes once more, I nodded subtly and he removed his hand from my mouth.

The deep burgundy of dried blood coated his body, streaking the line of his jaw and beneath his cheekbones, where I'd held his face. The strands of his hair curled about his ears in crimson-tinted clumps.

Rising to my elbows, my gaze fell to his wound. Angry, swollen flesh tugged at the stitches, and in areas , bruising showed in deep purple hues. Despite this, the threads held, even as Neirin's heavy breaths swelled through his chest and to his belly. The raggedness of his breathing spoke of the pain he still felt, though I sensed a complete absence of sensations through our bond. His gaze was focused and intent.

Following it, I turned my head to face the door. The sound came again, and bracing his weight on a shaking arm, Neirin pushed to his feet. A muscle at his jaw flexed, and he wavered momentarily before stepping to the wall to steady himself. Head hung, he panted and adjusted his hold on the dagger. When he raised his gaze to the door again, determination lined the set of his brows. Using the wall to support himself, he moved away from me, his steps creaking on the wooden floorboards.

The knocking came again. Neirin opened the latch and swung open the door in a fluid movement, standing without the support of the wall, and any prior trace of weakness vanished. His was the pose of a man accustomed to withstanding a great deal of pain, to holding himself as a wall of defense despite it. My heart caught at his strength, and at the implications of what he'd been through in his life.

"You're not dead." Maerel's statement came on a breath. Shock and perhaps relief, too.

Grunting, Neirin stepped back and lowered the blade. The tension in the air settled with the motion. He returned to the wall and braced himself against it, the effects of his brief efforts showing more clearly now as his breath came on a shudder and fresh red blood trickled from his wound.

"I am grateful to see you, too, Maerel," Neirin huffed. The edge of wit in his tone brought me fully to, and I stood, my muscles sore from sleeping on the hard ground.

"You need to sit down," I said as I went to him, my voice raw.

The innkeeper's gaze trailed down Neirin's body unabashedly as I approached, sending a prick of— It wasn't quite jealousy, for I knew that Neirin belonged to me alone, but something similar. Something inside of me that snarled, that raked, as deep and primal as the old magic that marked us.

No, I'm being absurd. Maerel is likely only gazing down to his wound. And what does it matter anyway?

Huffing irritation, I tucked my head under one of Neirin's arms, allowing him to lean on me as I guided him across the room. The amount of weight he put on me revealed his pain, the truth of his weakness. Yet still, he'd gone to the door to defend me. Something in my chest constricted at the realization, and when I helped ease him into a chair and covered his lap with the bloodied quilt, I kissed him. It was brief, a brush of lips, but full of meaning.

"Thank you," I said.

Neirin's brows drew together, but before he could question me, Maerel appeared at the bed, calling me to help with the sheets.

When all the soiled blankets lay in a pile, Maerel bundled them and left the room. She came back a few minutes later with fresh bedding and, on her next trip, a pitcher of warm water and a bowl with a stack of clean rags.

The innkeeper busied herself with mopping the floors, cursing under her breath, and lecturing Neirin as she did. Despite the state she'd been in earlier, Maerel's quick tongue had returned. I didn't share friendship with the innkeeper, but I did hold a level of trust with her. It had been Maerel who'd first found Aureus and me in her garden all those years ago after Mother had died. She had been the one to take us to Leighis, where we were nursed back to health. It was because of Maerel that Aureus and I came to have a home. There was something about such a situation that created a connection between people, even if they did not often walk the same paths or form a close bond.

When I'd finished redressing the bed, I walked back to Neirin and touched the back of my hand to his forehead to test for fever. His skin was still cool. Almost too cool.

He drew me into his lap by my waist.

"I don't want to hurt you," I cautioned.

"You won't hurt me," Neirin said, lowering his cheek to my forehead.

The comfort I found in his embrace was welcoming, and I relaxed against him, soothed by the steady thrum of his heart. Adrenaline faded, and my immediate concerns over Neirin's state eased. The weight of exhaustion tugged at me, and I released a long and heavy breath.

"You're about as much help as that routier of yours is," Maerel retorted as she wiped a bloodied handprint from the wall. "Stays in my inn free of charge, is out with you all day, kills a man in my garden." She was rambling, but Neirin flinched at her words nonetheless. I suspected the innkeeper took to sarcasm and quips as a way to soothe and conceal her true emotions. It was something I understood, recognized, and could empathize with.

"Has anyone come looking for me?" Neirin asked. I placed one of my hands over his in a silent offering of support.

Maerel met his eyes and sighed. "No, not yet. I cleaned the kitchen, but I'm not dragging that body out to the river for you. Someone will find him."

"As they must." Neirin's response came without hesitation, his words flat yet laced with abhorrence. "Thank you, Maerel, for what you've done."

She nodded. "There's nothing left to lead them to you, but come morning, I suspect someone will start asking questions around town. They'll ask if I know anything."

The hand beneath mine tensed. "What will you tell them?"

Tossing the rag she held over her shoulder, Maerel ran a hand through the loose strands of hair that fell in front of her brows. "Did that man deserve what came to him?"

"He did."

Maerel set her eyes to the hearth. "Tomorrow, you will explain." Turning her eyes back to him, she narrowed them. "No more lies, Lark."

"Neirin," he corrected.

I stroked the back of his hand with my thumb, knowing this was hard for him.

Nodding, Maerel gathered her things. "I will cover for you. Get some rest. You're both safe here."

The door closed behind her, and Neirin coaxed me from his lap. He stood, groaning as he did, and latched the door. Blood trickled from his wound, and the heaviness in his eyes and the paleness of his complexion spoke of his state.

"You've lost too much blood," I told him. "Sit back down. Do you need help?"

Trailing a hand along the wall, he made his way back to the chair. "No, I'm alright."

Pouring heated water from the pitcher into the ceramic bowl Maerel had provided, I scoffed. "You are not alright, Neirin." I gritted my teeth. "You should be—"

"Dead. I know. I should be."

I set my jaw. Instead of giving him a response, I soaked one of the clean rags and wrung it out. The cloth steamed, and as water trickled down my arms, I became aware of how cold the room was. I would add logs to the fire after getting Neirin cleaned, bandaged, and into bed. No, the fire would be out by then. I sighed and set the rag back down. Pacing to the hearth, I added a log and poked the embers.

"Why aren't you? Dead?" I asked.

"Because you saved my life."

I turned back to him, creasing my brow. "You shouldn't have survived that," I said plainly, though the words choked in my throat.

Returning to the ceramic bowl at the table beside Neirin's chair, I wet and wrung out the rag again and wiped at the streaks on his face. The crackling fire cast a warm yellow light across him, sharpening his features. A part of me remained hollow, afraid. Sniffling back my emotion, I cast my eyes aside.

"It is my blood. It heals me," Neirin said, though I knew that already. Concern hardened his expression. "Where is Calix?"

"Calix is fine. I've given him a tincture to make him sleep." A knot formed in my throat. "Neirin, I thought—" Despite my efforts, the tears that threatened before broke past the barrier, and one slid down my cheek.

Neirin hushed me gently. He took the rag from my hand and

returned it to the side table, hanging it over the ceramic bowl. Cupping my cheek in his palm, he sought my eyes. "I am alright now. Because of you."

To the soft crackling of the fire, I took my time cleaning Neirin's body, wiping him free of the reminders of the night. When I was through, he brought a clean cloth to my cheek, then to my hands. The tenderness of it released the last of my fortitude, and I released a trembling breath.

By the time we finished, the flame in the hearth was again burning low. I added another few logs and hugged my arms, cold in the light cotton gown I wore. My dress was ruined. It lay in a pile with Neirin's clothes. Maerel had left a gown for me on the dresser alongside a pair of soft, worn pants for Neirin.

He stood with his back to me as he pulled the dark pants up and tied the band at his waist. When he turned, he tilted his head slightly, and the corners of his lips curved up, revealing his dimple. My heart leapt. How close had I come to never seeing his smile again, to losing what I'd only just found, what I was still learning the depth of?

"Do not overdo it," I told him, and returned to his side to help him to the bed.

After cleaning his wound and before we'd dressed, I'd wrapped it. The blood loss seemed to be under control. Color had returned to his face, and though his eyes were still tired, he admittedly looked much better than he had only an hour ago.

With my aid, Neirin sat at the edge of the bed. He leaned back and lay with a sigh. Desperately, I wanted to join him, curl to his chest, take comfort in the steady thrum of his heartbeat beneath my ear. Yet I hesitated. Was it presumptuous of me to assume I could stay with him? To share the bed with him? It seemed like such a foolish thing to worry over after all we'd shared. But in my state of mental exhaustion, I fumbled over the concept.

"Please stay."

Blinking to clear my thoughts, I rubbed my eyes with my knuckles. "Are you sure?"

"I don't want to be alone tonight."

There was vulnerability in his words. My heart flipped, and with one last glance at the fire to assure myself it was going strong, I climbed onto the bed. Crawling forward like a child, I collapsed into the soft blankets with a grunt. Neirin huffed with his amusement. I let out a weary breath, and he drew me against his chest, pulling a quilt over us.

"Rest," he said and kissed my forehead.

Curling into his warmth, I yawned. My head fit into the crook of his arm in a way that felt so incredibly natural. Right. Like we were made for each other.

Trailing my fingers over the lightly raised lines of the scars left by Astraea, I hummed. "How does no one know about the Queen? About her messengers— and what they are?"

"To my knowledge, only the children and I know. They will not speak of it because they rely on her, on the blood—*my blood* —she supplies them with."

A lump formed in my throat, and I retraced one of the faint branching lines. "Is this truly the only way to aid the children? It … it makes me sick to think of what happened to you and what is *still* happening to them."

There must be another way.

Neirin fell quiet. The steady rise and fall of his chest lulled me. "I cannot attest to her conscience, nor can I make claims as to what is right or wrong in this. It is complex and, in truth, it seems there is no good solution. Though I despise the woman, I believe in her mind she considers what she is doing to be right."

"How did an Alidian become a Queen? How did she keep the secret so long?"

"Astraea comes from one of the most influential houses in the western lands. Her marriage to the King was arranged for political reasons. While I do not know all the details of her past,

I am aware that great wealth can afford significant discretion. When she came to the capital, my mother accompanied her as a lady's maid. No doubt her source of blood before I was born."

Nuzzling into Neirin's neck, I sighed.

"I must tell you something else," Neirin said, a sound of hesitation in his voice. "I must tell you who my brother is, who my father was." He swallowed, and I remained quiet, letting him speak. "My brother's name is Harlan. And my father..." He released a breath. "My father was King Kaius."

I sat up, all weariness gone, and gawked down at him. "You mean to say you are a prince? That is"—I shook my head—"not believable."

The corners of his lips quirked before laughter spilled out. The sound was rich, came from deep in his chest, and danced in his eyes. The dimple on his cheek warmed my heart.

"I'm not a prince," he said when his laughter ebbed. "As I told you before, I have no name. I'm a bastard. I have no right to the throne, and I don't want it. It belongs to my brother."

"You are being truthful?"

"I am, Evera," he said, the seriousness returning to his features. "Lie back down."

I curled against him again. "None of this feels real. Feels possible."

"It is a lot," he agreed.

Trying to piece things together, I twisted a curl of Neirin's hair with my finger. "Your mother, then, she was the King's mistress?"

"Yes. My mother was like me, a shifter. She carried the blood of the gods. Before I met you and learned of the bonds, I didn't know what she and my father shared. Though it was evident that he grieved for her even after all these years. I understand why now. They were mates." Neirin nuzzled the top of my head. "Your mentor spoke of infertility. Does that mean Harlan ..."

"Harlan is the late King's son. Or, at least, I have no reason to believe he isn't. The infertility only affects shifters. Just as I could have a child without you, you could not have one without me. Your father, being human, would have been able to have a child outside of his bond, would have been able to have a child with Astraea."

He hummed thoughtfully, as if my explanation resolved all questions. I huffed a laugh.

"What amuses you?" he asked, tone lighter as he pressed a kiss to my head.

"The absurdity of this all," I answered. "Each time I learn something about you, you become more elusive, more ... impossible."

"Impossible?"

"Yes," I said flatly.

"I do not mean to be elusive." He stroked his thumb at my shoulder. "But I understand why you would feel that way. It is fair."

Sighing, I gazed out the window. Only the murky blackness of night and the shadows of branches and leaves were visible through the glass panes.

"What of the man in the garden?" I asked. Though absolutely everything about what Neirin had just said was life-altering, what I needed to understand most was his character.

Quiet befell us. Embers popped and crackled in the hearth, and against the windows, a faint patter announced the start of rain.

"You saw him?"

Clenching my jaw, I nodded into the crook of his neck.

"And do you know what it means when a man is executed in such a way?"

The knot in my throat returned, thick and choking as images of the rod impaling the man through the chest came to my mind. "No."

"That man—" Neirin cut himself off. "He took girls, forced them. That is why his body must be found. It's a small penance for those he hurt. To be impaled as he is, is a mark that tells who he was as a man, what he died for."

"Like the other man you spoke of? Back in the stable?"

"The man I killed for my blooding? Yes. Such men don't deserve to live."

Outside the windows, the rain picked up, and a wind howled, echoing through the chimney. My fingers returned to tracing the faint lines of Neirin's scars. "I thought perhaps you'd discovered the assassin."

"No," Neirin confessed. "I considered his father, the commander, but now"—he wet his lips—"I am left without any reasonable suspect. It will be harder for my brother to take my word, I presume, if I cannot reveal the assassin."

"But you must return regardless, yes?"

"Yes. If someone is after the throne, Harlan's life may lie in the balance. I cannot abandon him."

"I understand," I said. "I would risk my life for my brother as well." And that's what it would come to for Neirin—risking his life. To save a King.

33

NEIRIN

Sunlight streamed through the windows, stirring me from my sleep. It was early morning, and the fire in the hearth was nothing but coals. My left arm tingled, numb, tucked beneath Evera just as it was when I fell asleep. Our fingers were intertwined, and the marks of our bonds lay parallel.

Though the room held a faint chill, Evera's body was warm beside me. I pulled the quilts up higher with my free hand so they cocooned us. With her in my arms like this, it felt like she was mine—just as I was hers. And would always be hers.

But what of Harlan? Fate and the cruelness of love and loss tugged me in two directions, wore me down, and strained at my soul.

Pushing aside my thoughts, I brushed my thumb against Evera's cheek. The curls of her hair framed her face, so peaceful in her dreams. I studied the slope of her nose and the soft pout of her lips. The gown she wore hung off one shoulder, revealing countless little speckles that matched the ones across the bridge of her nose. I could kiss each one and still not have my fill of her.

Evera's chest rose heavily, and she cuddled into me, waking. I kissed her temple. "Good morning, love."

She looked up at me through fluttering lashes, her eyes stunning this close. They reminded me of a pond I visited once in the western lands, its surface so tranquil and flat that it mirrored everything above it. Willows surrounded them, their sweeping branches painting the sanctuary in tones of blue and green. Perhaps one day I could take Evera there. Again, sadness clenched at my belly, the weight of our situation an ever-present cloak over us.

"Love?" She blinked sleep from her eyes and stifled a yawn. "You called me that last night, too."

The corners of my lips turned up. My mate was bold. "Do you not like when I call you that?"

Rising to her palms, bracing herself above me, she held my eyes, studying, contemplating. The ginger waves of her hair fell over her shoulder. There was such brilliance in her, such cunning and wit. I waited for her retort.

But her tone was sober when she spoke. "It is not something to say lightly."

My heart flipped. She was asking if I loved her.

Cupping her cheek in my palm, I studied her face. The early light of dawn poured into the room at an angle. It caught in her hair and lashes, illuminating the fire within her.

"I love you, Evera."

She wet her lips, and her eyes betrayed her reservation. I rose to my shoulders, cringing as the motion tightened my core and pulled at the stitches of my wound. Moving my hand to the back of her neck, I drew her lips to mine. If she was not ready to return the words, I didn't want her to. The kiss was brief but full of meaning. When I withdrew, I held her eyes and she smiled. One day she would tell me too.

A shout from outside broke the moment, and fear trickled through the bond.

"They've found him," Evera said on a hush.

"Do you trust me?" I asked, a knot in my throat.

After a brief hesitation, Evera nodded, and my heart leapt.

"I will keep you safe. Nothing will happen to you as long as I live." My words were a promise and a reminder of my fractured life.

"And what of you?" There was unease in her tone; it seeped into me. The voices outside grew in number, and a heaviness weighed me down. "What will happen if they take you? Will they—" Her voice wavered, broke.

Instead of answering, I kissed her again. No response would ease her worries. I would not lie to her. So I kissed her like it was the last time, and when she opened her mouth to me, I deepened it, intertwining our tongues and taking in all of her. Giving her all of me. When the kiss broke, she was breathless, but at least she was smiling.

Leaving her in bed, I went to the window. Outside, the soldiers from the capital gathered around Cyan's body. A few local soldiers stood beside Aaron and the garrison commander. In the rays of dawn, the metal rod jutting out of the fallen guard was a formidable mark facing the rising sun.

Evera rose and came to stand with me. She hugged my arm and rested her cheek against my bicep. My heart clenched at the position I'd put her in.

Turning from the window, I wrapped her in my arms, and she nuzzled into my chest. The stitches beneath my bandages itched when her body moved against me.

"Can you remove the stitches?" I asked.

Evera studied me with a crease in her brows. I traced the lines with my thumb, smoothing them.

"Not for at least a week—"

I shook my head. "Will you check them?"

She nodded and moved from my arms. The absence of her warmth sent a chill down my spine. When she returned with her bag in hand, she set it down and found the end of my wrap.

I remained still as she removed the bandage; her touch at my chest, torso, and sides was light. And the sight of her before me, the way her gown swept over her shoulder and revealed her neck and the upper swell of one of her breasts ... I clenched my jaw.

"Does it hurt?" She raised her eyes to mine, with concern tugging at her brows. The bandage, stripped down enough to reveal a red stain on the cloth, trailed to the ground.

Releasing a breath, I sought constraint, calm. "No, it does not hurt." My words came out thicker than I intended, and I swallowed.

A grin curled up Evera's lips, and she hooked one of her hands at the band of my pants. Rising to her toes, she spoke against my lips. "I can feel your emotions too, Neirin."

"That is valuable insight." I swallowed the knot in my throat.

Evera stifled a laugh.

I raised a brow and huffed at her reaction, though in truth I was grateful for the lightness it brought.

"Temptress," I teased.

She shrugged, not denying it, and turned her attention back to my bandages.

Once they were removed, she addressed the wound with a look of puzzlement, trailing her index finger just above the slash. Though the skin remained swollen, the bruising had dissipated overnight, and the familiar discomfort that came with healing told me that if the thread was not removed soon, it would become embedded.

"When I was a boy, I cut open my leg climbing in the apple trees," I explained. "The castle surgeon stitched the gash, and when I returned five days later to have it evaluated, he had to recut the wound to remove the threads."

Shaking her head, Evera nodded to the bed. "Lie down," she instructed and went to the nightstand to retrieve her dagger.

I lay back with my legs hanging over the side of the bed.

"Do not fidget." Evera crawled atop the bed and sat next to me on her knees.

Placing my hands beneath my head, I grinned up at her. "I'll be good," I promised, voice husky.

Scoffing, Evera took the tip of the blade and caught the end of the thread. Though the pressure was uncomfortable and the swollen skin still tender, I held still as she discarded the blade on the quilts and turned her attention back to the threads.

"Evera," I spoke her name to draw her eyes to mine, then pointedly tilted my head, gesturing.

When her glance turned to the unsheathed blade, she huffed through her nose. "You are insufferable."

"Might I remind you that you cut me with that very—" A flash of hot concentrated pain made me snarl as Evera tugged at the thread. I narrowed my eyes but held my tongue, and the corners of her lips turned up in amused satisfaction.

Humming, she looked up at me once through her lashes before setting back to her task, gentler this time as she worked the remaining threads, cutting sections as needed to make the removal easier.

As her fingers moved with nimble confidence, I found myself enthralled by her. Not just by her beauty—though that, in my eyes, was unmatched—but by her resilience and bravery. Not only had she saved my life, she'd known how to handle Calix with only the barest of information about his condition. She'd aided me without knowledge of the components that had led to Cyan's death, and did not question me until we lay in bed, until all was cared for. The words held in my throat, certain as I was that they would not be enough, would not express my feelings to their fullness.

Whatever lay ahead, I could not resent fate for the time it allowed me with her. These would be the moments I thought back to when death came for me. Whether that be in a fortnight or less, or, should life be kind to me, in old age.

I would cherish her for as long as I was given.

34

EVERA

"Stay here," Neirin instructed, his sturdy hand at my waist as we stood in the inn's kitchen at the base of the stairs. He wore the simple breeches he'd slept in and a loose cotton shirt Maerel had left outside the door, and I wore one of her dresses. It was plain and hung a bit too short.

Nodding, I stole a quick kiss. The silver of his eyes shone, and when he spoke, his words were full of depth.

"You're the most incredible thing that's ever happened to me. You know that?"

What response could I give to that? The fire crackled in the hearth, and I smiled wistfully. Instead of replying, I wet the pad of my thumb and wiped a streak of ash from above his brows. The coals of the fire were all we had to disguise his hair, and though it did darken it to a dusky ebony-gray, a better solution would be needed. Walnut shells could be used to produce a dye, though the thought of permanently altering the stunning natural silver seemed a crime. It would grow out, though.

A man's voice in the other room, at the bar, drew Neirin's attention, and his hand left my side. A feeling of slick unease trickled through the bond as Neirin left me, hesitating only briefly before pushing through the split kitchen door and leaving me alone.

"What is this about?" Neirin's tone, firm but not disrespectful, floated to me from the other room. I stepped closer to the door, careful to stay quiet and out of sight.

"A man of the guard traveling through here has been killed behind your inn," the man said to Maerel.

"No one has acted suspiciously," Maerel said. "If I knew something, I would tell you. It's fair to suspect whoever killed the man has left town already, no?" Her words were clipped, irritated. The innkeeper was a convincing liar.

The man grunted. "And what of you? Where were you last night?"

"With me," Maerel said, tone heavy with implication. "Kept me up all night. I doubt he heard anything either. I'm not quiet."

Heat flushed my face, and I sucked in a breath. Though I understood the reasoning for her words, they still stung. Neirin was mine. Only mine.

"Is that true?"

Neirin's response was nearly as convincing as Maerel's. "You don't think I'm sticking around here just for the cheap whiskey, do you?"

My heart sank.

I peered through the gap in the doors. The innkeeper's arm was wrapped around Neirin's waist, and his arm rested casually across her shoulders. Maerel reached up to him, and he kissed her. The air from my lungs left me in a rush, and I shut my eyes, leaning heavily against the wall.

The man, still out of my line of sight, dismissed himself. A moment later, the heavy front doors of the inn closed with a creak. Fire fueled me, and I left the concealment of the kitchen. Neirin turned to me and backed up as I pushed him against the bar.

I clenched my fists and set him with a stern expression,

resisting the urge to strike at his chest. Knowing such an action was uncalled for, still, I huffed, my emotions getting the better of me.

Beside us, Maerel laughed, and I turned my anger to her. Neirin's arm wrapped around my waist, and he pulled me against him, kissing the top of my hair. Damn him, I was trying to be angry.

"Are you jealous, love?" His words held a curl of amusement.

They were both teasing me. I set my jaw.

"Don't be upset with him. He was only playing along. It was important that Aaron believed our story," Maerel offered. "Though I will admit, I've wanted to kiss that man of yours since the day he walked into my kitchen naked."

That planted an entirely new image in my mind. Turning in Neirin's embrace, I scowled at him, and he grinned, revealing that damned dimple.

"I'm yours," he reassured and brushed my lips with his.

My cheeks flushed. When had I decided I wanted that? To be his. But I did. I swallowed the knot in my throat. It was time to talk to Aureus.

"Walk her home, Neirin. Then we need to talk," Maerel said.

Neirin's smile faded. His chest rose and fell heavily once.

"Do you want me to stay?" I asked him.

Neirin nuzzled against my ear, and the affection of the gesture warmed my heart. It was impossible to resist the truth of it. I was falling for him.

"It's alright," he said, brushing another kiss to my temple. "Your brother is likely worrying about you. Let's get you back."

The brisk scent of fresh rainfall hung in the air as Neirin walked me back to my family's shop. Dew clung to the grass and dripped from the leaves of trees that bordered the road. I held his hand, our fingers interwoven, and he stroked casually with his thumb. Kicking stones into puddles, Calix walked a few paces ahead of us.

"Evera." A gruff voice drew my attention.

Ruairc approached from the market, his brows drawn and his lips a thin line. Neirin's thumb stilled, but he kept his hold on my hand. It was a statement, and, gods, maybe it shouldn't have, but it made my stomach flip. Though he tried to hide it and give me control, there was still a possessiveness to Neirin. Despite myself, I ached for it.

"Where have you been?" Ruairc asked, his gaze avoiding Neirin entirely.

"I spent the night with Hadrian," I told him.

Ruairc's expression sank, and a coil of satisfaction held me at his dejection. But there was a bitterness to it, too. Because, despite his plotting with my brother, Ruairc was a good man. And at one time, we'd been friends.

"Who is this man, Evera?" His question was sharp and laced with judgment.

Any trace of sympathy I felt for him fell away. "It's none of your concern, Ruairc. You don't own me." I met his scowl with my own.

"And he does?"

"Evera belongs to no one," Neirin said, his tone light but assertive, effectively ending the path of conversation. He squeezed my hand reassuringly, and my anger lessened.

The tense set to Ruairc's jaw portrayed the hurt, the loss there. An uncomfortable quiet hung around us, broken after a moment by the distant chime of a bell. I raised my eyes to find Aureus in the doorway of our shop. Relief etched his expression. That was about to change, though. Gods, I was not ready for this conversation.

"I will be at the inn if you need me. I must speak with Maerel. Would you be willing to busy Calix for some time?"

"I can do that," I replied, knowing he only asked in the way he did to assuage me. If it eased Neirin's worries for the boy to stay with me, I could concede. After Calix's intervention the day before, I could no longer deny his value; he had made an excellent guardian.

I rose to my toes and pressed a kiss to Neirin's lips, uncaring of our audience. It was a goodbye but not a farewell. It was a reassurance that I would see him again soon. The slightest brush of his lips sent a spark through my veins.

Steadying myself, I offered Ruairc a half nod of acknowledgment for the sake of being amenable. The cobbler's eyes were cast aside, his brows tugged in, and his expression was tense. He was lamenting a loss. I'd hurt him. The realization caused a pang in my heart as I turned my back on the two men and crossed the market, Calix in my shadow.

"Are you alright?" Aureus asked as soon as I reached the steps. His gaze swallowed me whole as he tried to assess my well-being. It was the healer in him as well as the caring older brother.

"I am," I reassured him.

Aureus's chest fell with a heavy exhale. I stepped around him and entered the warmth of our shop. Calix skirted in just behind me, looking around with an expression of boredom before finding something to meddle with. The boy played well at feigning childishness. The observation left me feeling somber.

"Evera, you must explain." Aureus followed me as I paced to the front counter. "It's clear that the man you've been with has been wounded. All night I'm up worrying, and come dawn, soldiers are at the door speaking of the murder of a castle guard. When Ruairc learned that you were off with Lark, I had to convince him not to go to the inn after you. He's been pacing the market all morning. Evera, did Lark kill that guard?" He flicked his gaze to Calix. "And who is the boy?"

"The boy goes by Calix. He is training under Lark to be a routier." A half-truth, but I had no better explanation. The remaining of my brother's questions I left unanswered. I bit the inside of my cheek as I considered the possible repercussions of telling him the truth in its entirety. Would Aureus go to the garrison? Turn Neirin in? If he knew of our bond, would he respect it? If he knew of my feelings?

When I hesitated in my response, Aureus pinched the bridge of his nose. "There's so much of Mother in you, and it frightens me."

I drew my brows together. "Mother?"

Lowering his hand to his beard, Aureus's glance turned to Calix again. Catching his implication, I sent the boy off with orders to practice his studies in the back room. Though in truth, I was unsure of the expectations of a routier in training, or whether the boy even knew how to read.

When he left, I pointedly set my gaze back to Aureus.

He studied me. "Mother loved us, Evera, but she made poor decisions."

Shaking my head, I rose to her defense. "No, she did what she had to. To keep us fed." It was what Aureus had always told me and what I remembered of her.

"No," he said, forlorn. "She could have found another way. The situations she put us in were unacceptable."

Heart thundering in my chest, I sucked in my bottom lip and waited for him to go on. Light from the window shone on his dusty blond hair. We bore such little resemblance to each other, but our personalities were in tune, as they always had been, a mirror of each other in expressions and tones.

"Why are you telling me this?" I demanded.

Aureus released a breath. "Because I am frightened for you, sister." It wasn't the response I was expecting. Not a lecture or a reprimand, but an admission. He rolled his shoulders as if a great burden lay on them. "What do you remember of the night mother died?"

I sucked in my cheek and chewed at it. "I remember the cold —and your warmth beside me. I remember a hand at my wrist, yanking me away from you, then"—I swallowed hard—"Mother's scream."

Aureus took one of my hands in his. "All these years, I hoped you would forget, that the nightmares would fade, and that with them the memories would dissipate. You were so young then. I thought maybe—"

"What happened that night?" My voice was low, and apprehension quickened my heart.

My brother shook his head, gaze distant. When he answered, his words were hesitant, carefully chosen. "Mother got a position at one of the pleasure houses in the capital. We were very young, but I recall the man who owned the business. He told Mother that she had something his clients desired."

I shook my head. "I don't remember that place."

"We were not there long, and that is not the point." Aureus let out a heavy breath. "Mother did not ask what would be expected, did not press, did not ask any questions at all. She made decisions on impulse, never taking the time to properly think them through. She saw a place we could reside with a roof over our heads and grasped for it without consideration."

By now, I have understood the direction of his story. "You believe I am acting rashly?"

One of Aureus's brows rose, but he avoided a direct reply to my question. "There is a boldness in you, sister, one that I envy. But you do not temper it, and that is what frightens me. Though I try to be a pillar for you, to be a voice of reason, you resist me. The world may not be what you wish it to be, but there is nothing you or I can do to change that, and when you push ..." He swallowed. "I see the repercussions. And yesterday, when—"

"How did mother die?" A knot formed in my throat.

Aureus halted his train of thoughts and set his jaw. "Evera—"

"Whatever happened that night ... it darkens my dreams. I want to know."

Hesitancy held him for a moment, then he sighed. "The man

who was sent into our room … What our mother had that the owner of the pleasure house took us in for …" He flexed a fist. "It was not Mother he wanted."

Gnawing apprehension tugged at me, and I trailed my fingers over my wrist. The grasp that had pulled me from Aureus that night, that tugged roughly and spun me, pushed me to the bed … Images came back to me, strikingly vivid.

Small details and blurs of movement. Mother's face, tears on her cheeks that contradict the fire in her eyes. Her fingers grasped at the shirt of the murky dark shadow of a man who holds me down, straining to pull him away. He strikes her, and she falls back. A scream leaves her throat as her head hits the bedpost, then my vision is drawn from her again.

Fractured clips. Struggling, kicking, and lashing out, seeking something to bite. Aureus's eyes were wide from behind the dresser, fear in his expression. Grasping at the blankets, crawling to the edge of the bed just to peer over and find mother looking back up at me, the fire there quenched, void, her essence gone from her as blood pools beneath her head.

Then I'm flipped, and rough hands bruise my legs where they grasp. Left unrestrained, my hands claw, though my efforts are merely a hindrance to the shadow as he positions himself over me. In the welling panic, a glint of light reflects off the pommel of a dagger at the man's hip …

"Evera—"

"I remember," I rasped. "I remember all of it."

Aureus hesitantly took me in his arms. I let myself fall into his embrace as dull understanding and acceptance fell over me.

The first man I lay with as a woman was a soldier from the local garrison—Fenrick was his name. He told me it would hurt, and it hadn't. Not really. A little, perhaps. It had been uncomfortable at first. Hadn't lasted long enough to begin to feel good.

So I was broken, then, ruined before I'd made the choice for myself. And though I'd been with several others since Fenrick and none except for Neirin had meant anything to me, there was still a deep and clawing feeling that I was less … because of what that man did to me the night of Mother's death.

My legs trembled, and I slumped to the ground, leaning against the shelving. Aureus sat with me, an arm wrapped around my shoulder. There were no words that could be said, and though I felt I should cry, tears eluded me. A bitter dullness held me.

As the images replayed in my mind and I fought to keep the thoughts from moving further, the glint of the pommel returned to my consciousness. The short dress Maerel lent me gave easier access to the scabbard at my thigh, and I hitched my skirts to withdraw the old blade.

"This dagger," I said, hands shaking. "It was his."

Aureus tensed and stroked his thumb at my shoulder. "Yes."

The shadow of the man's face became clearer in my mind as I caught my reflection in the dagger's surface. Short black beard, slick. His hair groomed, his silk top bunched. The kind of man who could pay for discretion. But it was the look of surprise in his eyes when I drew the dagger and slashed out at him that held me. A painting frozen in time. His eyes were green with flecks of amber, the kind of eyes someone would trust.

Swallowing, I slid the dagger along the floor and into the shadows across the room. Finally, tears choked me, and I let them flow, hugging my knees.

Aureus hummed Mother's lullaby, and I sobbed, grasping for his shirt and burying my face against his chest. He smelled of basil and wormwood, of our shop, of home.

He wasn't strong in the sense Neirin was; he was built of a different disposition. It was clear his lack of action both on the night of Mother's death and at the farmhouse the day prior plagued him; that remorse lay heavy on his shoulders. For that reason, I could forgive him.

After Mother's death, Aureus had looked after me, kept me

fed, and kept us hidden from the dangers of the world. And when Leighis took us in, Aureus had never stopped caring for me. He was, as he said, a pillar. It was a different kind of strength. I fought him at each turn, but it had only ever been his will to protect me in the way he knew how.

"I'm sorry," I cried against his chest. For the bitterness I'd felt toward him, the trouble I gave him.

Aureus stroked my hair and stopped his humming. "So am I."

Sniffling, I fought to settle my uneven breaths. "I love you," I told him, voice faint.

"I love you too, sister." He rested his cheek on my head.

"Aureus." My voice was muffled against his tunic.

"Yes?"

"I think I love him, too."

"I worried as much," he said, defeat in his voice. "But you need to explain. No more lies, no more secrets. I must understand, must know you're safe with him."

Nodding, I wiped my tears with the back of my hand. As I did, Aureus's gaze fell on my tattoo. It was time to tell him everything. So, I started from the beginning.

35

NEIRIN

MENTALLY CHECKING off the last thing on Maerel's list, I thanked the young man at the market stall as I paid him, then rearranged the items in my basket. The ash in my hair kept attention at bay as efficiently as the hood had. Perhaps even better, a drawn hood could come across as suspicious when the weather was fair. To use the coals of the fire had been Evera's idea; my mate was clever.

Despite this, as I walked through the market my skin still heated as if eyes watched my back. It put me on edge even as I knew the sensation was only an illusion.

The castle soldiers were gone, checked out of their rooms yesterday after scouring the town for information on Cyan's death. It would take them some two days more to reach the capital. If the huntsman was not back within three days' time with word from my brother, I would have to make new arrangements.

For today, though, nothing could be done, and I resolved to press thoughts of the things that were out of my hands aside.

The time Evera and I had here, with this sense of normalcy, was limited. For now, I would take advantage of the simple moments and stolen kisses. I would share with her the positive memories of my childhood. And if she chose to share stories of her own, I would memorize each word, each moment of light-hearted warmth, each smile.

I scaled the few short steps to the front of the shop and pushed open the door. Aureus raised his eyes. A muscle in his jaw flexed, but his expression remained flat. "Evera is upstairs."

The apothecary's tone left no invitation for me to go upstairs, so I attempted casual conversation to ease the tension between us.

"Apples," I said, drawing one from the basket I carried. "All the way from Aldruil." I tossed it in the air and caught it again. "As a boy I—"

"She told me about you, Neirin," Aureus said, his tone edged. A chill ran through my veins. My grip firmed, and my nails indented crescents in the apple's skin.

"Can you keep her safe?" he asked.

"I would lay my life down for her."

Aureus nodded. "You love her?"

"I do."

"And this bonding she speaks of … it's true?"

Creasing my brows, I nodded.

Evera came through the curtain that separated the back room from the storefront, breaking our conversation. Her eyes lit when she saw me, and I smiled, warmed by her.

Her dress was a soft green that matched her eyes. It was more form-fitting than the one she usually wore, which was ruined, and it had mid-length sleeves. The neckline dipped, and a brass embellishment rested between her breasts. At her waist was a belt with coordinating copper fittings cinched loosely, with a small pouch attached to it.

She came to stand before me, and I dropped my forehead to hers. Our hands intertwined.

"You aren't covering your mark," I said on a breath.

"I no longer wish to conceal what we share." She released the apple from my grip and placed it back in the basket. "What are the apples for?"

"I would like to bake with you," I told her. To share with her the fond memories I held of time spent with Nyana in the kitchen. To take the time to get to know her heart, to show her all of mine.

Evera tilted her head and quirked a smile. "Bake?"

I nodded. "Muffins."

Evera hummed and brushed a strand of hair from in front of my eyes. The gesture was intimate and filled with a sense of casual comfort. When she withdrew, a faint dusting of soot marked her finger.

"Do you need help with anything before I leave?" Evera asked her brother over her shoulder. Aureus shook his head. And though I could tell he was still hesitant, there was undoubtedly a shift in his attitude.

"Where is Calix?" I asked.

"Weeding the garden," the apothecary answered, his tone flat.

"Should I call for him?" Evera asked.

I lowered my gaze to her. "No, the work is good for him." I turned to Aureus. "You will let him know where we've gone if he comes asking?"

The apothecary nodded, though he appeared uninvested in the sudden keeping of a young boy. That was fair, but it comforted me to have Calix near Evera when I could not be. And in truth, the boy was well-mannered and a hard worker.

"Is your brother cross with me for pushing Calix on your family?" I asked Evera as we exited the shop.

"Aureus doesn't need a reason to be cross," she said. "Calix hasn't been any trouble, and Leighis seems to enjoy having a youthful spirit around the shop again. When he is present, Calix brings him books and asks him questions. I can't help but wonder if Leighis sees Aureus and I in him. I think Aureus has wondered the same."

Keeping her hand, I went to the bottom of the steps and gestured with my other. "You spoke to your brother. Told him about our bond?"

When Evera reached for me, I took her into my arms, sweeping her off her feet in place of her taking the few short steps.

"It was time to tell him the truth," she said with a giggle. Expression softening, she brushed the tip of her nose to mine. "I hope you aren't upset."

"Never," I told her.

She graced me with a kiss, and when I lowered her back to her feet, she took my hand and we set off through the market. The square was busy, which offered its own disguise.

"I admit I feel lighter now that Aureus and I have talked," Evera said, "and I think he does too. Though I'm still not certain he likes the idea of us. Or of the bond. At least he's making an attempt at amenity, for me." The light hit her, making her fair skin glow.

"The idea of *us*," I crooned with teasing inflection.

Evera hummed—not quite an answer, but the ease with which she'd made the statement initially spoke for itself. Spoke of what her heart desired. If it took time for her mind to come to the same conclusion, I could be patient.

Looking past me, Evera's smile broadened.

Following her gaze to where her friends stood a short distance off, I released her hand and brought my touch to the small of her back, encouraging her toward them. When she raised her eyes to mine, they sparkled. I tilted my head in their direction, the only invitation she needed.

"Farren, Renna." The lightness in Evera's step as she went to them warmed my heart. Something had altered in her. Whether that was because of what we shared, or the talk with her brother, or something else entirely, I was unsure. But I was grateful for it nonetheless .

The two young ladies turned and grinned warmly. I stopped beside Evera, and they studied me. The one with a baby strapped to her sucked in her lips knowingly, and the other only blushed.

Evera made formal introductions, giving them my false name. The one named Renna—the bolder of the two—took my chin between her thumb and index finger. I cast Evera a side-long glance, and she giggled.

"Gods, good for you, Evera," Renna remarked, turning my head to the side. When she dropped her hold on me, I studied her curiously. She was the one who had spoken of kisses before.

"Renna, that's enough." Evera laughed and wrapped her fingers in mine. The gesture drew a smile to my face.

Farren sighed. "Oh, he's got a dimple."

The three of us looked at her, and her cheeks reddened.

Evera snuggled into me, wrapping her other hand at my bicep. She hummed her acknowledgement. "I like it too."

The dimple came from my mother, for neither Father nor Harlan had one. It was strange, but at that moment, the realiza-tion seemed all the more important. Like Mother had given me a gift, knowing one day my mate's eyes would warm when they fell upon it.

Evera turned back to her friends, and the conversation moved on even as I remained unable to break my gaze from the woman who held me like she wanted me, like I was hers.

"What were you shopping for?" Evera asked, peering around her friends to the stand they'd had been examining when we approached. An assortment of jewelry and trinkets decorated with colorful stones lined the tabletop. Several caught the sunlight, casting patches of green and blue on the linen tablecloth.

"Necklaces," Renna replied. "Espen has tasked me with finding one I desire."

"They're beautiful," Evera murmured. The merchant behind the stand nodded his appreciation to her. He was older, perhaps five and forty, and had graying hair at the sides of his head.

Leaning toward us, Renna added on a hush, "Espen claimed he would buy me whichever one I wanted if I modeled it for him with nothing else on."

Farren sucked in a breath. "Renna," she scolded, eyeing me.

Amused by the girls and hoping to fluster Evera a bit, I decided to play along. Lowering my voice to a rumble, I leaned in and spoke against her ear, just loud enough that her friends could overhear.

"Tell me, love, which one is it that you want? Your friend's husband is clever. I would like to follow his lead."

Evera narrowed her eyes pointedly but did not justify my remark with a response.

Amusement vibrated in my chest. I bent down and kissed her, letting my lips linger on hers. Pulling her against me, I deepened the kiss, and though her friends giggled, she melted against me and returned it. When she broke away and sucked in a breath, I grinned wickedly at her. A spark lit her eyes, and I left her with her friends to speak with the merchant.

There were many options, and I knew nothing about jewelry. Still, I liked this Renna woman's ideas. And even if Evera didn't model it for me naked, I wanted to give her something. I considered the green stone she wore, hung by a golden chain around her neck. I recalled an occasion when it had caught the light and gleamed with the same vibrance that painted her smile, shone in her eyes. The corners of my lips turned up at the memory.

I longed to give her all the things she desired. Though ... Evera had, in truth, expressed little wanting for physical things. Aside from the manor, nothing else came to mind. While the funds in my accounts back at the capital could have afforded it, those savings was lost to me now, and the single silver and few copper coins I had left certainly couldn't buy it. So, a necklace it was. Something she could touch when we were apart and think of me, remember my love for her.

"This one," I told the merchant, picking out something shorter that I thought would layer well with what she already had. The gold chain was simple, but the small stones at its center were stunning—shades of sage that varied from dark to light, like the many tones of her eyes.

I returned to the women, stood behind Evera, and draped her beautiful cinnamon curls over one of her shoulders. Giggling at my touch, she looked up, and I brushed her temple with my nose.

"Hadrian," Evera objected as I clasped the golden necklace at the back of her neck. I did not miss the teasing with which she voiced my false name, nor the glint in her eyes.

Leaning in, I responded against her ear, low enough that only she would hear, matching the teasing of her tone. "Cordelia."

The brush of my fingers across the back of her neck unclasped her old necklace, and I narrowly caught one end of the fine chain before it could fall to the ground. I studied its fastener briefly. It seemed loose, but what did I know of jewelry? Evera looked up at me over her shoulder quizzically, and I offered a quirked smile for my clumsiness before re-clasping the chain, along with her new necklace.

"I think he wants to see you naked in it," Renna crooned, a friendly tease in her voice.

Heat flushed Evera's cheeks; they reddened beneath her freckles.

"Your friend is correct," I murmured.

Sucking in her lips, Evera narrowed her eyes at me, and I offered a cunning smile in return.

"You're beautiful," I told her, meaning it with my entire being. Warmth fluttered within me as I let out a contented breath, eager for the morning we were to spend together. Our troubles were too numerous to count; the future was unknown. But the light in her eyes, the easy comfort of her touch, they spoke of her acceptance of the bond we shared. My smile softened to something deeper, and as it did, the corners of her lips rose faintly, showing that she felt it too. In that moment, everything felt just a little less heavy. Like together, perhaps, we could work through the tangled path of thorns ahead and come through the other side to something more than I'd ever even thought to yearn for before.

36

———

EVERA

IN THE DOORWAY leading into the inn's kitchen, I stilled my steps. Directly across from me, the door that led out to the gardens was closed, its white ceramic handle clean and polished. The wood flooring beneath my feet was worn, old, but clean, too. The air smelled of citrus. Maerel had done well in her fastidious cleaning. Not a single smear of blood remained.

"Are you alright?" Neirin asked. He stood before the central table, laying out the items he'd purchased from the market. The faint tug of his brows showed his concern.

"It's as if nothing ever happened," I said, feeling dislocated.

The crease in Neirin's brows softened, and he stepped to me. Pulling me into his embrace, he kissed the top of my head. "Is it too hard for you to be here?"

"No," I spoke against his chest before he could change his mind and usher me out. Because even though I'd teased him for it back at the shop, I wanted to bake with him. It was amusing to imagine him cooking, as gruff and rugged as he was. Much less baking. "It's only that the memory of how this place was the other night is …" I searched for the correct word. "Disconcerting."

Neirin cupped my cheek in his palm and met my eyes. "Then we shall make new memories."

I smiled and stood to the tips of my boots, brushing my lips against his. Neirin's arm at my waist pulled me in closer, and when the familiar rush of heat swept through the bond, I sought with a hand beneath his shirt, above the bandages. His breathing quickened, and I giggled at his reaction.

Neirin pulled back, and the corner of his mouth crooked up, revealing the indent of his dimple. "You are a tease."

Lightened by his candor and what had become a quip between us, I shrugged. "Perhaps a little."

Amusement danced in his eyes before he turned back to the table. "Come, help with the apples."

I followed him, a lightness to my steps. A warm breeze carried through an open window at my left and, as I came to stand at his side, I caught the scent of vanilla. "Do you want me to peel them?" I asked, gesturing to the basket of apples with a tilt of my chin.

He nodded. "And dice them."

While Neirin put away the rest of his purchases from the market, I prepped the apples. The peels and cores I set aside for the chickens, as he instructed me to do. The cubes of flesh I collected in a ceramic bowl. When I finished, I brought the knife and wooden cutting board to the washing tub on the counter.

"I'll wash those later," Neirin said, coming in from the back door with eggs nestled in the crook of his arm.

Various bowls and ingredients lay arranged on the table, and a fire crackled in the hearth, warming the room.

"Where did you learn how to bake?" I asked.

He set the eggs carefully in the dip of a folded cloth so they wouldn't roll off the counter. "The woman who raised me, Nyana, taught me. She's the castle cook."

"You were raised in a kitchen?"

Cocking his head to the side, he studied me. "That surprises you?"

I shook my head. It wouldn't have been my assumption. "Would you tell me more about your childhood?"

A glint of light caught his eyes. "What would you like to know?"

Considering, I leaned against the table and propped my chin on my hands. "Did you ever get into mischief as a boy?" It was a little question, but there had been enough heavy conversations in the past days.

"When I was very young," he said, turning his back to me to check several drawers before withdrawing a set of measuring cups. "There is a small orchard in the Queen's gardens." He measured out flour into the bowl on the table before me. "My brother and I would climb the trees and sit in them for hours, eating whatever was in season until we got belly aches." A faint laugh of remembrance tugged a smile at his lips.

"It is hard to imagine a prince climbing trees." I handed him a small container of cinnamon he'd gestured to. "Isn't your brother much younger than you, though?"

A darkness shadowed Neirin's eyes. "Not Harlan," he corrected, halting his movements. "Nyana's son, Thatcher. We were within a few weeks of each other in age."

Were.

"Neirin, I'm sorry." I sucked in my lips. "I didn't intend to bring up something painful."

For a moment, an uncomfortable air of unspoken words hung between us, and I teetered between encouraging him to open up about the brother he had lost and letting the conversation go, in pursuit of returning lightness to our morning.

"No," he said finally. "It was a good memory. Whenever I think of Thatch, my memories go to—" He sighed. "It is important to remember the moments of contentment we shared, too."

Still unsure how to respond, I skirted the table to stand

beside him and rested my head on his shoulder, offering comfort.

He kissed the crown of my head. "Like baking." He was smiling again, though it did not reach his eyes. "Apple muffins were always my preference, Thatch liked the blueberry ones."

Picking up the canister of cinnamon to busy my hands, I replaced its lid. "I would have to side with you. Cinnamon makes me think of fall and warm hearths and huddling up with a favorite book and a mug of spiced tea."

"That's a comforting image." He handed me a whisk. "Though I can think of more enticing activities than reading to busy ourselves in the cold season."

Heat flushed my cheeks, and I nudged at his side with my elbow to conceal my fluster.

He laughed and slid a bowl in front of me. "Too forward?" A hint of mischief shone in his eyes.

"No." I worked at my bottom lip, narrowing my eyes, then rose to my tiptoes and spoke against his lips. "Not too forward."

Neirin inhaled sharply, and a shudder coursed through his body.

Humming, I lowered back to the balls of my feet and refocused on my task, knowing full, and well the way my teasing stirred him.

An arm at my waist pulled me hard against his chest, and I squealed, whisk in hand, tossing a cloud of flour between us just as he pressed a kiss to my lips. Hard, firm. I melted against him.

When I drew back enough to meet his eyes, he laughed and ran his thumb beneath my right eye, brushing flour away. "The things you do to me, Cordelia."

Rolling my eyes, I shoved at his chest. "Hadrian."

His smirk widened, and he took the whisk from me. As he set to cracking the eggs, adding the yolks to my bowl and the whites to a smaller one, I watched his movements. Though I knew he was aware of my gaze on him, he did not look up again from his task even as he cradled the smaller bowl in the crook of his arm, muscles flexing as he whisked.

I wet my lips, admiring his strength and physique. A flush of heat warmed my cheeks, and a coiling desire shot straight to my center as yearning came over me.

Looking up and catching my blush, Neirin stilled in his task. Though the egg whites had yet to form stiff peaks, he set the bowl aside, a hunger in his eyes. I sucked in a breath, the sensations of desire, of need, intensifying.

"This was not in my plans," he said, voice lowered as he stepped closer and braced an arm behind me on the table, caging me.

My eyes flicked to his lips, then back up to the silver of his eyes. "What was not in your plans?"

Neirin drew my hair over one shoulder and traced his thumb beneath my ear. "This." He brushed his lips against mine, the kiss faint, shooting a need for more through my veins. Before I could speak, he sighed, a hesitation, despite the yearning that seeped through the bond. "You are the only woman I've lain with, and the effect you have on me makes it very difficult to—" He swallowed. "To hold back, when every instinct, every desire—"

"I want you too." Arching my hips off the table, I encouraged him. "I don't want you to hold back."

He withdrew from me and held my gaze. A muscle flexed at his jaw. "I do not want you to think I only lust for you, that I seek only your body."

"I do not think that."

Again, he hesitated, and his body shuddered. Knowing that I was the only woman he'd been with, that he belonged to me alone … I raised my chin, baring my neck to him.

"Tease," he rasped.

Unable to gain any friction from him like this, I hooked one of my legs at his upper thigh. "You are being the tease," I retorted, impatience lacing my voice.

He growled, low, rumbling, and the tension snapped.

Neirin took my leg by the crook of my knee, and in a single movement, lifted me and stepped to the table. I landed on it roughly; the desperation in Neirin's reactions lacked fluidity, his actions portraying his raw need.

He hooked both of my legs at his hips and leaned into me, bracing himself with one arm behind me on the table and wrapping my waist with his other as if he could somehow draw me closer to him, though our bodies already aligned. Through the cloth of his trousers, I could feel the firmness of his need.

Head hung, Neirin panted hot breaths on my neck. His hips rocked, thrusting against me, measured at first, then quickening as he moaned. The table rattled, and behind me, something fell over and rolled. The trickling sound of milk spilling over onto the floor followed a moment later, but neither of us made any move to right the pitcher.

"Kiss me," I pleaded through whimpers.

Neirin purred a growl against my neck and halted the movements of his hips. Trailing kisses up, he nipped at my ear, eliciting a sharp pinprick of pain. I gasped, then his mouth was on mine, stealing my breath and taking advantage of my parted lips, the exploration of his tongue almost forceful. The raw need alone brought me to the edge of release, and I ran my fingers through his hair, meeting his passion as our tongues danced.

He broke our kiss, rasping. "I *need* more." He groaned.

I swiveled my hips and hardened my tone to a command. "Then take more."

His grip at my waist tightening, he thrust hard against me. With my skirts bunched and the length of him right where I needed it, separated only by the cotton of his pants, I shuddered and cried out.

"Someone will hear," he panted, repeating my statement from the tower as he rutted against me once more.

Whimpering, I bit back my cry. *"Let them listen."*

"Maerel will have my head if she returns to this," he said against my lips. "Or is that what you want, love? For her to find us in the kitchens with my cock buried deep inside of you?" He nipped at my bottom lip. "Is that what you need to ease your jealousy?"

Too hazed by my lust, by the effect his words had on me to dispute him, I gripped tighter at his hair. "Yes, yes, that's what I need."

Breathing heavily, he worked quickly at the ties of his pants. I kissed and nipped at his neck, and when he shifted the cotton down, I grasped for him eagerly.

"Fuck," he hissed, thrusting into my hand.

I whimpered, working him, imagining the thickness of him inside of me. Wanting him, yet at the same time reveling in this control, in the power I had over him. "Tell me what you want."

Head hung, his hair brushed my neck. "You know very well what I want," he growled, nipping my shoulder.

"Say it." I quickened my strokes.

"I want ..." His words came in ragged gasps. "I want to be inside of you, I want your warmth, your slickness." Suppressing a moan, his body stiffened. "Evera, I need you now. I can't—"

The control was too intoxicating. To see him like this, to feel his raw desperation, to know how close he was to the brink. This powerful, gorgeous man, was practically trembling before me.

"No." Stilling my hand, I gripped him with a firmness that made him hiss and his body quiver.

He drew back enough to meet my eyes, a feral glow there.

Reveling in the rush, emboldened, I released his cock and brought both of my hands to his hair.

"I want *kisses,*" I coaxed, implication thick in my tone.

He rolled his lip, eyes sharpening. Without hesitation, he unhooked my legs from his hips and lowered to his knees. When I quivered, he stilled me with a firm grip at one of my thighs.

His rough hold twisted a nervous excitement through me, and sent little shocks of pleasure to my apex. He trailed his fingers along my inner thigh, nipping and kissing at the sensitive skin there as he worked up my leg. Teasing, stimulating wetness from my center, building my need. I shut my eyes and my head fell back as I gave in to the sensations.

"Your dagger," Neirin said on a pant.

"What?" His statement tugged at my haze, and I whimpered, coaxing him with my fingers in his hair, but he was set on his distraction. His thumb traced the spot my scabbard had been before I removed it.

"I don't want to talk about it now."

Neirin remained unmoving, seriousness in his tone. "You will tell me later?'

"Yes, fine," I acquiesced, fully aware that I was now the one begging, now the one under his control. "Later."

Seemingly content with this, Neirin further bunched my skirts to my lap, and the breeze from the window chilled my center, bare and vulnerable. He restrained my left leg with his arm and trailed his thumb through my wetness, and I shuddered at his touch.

I raised my head to find him between my legs, his silver eyes intent on me as if he'd been waiting to steal my gaze, hold it forever. The tousle of his hair begged me to run my fingers through it again. Smudges of ash streaked his brows and at the side of his temple. His lips, swollen from our kissing, brushed against my leg, and he applied gentle pressure at my apex with his thumb. His heavy breaths warmed my center.

"Tell me what you want," he rumbled, turning my own game on me.

Damn him.

"I want your mouth on me," I pleaded. "I want to feel your kisses."

With his eyes locked on mine, he slid a finger into my depths, and I gasped, letting my head fall back again in the sheer ecstasy of the moment.

In the next breath, his mouth was on me, and I all but lost myself. It started as a kiss, teasing, then his tongue parted me, and I cried out.

"You're so wet," he breathed against my center, and I hooked my right leg over his shoulder and ran my fingers through his hair, needing more.

"You like that, love?" he rasped, restraining me with his grip on my left thigh when I tried to grind against his face. "Do you like these kisses?"

"Yes," I whimpered, the word a plea. I rocked my hips, but he held me still, sliding his finger in and out of me as he breathed hot air against my sensitive skin.

Growling his satisfaction, his tongue lashed out again, and the coiling tightness within me began to build.

"That's my good girl," he said, his words nearly a purr as he left me briefly to nip at the inside of my legs. Each graze of his teeth shot a deepening need through me, a more vivid awareness of the lack of his mouth on me. I needed to be filled by more than just his finger moving slowly in and out, curling in just the right way.

"Do you know how long I've wanted to taste you?" he crooned.

Gasping, I fought to form words, but I could barely breathe. The climbing rush was building too quickly; I wanted more, needed more. As if he knew, Neirin thrust a second finger inside, and I bucked against his hand.

"You're close already, aren't you?" he growled, his fingers pumping. "The way you tighten down on me." He moaned.

Unable to do anything but gasp, I clutched at his hair, uncaring of the soot that darkened my fingers.

When he nipped gently at the swollen bud of my pleasure and sucked it into his mouth, pounding me with his fingers, I unraveled. Shuddering, rocking against him, I came. Hard. The orgasm undid my entire body, shooting jolts of pleasure through my veins. And when it finally settled, he licked my wetness once more.

I trembled, looking down at him, and he rested his cheek against my leg. With the edge of lust waning and my breath slowing, a flush of heat warmed my cheeks.

He scoffed. "Now you are shy?"

Sucking in my lips, I shook my head, denying the truth.

When he rose to his feet, the firmness of him was still apparent. Neirin caught the focus of my attention and lifted my chin.

"Do not worry over me," he said, abandoning his hold on me and adjusting himself, retying his trousers. "Pleasuring you is the greatest satisfaction you can give me."

"I very seriously doubt that," I retorted.

"There is your boldness." He tucked a strand of hair behind my ear. And though his chest still rose and fell heavily, betraying his restraint, his voice was soft. "Tell me, love …" He caught my lip with his thumb, his focus lingering there a moment before he raised his eyes to mine. "Have I succeeded in replacing your memories of this room with yet a more favorable one?"

"You have," I said on a breath, and through our bond I sensed a different sort of emotion. One I couldn't quite place. A calming warmth radiated through our connection. Like sitting by a crackling hearth in the fall. I smiled at the notion and inhaled deeply, the scents of cinnamon and vanilla in the air reminding me of brisk fall mornings and spiced tea.

Whether it had been Neirin's intention to leave me with this sense of contentment, I could not say. But the way he leaned in to gentle affection after pleasuring me instead of acting upon his own need, as pressing as I knew it to be, made me suspect it may have been.

I raised my hand and brushed my fingers through the strands of hair that hung over his brows, moving them to the side. Streaks of soot stained his forehead, a reminder of the fragility of our situation. There would be danger in what lay ahead, but I pushed such fears aside to linger in the faith and promise of this simple moment; in laughter, passion, and the closeness of two hearts bound to each other.

37

NEIRIN

EVERA SLUNK DOWN against the kitchen cabinets, and I followed her lead, sitting opposite her with my back resting against one of the table's legs. With one knee bent and an arm hooked over it, I studied her as she made happy little noises through bites of muffins. It was at least her third, and she'd yet to show any signs of slowing.

"Are you not going to have any?" Evera asked, licking crumbs off the tips of her fingers.

"Just making sure there is enough for you first." Of the dozen muffins we made, most of them remained. Still, I enjoyed teasing her.

She narrowed her eyes, but instead of forfeiting the bowl, she brought it to her lap as if guarding it and pouted. Carefully inspecting her collection, she chose one muffin and held it out.

"Here," she said. A dance of mischief sparkled in her eyes.

I reached for the muffin, but she drew it back and grinned.

Meeting her challenge, I sat forward and leaned over her until our eyes were level and our noses brushed. "Tease."

Stifling her smile, Evera looked up at me through her lashes, and again I was struck by the depth of emotions she gave me. I meant it when I told her I did not just crave her body, though I could not deny my attraction, my wanting for her. But I wanted this, too. This playfulness, this wit. The way she instilled a yearning for life within me that I'd not had before. Hopes for a future, for something for myself, for us.

I leaned in to kiss her, but she giggled and broke my intentions with the muffin.

Narrowing my eyes, I took it from her and kissed her anyway. For as long as I was hers, I would not squander any opportunity for closeness and affection.

"Oh!" Evera gasped, reaching for her satchel.

I sat back, giving her room to grab it, and took a bite of my muffin.

She set the bowl aside and drew the book of lore from her bag. "I intended to lend this to you the other night, but …" She handed it to me instead of finishing the thought. "How much of it did you get to read?"

When she was resting in the manor house, I scanned a handful of the pages. Though in truth, I spent most of my time watching her sleep. But I wouldn't tell her that, of course.

"A little," I said, taking another bite.

"Did you read the part about middle shifts?"

I drew my brows. "Middle shifts?"

Evera crawled forward and turned, settling next to me. The way we fit like this was perfect. I placed an arm over her shoulder, and she pulled her knees up and propped the book open against her legs.

"Here," she said, pointing to a page heavy with black script.

"The pages without pictures are dull," I remarked blandly, teasing her. It was something Harlan might say, though, and mean it. The thought lent me to a feeling of homesickness and a longing for the times when his youthful ignorance irritated me. What I would give now for him to be able to hold on to his childhood longer, to be safe, and to be unburdened by the expectations of rulership.

Even if Harlan's decisions were undoubtedly guided by the court and by his mother—an uncanny thought—it would still be an incredible shift in expectations from his prior innocence. The boy should have had more time to mature, to grow into his role. Had I not been distracted at the festival, would I have noted something off and intercepted the assassin who had taken Kaius's life? Guilt tugged at me, and an apprehensive jitteriness seeped into my bones. When would the huntsman return?

Evera wrinkled her nose. "Just listen." She began to read from the page. "Most children shift first between the ages of five and seven. Depending on the child's magic and power, they may experience middle shifts for anywhere from a few months to a year from the time of their first shift."

Middle shifts? The Queen never gave me a name for it, though I knew what Evera spoke of—the broken, horrid thing of nightmares I saw each time I met my reflection. Just as I saw it that day reflected in Thatch's eyes and the many times after, when the Queen forced me to stand before the great mirror beneath the castle as a reminder of what I was, what I was capable of if I lost control. Where she kept me hidden until I could regain my composure, tamp my monster back down. Conceal what lurked within me.

"Until a child develops a connection with their other form, shifts can be frightening and painful, even, at times," she read. "It is because of this—"

"Are you saying broken shifts are due to … what? A disconnect?" I shook my head. "I will not give power over to him. The fox is a monster. I know you do not see it that way, but that is the truth."

Evera cast her gaze aside, and dejection trickled through the bond like the slow and steady drip of gathered rainfall from a leaf.

"I should not have spoken so roughly," I apologized. What would Evera say if she knew the truth about Thatch's death? Would she understand my resentment for the fox then? Would the truth be too much for her? Would I lose her?

When she did not respond, I wet my lips. "The middle shift you speak of … horrid, cannot describe it. When it happened to me the first time, I was young and had no knowledge of what or who I was. The form is frightening, and though I will admit the fox does not favor violence over flight, I do not have control of him. And when he is cornered, threatened, he reacts."

"He defends himself?"

A pain stabbed at my heart, and the heat that accompanied distress coursed through my blood.

"Did the fox hurt someone?"

I set my jaw and released a shaky breath, fighting to suppress the claws of the beast that raked beneath my skin, testing my emotional instability and searching for an opening to take his hold.

"Yes." Behind my eyelids, images flashed, replaying the horrors of that day. I sucked in a breath through my teeth and blinked to clear the memories.

"Neirin," Evera's voice seemed distant.

Fingers cupped my cheek, then the touch trailed higher, into my hair as she coaxed my head to turn to her. She held me, both with the physical touch of her hand that grounded me and with her scent. In a way no one else ever had been able to, she soothed my panic and calmed my soul.

"There is something that I, too, am frightened to speak of," Evera said, her voice soft, soothing as she stroked my cheek with her thumb. "Not a secret, just—" She averted her eyes for a moment. "Something very painful to think about."

The sadness that seeped from her drew an instinctual need from me to put her first, to comfort her. And though my heart still raced, I reached for her hip, drawing her into my lap. As she shifted into my embrace, the book fell and became unimportant, as everything else in the room did. It all just … fell away.

With her forehead to mine, Evera found her voice. "When you are ready to speak to me about your fox, I will listen. And in time,"—she dropped her head to the crook between my shoulder and neck—"I hope that I will find the bravery to tell you about my dagger. So that we can share the weight of our pain. But for now, Neir … for now just hold me."

38

———

EVERA

Sitting in the study, I closed my eyes, immensely grateful for the calm. The door was propped open, letting in sunlight and a warm spring breeze. I took a sip of white wine—light and crisp with notes of citrus.

"Thank you for this, Farren," I said on a sigh, the tension leaving my body.

I watched her tear a piece of bread from the fresh loaf she'd brought from her family's bakery, still warm, and cut a small bit of soft cheese to spread over it. "We both needed it, I think." She smiled, but her usual warmth didn't reach her eyes.

"Is something weighing on you?" I asked.

Humming thoughtfully, Farren dipped the spreading knife into a jar of fresh blackberry preserves and added it to her bread, mixing it with the cheese. "Nothing that is of any interest."

"It is of interest to me," I said, filling her glass back up to nearly half full.

Needing little encouragement, she swallowed her bite of bread and sighed haplessly. "Father says I must choose a suitor soon."

425

From the time we were girls, Farren had always spoken highly of marriage and motherhood, and how desperately she looked forward to them. It wasn't my dream, but I understood her yearning, in a way. The comfort of a man in your bed each night, waking to the giggling of children and the warmth of your husband's smile. Those things, admittedly, were desirable. It was the complacency, the starching of self that came with marriage that dissuaded me. But Farren and I were different in many ways, and I had no intention of discouraging her.

"Of all the men who have come for your hand, you do not take to any of them?" I already knew the answer, but she needed to express the her thoughts aloud to fully accept them.

"It is not that. I am grateful, truly. For I've had more suitors than I can expect as the daughter of a baker, and there have been several that were kind and young and charming ..." Her brows drew together faintly.

Waiting for her to continue, I took another sip, letting the alcohol warm my belly and lighten my mind.

"I have been hoping,"—she sighed—"waiting, for *one*. But he has not come for me, and I do not think he will."

There it was. I offered her a look of encouragement. "I will see what I can do. But you must be brave as well. Between your shyness and his aloofness, there is only so much that I can do."

The corners of her lips quirked down, but Farren spoke no further on her feelings for Aureus. It was something she never fully admitted to, yet between friends, it was often not necessary for something to be voiced aloud to be understood.

"What of you, Evera? What of the guard?"

Heat warmed my cheeks as my thoughts turned to Neirin and to the *kisses* he'd given me. "He is a dangerous temptation," I said, swirling my wine. "One I believe I am falling quite heavily for."

The curtain to the back door swept open, and I tilted my

head, expecting to find Aureus. When I sighed deeply, Farren turned in her seat to see who approached us.

"What are you doing here, Ruairc?" I asked, sobering.

Aureus came through the curtain next, his eyes briefly scanning the study chairs where Farren and I lounged, undoubtedly questioning the effects I had on her propriety.

"I wish to speak with you," Ruairc stated, shuffling his feet, a look of hesitancy entering his expression.

I withheld my retort and softened my response. "There is another, Ruairc—"

"I am not here to court you."

I raised a brow and exchanged a glance with Aureus. The pinch of my brother's lips suggested he was not aware of this change in intentions, though he was not outwardly displeased, either. After our talk, Aureus had taken a step back on the topic of marriage. Being raised with Leighis, we'd learned of the lore and the magic of the bonds; we held a certain level of respect for such things. Though I was certain that in his eyes, Ruairc was still the better match. And I could not, in all fairness, blame him for that. The cobbler was a safe choice.

"Then why have you come for me?"

"There is something I must say. It is important." Scaling the few short steps up to the study, Ruairc nodded a greeting to Farren and held his hand out to me. "Please, Evera, walk with me."

Though my first reaction was to deny him, the longing in his eyes made me uneasy—his intrusion presented the perfect opportunity to give Farren and Aureus a moment alone.

Leaning in, I spoke against Farren's ear. "Feign that you are intoxicated."

She faced me with a confused draw of her brows, but when I subtly raised a brow toward Aureus at the bottom of the steps, she flushed and nodded.

Sighing, I took Ruairc's hand and allowed him to help me

stand. It was the kind of thing a gentleman would do, yet it itched at my skin. Everything Ruairc did spoke to my inadequacies as a person, my need to depend on a man for every action.

"Farren is drunk," I told Aureus as I straightened my skirts. "Stay with her until I return?"

"The shop—"

"It is slow, and I will lock the door on my way out."

Frustration creased Aureus's brows, but he was, like Ruairc, a man of chivalrous intent. "Very well."

Farren flushed a deep crimson. Addressing her glass and the half-empty bottle of wine from which I'd poured only once for myself, I questioned how much of an act she would truly have to put on.

I followed Ruairc down the steps, calling for Calix over my shoulder, wanting to give Farren and my brother time alone. In truth, the boy was barely noticeable, tucked against the bookshelves, deep in his own world. He'd become increasingly interested in Leighis's books, and scrolls, and journals, and I often found him reading even when I woke in the night to relieve myself. I'd asked him on several occasions what he was so interested in, but he always brushed the question aside. It was Leighis he took his thoughts to.

Abandoning his book, Calix stood and hurried to catch up to us. As Neirin had claimed, the boy was extremely well-poised. Never did he complain or act with reluctance. A part of me was grateful for this, as he had more or less been placed in my care. But this discipline came from ill treatment in his past, and that was a sobering thought.

We left the shop, and I locked the front door behind us.

"Did you only accept my invitation to leave the two of them together?" Ruairc asked.

I turned my gaze to him and narrowed my eyes. "How—"

The cobbler laughed, though it did not reach his eyes. "It is not a difficult thing to do, to fall for someone you grew up with." He ran a hand through his hair. "And they do not hide it well, though they seem adamant in their refusal to admit their feelings to each other or to themselves."

Calix, apparently having no interest in conversations about romance or courtship, ran ahead to the central well and worked at the rope, pulling up a bucket for himself. On this day, the market consisted of barely more than half a dozen stands, so it was easy enough to keep an eye on the boy.

"Aureus worries too much about the shop to consider a relationship for himself, and he is blind to her affections."

"Is it that he worries about the shop, or that he worries about you?"

Frowning, I considered stepping down the few short steps to the market square. "Perhaps it is both."

Leaving the faint hum of the market, we made our way to the road and set off at a leisurely walk toward the cliffside. Calix followed dutifully as I had anticipated, keeping a respectful distance back.

"What is it you wished to speak of?" I asked, bypassing idle chat.

Ruairc kicked at a stone as he walked. It skipped ahead of us, stopping in a crack where a puddle of water gathered from the prior night's rainfall. "Your brother gave me your dagger."

I balked.

Before I could respond, he held up his hand. "Though I am not a blacksmith, I understand the mending of things. When I saw it, I asked why you did not carry it, and Aureus would not confide in me. Yet he did offer it to me to repair when I proposed the idea."

Unease twisted my stomach, and I stopped walking. "Speak plainly."

"Very well." Ruairc drew a bundle cloaked in burlap cloth from a leather bag strapped over his neck. Unwrapping the layers, he revealed my dagger, though it was not my dagger.

"You repaired it," I observed on a breath.

"Yes. That is what I wish to speak to you about, and why I have decided to step down, to no longer court you."

A short distance off, I caught Calix's gaze. The boy seemed to have some form of intensified sense of hearing. Whether that was simply his observational skills, or whether he could read lips, or whether it was an effect of what he was, I could not say.

When I gave no reply, Ruairc continued. "It has always been in my nature, I believe, to fix that which is broken. As I did with your dagger." He did not offer it to me, only held it in his hands, his eyes lowered to it. "It is a common blade, really. I've seen several similar ones before, just like it. It is because of that, that I was able to repair it to such a likeness of its original state. Yet … When I did, I realized how incredibly wrong I had been to do so."

"This is what you came to tell me, that my dagger is exceptionally ordinary?" I fought to keep my impatience from my tone.

Ruairc raised his gaze, and I met his honey-brown eyes. "I've always measured things by their usefulness or adequacy. I deem an object valuable using my standards alone, but … perhaps it's not my place to—"

Shaking my head, I cast my eyes to the coastline, where seabirds hovered and squalled. "A dagger is only useful if it's sharp, Ruairc. That is my measure of value."

"Evera, look at me, please."

Reluctantly, I did.

"How many times have you used this dagger over the years? Countless times, yes? What have you used it for?"

Considering, I crooked my lips. "Cutting ties for orders for the shop, splicing plants in the garden. The handle I have used to mash dried leaves on occasion, or to loosen the seal on a stubborn jar." In truth, I used the blade often for everyday tasks. And although it was not well-kept in the sense of being sharpened, I kept it clean and sanitized, for the off chance I might need to use it, as I had when removing Neirin's stitches.

Ruairc's low laugh disturbed me. He looked out at the sea, giving me his profile, and I saw in him what I had not seen in many years. There was a warmth to his smile, and not just that, but a familiarity. A comfort. A pang of regret struck me for the way time and the course of aging had affected what once was a close friendship.

"To loosen the seal on a stubborn jar," Ruairc repeated, drawing me back to the present.

"Yes," I said, a bit defensive, if only for the unexpected shift in my feelings.

"That explains the condition of it."

I huffed. "What is your point?"

"My point, Evera …" He took one of my hands, holding my dagger and the cloth it was loosely wrapped in at his side.

My eyes fell to where our fingers intertwined, but I did not draw back.

"You are broken," he said.

Setting my jaw, I made a halfhearted attempt at withdrawing my hand, but he held it still.

"Let me finish," he insisted. The subtle upturn of his smile tempered what may have otherwise seemed an imposing gesture.

I nodded.

"There are parts of your past that you revealed to me when we were young, and many parts I know of that you still have not told me, or perhaps that you keep even from yourself. My point is that we are all broken, to various degrees. I have felt for you from the time I was first old enough to yearn for a woman. I have loved you even longer."

Swallowing, I lowered my eyes but let him continue.

"If I were to have you, though, I would press my concepts upon you, seeking to fix you. Not purposefully, but I believe I would. Just as I did with your dagger. It was only when I finished repairing it, when I held it up and viewed it as nothing more than a replica of others of its kind, that I realized I was wrong."

"You were wrong?" I looked up to him again.

"You do not need to be *fixed*, Evera. Embrace your brokenness. You are distinct, extraordinary, just as you are. It would be a disservice to attempt to conform you to the mold of what others consider respectable and acceptable. This"—he held out the blade and shook his head—"it is not what is best for you."

"Why are you saying this?" My words caught in my throat.

"Give me some credit where it is due. I am not daft. I have seen the way Lark speaks to you, how he treats you. As much as I resent the man, it is clear he does not try to change you. Does not try to fix you. That is what you deserve. That is how you will flourish."

Keeping Ruairc's hand in mine, I hovered over the blade with my other. Thoughts of the night of Mother's death came back to me, and I chewed the inside of my cheek to hold down the emotions.

"Have I misjudged?" Ruairc posed.

"No," I said, releasing a breath. "No, you have not misjudged. It is only that it is not as simple as that."

"Is it not?"

Trailing my middle finger in a little circle where the latticed leather wrapped the blade's handle, I considered Ruairc's words. It was true that Neirin had not tried to force me into the constructs or views society deemed proper. That I had come to see already. It was the concept of brokenness that held me.

In all my life, not once had someone told me that I was broken so boldly. It was something whispered, something seen in the eyes of others on occasion, especially when I was younger, but never voiced to me. There was an overwhelming self-acceptance in what Ruairc stated.

My life had been composed of an endless cycle of attempting compliance, for Aureus's sake, for the sake of our shop. Of holding my tongue. Of hiding my abilities, my skills, my dagger. Of concealing my past, even from myself.

"I do not want to be fixed," I said, more to myself than to Ruairc as I took the blade and held it up to the light of the sun. It was still my blade, but it lacked the wear of time, of use, of the scars inflicted upon it. And it was as Ruairc said—it no longer held any importance or any value at all to me.

"Embrace the broken." Ruairc squeezed my hand. A warm sadness shone in his eyes—the acceptance of letting go, even when it ached him deeply to do so.

Embrace the broken.

The rattle of wheels behind me shattered the stillness. Ruairc dropped my hand to coax me to the side of the road, his touch at my waist gentle. The moment fell away as we stood to the side, quietened as the wagon passed. When it did, I turned the blade over in my hands. It was still the blade of the man who had hurt me, the one responsible for Mother's death.

"I appreciate your words, Ruairc, I truly do," I said, holding the dagger back out to him, "but I do not want this."

He held my gaze with a considering look. Perhaps he could see that there was more, that I was withholding, but he did not press. Instead, he rewrapped the blade and returned it to his bag. "Then I will hold it for you, as long as you need me to."

Words held in my throat, ones I was not yet ready to put voice to.

Calix, suddenly beside me, tugged at my shirt. The boy's stealth, the way he so easily evaded detection, made him seem at times more ghost than child. It would not be difficult for him to survive on the streets as a pickpocket. Though it was more than coin that Calix needed. If he were dependent on Neirin's blood, would he always be with us? A fondness settled over me at the thought.

"Evera, look, in the center," Calix's voice was hushed, thick with unease.

Two men stood near the well, alternating between conversing and scanning the crowd. Both wore leather, worn but of good quality. One rested a hand atop the pommel of his sword. The other bore two shorter swords strapped to his back. "Huntsmen," I deduced. No one else would use a double-bladed sword, save for a huntsman or an assassin. An assassin, however, would keep to the shadows, wear a cloak, not heavy leather armor.

I reflexively coaxed Calix behind me, concealing him with my skirts, grateful Neirin had had the forethought to purchase the boy simple clothes to replace his uniform of indigo and silver. He gripped the fabric of my dress.

"It is alright," I said, placing my hand in the midnight curls atop his head.

The boy sucked in a shuddering breath. "They have Eaumond."

Frowning, I looked back to the huntsmen, and then I saw him—the boy from the festival who'd stood beside Calix. Deep shadows created dark crescents beneath the boy's eyes, and he stood with hunched shoulders as if a great weight wore on him. The weight of his own strain for control of his magic.

"How does he know that boy?" Ruairc asked, suspicion in his tone.

I shook my head. "If you truly care for me, you will not press this. Will not question it."

Ruairc's fists flexed at his sides, but he did not speak out.

"Come, Calix, let's return to the inn." I lowered my hand to his shoulder and encouraged him to walk with me, our backs to the huntsmen.

"Are you in danger?" Ruairc asked.

I glanced back at him. Evidently, my features answered where my words did not, for he came to my side, so close that we nearly touched. So close that when he looked down at me, I could detect flakes of gold in his irises.

"Let me help you, Evera," he said, his tone almost pleading, despite the low hush of his voice.

"This isn't your concern."

"It is now," he said. "I made an oath to Aureus that I would protect you. That does not change now, just because your heart belongs to another."

I drew my brows together. "You made an oath to Aureus?"

"I did." His hand went to my waist as he encouraged me on down the path. "Just as I did to you when we were only children."

I let him guide me, Calix still holding to my skirts.

Just as I did to you when we were only children. Remembrance came over me. Summer heat dampens the back of my neck, dirt and grass stains on my dress, and brambles in my hair. Ruairc, his honey eyes round still with youth, his chest heaving as he caught his breath. What had we been running from before we tumbled down that hill? Did it matter? Was it only something we'd made up?

"I'll always protect you, Evera."

"Who is to say it isn't I who will protect you?"

"That was just a game," I said.

"I meant it all the same."

NEIRIN

WHEN THE INN WAS BUSY, it was easier to distract myself, to keep my thoughts from wandering.

Late morning often left the bar with a lack of patrons, the remains of breakfast cleaned up, and some time still left until lunch. In addition to the time of day, the rooms were only at half occupancy—the influx of travelers coming from the festival had dissipated, and that, too, contributed to the quiet.

To busy myself, I'd left the bar to wash the morning's dishes in the kitchen. The scents of new grass and early flower buds carried on the breeze through the open window, and the clucking of the hens in the garden lent a peacefulness to the day. Still, I could not shake the troubles of my mind.

There was a helplessness to the situation I found myself in, one that plagued me deeply. My thoughts looped, each time further frustrating me as I came to the same conclusions again and again.

Each day I spent in Elrune was a day Harlan was left vulnerable, unaware of the threat within the castle walls. The need to do *something* consumed me, a constant itch that would not dissipate. Yet even as my heart urged me to action, my training told me to practice patience, to use reasoning.

Without Harlan's blessing, I would not get past the guards at the bridge crossing, and there was no other way to reach the castle. Dead, I was useless to him. There was the chance that Harlan may have issued the order for my capture, not my execution, as Cyan had stated. If so, perhaps I could speak with him. But it was too much of a gamble. The sensible option was to wait for the huntsman, Nox.

Thoughts having again come full circle, I lowered my gaze to the shiny metal tankard I held and gave it a final wipe with a rough rag before adding it to the stack of drying dishes beside the wash basin. My reflection glinted off the metallic surface, and I released a weighty breath. Astraea's words returned to me. *"If you ever forget what you are, ever question that you are a monster, let your reflection stand as a reminder."*

Anger prickled at my skin. I shut my eyes and clenched my fist, resisting the urge to lash out, to push the dishes to the floor just to hear the glass shatter, the metal hum.

The heavy front doors of the inn opened with a groan. In the next heartbeat, I detected Evera through the bond, her emotions a slick unease. Although her unsettled state was troublesome, knowing that she was near and had come to see me, steadied me.

I left my task and pushed through the split doors. She stood with Calix and, to my displeasure, the cobbler. Was he the reason for her unease?

Passing the unlit hearth, I drew my mate into my arms, disregarding Ruairc. Evera relaxed in my embrace, and one of her hands came to the back of my neck, her fingers brushing through my hair. I drew back and beheld her; the light from the open door illuminated the side of her face, paled her skin, and added to the contrast of her countless dappling freckles.

"What troubles you, love?" I asked, tucking a strand of hair behind her ear.

"There are huntsmen in town," Evera said, the warmth in her eyes fogging over.

For a moment, adrenaline coursed through my veins. Could Nox be among them? No, he didn't dress like a huntsman. Evera would have no reason to pick him out of a crowd. The men she spoke of were more likely after a bounty on my head.

"They have one of the messengers with them," she added.

That explained Calix clinging to Evera's spare hand in a manner very unlike the boy. Did he, too, draw comfort from Evera's presence? Surely not as I did—not on base instinct, not with the rawness of the magic of our bond—but perhaps on a different level. Children such as Calix were nearly always abandoned by their families when signs of their affliction became apparent. Cruel as it may seem, the only other choice was risking the rest of one's family.

The reasons were unimportant, but I could understand his baser need for comfort from a woman when he had no mother. Every boy needed a mother; one to whom emotions could be laid bare... They were a place of safety when every other set of eyes on us expected stoic rigidness, fearlessness. Expected us to be a shield of defense, a stone of unwavering strength.

"Who do they have?" I asked Calix.

"Eaumond," he said, his voice broken.

Sighing, I dropped to one knee and placed a hand on the boy's shoulder. His indigo eyes held me, their orbs the color of the sea. There was a sadness to them, but they did not flicker at least. Again, I found myself struck by his restraint, his control over his magic, even when emotions weighed on him.

"Find your strength," I told him, keeping my voice level. If it was a mother's job to comfort, it was a father's job to instill courage when it was needed.

Calix nodded and sniffled once before raising his chin, a new resolve to his expression.

When had I become fond of the child? When had I begun to care for him? Standing, I pondered this even as a flutter of pride rushed through me at his bravery.

"I want to help, however I can," Ruairc said.

I'd nearly forgotten about the cobbler. The corners of my lips turned down as I addressed him, wrapping one arm at Evera's waist as the other held Calix's shoulder. The responding flex of Ruairc's jaw and the deflection of his gaze spoke of his submission.

"Neir." Evera's voice was coaxing, comforting, a warming reminder of who she was to me, of the unique connection we shared that allowed her to detect my emotions. "I trust him."

I offered a gruff sound of consideration, then nodded to Calix for him to take a seat at the central hearth before leaving the group to walk across the room to the bar. A knot was forming in my throat at the concept of Ruairc becoming privy to such fragile knowledge, and I needed a moment to consider. Why Evera wanted to draw him in, why she seemed more receptive to him than she had in the past, I could not guess. Those were questions for later, though.

At the bar, I poured three cups of whiskey, then took a considerate swallow from one of them. The split doors behind me swung, and Maerel came to stand beside me. The kitchen door creaked as her most recent dalliance slipped out.

"How do you plan to repay me for those drinks?"

"By preparing the morning meal, serving it, tending tables, and managing guests checking out while allowing you to stay abed with a recently arrived traveler all morning?" I offered.

She huffed, something between irritation and amusement, and retrieved her satchel from beneath the counter. "He was a disappointment, in truth."

"Maerel," I said, "it is nearly midday."

Shrugging, she returned to the kitchen. I took the three drinks to the hearth and offered glasses to Evera and Ruairc. Studying Calix, the heels of his boots kicking the stone of the hearth as he sat at its edge, I took a sizable drink from my own glass and offered the half-filled cup to him.

The boy's eyes widened, and a faint tug of a smile pulled at his lips as he took the glass from me. Suppressing my amusement at his reaction, I ruffled the black curls atop his head and leaned back against a table, facing Evera and Ruairc.

"What does he know?" I asked Evera, raising my chin to the cobbler.

She shook her head. "Nothing."

I pinched the bridge of my nose.

Maerel, now cloaked and with her satchel hung over her shoulder, rejoined us in the main room and set me with a frown. "Must you do your conspiring here?"

"No one visits an inn this time of day," I pointed out.

She rolled her eyes, and at the hearth, Evera suppressed a giggle. There was, in truth, some similarity in the two women. Both in their candor and in their refusal to adhere to convention. Perhaps that was why I got along with the innkeeper.

When Maerel left, I bolted the doors behind her for the sake of caution and turned back to the group. "Evera says I can trust you."

Ruairc nodded.

"What is your stake here. Why do you care?"

"I care for Evera. I want to ensure she is safe."

Narrowing my eyes, I measured his words. There was a slight condescension behind them, as if I were incapable of assuring her safety, or perhaps it was only that he disapproved of my bringing her into this position to begin with. Fair enough. I let it go.

Holding up my arm, I revealed the marks of our bond. "What do you know of the old magic?"

The cobbler frowned. Evera stepped in, covering the basics of what I was and who we were to each other. When she exposed Calix for what he was, the boy flinched visibly and turned up the end of his drink.

"Magic binds us," Evera said, "but what you said before the market stands true. Magic alone could not speak for my heart."

I wrapped an arm over Evera's shoulder and curled her into me, smiling as I spoke against her hair. "Your heart speaks to mine?"

Elbowing me playfully, she huffed. I laughed in turn, grateful for the lightness she gave me even when the stakes were high.

"I suspect that the Queen sent Eaumond with the guards. It is a great error in judgment on her part."

Evera pouted. "How so?"

"Though Queen Astraea's restraint far surpasses that of the children, she still is one of them. It has been nearly a fortnight since she … Since the festival. Without my blood, her reasoning will begin to waver, and she will act more brashly. This is a sign that she is becoming desperate. Sending the boy with a pair of huntsmen means both that she has exposed the child's abilities to detect me on a baser level, and that she is avoiding the involvement of the King. If not, she would send the guard."

"Will you help him?" Calix's soft voice drew my attention.

A bitterness rose in my throat. "I will not treat you like a boy, not when you've proven yourself capable and earned the respect of a man."

Calix nodded, and his throat bobbed.

"Taking you in … I do not regret it. You've earned my trust, Calix. You have a place with me—"

"With us." Evera reached for the boy's hand, offering it an encouraging squeeze.

His eyes rounded, and he sucked in his lips.

I sighed. "But I cannot simply take on the care of any child who needs aid. It is much more complicated than that."

"I understand." Calix raised his eyes again, a resoluteness there. "But will you let him feed? Once?"

My heart fumbled. Calix was not ignorant. He knew, as I did, that to let one of his kind feed only prolonged the inevitable. If they did not continue to receive the blood, it was a temporary kindness. A swift death would be more forgiving. Yet I understood his concern and could empathize.

"If it does not risk anyone else's safety," I conceded.

Nodding, Calix turned his eyes back to the empty glass in his hand without further note.

"So, what is your plan?" Ruairc leaned forward, bracing his forearms on his knees. To his credit, he'd listened with few questions and had shown no outward sign of disbelief. Whether this was due to a trusting nature or simply a desire to stand by Evera, I was unsure.

"Calix will have to stop feeding," I said decisively. If I didn't draw my blood, the huntsmen would not be able to use their leverage. "It's the scent of my blood that attracts their kind." I met Calix's eyes. "At a baser level, they can pick it up from quite a distance." I turned back to Evera and raised a brow. "And you, love, will have to refrain from stabbing me."

"That was an accident," Evera quipped, wrinkling her nose.

Ruairc laughed, then stifled it with feigned coughs as the attention turned to him.

"So, what do we do?" Evera asked.

"We wait for the huntsman Nox, the one I spoke with the night of the fire. He's to bring word from my brother. For now, that is all we can do. Attempting to return to the castle will result in my capture at the bridge. There's no alternate route, and charcoal in my hair alone will not deceive the guards stationed at the checkpoint."

Twisting her lips in a thoughtful way, Evera studied the floor for a moment.

"What if there is a way to pass the guards at the checkpoints without suspicion?" she queried.

"I've pondered every option—"

"Not every option," Evera said. "If you were to shift—"

I hardened my expression. "The fox cannot be controlled."

"Curled up in the back of a wagon with Calix; at a quick glance, the guards will assume you are a dog." She spluttered the words out as if speaking them quickly could alter my resolve.

Raking a hand through his hair, Ruairc sighed deeply. "He can truly …" He flashed a quick glance in my direction. "You've seen it?"

"I have."

"It is a lot to expect someone to believe," I said.

When Ruairc did not reply and posed no other questions, I spoke to Evera. "We wait for Nox."

She nodded, though the dejection that flitted through the bond betrayed her disappointment. What she spoke of, though, what she proposed, was not possible. The fox was dangerous.

Biting her lip, Evera raised her sage eyes. "Can I stay the night with you tonight?"

Again, using a forced cough to poorly conceal his reaction, Ruairc pounded at his chest. Could I sit so calmly if I were in his place? Was his presence here a testament to his devotion to her, his willingness to put her desires first, or was this all a ploy? Despite Evera's confidence, I could not bring myself to share her full faith in the man. Had it been a mistake to tell him as much as we had? It would be all too easy for him to betray me to the huntsmen in town or to the local commander, to feign no involvement and stand as a comfort to Evera after my execution.

I had to put my faith in Evera, in her reasoning for involving the cobbler. A knot formed in my throat. I'd not put just my own life at risk, but Harlan's, all in the trust I placed on Evera.

Brushing my thumb her cheek, I held her gaze. My mate. My heart. "I would like nothing more."

40

NEIRIN

THE FIRE POPPED in the hearth, orange flames licking eagerly at the charred logs. Though it was not particularly cold, building up the fire gave me a task to busy myself while Evera settled Calix to sleep.

It wasn't like Calix to be dependent on comfort. Clearly, seeing Eaumond under the control of a pair of huntsmen had troubled him. After such a length of time, it was reasonable to assume that the boy, too, was suffering. Again, I found myself impressed with the control Astraea's messengers had. For them, though, the alternative to control was death.

With the fire built, I left the hearth and crossed the room to the doorway. It stood cracked, and, cautious to be quiet, I pushed it further open. Evera lay on the chaise, eyes shut, with Calix tucked into the curve of her body. One of her thumbs stroked his shoulder, the only sign she remained awake.

For a moment, I only watched, unable to break the gentleness of the moment. Never had I considered children to be something I desired, not even as a fleeting thought. Though I loved Harlan, I'd never looked upon him and yearned for a family of my own. He was my brother, my kin. I was fiercely protective of him, but it was different … in a way I could not quite place.

Evera yawned, and her lashes fluttered. When her eyes opened and her gaze met mine, a deep, rich warmth coursed through our bond, and I smiled softly, entranced by her. If only things were different, if my seed would not contribute to the forging of another monster. Evera would make an astounding mother. A selfish thought, admittedly, as I was unsure that life suited her. Still, it would never come to fruition, so I allowed myself to bask in the glow of the fantasy.

Careful not to wake Calix, Evera rose from the chaise and pulled a thick, woven blanket up over his shoulders. She stroked curls of hair from in front of his brows before turning to me.

"What are you thinking?" she asked when she joined me in the doorway.

I wrapped my arms around her middle. "Truthfully?"

"Always."

"That this feels like a family."

Again, the thick warmth flowed between us. I did not have a word for the sensation, not one I could utter with certainty. It was reminiscent, though, of Nyana's arms around me or the gleam in Harlan's eyes when he looked to me with the kind of admiration that only he showed for me.

A murkiness seeped through, and Evera turned her head sideways to rest on my chest. "Why do I feel we are about to lose it all?"

I held her tighter, having no words to ease her worries. Not when they were so valid. A knot formed in the pit of my stomach, and for the first time, I considered running away. Considered taking Evera and Calix to the western lands and starting a new life there, where it was unlikely I would be recognized. Where I could get a laborer's job, make an honest wage, and provide for them. A cottage at the edge of a smaller village, overlooking fields.

"I must protect my brother, Evera," I said, sorrow thickening my words as I knew very well the cost I bargained with.

Though I expected her to counter me, to point out that my capture would lead to Calix's death or to her despair, she only nuzzled against my chest. When she drew back, she reached between us and cupped my cheek, the smoothness of her palm a contrast to the short stubble growing in at my jawline.

Barefoot, she raised to her toes, arching into me, and brushed my lips with hers. The kiss was slow, gently seeking as her lips parted and she sought to deepen it. She tasted of cinnamon, with a woody and sweet flavor. Like spiced cider.

When she broke the kiss, I lowered my forehead to hers, immensely grateful for the gift of her presence. For this unexpected spark that made my life worth living, beyond simply fulfilling a task. For the way she lent me to dreams of a simple life, with such wistful longing.

"My soul is yours," I said on a breath. "Until my dying breath, it is yours."

Lowering her hand to my chest, Evera drew back enough to meet my eyes. There was such sadness there, and it ached at my heart.

"Neir, I want you to shift for me."

Shift. I couldn't. Not even for my mate. "Evera—"

Huffing a breath, she wiggled from my arms and took my hand, leading me into my room. She dropped her grasp and closed the door quietly behind us, allowing Calix to sleep in the hall, undisturbed by our conversation.

"Please," she said, "allow me to speak before dismissing the idea entirely."

Setting my jaw, I nodded once and leaned back against the door, crossing my arms.

She paced from the bed to the dresser and back again several times, her feet showing beneath her dress as she walked. The dress was a bit shorter than the others I'd seen her in. Everything about her was so small compared to me.

"Neirin."

I looked to her. "I apologize. I was pondering how fair and delicate you appear. It is an exquisite complement to the fire within your soul."

She narrowed her eyes. "Are you attempting to flatter me?"

"No," I said truthfully, then leaned into playfulness in an attempt to lighten the conversation. "My thoughts began to wander, as it was taking you some time to gather your thoughts."

"You are insufferable." She huffed, but the corners of her lips turned up.

Stepping to her, I took her hands in mine. "Admittedly so, at times." I trailed my thumb over a freckle between her index finger and thumb. "This is important to you? That I shift?"

"It is," she said. "You believe the fox to be a monster, and I will not force you to speak on why if you are not ready to. But Neir, when you were wounded, I held him in my lap. There is more to him. I know it in my soul, and I know that he will not hurt me."

"The fox sees you as his," I agreed. He wouldn't hurt her.

"The book of lore states that children experience middle shifts until they come to accept their animal. I have faith that there is a possibility this is true for you as well. That in giving yourself to him freely, in fostering a bond with him, you may ease the battle between the two of you. It is possible you may unlock your abilities, too."

"To perceive magic," I recalled.

"Yes. And to manipulate it."

"Why does this matter? Why now?"

Dropping my hands, she held the front of my shirt, the cotton loose and light. "Eaumond is important to Calix. I want to try to help him. If you shift, show your fox some acceptance, perhaps you would be able to control his–"

"Rescuing that boy is not our priority," I reminded her. It couldn't be.

"If there is a chance you may be able to control his magic, temper it ..." She pushed. "Will you attempt this? For me? Will you give yourself to your fox and see if you gain some connection? Some flicker of access to your abilities?"

Sighing, I gently raised her chin. Was her theory true? If I gave myself freely to the fox, would he become more manageable? Would my abilities come forward? And would that give me an advantage in aiding Harlan? No. I could never shift outside of this room. With Evera, I knew the monster was no threat. But outside of these walls, with others, if he felt threatened ... "This is truly what you ask of me?"

"Yes."

A weight fell over me, and when Evera cast her gaze to the floorboards, I suspected she sensed my hesitation, my fear, through our bond. Still, she held firm, unwavering.

I heaved a sigh and left her to stand before the dresser. With my back to her, I stepped out of my pants, folded them, and placed them neatly in one of the drawers before pulling my shirt over my head and placing it there as well.

When I peered over my shoulder, Evera turned her eyes quickly away. For all she frustrated me at times, I could not bring myself to feel any bitterness toward her, not when her bashfulness reddened her cheeks and caused her to flutter her lashes and suck in her lips.

"Your shyness amuses me," I admitted, returning to her.

"I am not shy," she countered, finally breaking her gaze from the hearth to meet my eyes.

"No? Are you certain?" I took one of her hands and placed it on my chest so that she might feel the beating of my heart, quickened by her presence and by the trickle of desire that came to me from the invisible threads of our bond.

"I—" Her eyes lowered, as did her hand. She trailed her touch over the ridges of my muscles.

I began to stir for her. The sensation was still so new, so conflicting. While my aching for her was truly unlike anything else, it also troubled me. It signaled a lack of control.

Closing my eyes, I released a steadying breath and focused my thoughts. "This may do nothing," I warned. "It may be that I simply do not have abilities."

Raising her gaze again, she lifted her chin in a show of stubbornness. "I understand."

A faint nervousness tugged at me, and I dipped my forehead to hers for support. "Close your eyes. I don't want you to see this."

Evera's body trembled in my embrace, and a swirl of muddled emotions rushed through the bond. I kissed each of her eyelids in turn.

Taking a step back, I let out a breath and released my control to the monster, the beast that stirred within. He took it without hesitation. Eager, greedy, desperate. Fear, raw and unhinged, surged. Squinting my eyes shut, I gasped as the heat began to build.

Lips brushed mine, and my eyes shot open. Evera, having stepped to me, cupped my face in her hands, and I lowered my forehead again to hers, my breathing ragged.

"Do not resist this. Give him your control. You must do so willingly. Please, Neir, try for me."

Neir—what Harlan called me. What Thatch once had as well. Trembling, I fought back as waves of surging heat rolled through me.

"Close your eyes," I rasped through gritted teeth.

"No."

I sucked in a breath. Evera couldn't watch the transition. For her to look upon me and call me a monster … I trembled.

Kissing me again, firmly this time, Evera drew me from the nightmare of my memories. She spoke against my lips, her words a command. "Give in willingly. Trust me."

Trust her. Scrunching my nose, I shuddered, then I let go. I released all control and hooded my eyes as the searing heat built. And then … it disappeared. The burning ebbed to a liquid warmth. Fluid, as it was the night death had loomed over me. Calmed by Evera's scent, already more potent as my senses heightened, I relaxed.

Instead of breaking, my bones warped. Though there was still a tightness to the pull of my skin, it didn't rip or tear. There was no scent of blood in the air aside from the lingering traces from the night Cyan and I fought.

As the shift took me, my legs gave out, and Evera's arms supported me as I fell to the floor. Blinking blearily as if in a haze, I held her gaze as I shed the last of my control. I closed my eyes and a chilled breath left my lungs, soothing, calming. New.

When my fox opened his eyes, Evera knelt before him. Awe laced her features. Not fear, not disgust.

My fox keened, and she stroked the side of his face. He rubbed against her touch.

"He's incredible," she breathed.

Incredible.

Putting his paws on one of her knees, he sought her scent at her neck. With Evera kneeling like this, the animal stood roughly the same height as her. He was big for a fox, nearer to the size of a wolf.

Evera giggled as his nose brushed beneath her ear, leaving a trail of wetness. How easily his jaws could clamp around her neck. Yet, she trusted him completely. The animal whined and drew back to meet her eyes. In this form, their vibrant sage was a pale, muted gray.

"It's alright," she said, though I was unsure if she was talking to me or the fox. Was she sensing my emotions? Or his? Or simply responding to his whimper?

It was foolish to think an animal could understand anything. Still, he seemed to respond to her tone, at least.

A sound from downstairs drew his attention. Fully alert, he curled his lips into a snarl. The stairs creaked, and a pale-yellow warmth from a lantern shone beneath the crack in the door. Moving toward the threat, he pinned his ears, eyes hard on the dancing light.

Maerel's door opened, then closed as she retired to her room.

"We're safe here," Evera said, and he looked over his shoulder to where she sat, silhouetted against the pale flames in the hearth.

Returning to her, he prodded her with his nose, circling, scenting her as if to detect nothing was out of place. She giggled at his touch, her smile light, full of whimsy.

Seemingly content, my fox lay down and rested his snout on her thigh. The warmth of the fire heated his pelt, and he yawned.

For some time, Evera stroked his fur. My fox's heavy eyelids fluttered, and I, too, became weary, soothed by the touch and comforting presence of our mate. Thoughts of returning to my form seemed distant, unimportant. For the first time in my life, I was entirely content like this.

"Will you give him back to me?" Evera asked, cupping the side of my fox's face in her palm.

The animal raised his head, studying her. Outside, the wind picked up, and a branch scraped along one of the old glass windows with a cringing screech.

The sound was much too loud in this form. My fox swiveled an ear, intent on it, and his flank quivered. The creations of man disconcerted him. He preferred the woods, the scent of earth and rain on the air, and the scurry of hares in the undergrowth.

In this place, the ground was flat and uniform. Everything had sharp edges and harsh shadows. There was the fire, though, and he seemed to like that. And there was Evera, and she was everything to him. Just as she was everything to me.

With her gentle touch, Evera turned his gaze back to her. She touched her nose to his, and he sniffed the scent of her encompassing.

"Please, give him back to me," she repeated. The words were a request, not a command, spoken with such caring that it confused me.

All my life, I'd seen my fox as only a monster, a vile, selfish creature that caused horror and suffering. But Evera ... she treated him with affection, with a caring he had never experienced from anyone else.

In a wave, he released his hold on me. Not in a lapse of awareness, but in the act of giving freely, as I'd done for him. And when the warmth heated my veins, foretelling the shift, I braced for the pain that didn't come. It was fluid and swift.

Back in my own body, I held Evera's gaze. Knelt before her, bare to her, vulnerable. She'd seen the worst of me, yet she hadn't faltered.

"I love you too," she whispered and brushed her lips to mine.

41

———

EVERA

My LIPS LINGERED on Neirin's lightly as my words hung over us. His breath left him in a shudder. Brushing my nose along his, I encouraged him, and when he accepted my kiss, it was sweet and slow.

He pulled back enough to meet my eyes. His lashes were dark, curled, and so damn pretty, and a tousle of hair fell in front of his brows, disheveled in the best way.

And his eyes—gods. Silver orbs like the moons, searching my soul. They were the same eyes as his fox's, symbolizing what they shared. Both fighting each other, afraid because of abuse, loneliness, and self-loathing. Because of a memory too dark to even speak of. But one day, he would open up, and would share. And when he did, I would be there. I would love him, not in spite of his brokenness, but because of it.

Broken together, just as we were meant to be.

"I love you," I said again, needing him to understand the depth of my words, to know I accepted every part of him.

"I love you too," he echoed, but his brows drew together as if he didn't believe me. I would have to show him, then. Today and every day. With casual touches, lingering looks, and stolen kisses.

I ran my fingers through the waves at the back of his neck and drew him to me. Balanced awkwardly from his shift, he nearly fell on top of me, and I wrapped my arms around him reflexively.

He braced himself with one hand to keep from crushing me and, with his other arm at my waist, lowered me the short distance to the wooden floor. Giggling into his hair, I released my grip and relaxed back, drawing my knees up on either side of his hips. The way we fit together was perfect.

Neirin studied me, his faint smile tugging at his dimple. He tucked a strand of hair behind my ear with a contented sigh. There was so much intimacy to it, so much caring. "*You* are incredible, Evera."

I offered a bashful smile and rose to my elbows, closing the distance between us so I could press my lips to his. Like before, it was languid. We took our time to learn one another , memorizing every touch and reaction.

When he broke the kiss and cringed, my heart fumbled.

Noting my concern, he smiled and took one of my hands, drawing it to the rough skin of what felt already to be a scar from his duel with the guard.

"It still hurts sometimes," he said.

Of course it did. It was so easy to forget, with the miraculous way Neirin healed, but it had been only days. "I'm sorry."

"You have nothing to be sorry for." Keeping my hand, he stood, pulling me up with him.

Though I kept my eyes on his, I was aware of his obvious desire, and I wet my lips at the thought of being with him again. "You should rest," I said, voice hesitant. "Let it heal."

The bond drew me to him in a way I'd never experienced with another man. It was a yearning that sparked at the slightest implication. It was the need to be claimed, to become one in the most intimate of ways. It wasn't on my mind when I stepped forward. Yet now, standing so near to him, the call tugged on me.

Neirin huffed with his amusement. Drawing me from the depths of my thoughts, he brought my hand to his cock with a glint of wickedness in his eyes. My fingers wrapped, and his length pulsed beneath my grasp.

"Does it seem like I want to rest?" he challenged.

Flushing, I lowered my gaze, nervous and eager all at once. But this was different than what we shared before, different from our exchange in the kitchen as well.

"I'm nervous," I admitted.

"Then we don't have to do this." Neirin withdrew my hold on him, intertwined his fingers with mine, and lifted our shared grasp to his chest. His gentle words coaxed me to raise my eyes to him.

I shook my head and leaned into him, resting my forehead on the bold black markings across his heart. I took a deep breath. "I want to."

Nuzzling my hair, Neirin wrapped his arms around me. His thumb traced lazy circles at my shoulder. "What are you nervous about?"

Heat flushed my cheeks. "This isn't just sex."

Quiet befell us, and Neirin's thumb stilled. With a heavy exhale, he drew back enough to bring a hand between our bodies and coax my chin up. "No, love."

"That is what scares me."

Lines creased between his brows, and despair seeped through the bond, like grasping for something out of reach. Slick—an inability to gain footing, choking as if water filled my lungs, like a depthless sea pulling me under.

A muscle at Neirin's jaw flexed, and he looked away, eyes darkening.

"Neir, look at me."

He did, and I drew a breath.

"At the gatehouse, I kept my name from you because I feared attachment. Because it was easier that way. Because I yearned for an escape from the expectations placed on me. And now—" I worried my bottom lip, memories of the night of my mother's death coming back to me. "With what I know now, maybe I should fear intimacy."

"With what you know now?" Concern laced his expression.

Shaking my head, I sucked in my lips. "Later. I'm not scared … because of that. Not scared of closeness, either. I suppose." The words caught in the back of my throat, but I pushed through. "I'm scared that I *am* attached and that if we do this, I won't be able to move past it. Move past you. And if you leave me, if we fall apart, I will never heal from it."

Neirin's voice thickened. "Evera…" With a breath, he ran a hand through his hair. Turning from me, he paced to the hearth. For a moment, he studied the flames, then he turned back to me, though our distance remained. "I have an obligation to my brother, and I must go to his aid before I can offer you any form of comfort of a life or at home. There is a great risk I may never be able to offer you these things, that I may not return from the castle at all. To be with me puts you in danger, this I know. And yet I cannot let you go. Will not. Unless you ask me to. And if you do, it will destroy me."

Outside, the wind howled, blowing down the chimney. The flames in the hearth shuddered. And when I stepped toward Neirin, the loose boards beneath my feet creaking, I accepted.

Accepted Neirin in all his forms, the life that lay before us, and its perils. Accepted myself and the broken parts of me that would always exist. They formed me as Neirin's hardships formed him. So, I accepted it all. And when he lowered his lips to mine, I accepted his kiss. The tribulations of our pasts and the unknowns of our future didn't matter. Only this mattered, this moment.

Sweeping my hair over my shoulder, Neirin kissed first my neck and then my shoulder as he worked the ties of my bodice. With a single finger, he loosened the ribbons at my breasts, taking his time, and I closed my eyes, reveling in the way he set my heart to racing.

The bodice fell to the ground, and without it, my dress loosely gaped at my chest and slipped over one of my shoulders. Drinking me in with his eyes, Neirin briefly took my jaw in his hand, then trailed his thumb back to my ear, down the side of my neck, and to the flowing fabric of my dress. With ease, he unhooked it from my shoulder, and it, too, fell to the floor in a swaying motion.

Bare before him with only my necklaces on, I sucked in a shuddering breath, needing his touch on me again, but he only held me with his gaze.

"I want you to say that I am yours," I said.

Breaking from his trance, Neirin trailed the fingers of his left hand from the dip beneath my breasts to my navel, the bold marks of our bond at his arm a stark contrast against my pale skin. He made a low rumble deep in his chest.

I pressed my body to his. There would be time to run my hands over his muscles and scars later. It would be time to revel in his strength and discover every part of him. But in this moment, I needed to be one with him. To belong to him, and for him to belong to me.

I rose to my toes and kissed the soft skin beneath his ear. "Claim me," I whispered.

He kissed my neck eagerly, and between us, his cock throbbed against the dip of my belly. His teeth raked my skin, a caress that shot tingles through my veins.

"Don't you see, Evera?" He nipped at my jawline. "That it is you who has claimed me? I was yours from the first time you told me you didn't fear my monster."

"Say it still." I ran my fingers through his hair. "If you want me, if I am yours, claim me."

Without hesitation, Neirin grabbed me by my thighs and lifted me. I wrapped my legs around his hips, and he hissed his exhale. The tightness in his expression revealed the pain of his wound, but he didn't waver. I made an objection, but he cut me off with a kiss, harder this time, searching, and when I parted my lips, his tongue found mine.

He carried me to the bed and laid me down. Scooting me back so my head rested among the pillows, he moved over me, his thigh between my legs, encouraging me to open to him. My body responded, arching, as if I needed him. The fevered movements rewarded me with a brush of the head of his cock, and Neirin groaned.

He braced me against the bed with his thumb beneath my chin and his fingers curled at my neck. There was no pressure on my throat, but the dominance of the action spoke loudly all the same.

His silver eyes held mine with such an intensity I nearly came undone. With the fire crackling, sending warm yellow light across the room, shadows played on the ridges of his muscled torso and arms. His lips were parted, slightly swollen, and eager.

Tilting my head to the side, Neirin lowered his lips to my neck, and the heat of his breath shot tendrils of excitement through my veins. Anticipation. He dropped his grasp at my neck and moved his hand to cup one of my breasts, running his thumb over my nipple until it hardened. Then his touch lowered, following the curves of my body to my hips.

With a rasping breath, he spoke against my neck. "Mine."

The word resonated through my body, my soul, and when he bit down, the sharp pain throbbed with my heartbeat. I cried out, and in the next moment, he was pressing at my entrance.

He thrust in, and I gasped, taking the length of him.

Breathing heavily, he licked once over my neck, soothing the sore spot, then kissed it. He drew back to gaze down at me, rocking his hips. I shuddered.

With his left hand, he sought mine, and our fingers intertwined between our chests. The marks of our bond overlapped, and the softness in his eyes spoke of such great depth and longing. It was something more profound than lust. It was love. Undoubtedly, unabashedly, raw and unrestrained.

With my arm bent so our shared grasp lay at my breasts, our skin brushed as he moved, our panting heady against each other's lips. Already the coil within was building, and I moaned, hooking my ankles and arching my back. When Neirin thrust in again, he hit the deepest part of me, and I trembled.

Between the dip of my belly and the defined ridges of his abs flexing with each movement he made, my eyes fell to where we came together. The slick length of him drew out to the tip, glistening, coated with my wetness.

He stilled and lowered my hand, trailing it down my torso, and further still. "Feel our connection," he rasped.

I whimpered. Pushing his length back in just enough to secure our binding, Neirin encouraged me, drawing my fingers to where we came together.

Exploring with my touch, I let my head fall back, eyes closed. And slowly, so fucking slowly, he pushed in. His cock, slick and smooth, moved across my fingertips and sank in as I encompassed him. And fuck, it was like nothing I'd ever experienced.

"You're made for me, just as I'm made for you," he said against my lips, setting a pace. I reveled in the sensation and in his words. "The way you take me to the hilt—" He thrust in deep, and beneath my fingers, no gap remained between us. "You're shaped just for me. *Mine.*"

My core tightened, and I rocked, but he held me still beneath his solid weight. Panting, I drew my hand from between us and buried my fingers in his hair, needing to touch more of him, encourage his kisses, and succumb to the desperate need for release.

"Look at me when you come," Neirin commanded.

When I opened my eyes, my breath caught. He held my gaze, jaw tight. His ash-dusted hair fell about his face. Then he quickened his pace, fucking me hard enough to rattle the headboard against the wall.

The lock of our gazes held us, grounded me as the sensations became too much. As white light fluttered at my vision, I cried out. The orgasm shattered me, building and coiling until my body trembled with release.

With my legs at Neirin's hips, I held him tight, and he moaned as his last shuddering thrusts came shaky and uneven. Gasping, he lowered his head, and his hair tickled my breasts. He gently kissed the upper swell of one, then collapsed beside me, pulling me with him by my hip so our connection didn't break with the movement.

"My everything," he breathed, his words thick and relaxed.

Coming down from the rush, I curled against him. The thrum of his heart slowed, and mine matched its pace. *My everything.*

42

NEIRIN

I COULD BECOME accustomed to waking with Evera in my arms. My mate. My love. My everything.

A soft whisper of a snore escaped her lips with each exhale. I grinned at having something to tease her for later. Brushing a kiss to her forehead, I woke her.

"We've slept in," I whispered.

The light of late dawn illuminated the room. Downstairs, Maerel moved about the kitchen, no doubt making more noise than necessary to wake me. Evera stirred and pouted. With a stretch and a yawn, she curled back into me, wrapping me with a leg and holding me in place.

I chuckled. "Your brother will be worried, love. It's time to get up."

Outside, a raven cawed, an ominous sound like the threat of a choking fog rolling in. I frowned.

"What's wrong?" Evera smoothed out the creases of my brow with her thumb.

"I do not know what I will do if Nox does not return. Each day that passes, the danger to my brother grows, and the deception within the castle goes uncovered. I must reveal the threat.

And with the two huntsmen under Astraea's hire in town now, everything seems all the more fragile."

"It is not your job alone to protect your brother, Neir. There are other guards."

Nodding, I cast my gaze aside. "I cannot risk losing another brother."

"Alright." She cupped my cheek, drawing me back to her. "Then we will leave today."

"How—"

"Your fox." Scooting back, she sat, leaning against the headboard. "It will work. I know that it will. Once we pass the bridge and the checkpoint, we can further devise a plan. Is there a concealed way into the castle?"

"There is." I sucked in my cheek and chewed on it. Giving in to the monster still unsettled me, though Evera had proven that he listened to her, at least to an extent. I feared how he may react to Calix, or to any other who approached him. Deflecting, I voiced another hesitance—Calix's friend. "What of Eaumond?"

Evera sighed. There was no good answer, and I knew that. But what could the boy expect? I could not take on another child. Already, I'd taken on one, which was more responsibility than I ever intended to have.

"What is the risk in retrieving the boy from the huntsmen?" she asked.

"Considerable." And giving myself willingly over to my fox hadn't given us a magical solution to our problems. The unsaid words held in the air.

Evera wet her lips. "I will talk to Calix."

Cupping her cheek in my palm, I lowered my forehead to hers. Never had I known someone so selfless, so determined to help others. If only there were some way I could alter our reality, aid her in her goals instead of holding her close, holding her back. Being the voice of reason left a bitterness in the back of my throat.

TOGETHER WE WALKED the main road and turned right, heading toward the market. Despite my foreboding, the morning was fair. The sun, still low in the sky, sent long shadows and warmth in our direction as we made our way along the cobblestones.

Calix had stayed at the inn, claiming he desired to aid Maerel in some of her morning tasks. I believed he lied. After Evera spoke to him about leaving Eaumond behind, he distanced himself, hardened his eyes, and withdrew from me. I could not expect him to understand, not when I asked him to risk his life—to be in the presence of my fox—so I could save my brother. Yet he had no choice in the matter, and he knew this. I suspected it made him bitter, which I could not fault him for. To be fully reliant on someone was a hollowing thought.

"Do you think Calix will forgive me?" I asked Evera.

She squeezed my hand but did not answer right away. When she did speak, her words were measured, considered. "It's not a simple situation. He understands that. He seems to hesitate between speaking his mind and remaining obedient, though. Like, there is something he is holding back." She halted in her steps. "Also, Neirin … he told me that the Queen offered to let you live out your life in one of her estates outside of the capital, and let the messengers take what they need from you there."

"To accept her proposition would remove me from my brother indefinitely. In addition to that, you would not be safe among those children, should she even allow you to come with me. Astraea is controlling. It is why, I believe, she feeds from me in the places that she does. It is a mark of ownership. I suspect she would not take kindly to me having formed a mate bond."

"Do you think she is capable of violence?"

"Of killing, you mean?"

Evera nodded.

"If it were a matter of her magic alone, yes. But Astraea is thoughtful, considering. I do not think she would act upon impulse or kill with her own hands if she could have another act in her stead. That is, when my blood is helping her control her powers. There is no way to say what her current condition is, and I will not risk you spending your life there. The woman is, most certainly, capable of violence. I believe she takes a thrill in the 'lessons' she forces on the messengers, that she forced upon me as a child."

"Do you believe she could be behind your father's death?"

My father.

"What would she gain from Kaius's death?"

Quirking her lips, Evera shrugged and began walking again. "When I first met her, I felt a closeness to her, a connection I'd not expected. It is my belief that a woman capable of hurting children and so easily disguising her true nature is not to be trusted."

I'd not considered Astraea for the killer, yet she told me the night of the festival when she took me into the lounge room that she would ensure Kaius did not send me away to the western lands.

"If Astraea did orchestrate all of this," I said, "why would she frame me when she needs my blood?"

"Perhaps she thought your brother would spare you? Jailed, you are still at her disposal, are you not?"

The thought sobered me. Everything Evera said made such sense. Yet Astraea had been giving a speech at the time of Kaius's death. And should Cyan's words be believed, Rion had been preoccupied at the time as well.

Sighing, I turned Evera toward me and rested my hand at the curve of her waist. "What have I done in this life to deserve someone like you, love?"

She shook her head, but before she could object, I pressed my index finger to her lips. She giggled, the mood lightening.

"Your sharp mind, the way you challenge me, show me things from a new perspective." Wrapping my arm at her waist and pulling her against me, I spoke against her ear. "The way your body drives me wild—"

She set me with a mock glare.

"And the way your candor sobers me."

"Hm. What did you do to deserve me? That *is* a fair question," she quipped. "You truly can be insufferable at times."

"Yes, I know, love." I kissed her forehead, and as I did, I caught sight of a man behind her, riding down the road toward us on a chestnut stallion. His hair was short, dark, and curly; his attire was unfitting for a huntsman. My heart leapt in my chest. Adrenaline, fear of the unknown, of the inevitability of answers just out of reach, sent a sinking feeling to my stomach.

"Gather your things, speak with your family." My words came quickly, hushed. "It is not goodbye, only farewell for now."

"You are not coming with me?" She met my gaze with her green-blue eyes.

"Nox has returned. I must speak with him."

4 3

NEIRIN

NOX MET my gaze briefly as he drew near. To his credit, he took his discretion seriously, not offering even so much as a nod of acknowledgment as he passed us by at the market and continued toward the inn. The thrum of my heart sped up at seeing him, at the questions that would soon be answered.

With a departing kiss, I left Evera to gather necessities for our trip and speak with her brother and mentor. It was fair to expect that Aureus would be displeased, but I had no doubt Evera could manage him on her own. So with my back to the rising sun, I followed in the path of the huntsman.

At the base of the cliffs below, the waves crashed. A pressing unknown tugged at the back of my mind, stuck there like a thorn. The two huntsmen hired by Astraea had checked in with Maerel at the inn the night before. I'd not caught sight of them nor the messenger, Eaumond, since.

As long as I remained unwounded, Eaumond would not be able to use his abilities to seek me out. The Alidian's senses fed off blood. Without it, the child would do the men little good. Yet if I stumbled upon them by chance, or if they remained at the inn … I pushed the thoughts away.

473

In all my years of training, I could rely on my observation skills. Distractions were my only concern. That, and leaving Evera alone without Calix or myself to defend her while she spoke with her family. I would need to teach her how to defend herself. Still, she was cunning, and wit alone was a weapon that could be honed.

I entered the inn through the kitchen, sweat beading at the back of my neck as my nerves allowed the fox an opportunity, a window. Though he scratched, the writhing did not come. Could Evera have been correct in her assumptions that, in giving power to him freely, he would, in turn, fight for it less often?

I found Calix sitting with his back against the wall, spinning a coin between his legs with an absent look in his eyes. Though I could have chided him for being neglectful when he'd claimed he would help Maerel with her busywork, there was a barrier still between us, and I didn't wish to add to the divide.

"The huntsman Nox is here," I said.

He looked up at me but gave no response.

"Are you prepared to leave?"

He nodded.

Setting my jaw, I wished for Evera's easy way with the boy. She had connected with him and always knew what to say. She was like that with me as well.

"Calix," I said as a thought came to me, "you can control your magic, to some level at least. Could you raise just a note of it to the surface? Not enough to darken your eyes."

The boy drew his brows. "Now?"

"Yes."

Lowering his gaze back to the coin, Calix's chest rose and fell as he let out a breath. The hum in the air, the charge, did not come. Yet his eyes darkened, and from his chest a glow of light formed, faint but steady.

"Evera was right," I said, the words leaving on a gasp. I could sense magic.

Calix turned his head to the side, puzzlement crooking his lips as his irises returned to their bold blue.

I flexed my fists at my sides. There would be time later to muse over the implications, the possibilities of this new ability.

"Stay out of sight," I told Calix and crossed to the split doors.

Pushing them open a crack, I scanned what I could see of the inn's main room. Nox sat at the bar, talking with Maerel as she poured him a drink. Otherwise, the large entry room remained empty, the hearth unlit.

"Stealth does not suit you," Nox said, his voice raised a note.

I released a breath to steady myself and pushed the doors open to join Maerel behind the bar.

"It is not my strong suit," I responded flatly.

"No." His lips turned up in a friendly gesture. "It is not."

"Timeliness is not yours," I retorted. "A fortnight to the day."

Setting his glass down, Nox patted the barstool beside his own, an easy smile broadening across his face. "Come, sit, I have a response for you. A letter from the King himself."

My heart flipped. "The word is good?"

"That is for you to tell me, friend," Nox said. He withdrew an ivory letter, sealed with red wax and embossed with the royal crest, from his jacket. "Another drink, please," he said to Maerel as I skirted the bar to take a seat two down from the huntsman.

Taking note of my gesture, he laughed. "Do you always keep people at sword's length?"

"What kept you? The trip should not have taken as long as it did." I refused to give weight to his jeer.

"Life." Nox held his hand out to Maerel, and she passed him the drink. Placing the letter atop it, he slid both across the bar to me. "The journey is short but beautiful this time of year. To rush would be to miss things."

"To perform your task should be your priority." I held the

letter up and examined the seal. The truth of my brother's state hung within the parchment. How he fared and if any new threats had been detected. Perhaps, too, why more guards had not yet been sent to Elrune after Cyan's death. That, in itself, gave me hope. Perhaps Harlan had heard of how Cyan was killed, took my action as the penance for his ill deeds, and, having read my note, called off further searches. It would explain, too, why the Queen sent huntsmen herself.

Nerves fluttered in my belly, and I set the letter down, taking a deep drink of the whiskey. It warmed my throat if nothing else.

"You have a shadow."

I placed the glass on the bar top and drew my brows together, but before I could question Nox, the split doors opened and Calix set me with an apologetic look.

"Typically, he is prone to stealth," I said, annoyance leaking into my tone. "Perhaps it is only that you are very perceptive."

"And you are not?" Nox asked, a quirk to his lips.

I am. Normally.

Was I letting my unease hinder my observation skills? The thought displeased me, but I brushed it aside. It was unimportant. "Come, sit," I told Calix.

He skirted the bar and took the barstool beside me, at my left, leaving the space between Nox and I.

A subtle hum in the air lifted the fine hairs on my arms. Too faint, I suspected, for anyone else to take note of. Calix was troubled, but this was not the time to create a scene, and it had not been an excusable time since his last feed for him to slack in his restraint. Casually, I slid my glass, still roughly a third full, to the boy to take the edge off, even as irritation prickled that I should have to worry over such a thing in this moment.

Calix took to the drink without hesitation. Huffing, I set my attention back on the letter.

"Do you recall what I said when you sought my services?" Nox asked.

"You say many things, huntsman," I snapped, tearing the wax seal off the letter. I hesitated, the feel of the paper beneath my fingers course. It was unlike me to speak without thought, and my response had been sharper than necessary. Yes, the man maddened me, but … I rubbed between my brows, a pressure building in my head.

"That is fair." Nox turned and leaned against the bar top.

I blinked, clearing a fog from my mind. Again, anger swept through me. I slapped the letter down and flexed my fist. "Why pose a question and let it fall off?" I wanted to grab the man, shake him.

The energy in the air intensified, splitting my attention. Maerel stopped her task, though she kept her eyes cast down to the cup she held. Nox gave no notable response at all. Time felt … wrong, somehow. Slow, thick.

A dizzying hum filled my head.

"Dammit, Calix." I spun on the boy, fury heating my blood.

Calix grabbed at his hair, then lowered his hands to his side. He stood, balling his fists. "Damn *you*, Neirin," he countered and, with fair force for his scrawny form, struck me in the face with a closed fist.

Taken entirely off guard, I balked and brought my thumb to my lip, the metallic tang of my own blood foretelling a split lip. Had he just struck me? Had I imagined that? *No, I didn't.* Snarling, I seethed and grasped the boy by the front of his shirt.

"Eaumond's my friend." Calix spat the words. "You could have helped him, helped all of them." Tears welled, and he blinked, the white of his eyes bloodshot. He began to cry. "You could have helped all of them."

"Neirin." Maerel's voice drew me back, and I spun to look at her. The movement was too quick, my vision blurred, and I firmed my jaw and narrowed my eyes, trying to keep focused.

Was I drunk? No, I couldn't be. Why was everything so delayed, so hazed?

"What is it?" I growled.

Why does everyone need something from me?

The innkeeper looked past me, and she nodded with her chin.

Why does she look so ... defeated?

Turning in my seat to see where she gestured, I let the world catch up to me, slow in its spinning. My hand still gripped Calix's shirt. At the hall that led to the lower floor of rooms, the two huntsmen stood, Eaumond between them, his eyes black as coals. It was not Calix, then, whose control had faltered.

"No!" Calix screamed.

Eaumond fell to the floor sideways, eyes wide and dark, void as he grasped at the slit in his own throat, crimson spewing. I gaped my lips to question what I saw.

"You did not say you would kill him," Nox snarled.

I turned to him, nearly swaying from my seat this time at the rush of movement.

Kill him? He is dead? Of course he is, or dying at least. His throat has been slashed.

My head throbbed. Something was wrong. Terribly wrong. With me.

"It was not my intention for anyone to get hurt," Nox said.

Is he apologizing to me?

"And I did not expect you to pass your drink to the boy. I— I am deeply sorry for that."

Moving more slowly this time, I turned my attention again and focused on the white of my knuckles where I clung to Calix's shirt. Drink? The boy? Had he ... What had Nox done to us? I released my grip, and Calix fell to the ground with a heavy thud.

"Calix—" My hands trembled, and I reached for the bar, needing to steady myself as everything moved both much too slowly and much too fast at the same time. At my feet, the form of the boy I'd come to love lay lifeless.

"When you solicited my help …" Nox said, his voice no longer behind me but directly to my left. The touch of his hand as he took mine was warm, tingling almost. He slid a cool band on my index finger. Mother's ring. "I told you that my loyalty was dependent on honorable intent. Imagine my surprise when I learned of your ploy to kill the new King. Your own brother, Neirin. There is no honor in that, no forgiving that."

"No, you are wrong—" The weight of my own head was nearly unbearable. My arms, too, had become leaden. I gasped to fill my lungs with air. Falling forward, I watched the floor grow closer until my head struck it. I blinked, looking at Calix just as I had at Cyan when he had died. But Calix looked so peaceful. Now that I was close, I could see that. Like he was sleeping. Like when Evera lay with him, stroking his shoulder, humming.

"My family," I mumbled, the words incoherent even to myself as my ears hummed, as darkness swept over me.

44

—————

EVERA

Whatever misconception I'd had that this conversation would go over well was lost to me the moment I walked into the shop to find Ruairc leaning up against the front counter. Aureus's stern expression told me he suspected something, but that the cobbler had refused to give him the information he sought. Apparently, he'd been in the shop for some time, waiting for me to return home.

"This is truly what you want?" Aureus asked some half an hour later, as he sat in one of the padded chairs in Leighis's study. He leaned forward with one arm resting on his knee and the other hand smoothing the creases at his brows.

"It is," I said, keeping my voice steady. The explanation had taken the breath out of me, leaving me burdened by the guilt of the lies I'd given with little effort. I wished it were different, that I didn't need to deceive Aureus, but keeping the entirety of the truth from him in this situation was a kindness to him. Whether Neirin had received word from Nox that he'd been pardoned or that his brother had refused to read his letter, we would be returning to the capital. Neirin could not stand by while his brother's life was in peril. I could empathize with that; I would

481

do the same for Aureus. As far as my brother knew, everything would go as planned, and we needed only to walk into the castle, speak with Harlan, and Neirin would regain access to his funds and clear his name so that we could live an honest life together.

"This is not just due to the magic, the bond? You truly love him?" Aureus asked.

"I do," I said. That, at least, was the full truth.

Ruairc, who'd taken it upon himself to linger, held my gaze, aware of the faulty facts I'd laced my story with.

There was an uncomfortable quiet, then Ruairc pushed off the railing and stood beside me, taking my sack from the table and adjusting it over his shoulder. "I will still escort her to and from the castle to ensure there are no run-ins with thieves through the pass."

I had suspected Ruairc would volunteer to come along, and had dreaded it when I first arrived at the shop. I had no desire to embrace the discomfort of traveling with two men who both desired my heart. But I found myself with nothing to say. I should have dissuaded him, yet the way he stood at my side despite the situation I'd put him in, despite my heart belonging to another, caused me to hold my tongue. Could I do the same? Support someone I loved after they'd chosen another? I looked up at him, expression soft, and turned the corners of my lips up in a subtle smile. *Thank you.*

He nodded, returning my expression.

Aureus sighed. "There is no talking you out of this?"

"No."

My brother tapped his fingers on the armrest, casting his gaze away from us. His worry, his lack of ability to protect me himself, set his forehead with wrinkles. After a moment, he turned his attention to Ruairc. "You will ensure her safety?"

"I will." Ruairc's response came without hesitation. And while I didn't particularly like the concept of Aureus *allowing* me to go because I was being escorted, I held my tongue. And Ruairc, I knew, was only trying to keep tensions from mounting. He was trying to help.

"Why?" Aureus addressed his friend.

"I no longer aim to court her, but that does not nullify the promise I made to you. I will stand by her, protect her." Ruairc placed a hand on my shoulder, the gesture friendly, and smiled at me. "If she will allow it."

If she will allow it. I offered him a smile to show my gratitude for his gesture, for letting the decision be my own, and not making it for me. "You can come with us. Thank you, Ruairc."

His beaming grin sent me back to the days when Ruairc and I had played as children, oblivious to the matters of adults—of desires, commitments, and obligations. He hadn't been courting me. He'd been my friend.

As Ruairc spoke with my brother, disclosing our timeline and the simpler details, most—if not all of which were lies, I gathered the items I would need. Basic necessities—skins of water, bread, miscellaneous other snacks for the road, along with a blanket rolled tight to conserve space, and a spare cloak to conceal Neirin's silver hair if it rained or the charcoal washed away for some other reason.

On a last thought, I gathered three vials of the sleeping tincture I'd used on Calix before.

Kissing the crown of Leighis's head and hugging Aureus, I took one last glance over the study, over my home. This was not goodbye, only farewell for now.

"Are you ready?" Ruairc asked.

"Yes," I said, "I've got all I need."

ANTICIPATION COURSED THROUGH MY VEINS, each passing moment increasing my worry. It had been too long. Neirin should have been at the stables by now with Calix.

"What is keeping them?" I asked, needing to air the words.

"It could be anything, Evera." Ruairc adjusted the straps on his mount's saddle.

I patted Sorrel's neck. Taking the wagon would cause suspicion, but Aureus was out with Farren, and that would give us time, at least, to get out of town. By the time my brother noticed it was missing, we would be gone. It was an inconvenience to travel in such a way, but it was the only plan I had. In the back with Calix, half-covered by a quilt, we could pass Neirin's fox off as a dog. As long as his tail was hidden, it wasn't such a stretch.

"Evera," Ruairc said.

I raised my gaze and found him staring out through the stable doors behind me. I followed his line of sight.

My breath caught.

Passing the open stable doors, making their way down the cobbled road, the two huntsmen rode in front of Nox, a body draped over the rumps of each of their horses. One, a boy, with dark and curly hair. The other form, larger, dusted the horse's leg with the ashes in his hair.

"No," I rasped beneath my breath.

Ruairc wrapped his arms at my shoulders and hushed me as the small group passed.

No.

When the road before us stood clear again, I spun in Ruairc's grasp and struck at his chest, anger and fear coursing through my veins with the rapid beating of my heart. Keeping his hold firm around me, he allowed my pounding fists until they settled, replaced by tears. I crumpled against him.

"Nox took them. He betrayed Neirin. He—" My words came out nearly a wail, and new tears swelled with them.

Ruairc stroked my shoulder.

"I need them, Ruairc. They are my family. Do you think—" I choked back the word that stuck in my throat.

For a moment, only my tears broke the quiet. The rough leather of the apron Ruairc wore smelled of his workshop and brought back memories of playing in the back room together as children.

"They are alive," Ruairc said finally. "If they were not, the huntsmen wouldn't have wasted the time to bind their wrists and ankles."

Overwhelmed, I shuddered. How had I not noticed? But Ruairc was right. There would be no reason to secure them in such a way if—

"What do you need?" Ruairc asked.

I pulled back to glance up at him. "What?" I asked, fighting against the waves of panic.

"Dammit, Evera. What is our plan?"

His sharpness grounded me. "Our plan?"

Dropping his embrace, Ruairc ran a hand through his beard, then took my hands in his. "Since we were young, Evera, you have had more fire than Aureus and I combined. I can fight, but I can't take three men. So, what's your plan?"

My breath hitched, and a faint tendril of hope took root. I latched on to it. Ruairc was right—now was not the time to lose my composure. Not when my family needed me. I'd lost myself for a moment in the possibility I'd lost Neirin and Calix, but if I was going to get them back, I'd need me—stubborn, determined me. The me Neirin loved, and the me I loved too, who followed her own path no matter how many people whispered *witch*.

"There is a tincture." I withdrew the sleeping tonic I'd used on Calix from my satchel. "If we put this in their drink, the huntsmen will fall into a deep sleep. Nothing will wake them, aside from time."

"They will stop before the mountains," Ruairc said, nodding.

"It would be too much of a risk to take the pass with such a valuable bounty on the back of their mounts, not when they would still be riding through dusk. They will camp and leave at dawn."

"Then we must follow them." I tucked the vials back into my sack and led Sorrel to a stack of crates I could use to mount her.

"You can ride? What of the wagon?"

"Yes," I said. "Neirin taught me. And there is no time for the wagon. We will sort out a new plan once we get them back."

Without response, Ruairc mounted his own steed. "Let us get your family back." There was a glint of sadness, of loss in his eyes as he kicked his stallion's sides and passed me, crossing the border of shadow into the sunlight of the open air.

45

NEIRIN

I awoke with a start, my heart pounding and the weight of a nightmare lingering. With my eyes shut tight, I tried to still my breath. My head throbbed, and when I removed a makeshift wrap of cloth to investigate, I found a welt just above my left ear, raised and tender. Surrounding it, my hair was matted, clumped with what was probably blood and charcoal.

Rope bound my chest, holding me upright against the trunk of a solid oak tree. My wrists, at least, remained unbound, though red markings indicated they had been, not long before, tightly tied.

As the fog in my mind cleared, I blinked, taking in my surroundings and trying to make sense of what had happened. The last thoughts I had were of Calix falling to the ground.

Calix.

Panic searing in my chest, I lashed at the bindings, but they held me firm. Beside me, a faint mumble drew my attention, and panting, I turned my head. A quarter way around the tree, the boy sat upright, restrained in the same position as I. Relief flushed over me.

"Calix," I said beneath my breath, aiming to rouse the boy

489

without drawing the attention of our captors, whose voices carried from a short distance off.

He only mumbled again, his eyes heavy and lips pouted. Deep in sleep, but alive. Whatever Nox had laced my drink with was potent, then. Calix had consumed little, but still, he was unconscious. His slighter size, too, could account for his prolonged sleep.

The twin moons shone down, waxing crescents that gave off only the faintest amount of light. Still, it spilled, catching on the blades of grass in the clearing before us. I craned my neck to seek out the direction of the voices. Down a short slope, the three huntsmen sat around a fire, its lapping flames vibrant, casting pools of yellow warmth upon their faces.

The two I did not recognize laughed, drank, and shared stories, but I was too far off to make out their words. Nox sat off to the side, his face pinched, eyes cast to the shadows of the woods beyond, to the Edthiel mountain pass.

"Calix," I rasped again, tugging at the ropes, knowing they would not break but hoping the rough action might wake him.

When he mumbled a second time, there was a faint wakefulness to the sound. I called for him again. At the fire, the three men remained oblivious to our waking, as we sat some distance off beneath the patchy shadows of the oak's canopy.

"Neirin?"

"There are three men by the fire. Can you strike them with your magic?"

Foggy, Calix mumbled. "No, I"—he heaved a breath—"my magic feels … weak."

The drug was still wearing off, then. Closing my eyes, I did as Evera had instructed me at the inn and released power to my fox, desperate to get free of the binds, but he did not answer the call.

"What happened?"

"Nox drugged us," I hissed, bitterness in the back of my throat.

For a moment, Calix remained quiet; then he sighed. "Eaumond is dead."

"Yes." I did not have a better response. The smell of the campfire carried on the breeze sending a chill down my spine. I drew in my lips, biting back the emotion that tugged at me. How long had I been unaware of the cold, uncaring of it? Yet now, restrained and helpless, it was all I felt. Cold desperation and a choking panic. Hopelessness.

Amid the distant chatter of the huntsmen, my thoughts turned inward. Of all things, they went to Evera's dull dagger, the one she no longer wore. Why did she no longer wear it? I'd told her she could tell me when she was ready to talk about it. The missed knowledge of something that weighed on her, that was important to her, drew me to clench my fists.

Will she think I abandoned her when I did not meet her at the stables as we planned? When she could not find me?

The hoot of an owl somewhere out in the woods beyond the clearing rang through the night. When the wind shifted, sending the scents of the forest past us, I closed my eyes.

"When our magic returns," I told Calix, "we must use it to free ourselves."

"It was as you said before, Neirin. My life—Eaumond's life—we are not worth the cost of our existence."

Craning my neck, I stared at him with drawn brows. "I did not say that."

"You said that to let us feed only prolonged the inevitable, that it would be more compassionate to kill us."

"Before I thought only with my mind," I said. "What I said was true, logical, yet now my heart speaks against it."

"You do not grieve for Eaumond," Calix retorted, bitterness lacing his words.

"No," I acknowledged, "but for a moment, back in the bar, I

thought you had died. And … I care for you, Calix. What I said is not incorrect. You and I … we are monsters, and I have no intention of bringing another into the world, but you are—"

"I am not your son."

The coldness in his tone caused me to draw my lips in.

"No," I admitted.

Stillness hung between us.

"My father was a good man," Calix said. "I killed him, along with my mother and my baby sister. I did not mean to."

"Unforgivable truths," I stated. A breeze ruffled my hair.

"Unforgivable truths?"

Letting my head fall back and rest against the trunk, I watched the leaves rustling in the canopy overhead. "I killed my brother, Thatcher." The admission stung my throat. Yet as I spoke, a freedom accompanied the pain, like a weight lifted.

"The first time I shifted we were sparring, just boys playing with toy swords. The middle shift took me, and I did not know what it was, did not expect it. The creature within me, it was horrid, and Thatch, he—" I shut my eyes, and the nightmare returned to me. Not a nightmare, a reminder of what happened all those years ago. I swallowed. "He called me a monster."

"Your fox killed him?"

Wetting my lips, I let the images come to me. "The full shift took me, and Thatcher, he was a fighter. As young as we were, he bore his wooden sword and advanced upon the creature, spitting out the worst words he knew, tears welling in his eyes as he believed it somehow possessed, perhaps. 'Monster, monster, monster,' he kept saying." I swallowed. "He cornered the fox. There was no escape and … and I watched it all, unable to restrain the monster as he lunged at Thatch's leg." Thatch's screams flooded my ears. "Thatcher struck him again and again with the wooden sword, and the fox, he … he went for his neck, and then it was over. To watch a life leave someone—"

"The absence of a soul."

"Yes."

How long had I kept the story of Thatch's death to myself? Only Astraea knew, for she had witnessed it, sitting overlooking the gardens. The gardens Thatcher and I were not even meant to be in. We were so foolish. Had we been in the castle, somewhere else, perhaps things would have been different.

"There are some truths, some events, that are unforgivable. Yet we must live with them. Living with them is our punishment."

"The deaths I have caused—"

"You must live with," I said, my tone stern. "Do you remember what you told me about Evera? You said she was good, do you recall that?"

Calix sighed. "I do."

"We live on for those who are good. To protect them, to cherish them. It is why I must save my brother. And once I have rid the castle of the bastard that killed Kaius and I know that Harlan is safe, I can make a life for Evera and I. And for you, Calix. I am not your father; I will not try to take that role. But I care for you. Evera and I both do."

The boy sniffled, and when I turned my head, resting my cheek against the bark, he looked away and drew his knees to his chest. My heart ached, but again I did not know the correct words to say or how to comfort him. Calix muffled his cries. On my inhale, I detected the coming of rain.

For now, all we could do was wait for our magic to return. More waiting. More helplessness. It was one thing to speak to another, especially a child, and offer words of comfort. But the future I spoke of felt so unreachable, every possible outcome bleak.

If our magic did return, we stood a chance. But without it, Calix could not fight, and I was one man against three. Huntsmen, at that. Known for their tricks, they do not fight fairly.

What did Nox poison us with? Will our magic return at all?

Evera would know. But she was back in Elrune, likely believing I'd abandoned her. Was she held up in her room? Was she hurting? Or would she seek me out for leaving her behind? That seemed more likely. That realization brought with it a new fear. If she were to come after me, thinking I'd merely left her and not knowing of my capture, she would put herself in danger. Capable as she was, she could not fight these men off, and it was not in her disposition to do so even if she could. She was a healer. Not a killer.

Beside me, Calix's sobs softened until they ebbed to the occasional shudder or gasp for breath. It was easy sometimes to forget that he was only a boy. I had to protect him. Had to ensure he was safe, as was Evera. I would not give up. I would fight the three men if I had to, my fists against their swords. It would be futile, yet what else could I do? My exhale fogged in the night air. What had I done putting Calix and Evera in such a situation? Would I lose them, too? Was I cursed to watch those I loved die because of me?

46

———

EVERA

As we neared the mountain pass, the light of the moons filtered through the sparse trees we passed along the main road. Stillness lurked in the shadows, which were devoid even of the chirp of insects. No sound but the distant hoot of an owl and the hoofbeats of Ruairc's mount and my own.

I carried my satchel, heavy with the weight of traveling goods, in addition to a small bottle of concentrated alcohol for cleansing wounds, a ball of wound bandage cloths, and an assortment of medicinal plants for fever and fighting infection. They were items I'd gathered on my second trip into our shop before departing, grateful that my brother was out with Farren. The healer in me felt better being prepared.

"What if the huntsmen are not drinking?" I whispered, my throat dry.

"They will be drinking."

Ruairc's confidence eased my worries, if only slightly. If he were wrong and the men weren't drinking, there would be nothing for us to fall back on aside from his rudimentary swordsmanship skills and perhaps Calix's magic, if the boy was conscious.

497

The distant hum of voices carried to us, and ahead, I caught the warm light of a fire flickering a short distance off the path. Ruairc drew back on his mount's reins, and the stallion stilled, snorting a cloud of mist into the chilled air.

"That'll be them," Ruairc stated. "No sensible traveler would camp so close to the mountain pass. If I tell you to stay with the horse—"

"You know very well I will not."

He huffed. Without further pressing, he dismounted and came to Sorrel's side, offering me his hands. Swinging my legs to one side—something I was becoming a bit less clumsy at—I took his hold and hopped down, landing roughly on the packed earth.

A pang ached at my heart as I considered each of the times I'd dismounted with Neirin. My stubbornness, the way he stood close enough that my body pressed against his, the way his hands held me at my waist. This had to work. There was no alternative. Neirin brought me laughter, frustration, tears, and love. Each time he looked at me it was as if no other woman existed. He made me feel beautiful. And beyond that, he made me feel confident, bold, and empowered.

"If these men catch us …" Ruairc said, his face near to mine as he stood before me, my hands still loosely in his. He swallowed.

"I know." There was, in general, little honor among huntsmen. They worked parallel to the law, making their own rules as opportunities presented themselves. Most were known to have few morals, and I … I was just a woman to them, something to be used. Ruairc was a man with a sword. If he drew it, they would not hesitate to take his life and leave him where he lay.

"Then do not let them catch you," he said.

The depth in his eyes held the faintest flicker of yearning. Though our closeness was something I gave as little thought to as I would being close to Leighis or my brother, my heart fumbled at the realization that Ruairc's feelings were not the same. In the stillness of the moment, I almost stood to my toes and kissed him, just to give him that, to show him I appreciated all of this. But I couldn't. Something had changed within me. A kiss was no longer something light to be given. Sighing, I wrapped my arms around his back and hugged him, taking his warmth and comfort and giving him mine.

Though he was stiff for a moment, he relaxed against me and held me close, cradling my head in one of his hands. His breath was warm against my ear where he rested his head atop mine. Should I echo his words, they would be lost on the wind. Ruairc would not lay his sword down and flee, not if he believed his resistance could buy me a chance at escape. So instead, I nuzzled against his chest and breathed in the scent of him. He smelled of childhood, of playing in his shop beneath the workshop table, whittling little figurines using sharp flakes of rocks we found in the woods.

"Thank you," I said. The words weren't enough.

He sighed into my hair, then his arms left me and he stepped back. When he turned his attention to the glow of light in the field, I swallowed the knot in my throat and reached for the peridot at my neck to clasp it as I'd done so many times before.

"Ruairc," I rasped, panicking and heat rushing through my veins as my fingers found only the shorter necklace Neirin gave me, and not the green stone that hung to the dip of my breasts. "My necklace—" I swallowed. "Leighis gave it to me."

Brows pulled in slightly, Ruairc looked back to the trail behind us. The clasp could have broken at any point along the road. I pushed down the feeling of loss of something I'd so long held dear to me, held as a comfort. I inhaled briskly and trailed my fingers higher, to the shifting stones along the chain Neirin gave me. It brought back memories of his touch as he brushed my hair aside and placed it around my neck.

Ruairc only studied me, as if knowing I needed a moment to gather my thoughts and rationalize my priorities.

When I did, I met his gaze. "Let's go."

Leaving the horses behind, we approached the huntsmen's camp on foot, keeping to the shadows of the occasional tree or higher-growing brush.I took each step lightly, testing before I set my weight, to avoid snapping twigs and drawing attention. Ruairc, too, moved quietly despite his larger figure.

I paused beside Ruairc, tucked behind a stone outcrop that backed up to a section of closely growing trees. I allowed myself a breath. As Ruairc had predicted, the huntsmen were drinking from tankards. One of the men went to the edge of the clearing and refilled his drink from an open-topped barrel, small enough to be strapped to the back of a saddle when sealed.

Swallowing my nerves, I withdrew the vials of mandrake and opium from my satchel, the glass container smooth beneath the shaking stroke of my thumb.

When the man rejoined the others, Ruairc nodded to me. I removed the corked seal on my vial in preparation and made my way closer to the barrel, keeping low among the bushes. My heart thundered in my chest even as I knelt, concealed by the undergrowth. Through the brambles, I could make out two forms strapped to a freestanding oak a short distance up a slope. Both figures remained motionless. Through the bond, I caught no notable trace of emotions from Neirin.

He is fine. He has to be. They both will be fine.

Motion from the campfire drew my eyes up, and I lowered myself further amid the tall grass. The eldest of the huntsmen approached, tankard in hand, talking over his shoulder. Already, he was intoxicated if his slur indicated anything. The tincture would work quickly, then.

I poured the contents of the vial into the barrel, then crept backward into the shadows. Ruairc's hand came to my waist as I reached him, friendly this time and perhaps a bit protective. Heart pounding, nerves consuming me, I allowed myself to take comfort in his touch as the huntsman dipped his tankard into the barrel, then retreated to the fire. Finally, I breathed.

"Evera." Ruairc's hushed voice drew my eyes from the makeshift camp. From his overcoat, he withdrew my dagger, wrapped in cloth as it had been before. "Lark— Neirin would say you should be able to defend yourself."

My blood ran cold, thoughts of the night of Mother's death returning to me. "What would you say?" I asked, eyes wide and focused on the blade.

"To stay back at the shop with your brother," Ruairc quipped, a glint of amusement in his honey-brown eyes. "But I would be wrong. So instead, I will tell you to break what I have wrongly fixed."

I frowned.

"The dagger." He offered it again, and this time I took it, examining its sharp edges. "Use it well. Make it yours again."

"Embrace the broken?"

"Yes, Evera." *Ever-ah.* He smiled, though his eyes remained sad. "Embrace the broken."

THE NIGHT WORE ON SLOWLY. My boots were too stiff, and a cold breeze caught at my ankles and made its way beneath my skirts, raising gooseflesh on my legs. Two of the huntsmen had come to dip their drinks, and both now slept soundly, their heads propped on rolled-up travel blankets. Nox, however, had not come to fill his drink. He sat with his back to us, leaning against a tree with his arms crossed.

"Do you think he is sleeping?"

"I cannot say," Ruairc replied, voice hushed. "How long will the tincture last?"

"A few hours, at least," I said, confident in my assessment. "Perhaps through the night."

Searching for courage, I rose, nearly tripping over my skirts, legs aching from kneeling so long, and left the shelter of the undergrowth. With hesitant steps, I neared the fire and squinted, assuring myself Nox was sleeping. When his chest rose and fell heavily, the tension in my muscles ebbed.

I bunched my skirts to keep from tripping over them, scaled the short slope, and fell to my knees before Neirin. His eyes shot open.

"Evera." He rasped my name, and beside him, Calix woke too.

Warm relief coursed through the bond, sweet and thick. Eagerly, I cupped Neirin's face and pressed a kiss to his lips, tears welling at my eyes. When I pulled back, I drew my dagger from the scabbard at my waist that Ruairc had lent me.

"I'm going to cut you both loose," I told them.

Behind me, steps sounded. I turned briefly to meet Ruairc's eyes as he scaled the hill, his smile broad, satisfied. *"Thank you,"* I mouthed, and he blinked his acknowledgement. Immense gratitude welled up in me, swirling with the relief of finding Neirin and Calix unharmed.

Past Ruairc, my eyes fell to the fire, to the two huntsmen's shadowed forms lying in the grass. Against the tree, Nox no longer slept. He stood, a crossbow drawn. The huntsman's hands trembled, their shaking clear even from this distance. I sucked in a breath, and when the arrow loosed, I saw its trajectory, the spinning arrowhead cutting the air.

47

———

EVERA

As the pointed iron bolt of imminent death approached, time slowed. A slick horror flushed through the bond. I was faintly aware of Neirin lashing at the ropes that bound him behind me. I tried to move, but my feet had frozen. A drop of rain fell to my forehead and dripped along the curve of my brow to my temple.

Just as I drew my breath, my last solid breath, a figure jumped in front of me, then a great impact sent me to the ground. My head throbbed, and I gasped. Air rushed out of my lungs, but I was still breathing, uninjured aside from the impact of a rough fall.

Pushing past the ringing in my head, I rose to my elbows. A weight lay heavy on my legs. Nox held my gaze from the bottom of the hill, stark panic rounding his eyes. The huntsman dropped the crossbow and took a step back, bumping into the tree. And then he was gone, retreating into the shadows.

"Evera." *Ever-ah.* Ruairc rose to one arm beside me, and I sucked in a breath. Mottled brown feathers, white at the tips, held my attention. Three of them, too perfect, too beautiful to be attached to the arrow that was embedded in Ruairc's back.

505

He coughed, and blood splattered my arm, mixing with the speckling of my freckles.

No.

He lay half on top of me, his legs holding my lower half in place. I tried to rise, to pull from beneath his weight, but my head spun and the world tilted. A throbbing where my head had struck the earth pinpointed my pain, nearly pulling me to unconsciousness. Blinking away the fog from my vision, I rolled to my side to face my friend and cupped his cheek with my palm. A tear fell across the ridge of my nose and caught in my other eye.

Beneath my hand, Ruairc's jaw flexed. His breathing was uneven, but there was a calmness to him, a depth to his eyes, a warmth. My lips quivered, and deep inside I knew—*knew*—he was going to die.

A drop of rain fell to his cheek, and I wiped it with my thumb. Another fell and caught on my lashes.

The breath I drew ached at my lungs. Blinking back my tears and fighting to still the trembling of my hand as I traced my fingers along the coarseness of Ruairc's beard, I hummed my mother's lullaby.

The melody was choked, broken by my emotion even as I tried to stop my tears. The rain came down harder, darkening Ruairc's sandy-blond hair and slicking it to his brow. I combed it aside with my fingers, then leaned in to him.

The shuddering of his breaths fogged between us as I hummed. When his shaking ceased, and he exhaled on a sigh, I bit down on my lip. Seconds passed, the stillness consuming. The iron taste of blood met my tongue, and I scrunched my nose, burying my fingers in the hair at the back of his head. The tune of my hum faded with his breath until only the pattering of rain in the leaves of the oak's canopy remained.

48

NEIRIN

THE RAIN CAME DOWN, wetting my knuckles where they clenched the ropes confining me. Thick, heavy loss came with the storm, and I sat unmoving. Just beyond my reach, my mate, my love, my world lay entangled with a man I'd spent the last fortnight despising. Yet as I sat, immersed in the moment, grief for the loss of his life held me.

In the clearing, the fire hissed. Its faltering light flickered, silhouetting the shaft of the arrow protruding from the cobbler's back. From Ruairc's back. The arrow he'd taken in Evera's stead.

I sought to form words, but they fell away with the rain. There was no comfort, no solace that words could bring. I yearned to go to Evera, to embrace her, but my bindings held me back. And, even if they hadn't, a heavy knowing told me she needed this moment as it was, without me. Needed to hold the man who had sought her heart and offered his aid to ensure her safety despite knowing she would never be what he wanted her to be.

Another unforgivable truth. Another casualty to my cause, to my search for redemption.

Looking to Calix, his eyes round and knowing, I considered his words. *"The deaths I have caused."*

Swallowing the knot in my throat, I relented to the moment, to the rainfall on my face, to the muffled cries of the woman I loved. To the absence of a soul.

The fire sizzled and died, the last of its flames quenched by the rain. Dim moonlight shone down on the scene through a patch of clouds, faintly illuminating the shadow of a man on horseback as he approached through the brush. Straining my eyes, I blinked back the blur of wetness to make out the familiar features of the apothecary. But he'd come too late.

Dismounting at the top of the slope, he fell to his knees and cradled Evera in his arms, drawing her out from underneath Ruairc's weight. The chain of her necklace glinted, catching my attention as he clasped it in his fist. Why did he have her necklace?

For a moment, Aureus only held her. When the trembling of her body lessened, they exchanged hushed words, lost in the downpour, and then she curled her knees to her chest and turned away from Ruairc, burying her face against her brother's chest. Aureus's eyes rose to mine and held.

For a long moment, I sat, watching, feeling entirely helpless. Finally, Evera sniffled and drew back from her brother's embrace. She turned back to me without meeting my eyes and used her dagger to free me from the rope.

When the last thread finally snapped, the tightness of my bindings slacked, and I drew Evera into my arms. Her cinnamon curls lay flat to her head, darkened to an almost umber tone by the rain. Her body shook.

There were no words to be said. Her heart was broken, and it was my doing. I'd let Ruairc get involved. Yet, if I had not … if he had not been there to take the bolt in Evera's stead …

Swallowing the knot in my throat, I cradled her head, drawing her into my lap, her face turned away from the cobbler's still form. I rocked and pressed a kiss to her brow; her skin was chilled against my lips.

At the bottom of the slope, Aureus moved through the shadows, releasing the remaining two horses from their ties. Their flustered nickering and disgruntled snorts accompanied clicking and the wet slap of the apothecary's hand on their flanks as he sent them off. They would return to their stables. All horses returned home. He moved to the tree Nox had rested beside and knelt to pick up something off the ground.

Calix, free of his bindings, went to stand before Ruairc, and when he cast his eyes to me, I knew his thoughts walked the same path as mine. *The deaths we'd caused.*

"We need to go," Aureus said to Evera as he scaled the hill again. A new resolve set his features and firmed his jaw. "You lied to me, Evera. Had I not found your damned necklace and thought to come after you to return it, knowing you would camp for the night—" He shook his head. "This is your fault as much as it is his." Aureus turned his cool blue gaze on me and tossed an ivory letter, its seal broken, to the grass.

"I'm not going back to Elrune," Evera snapped, setting her brother with an expression that perfectly mirrored his own. In my arms, her body quivered.

The two argued, and while part of me thought to intervene, to tell her brother to back down, I'd made that mistake once before in their shop. Evera could stand her own ground, and now, especially, I felt she needed to. Especially since , in truth, I sided with her brother on this. As much as I wanted her at my side, I'd put enough people at risk.

"Neirin." Calix held the letter out to me.

The boy exchanged a glance with Aureus. The apothecary had read the letter before rejoining us atop the hill. Aureus's cheeks turned red, and he turned sharply from me, from the letter, shoving his hands in his pockets. Actions that spoke a bit of shame; he'd pried where he should not have. With trembling fingers, I unfolded the paper and read.

NEIRIN,

For as long as I can remember, I have looked up to you. I have seen your courage and your skills in battle. When I first received your note, I will admit I considered your words for some time. It was only when the huntsman, Nox, pestered me for a response that I sat down to write this note.

Mother is unwell. She has shared with me her affliction and her reasons for keeping it from me. She has shared, too, your affections for her, and likewise. While matters of the heart are new to me, I am learning about them. In all ways, I am learning. How to be a King, how to be a man, how to make difficult decisions. There is a great weight to it, but I know that, in time , this, too, will lighten and ease.

Mother takes some fault in Father's fate. Guilt riddles her for imploring you to stay when Father planned to send you away, for begging with you not to leave her, both for your blood and for your affections.

While I cannot forgive her, or you, for what transpired, she is my mother, and I do not wish for her to suffer any longer.

I have held off the guard, even after word of Cyan's death. I believe that your intentions with him, at least, were honest. Mother has argued this as well.

You will remain at the country estate, where you will provide what Mother needs from you. What this is, I do not wish to know the details of. I seek only to keep her alive. And to help her stave off this sickness of her mind so that I can turn my focus back to what lies ahead, to the kingdom.

Best regards,

King Harlan

· · ·

TOSSING the letter to the ground between Aureus and I, I snarled. "This is full of lies."

Aureus's jaw firmed.

"Your mentor spoke of the laws of the old lore, so I presume you know them as well." I held up my arm, revealing the marks of my bond. "I've lain with no one else, had affections for no one else, certainly not the Queen."

"Stop, both of you. Just stop," Evera said, her voice almost a cry, bold but broken. Pushing from my arms, she wiped her face, a futile attempt as she stood with her back to us. She knelt back beside Ruairc, running her fingers through his hair. "Aureus, take him back to Elrune. Write to his family in the western lands."

Her voice sounded cold, empty as she dropped a kiss at the cobbler's cheek, then stood again, taking Calix's hand in hers. Together, they paced a short distance off, then Evera stopped. Calix looked up at her, their figures barely more than shadows. Cries broke from her again, and she fell to her knees. The boy wrapped his arms around her shoulders and turned his gaze to me. Even unable to make out his features amid the rain and shadows, I could feel the physical force of his sorrow. I suspected more for Evera than for the cobbler.

"What is your course of action now that your brother does not plan to pardon you?" Aureus's gaze remained on his fallen friend. "How can you assure me you will keep Evera from this fate?"

"I cannot," I admitted. "Though I suspect telling her to return with you will do little good. I've promised her I will not leave her unless she wishes it, and I intend to keep that promise."

"So you still aim to return to the castle?"

"The Queen lies with her every word. She would only do so if she were the one to order Kaius's death, if she were the one who framed me. Harlan is not in any danger from her. He doesn't need me. And he can make his own mistakes in ruling the kingdom." I swallowed, the knot in my throat thick as I released the weight of responsibility, of obligation I'd so long lived with. I watched the shadows of Calix and Evera wrapped in each other's embrace. "They are my family now. I will take them to the western lands and start a new life. An honest one."

49

NEIRIN

Dawn came so subtly, I hardly recognized it until I glanced up to the break in the trees and found the sky a dusky gray. Time was running short; the tincture Evera had laced the huntsmen's drinks with would soon wear off, and they would wake. Even if they were able to find their swords, which I had cast out in the trees and covered with leaves, I could take them now that I was unbound. Still, I didn't want it to come to that. It would have been better if they were still deep in their sleep when we left.

"We need to go," I said to Calix.

He sat beside me with one arm propped up on his knee, the other hand busied with pulling up blades of grass. "Are we really running away?"

I turned my gaze from the bottom of the hill where Evera was making her goodbyes with her brother, the form of the cobbler over his mount's back. Calix had overheard, then, when I spoke with Aureus. Perhaps the Alidian did have heightened hearing.

"My brother doesn't need me; he's not in danger as I thought he was," I said. "The Queen is malicious, selfish, but she would never put her son at risk."

Calix held me with his cobalt eyes. "And what of the messengers?"

Releasing a breath, I ran a hand through my hair. How could I make him understand? "It is not—" I tilted my head back, resting it against the tree and looking up to the branches above, black silhouettes against the lightening sky. "It is a hard truth, but there is no outcome in which your friends survive. Even if we were to free them, I could not feed them all at once, and there is no way to travel with such a large group. I've no coin to my name. I can't provide for them all."

The boy shifted and tossed aside the blades of grass in his right hand before turning to fuss with his tunic. "What if there was another way?" He withdrew a folded piece of paper from his waistband. "What if they did not have to feed off your blood?"

"Calix—"

"Read this." He swallowed hard. Interrupting went against his training, and his boldness spoke of his determination. Or perhaps desperation.

Nodding, I took the paper just as Evera climbed the slope and sat before us, crisscrossed in the grass. The slow patter of hoofbeats in mud sounded as Aureus left, heading back toward Elrune at a walk. Raising my eyes to Evera, I offered an encouraging smile.

She nodded subtly. Dark circles lined her eyes, which were red from crying. She sniffled, her nose slightly swollen. Her shoulders sloped, and her hair tumbled unkempt around her shoulders. To see her this way broke my heart. If only I could take her pain away, put it on myself instead.

Sighing, I turned my attention back to the paper, unfolding it to reveal Calix's scribbles and sketches. His penmanship was rough in some areas, slanted as if he'd written quickly. In other areas the scroll was more elegant, practiced, with carefully drawn diagrams and images.

"What does this mean?" I asked, trying to keep the frustration from my tone. At that moment, I needed to focus on Evera, comfort her, and make a plan to get my family to safety before the huntsmen woke.

"Reiterations of Leighis's studies," Calix said.

Evera furrowed her brows and shifted to her knees, looking over the paper from where she sat in front of me.

"I've been researching whenever I had time, and talking to the old man. He traveled to the ancient library of Vitalis once, and the notes I found from his time there—they gave me an idea. It took me some time, but I found this"—he pointed to an illustration of a flower with delicate cupped petals and tendrils beneath its bud—"in a children's book, a fairy tale. However, it aligns with Leighis's notes and descriptions found in several other studies. I believe that whatever this flower is, it can work in place of your blood."

Evera held out her palm, and I handed her the paper. "There's no such flower," she said, examining the drawing.

I rubbed the bridge of my nose. If I were to voice my thoughts aloud, there would be no convincing either of them to flee with me. They were too stubborn; Calix was too intent on helping his friends, and Evera was too invested in aiding anyone in need. But this was what she'd wanted all along—to use her abilities, to do good. Was it wrong of me to keep knowledge to myself if it kept her safe but stifled her?

"I know of the flower," I said, breaking off the conversation the two were having without me. They both quieted and turned to me. "I've seen it before. They grow at my mother's grave."

As if too nervous to speak, Calix remained still as a statue.

Evera, studying the paper again, shook her head. "How did you learn all this, Calix?"

"When you care enough for someone," I said, speaking for Calix, "you cannot give up in your search to save them, even when it feels impossible."

He nodded, understanding perfectly.

"If these findings are accurate,"—Evera traced a finger over the scribbling—"then we may be able to save them, Neirin."

May be able to. "I can't risk it, can't risk your safety for a possibility—"

Evera's eyes gleamed with determination, and her features sharpened. "I can do this, Neirin. Let me do this."

I shook my head. Every instinct told me this was wrong, that leading my family to the very place we needed to escape could only end in disaster. I should list the reasons such a plan was foolhardy. This was merely the hopes of a child, based on fairy tales and the findings of old notes and texts. Would Evera resent me if I denied her this? Would she try to go about the task without me?

Could I support her, even as I feared for her safety, for her life?

"Evera, what am I to do?" The defeat that rang in my voice echoed in my mind long after the words had disappeared from the air.

She reached for me and stroked my leg with her thumb, holding my eyes. "Put your trust in me."

5 0

———

EVERA

AT THE EDGE of the woods, Neirin dismounted and peered over the river's edge to the rushing water below. This was the sixth time we'd stopped, and he was growing irritated. "It is as I said." He kicked a rock, and it splashed as it met the rapids. "There is no place this river can be crossed, aside from the bridge."

In front of me, atop my mare, Calix remained still, his back warm against my chest, his frame slight. I, too, held back any response, knowing Neirin would only shut me down as he had at my last suggestion. This side of him was new to me, but I empathized with it to an extent. He was only frightened for our safety and unnerved by the position Calix and I had put him in when we insisted upon this path without any plan.

A plan was what we needed.

When Neirin rolled his shoulders and sighed, turning back to me with tired eyes, I held a hand out to him.

He cleared the short distance to Sorrel's side. "I'm sorry for being so sharp-tongued."

Shaking my head, I offered him a smile. "It's been a long day." As I spoke, the corners of my lips turned down, my

523

thoughts returning to Ruairc. A knot formed in my throat, and Neirin squeezed my hand, a gesture of support.

"We'll rest, reassess things at dawn."

"What of the huntsmen?" I queried.

Lifting Calix off Sorrel's back and setting him to the ground, Neirin turned his gaze to the Edthiel Mountains, just visible above the treetops to the south. "I suspect they'll return home to nurse their wounds and retrieve their horses. Only a fool of a huntsman would return to Astraea after failing her. It's likely they'll avoid her and avoid the capital, as we should be doing." His statement ended with pointed inflection.

"You know I can't stand by knowing those children—" I glanced at Calix. "Not when there is something I can do to help."

Neirin only huffed and helped me dismount Sorrel. I'd spent the better half of the morning while we rode going over Calix's notes and discussing his findings with him. While some plants' potency lay in their petals, others in their seeds or roots, I could not be certain what part of the elusive plant we would need to create the brew. We would have to use the entirety of it. In time, I could analyze the results of my findings and create a more precise tincture. For now, a general tea would have to suffice.

But what if it doesn't?

It was Neirin's concern too. If we were to produce the brew, break into the castle, seek to remedy the children, and the tea proved ineffective— No, there was no use riddling over what-ifs. I would leave the worrying to Neirin, as he seemed intent on doing so regardless.

By dusk, we'd tied the horses and set up a makeshift camp for the night. We had no fire, as Neirin suspected it might draw the attention of soldiers stationed out at the bridge downstream, but the evening was comfortably warm, and we had prepared rations to fill our bellies.

Propped against a boulder, I sat with Calix leaning against me as I stroked his hair, the curls atop his head thick and soft.

The last rays of light cast through the trees and fell upon cheeks still rounded with youth as he dozed.

"When we were tied to the tree," Neirin started, voice low so as not to wake the boy, "my thoughts turned to your dagger. I know you are not ready to speak of it, but I resented not knowing something so important to you as I faced death."

My fingers stilled in Calix's hair just as a breeze caught, sending a shiver down my spine.

"You carry it again."

The dagger remained sheathed, strapped to my hip with the belt Ruairc had lent me.

"Yes," I said.

"If you are not ready to speak of it—"

"No." I resumed my absent stroking through Calix's hair. The boy's nose scrunched as if he were in a dream, then the creases softened again. I sighed. "I am ready." Not because Neirin had broached the subject, but because of the child who leaned against me. Because of those we were going to rescue from the Queen's hold. Because of Ruairc's words, when he told me to embrace the broken parts of myself.

"Aureus and I lived on the streets with our mother when we were children," I said. "One of the men that Mother took to bed —" I swallowed. "He did not want her. He took my innocence, robbed me of the chance to choose for myself how I wanted to give my body, and killed Mother when she tried to fight him off." It was easier, somehow, to say the words than I'd expected it would be. Painful, but freeing too. Like I'd needed to voice them, needed to no longer carry the burden alone.

Sitting beside me, Neirin tensed, but he said nothing, only let me speak.

"It wasn't until a few days ago that I recalled the events. The nightmares I've had all my life—they were fragmented glimpses into that night. Mother's scream, Aureus hiding, my wrist being grasped, being tugged from my brother."

When I quieted, Neirin buried his nose in my hair, his breath warm as he exhaled heavily.

I carefully moved my arm, and Calix snuffled in his sleep, readjusting himself with his head turned away in my lap. Drawing my dagger, I held it up to the last light of the evening. "It belonged to him—to the man who hurt me."

"You defended yourself." Neirin's words came across as a statement, not a question, and I turned my chin to look up at him and meet his eyes. I began to form the words to question him, but he spoke first. "You're brave." He placed his left hand on my heart. "You have a fire within you. I saw it the first time I set eyes upon you."

Turning my gaze back to the dagger, I let Neirin's words sink in. Was I brave? Or was I only rash, a fool, always lunging before I thought? Perhaps there was no difference between the two. "When I slashed the man across the face, his eyes pooled with hatred. I thought he would kill me, too, but a knock on the door of the pleasure house room we were in startled him, and he fled out the window. It didn't matter that I cut him. It didn't make a difference or change what happened before I got my hands on his knife."

Neirin took my hand in his, coaxing me to turn the dagger. Its mirrored surface not only reflected the light, but it also reflected us. Neirin's eyes were pained, as if he'd seen a ghost. "It made a difference," Neirin said, swallowing.

I looked up to him again and found his face had paled. "Neir—"

He blinked as if clearing his thoughts. "You showed that man you did not fear him. And even if you could not take back what he took from you, in standing up for yourself, I believe you set forth on the path you're on today. I believe your action was the first spark of your fire. And now—" He smiled, and the color returned to his face as he kissed my forehead. "Now you burn brighter than any hearth, any wildfire."

His words melted the edge of nerves the subject had brought, and I hummed, the corners of my lips turning up. I sheathed my dagger at my hip, and with that, released the remnants of my fear of the man who'd hurt me all those years ago. There was no way of knowing if the man was dead or alive, living in the streets or in an estate. If he did live, he would see the scar of my mark each time he caught his own reflection. And if he were to cross my path again, I would detect him in a heartbeat. He wouldn't hurt me again. Though that pain would always exist to an extent, I didn't have to let it weigh me down anymore. Neirin was right, something had sparked in me that night.

Embrace the broken.

Was that what Ruairc had meant? That without the moments that shape us, we are nothing more than a mold of everyone else? Was it my broken pieces that made me unique, bold, and that fed my fire and strengthened my resolve? And Neirin—he, too, was broken in his own ways. Perhaps I was the broken piece to complete his puzzle, and perhaps he was the same unto me.

"Neir," I said, breaking the quiet. "What happened to your guard uniform? The night of the festival?"

He nodded across the river, to the thick forested wood on the other side. "It's still there, I suspect. I shed it when I shifted."

I sucked in my bottom lip as an opportunity came into view before me. One Neirin would never agree to. Perhaps it was time for me to be brave again, to take the first step.

51

———

EVERA

Warmth cocooned me. Neirin slept at my back, his arm wrapped at my waist, and Calix was curled against my chest. The cold breeze caught my nose and sent a chill down my spine, but in the warmth of my family's embrace, I felt safe from anything that lay beyond us. Secure. Was I wrong to push this pursuit? Was I putting my new family at risk for the sake of the children held in the castle? Could I live with myself if something happened to one of them? They were the same questions I'd asked myself time and again as I'd waited for Neirin's breathing to slow with sleep.

I studied the outline of the treetops, silhouettes against a sky speckled with stars. Though I knew my plan held the possibility of failure, it was the only option I could see before us. The river flowed too fast for us to swim, or at least it was for Calix and I. Neirin could, as his fox, but he would never agree to a plan that involved having to shift. However, if he woke to find Calix and I already at the other bank—if shifting were his only way to reach us … It was the only way.

"Calix," I whispered the boy's name, stroking his cheek with my thumb. He mumbled but didn't rouse. "Calix, wake up."

529

Yawning, he half opened his eyes, his lips pouted. "Wha—"

"I have a plan. We can't wake Neirin," I said, hushing him.

He sighed, and I wondered briefly whether he would go along with my plan or if he would question it. Leaving Neirin, I knew, went against his instinct and his loyalties. But he was loyal to me, too. He trusted me, and I hoped that was enough for him to put his faith in my plan. It was the only chance we had.

Without further word, he shuffled away from me and sat on his knees, his eyes studying as I carefully moved Neirin's arm aside and wiggled out of his hold. The chill at the lack of his body heat hit me instantly, and I resisted a shudder.

Looking down at my mate, my love, my world, I hesitated. But this was the only way. I'd turned countless options over in my mind, and no other path seemed possible. It was time for me to be brave, to be strong. To put into place what would move us forward. Once we were across the river, though, there truly would be no turning back. As if the rushing water itself were a physical representation of the last barrier between the war that waged in my mind—the war between running away and keeping my family safe or risking everything to do what was right.

Adjusting the single small blanket we'd shared to keep Neirin warm, I resisted the urge to kiss his brow before standing and turning my back to him. My heart thundered in my chest, and I let out a breath to steady myself, focusing on the rushing of the river, the gurgles and splashes, the smell of fresh water in the air.

Calix stood beside me, handing me my bag which contained the remains of our rations and supplies. Nodding, I took it from him, letting my right shoulder take the brunt of the weight, and set forward, following the course of the river.

WE WALKED IN SILENCE, even as the bridge came into view. The twin moons shone down, both waning, denoting the passing of time. Had it been only just over a moon, then, since the festival? Beside me, Calix's steps shuffled the stones as he dragged his feet, showing his exhaustion. I was responsible for him, for a child. So recently, I had dismissed the thought of marriage and motherhood. But this family with Neirin and Calix wasn't confining, wasn't stifling. They both supported me, believed in my abilities, in my mind, and in my heart. The corners of my lips turned up, and I wrapped an arm around Calix's shoulders, drawing him closer to me as we followed the river.

The loose stones and dirt underfoot gave way to a cobbled road, and I slowed my pace. Calix tensed but showed no other sign of hesitancy. He kept his eyes down as we stopped before the bridge.

Two soldiers leaned against the bridge's stone railing on one side, and a third sat with a waterskin in hand. One of the men standing nudged his companion, and both smirked as the first nodded at us. "What are a woman and a child doing traveling alone, and so late?" He stepped toward us, his eyes dark even in the glint of the lantern propped atop the railing.

Calix could take down the three of them if it came to it, but that would rouse suspicion if a change in the soldiers' shifts occurred, or if another traveler crossed the bridge and alerted someone within the city. No, we had to cross without drawing suspicion. Otherwise, this task would be in vain. There would be no sneaking into the castle if the guard were on alert.

"Thieves overtook us in the mountain pass," I said, allowing my voice to shake, hoping I would come off convincing in my lie. Calix's eyes remained downcast. The reputation of the thieves in the pass, I hoped, would be enough for the men to take pity on us. I'd considered using a prickle brush to give Calix and I the appearance of an ailment, but that could have gone wrong. The guards might have turned us away from the capital in an attempt to keep the contagion from spreading. As it was, there was no reason for the men to turn away a woman and child. That did not mean we were perfectly safe. At this time of night, the guards could easily take advantage of us. Calix would protect me, I knew, but it was my role not to let it come to that.

The first guard looked back, but his companion against the railing lent him no guidance. Turning back to us, he huffed. "Who else were you traveling with?"

"Just my—" I cast my gaze aside and sniffled, wishing I had the ability to fake tears.

"Father," Calix said, squeezing my hand. He raised his chin, meeting the guard's eyes. As young as he was, in such a situation, Calix would become the head of our house if it were just him and I left. "He distracted them while we fled."

"Why did you take the pass at night?" The guard's tone held no sympathy, though the tight downward turn of his lips told me it was likely we'd shifted his mindset just a little.

"Father is—was—a healer. Word came for us to come urgently. One of our customers is suffering with her pregnancy." Calix sighed. "Now I will have to take Father's place in aiding her until her delivery. I was Father's apprentice."

The man before us flexed his fist, hovering just above the pommel of his sword as if struggling over how to respond to our story.

"Back down, Renfred." The voice that spoke up was gravelly, aged. Taking a swig from his waterskin, the older soldier propped against the railing, coughed once, then took another drink. "Let them pass. Can't you see they've had enough of a night?"

Renfred flexed his jaw, and his companion standing a short distance back stifled a laugh at the lecture. He stepped aside, and as Calix and I passed the older man, I touched a hand to his shoulder.

"Thank you," I said, voice quiet. He looked up at me, wrinkles creasing beside his eyes baggy with exhaustion. I could smell the alcohol from his waterskin this close, and for a moment, as I held his gaze, I wondered why he looked so solemn. Had he lost someone? Apprehension tugged at my gut, and again I let the fear of what lay ahead take hold of me.

Calix squeezed my hand, and I let him coax me the rest of the way across the bridge. Was I leading Calix to a fate similar to the old man's? Was I to leave Neirin to grieve the rest of his life for Calix and I? Was I to be left to grieve for one or both of them?

5 2

___

NEIRIN

"Bested you again!"

I blinked, the sun beaming down on me as I lay in the cool grass. Squinting, I followed the line of the wooden sword held to my chest. A familiar, rounded face looked down at me. Freckles dotted the boy's nose and cheeks, and his short-cropped hair stood on end.

Thatcher.

I scoffed and pushed the pretend weapon aside. Getting to my feet, I dusted autumn leaves off my tunic, which hung over one shoulder, a bit too large. "You distracted me on purpose," I said, my voice youthful.

Thatcher grinned, not denying the fact, and playfully skipped back a few steps, his sword held straight out. "You'll get me this time, little brother." *Little.* I was younger than him by less than a fortnight. In truth, I stood an inch taller than him. He was agile, though, and clever. And admittedly, I was easily distracted.

"I don't want to play anymore." Tossing my sword to the ground, I picked up my waterskin from where I'd left it atop a stone bench and took a deep drink. It did little to cool me, so I dumped the remaining water over my head. Beads dripped from clumped silver strands of hair and made wet paths down my face.

"Why'd you do that?"

"It's hot," I said, tugging at my tunic.

"No, it's not. Are you daft?"

I readied a retort, but something told me Thatcher was right. It was the season of falling leaves. Overhead, the sun shone in a clear sky, but it had not been warm in several fortnights. The mornings were frigid, and the days not much better. I was distantly aware of icicles dripping from the bird bath just beyond the flower beds to my left.

Heat surged through me.

"I think I might be ill," I said, recalling the last time I'd caught an ailment. The flashes of heat had come before I spilt the contents of my stomach.

"You just don't want to lose to me again," Thatcher said boldly, though he took a step back anyway, just in case I did lose my midday meal.

Feeling dizzy, I sat down. The heat was becoming as unbearable as grabbing a pot hung over a hearth. Burning, searing. A writhing panic rose in my chest, like a nightmare, like snakes beneath my skin.

"Neirin?"

A sharp pain in my head sent me curling forward. I held my head atop my knees, hands cupping my ears to fend off the ringing.

"Neirin ..." The voice, smaller and frightened this time, seemed so distant I almost didn't hear it.

Intense pain took me, blurred my vision until darkness consumed my sight as I fell to my side. Half-unconscious, aware only of agony, time fragmented. Cloth confined me, but when I sought to push it from my face, I could not. I had no control over my limbs. I tried to cry, to scream, but I was trapped within myself.

On shaking limbs, the body that bound me got to its feet. The world took on a lower vantage point, and I beheld my brother before me like a giant, the colors of the world around him all off. Again, the wooden sword was pointed at me. This time, tears gathered in Thatch's eyes.

"Monster," he cried, his voice broken. "Give me back my brother!"

I am your brother. Monster?

Thatcher jabbed at the air in front of me, and the body that held me leapt back, snarling. My brother stepped forward, cornering me against a garden hedge. The tears that welled in his eyes created paths down his cheeks.

"Monster!"

This time, the wooden sword struck my head, radiating dull aching pain, sending the world sideways. Again, I growled, getting to my feet. But the sound was not my own. Neither were the steps that took me toward my brother.

When Thatcher struck out again, the monster leapt at him. And in the next moment, the taste of iron consumed my senses. My brother's neck snapped within the grip of the monster's jaws. So fragile. The gasping gurgles silenced, and from a place outside of myself, within the confines of a monster, I watched my brother's eyes loose their life. All I could feel was the pounding of the monster's heart. Shock consumed my thoughts, even as the monster licked the blood from its snout.

The murky darkness of a nightmare held me. But this was not a nightmare. It was a memory. I'd seen this before, been here before.

I'd killed my own brother.

I woke with a start, heart thundering in my chest.

Reality came back to me in a rush. I became aware of the lack of warmth, of the quiet, of the absence of my mate.

Evera and Calix—they were gone.

Rushing to my feet, I forced the memories of my brother's death down. The small blanket that had covered me in the night fell to the earth. The only remains of our supplies aside from Sorrel, who nibbled at the short grass. Panic, anger, and worry sent me pacing. I'd slept in my boots, and twigs snapped beneath my feet. Sweat beaded on my forehead.

Where did they go? Why would they leave without me?

Through the rasping of my breath, I fought to make sense of the situation. How had I not woken? I cursed to myself. With Evera, I slept more soundly than I did on my own. But that was no excuse. If anything, I should sleep lighter when I have my mate to protect. Was it the nightmare that had held me in sleep and kept me from waking?

"Neirin." A voice carried from across the river, and I turned.

Evera.

She stood at the far bank, Calix beside her and a sack of supplies over her shoulder. Relief fell over me to see them safe, though in the next instant, frustration took its place.

"Dammit, Evera," I growled. I didn't want to snap at her, but what she'd done was reckless, and she'd only done it in the dead of night because she knew I would not agree to the plan. "How did you cross the bridge?" Soldiers were mostly young, selfish pricks of men who would take such an opportunity to— And after what she'd told me the night before ... "Did they touch you?"

"No." Her level tone spoke for itself. She'd known, then, that it had been a possibility that one of them would try something.

Clearing the few short steps to the river's edge, I ran a hand through my hair. "You shouldn't have gone without me."

"We couldn't have crossed with you; those soldiers are posted there in search of you."

She wasn't wrong. Still, she'd put herself in harm's way. Equal measures of guilt and fear flashed hot and cold through me. I should have woken.

"What now?" I asked, knowing the answer. There was only one reason they would cross without me, just to meet me at the opposite bank.

"You can't swim the river," Evera said calmly, "but your fox can."

"That's a bold assumption." My worry tainted my tone with sharpness.

"I've seen foxes swim rivers, back in Elrune."

Huffing, I held her gaze. The woman was stubborn as ever. "Fine," I growled, even though the thought of giving power to the fox still frightened me. Despite my bitterness over how it was handled, it wasn't a poor plan. Though I couldn't control the fox, it was sensible to assume he would go to her. He always had in the past. The draw of the bond was stronger than any other instinct that drove him. But Calix … Even if his magic was strong … I swallowed, images from my dream returning to me.

"This is why you asked about my guard's uniform?" I removed my boots, trying to focus my thoughts.

"Don't need you traipsing into the castle naked, now do we?" Her tone was too light for the moment.

I grumbled and raised my eyes to the pair of conspirators once more before pulling my cloak and shirt over my head. An idea came over me with a rush of relief. "My uniform has some of my own blood on it; can you find it, Calix?" I didn't want him here. Not when I was not in control.

The boy considered for a moment, then nodded. I was unsure how the sense of smell worked with his kind, only that they detected my blood. But from how far off? I suspected it was at least a mile from here that I shed the uniform. At least Astraea would have had no reason to send her boys out in this direction, so it should have remained untouched.

"Off you go, then," I told him, an edge of command in my voice.

He narrowed his brows but didn't object. When he disappeared through the trees, I turned my attention back to undressing, working at the ties of my trousers.

My monster will not hurt Evera. My fox would not hurt his mate.

"I'm sorry to force your hand like this," Evera said, her voice quiet, words almost undetectable beneath the rushing of the water.

"Do not exclude me from your planning in the future," I said, stepping out of the last of my clothing. I did not want to fight, nor did I want to stifle her, but it was hard to force the bitterness from my tone. Did she not see how she worried me? How did the essence of my being seek to protect her? Capable or not, I wanted to stand at her side, not be left behind without knowledge of where she went or why. Remembrance of the panic I'd felt when I first woke rose a knot to my throat. No, this was not entirely her fault. The nightmare was to blame for at least some of my distress.

When she gave no response, I sighed. Quickly, I checked that Sorrel was secured so that Calix or I could find and retrieve her later, then I closed my eyes and released control to my fox. He took it, and as it had been before, the shift was fluid, painless, and lasted only the briefest of moments. Again, I found myself trapped within his form, the world muted, lacking color. Sound and scent intensified.

At least the forest calmed him.

When Evera coaxed him forward, my fox swiveled his ears. Two small steps brought him to the river's edge, the span of water appearing even more daunting from this lower vantage. He whimpered, stepping in place.

Evera crouched. "It's only a short swim. You can do this." Was she trying to reason with him? Could he understand her words? I doubted it. Either way, her voice tugged at him, the draw of the bond a physical force.

Panting, he keened, then leapt.

5 3

EVERA

Awe filled me as it always did when I witnessed Neirin shifting. To be told stories of magic as a child, then to come face-to-face with the reality of it as an adult—it seemed other-worldly. Neirin was real, though. He was my mate, my companion, the one who called to my heart.

When his fox reached the bank and scrambled up to stand before me in the short grass, I reached out a hand. The animal addressed me but did not come forward. Instead, he shook his mottled gray pelt, sending droplets of chilled water into the air. I withdrew my palm and wiped off the few that landed on my arm.

"I knew you could do it," I whispered, admiration warming my heart.

The fox looked to me, his eyes silver orbs. Could the fox understand me? I liked to think he could. He was smarter, surely, than Neirin gave him credit for. There was wisdom there, something that held more depth than instinct for survival alone.

I held my breath as he shifted back, wet clumped fur giving way to smooth skin, still slick with streams of water.

"You must be freezing," I said as Neirin held my eyes, his hair silver again. Whether it had been washed by the river in some way, or restored by the magic of the shift, I couldn't say.

"The only cold I felt was when I woke to find you not in my arms."

"I'm sorry—"

"I know." He cut me off, cupping my cheek in his palm. The chill of his skin sent a shudder down my spine. "All that matters now is that you are okay. I apologize for being sharp-tongued with you; it is only that fear overtook me when I woke."

Shaking my head to dismiss his apology, I leaned in and pressed my lips to his, the touch light and gentle. His hand at my cheek moved back, twining through the hair at the back of my neck as he firmed our connection. He did not seek to deepen the kiss, only strengthen it, as if he were afraid that I might slip away from him again.

When he finally broke the kiss and sat back, he wrapped his arms at his knees and sighed heavily. "I dreamt of the day my brother died." He wet his lips and cast his eyes to the trees. "I suspect that only worked to hasten my panic when I woke. I should have remained calm. Rational."

I sat beside him and rested my head on his shoulder. Even through my dress and cloak, I felt the coolness of his skin. Trailing my left hand down the length of his arm, I traced the marks of our bond until my palm lay above his. Reflexively, he took my fingers, intertwining them with his own.

"Do you want to talk about it?" I asked.

Neirin tensed. "I—"

Rustling in the brush drew our attention to the dense woods, and our conversation fell away. A moment later, Calix rushed forward, carrying a stack of folded black leather clothing. Neirin's uniform. A strap hung diagonally over Calix's shoulder with a sword sheathed at his back, and in his hand was a coin sack.

"You rummaged through my pockets," Neirin scoffed.

Calix shrugged and tossed Neirin the coins, which he caught effortlessly.

My thoughts returned to the night of the festival, when Neirin had spent an exuberant amount of coin on liquor. Now he weighed it in his hand, and I couldn't help but wonder if his perspective had changed. If now, instead of viewing the silver as nothing more than metal to toss at drinks, it was the potential for a new life for us. That kind of coin could buy us passage to the western lands. We could live off it for several moon cycles. It was an opportunity for safety and a fresh start.

A knot formed in my throat, and again, the trickle of unease that I was making the wrong choice here, risking too much, chilled me.

5 4

NEIRIN

FROM THE WOODS to the east of the castle, I led our group to a ruined section of the outer wall that led into the aspen grove surrounding Mother's grave. It was the same crevasse I'd snuck through as a boy to play in the woods, only now it was a challenge to fit.

Within the walls, I slowed our pace, letting the sun ascend enough to cast shadows through the trees and raise mist from the chilled earth. My companions remained quiet until we reached the monument and the bed of flowers that surrounded it, then they left my side, exchanging excited whispers as they began their work.

I stood back a moment, my nightmare still weighing on me. The coin in my jacket pocket was my escape, a real way to care for my family for some time, to get us as far from the capital as possible. I knew this, yet I could not broach the subject. Not as we'd walked, and certainly not now while I watched Evera kneeling, instructing Calix with a smile on her face. This was her purpose, what she had been searching for. How could I take that from her?

"Can I help?" I asked, joining them.

Evera raised her vibrant sage eyes and held out her hand. I took it and knelt beside her. She explained her strategies for harvesting the plants. We would leave most of the flowers, taking only what we needed for the children.

Though I followed Evera's instructions to the best of my abilities, I was frequently corrected by her or the boy. It was amusing the way he'd picked up her skill over the past moon; endearing, too. After one too many corrections, I was dismissed and tasked with keeping watch. A kind way of telling me my aid was not needed, but I didn't mind. In truth, I preferred to watch the pair.

"Why would the flowers grow here?" Calix asked as he carefully pulled back the petals of a young bud and collected the seeds within.

Evera hummed thoughtfully. "I can't be certain, but I believe it may have to do with the courses of nature. There are plants that grow only in certain climates, and others that grow only when given a specific nutrient."

"You think they grow here because they feed off the body—"

Evera shot Calix a hardened look, and he cut himself off.

Was it Mother's blood that caused the flowers to grow? Was it the return of her body to the earth that lent this place a sort of magic? Though I appreciated Evera's instinct to intervene on the delicate subject, I found the concept intriguing. And, in a way, reassuring. The mother that I never had the chance to know lived all around me, just in a different form. Each time I came to this place as a child, it was her gift to the soil that brought life to the flowers. A breeze caught the aspens around us, bringing their song to life. Was she a part of them, too?

Closing my eyes, I let the sound take me back to all the times I'd sat before Mother's monument. How many times had I asked her for guidance? How many times had I sought comfort here? Looking for anything to tell me that I belonged, that I was not alone.

The wind stilled, and I gazed at the marble statue. Its eyes of peridot gleamed in the early dawn light. Peridot.

Drawing my brows, I let my gaze fall to the necklace strung about Evera's neck, the one her mentor had given her that hung between her breasts. Though the stone was rough and unpolished, unlike the ones embedded in the statue, it was otherwise the same.

I huffed a laugh, and when Evera looked back at me, confused, I smiled.

Peridot—the symbol of union between mind, body, and soul. Had it been so clear all along? Was Mother telling me I needed to give control over to my fox, for clarity, for unity, as Evera had read to me from the book of lore? My smile faded. How was I supposed to fully accept my fox when I could not trust him not to hurt the ones I loved?

5 5

EVERA

At the edge of the aspens, Neirin dropped my hand and drew up the hood of his uniform to cover his hair.

"I'll go first," he said.

"No." I retook his hand and squeezed it reassuringly. "We go together, we will stand out less that way." It was more of a hunch than something I was sure of, but I stood by my statement all the same. "The guards are expecting you to be alone, are they not?"

He grunted and raised his fist to just beneath his chest, adjusting my hand so that it rested more formally in the bend of his arm. Calix took my left hand, his fingers small in my grasp, and together we stepped into the open courtyards as a family.

The castle lay ahead of us. Gardens of roses and lilacs stretched in its shadows. They were all manner of other flowers too. Beyond that, the top foliage and little white buds on orchard trees showed above a row of hedges.

Though it was early, a few servants were out working in the garden. Most looked up to us briefly before turning back to their work. I supposed that, in our state, they mistook us for the family of a guardsman. Quickening my steps to keep up with

551

Neirin's longer strides as we followed a small footpath skirting the side of the castle, I became aware of the mud lining the bottom of my dress. Would it be evident that Calix and I did not belong here? Was a man of the guard expected to marry well? My heart sank. What was I but the sister of an orphaned apothecary?

We approached a side entrance to the castle, the door was left propped open. The smell of bread came from inside, and chattering voices filled the air.

"Nyana will have what you need to brew your tea," Neirin said, halting a few paces from the door.

Nyana, the woman who had raised him. My heart fumbled in my chest as a rush of nerves and excitement overtook me at the prospect of meeting the woman. Again, I wished for a nicer dress. Never had I been self-conscious before of my status or what I wore, but I wanted Neirin to be proud of me, not ashamed. I looked to him as if I could find the answers to my unasked questions and worries in his eyes, but I found nothing more than trained indifference.

A girl a few years younger than I greeted us. Her cheeks flushed, and when Neirin asked after Nyana, she nodded and led us into the kitchen. We stopped in the entry, and Neirin shifted his arm, removing my hold on him.

By a crested opening in the wall that looked out to the gardens, the girl nudged an older woman and spoke quietly to her. The older woman turned, a small towel in hand. When she saw us, she dropped the rag, and her hand went to her chest.

"Nyana." Neirin's tone held a deep warmth when he spoke her name. He went to her, leaving Calix and I behind, and took her into his arms. "How I have missed you."

The woman, a fair two heads shorter than he, held tight to him. Her knuckles were white where they bunched in the leather of his jacket as tears streamed down her cheeks. When he broke the embrace, she sniffled as she held his gaze.

"I promised I would return," Neirin said, offering a smile.

"You shouldn't be here." Her voice broke. "The guard is searching for you. They believe you killed Kaius."

"I know, but I have matters to settle."

She shook her head, then turned her gaze to Calix and I.

Neirin held out a hand, gesturing for us to join him. "My family. Calix"—he ruffled the boy's hair playfully, drawing him to stand in front of him with a hand on his shoulder—"and Evera." I took his hand, and he pressed his lips to the back of my palm. "My betrothed."

Betrothed.

My heart raced. Perhaps I should have been cross with him for making such a statement without asking me first. But it was only a gesture, a way to show what I meant to him. He was mine as much as I was his. Equals. And what we had to face ahead, we would face together.

NEIRIN

WHILE EVERA and Calix prepared a tea for the Alidian children, I filled my time in idle chat with Nyana. Around us, the bustle of kitchen life went on as Nyana's girls prepared the morning meal. The scent of rosemary hung in the air, and loaves of bread sat in the stone oven, their pillowed tops rising as they heated through.

Nyana had never believed I killed Kaius, but she expected explanations nonetheless, so I caught her up to the best of my knowledge. I told her first about how Evera and I had come upon the King, and finished up with the letter from Harlan and my belief that the Queen was behind Kaius's death.

"The woman is unwell," Nyana said, sitting atop the crate I'd propped myself upon so many times in my youth.

I pushed off the counter where I'd leaned to pace anxiously, running a hand through my hair. "Unwell?"

"Her mind is … unsound. The few times I've seen her, she's seemed short-tempered, on edge. Though in truth, I don't believe she's left her room in several days now. I've been having the girls take tea and meals up to her chambers."

The lack of my blood was affecting her, then. I'd suspected it would, though I was unsure to what extent. Nyana, however, did not know the truth of what I was, nor of what the Queen was. The riddles of lies woven out of desperation to conceal what happened to Thatcher all those years ago stung my throat. "Perhaps her conscience has finally come forward to haunt her for the role she played in her husband's demise," I offered, wanting to move away from the topic.

"Neirin ..." Calix approached, then hesitated. As a messenger, he'd been trained not to interrupt, but he'd begun to adopt a more casual disposition with Evera and I. He was learning how to balance cautious habits with this new comfort.

"What is it?" I asked.

"The tea is ready." The boy's eyes shone with excitement. Something about him seemed different.

"Did you try it yourself?"

He nodded.

"And it works?"

"I believe so." His energy seemed improved, and the dark circles beneath his eyes were less noticeable.

I dismissed the boy and held out a hand to Nyana. When she took it, I helped her to her feet and pulled her against my chest, wrapping my arms around her. Would I see her again? I breathed in the scent of her, the familiar warmth she gave me.

A thought crossed my mind then, and I withdrew the coin sack from my jacket pocket. Counting out the remaining silver, I hesitated. The coin would buy Evera, Calix, and I passage to the western lands. It would give us an easy life for some time. However, I could not be comfortable in an easy life knowing that the woman who raised me was growing old and tired without some funds to her name. What I had would not provide for her the rest of her life, but it would be something.

After a moment of thought, I kept one silver aside, knowing it would at least buy Evera passage. Calix and I could offer our services on board the ship in exchange for the fare, but I would not subject Evera to swabbing vomit and sleeping in the crew's quarters among vile, immoral men. The rest I placed back in the pouch.

Nyana rejected the coin at first, but I placed it in her hand stubbornly and curled her fingers. "If I do not return, I need to know that I have done something to keep you cared for. It's not much, but it's all I can spare."

"The girls will care for me, if need be," she said, though she did not try again to give back the small pouch. I frowned, uncertain.

Calix returned, chewing at his bottom lip. Whether he was nervous about the potential danger ahead or simply excited to reunite with his friends, I couldn't say. Though I was getting to know him, he was still a difficult boy to read.

I released a breath, heavy with the burdens and responsibilities I bore, and the worry I felt for those I loved. I followed the boy to where Evera waited for us by one of the smaller hearths, where a pot remained hooked over the flames, nearly empty of its contents.

"This should be enough," Evera said, wiping her forehead with the back of her hand. Two baskets arranged with an assortment of water skins, bottles, and clear glass canisters sat before her. The containers that could be seen through held a slightly murky-looking liquid, with a color somewhere between light brown and faint green. Steam fogged what little space there was for air beneath corks or glass tops.

Apprehension nearly swallowed me whole as my eyes held the collection. If this tea did not work—

"This will work," Evera said, placing a hand on my arm and drawing my gaze to hers.

"You are reading my emotions again," I said beneath my breath, a faint smile tugging at my lips as I beheld the woman I loved. Her cinnamon hair, which usually framed her face in soft waves, had sprung into all manner of chaos from working over the boiling water. A particularly stubborn curl stuck out just above her left ear, and when I tried to flatten it out, it retaliated, sticking out even further. Unable to resist, I laughed and she joined me. "You're beautiful," I told her, cupping her cheek. "From your unruly hair to your stunning eyes." I trailed my hand lower. "To your heart, the way you care for others. What you are doing here is—" Selfless? Kind? Pure?

Not needing me to finish the sentence, she nodded and rested her hand over mine, her smile full of warmth. Full of love.

THE WALLS of the narrow lower-level corridors of the castle felt as though they were closing in on me, even though two or three could walk side by side. In this section, occasional pane-less windows lined the left wall, allowing light and fresh air to enter. Still, it was too dark, too confining. And soon all daylight would be gone. Only the dark would remain. Only horrors I wished desperately that I did not have to expose Evera to. I glanced down at Calix, and he met my gaze, eyes solemn. He, too, knew what remained concealed beneath the stone we walked on.

On the right, a doorway opened to a rounded stairwell. We took it one by one, with myself at the lead and Calix falling in line behind Evera. With each step down, the air became more musky, thick, and choking. Just as the steps became nearly impossible to make out, the yellow flickering light of a mounted wall torch seeped around the corner.

"This area won't be guarded," I said, clearing the last step and retrieving the lantern.

Evera remained close to me. Calix, however, held back at the bottom of the stairwell.

"I won't let her hurt you," I promised the boy. He raised his eyes, and in the flickering light his throat bobbed. I was unsure what brought me to speak the words. Of course, I had no guarantee, but if it was true that the Queen was unwell in her chambers, there was no reason that we shouldn't be safe here. Safer, in fact, than anywhere else in the castle. This section was used only occasionally for the storage of extra wine, ale, or the occasional collection of dried meat if a hunt was particularly successful.

Nodding once, Calix stepped forward, a visible shudder racking his body. It was a reminder that I was not alone in the residual fear left from the Queen's lessons. She'd used her magic and her abilities to train all of us, to push us down, make us submit.

"This way," I said. The words came out raspy, and I cleared my throat as I passed the torch to Calix so I could hold my basket with both hands. Evera pressed her side against mine, a subtle show of comfort, likely for us both.

After passing several open storage areas on the right, where the back wall was composed of hard-packed dirt and clay, I stopped before a simple, old door. The handle, rusted with age, looked nearly ready to fall away. Just above the handle, a sliding iron bar locked the door in place from the outside.

"Let me assess the situation first—"

"No." Calix stepped forward, determination behind his objection. "If they …" He swallowed and started again. "If they are alive, they will swarm you, desperate for your blood. I will go first."

"Calix—" Evera's voice was filled with worry.

"The boy's right." I set my basket down and sighed. Turning from the door, I placed a hand on Calix's shoulder. "Do not hesitate to use your magic on them, to any extent, if there is no other choice; if they have lost control to the point of being unable to see reason or thought."

He gave no reply, only lowered his gaze to the dirt floor.

"In life, we are faced with unforgivable truths," I reminded him, lowering to one knee so he was forced to meet my gaze. "But when we can, we must aid those we love, do what we can. Even if we cannot right our wrongs." I could never bring Thatcher back, but I could devote my life to protecting, supporting, and loving my mate and Calix. Even if I could not be Calix's father—could not take that place—he was family. Unfortunately, supporting them both now meant putting them at risk. But what choice did I have?

His brows drew together. "What if we can right a wrong?"

Though I was unsure what path his thoughts trod, I drew my lips into a fine line, considering. "If we have that opportunity, we should always take it." I lowered my hand from his shoulder and stood, joints stiff from the damp coolness of the underground corridor.

Calix sucked in a deep breath, nodded, and passed the torch to Evera. Her eyes watered in the dancing light.

Lifting the wooden beam, I released the door of its lock. It creaked as it swung open to silence and encompassing darkness. My muscles twitched, prepared to pull the door shut and bolt it again if necessary to protect Evera. The children within, they were— No, I would not call them monsters. I could not even understand the effects of their withdrawal. It was different for me. While I'd been a student to Astraea's lessons, the same as them, I did not rely on any substance to temper my magic. It was more a matter of training my mind, my body, my reactions. For them, I suspected it was as well, to an extent, or the lessons would have been in vain. But the suffering they were experiencing now ... I could not truthfully say I empathized with that.

Raising his chin, Calix took a step into the void and then another, his dark curls disappearing into the black of the room. Small as he was, his bravery was commendable. A wave of pride rushed through me, even as fear choked my throat, heated my skin. If I had to, to protect Evera—if I had no choice—could I bolt the door with him inside?

Another step, and he remained nothing but an outline, like the dark gray clouds silhouetted against a midnight sky.

From somewhere inside, metal scraped, the rattling of chains against stone. My blood ran cold.

57

———

EVERA

THE THUMPING of my racing heart was nearly painful against my ribs.

Calix was gone. He'd disappeared into the darkness as if it had swallowed him. And while I knew this to be irrational, that he was just out of my reach somewhere within the room, I could not bring myself to listen to the voice of reason.

"I can't do this," I said, breath rushing from my lungs, tears welling. I could not stand back and do nothing.

Torch in hand, I rushed past Neirin and into the damp, cold room. A hand reached for my cloak but missed. The light came with me, illuminating the low ceiling and Calix, who stood just in front of me.

"Evera." Calix's chest puffed as he sucked in a breath.

Boot steps sounded behind me, then Neirin's arms were around me. As if he could shelter me somehow, shield me with his body. But there was no danger here. Nothing to shelter me from. It was nothing more than intuition, and perhaps a foolhardy one at that, but it was simply as if all fear fell away.

"It's alright," I coaxed Neirin, using my free hand to work at his arms. He clenched me tight, his face buried in my neck, raw,

563

unfiltered panic coursing through the bond. "Neirin." I squirmed in his grasp, and reluctantly, he released me. I caught the glint of tears forming in his eyes as I looked back at him before finding my courage and moving toward the back of the room.

The pungent scent of death came on a wave, and I resisted the bile rising in my throat. The stench of urine and sweat nearly outweighed the scent, but it did not completely conceal it. Swallowing the sour taste in my mouth, I took another step, letting the light of the torch fall upon the scene before me.

We were too late.

Bodies lined the wall, all sitting, most leaning on each other. The oldest could have been no more than three and ten, the youngest—gods, younger than Calix. I fell to my knees, and the torch flickered as it hit the floor, sending the room into darkness for a moment before relighting. Distantly, I was aware of Neirin behind me picking it up. Before me, a boy with sandy-blond hair lay with his cheek against a child slightly older. The boy's cheeks were pale, gray-hued, where they should have held the rosy pink of youth.

He was so young.

Calix rushed past me to work at the metal chains. Tears filled my eyes. "Calix, stop," I rasped. "They're dead. All of them. We're too late."

Neirin's hand came to my shoulder, but I brushed it off roughly. Anger and grief coursed through me.

"Evera," Calix called to me, voice desperate.

I scrunched my nose, bitterness rising to my throat as I readied to snap at him again. In a time when he needed comfort most, I was useless to him. But the suffering that had happened here, the failure on my part to do anything, the knowledge that there was nothing I could do now but hate myself … These children, had they accidentally killed each other when they lost their ability to control themselves? Or had they simply died of dehydration, forgotten by Astraea in her own selfishness as she locked herself away?

Someone coughed, a rasp.

"Evera, help him," Calix pleaded, now pulling at my hand. When had he come to my side? "Seros, he needs help."

"Is his magic stable?" Neirin asked, his hand firm on my shoulder now.

"He's too weak, I think, to be of any danger."

"Are you positive?"

"No, I—" Calix swallowed his words.

He's still alive. I can help him. I have to.

Brushing Neirin off again, I went to where Calix had found the boy who was still alive only moments ago. Head resting back against the stone wall with two younger children, days gone if not more, resting against his sides, the older boy fluttered his eyes and closed them again.

"Seros," I spoke the name Calix had used, hoping it would stir the boy. "The tea," I called over my shoulder when I got no response. "And my bag," I added as an afterthought. "It's in the smaller basket, the one I carried."

Footsteps pattered on the floor, and I checked the boy for a pulse while I waited. It was faint, but there. I carefully pinched the skin on his arm, testing for signs of dehydration. Minor, perhaps.

"Your bag," Calix said, dropping it beside me as he knelt, waterskin in hand. He brought it to Seros's lips, and I helped, raising the boy's chin.

"Just a little," I instructed Calix. I ran my thumb over the boy's throat, coaxing him to swallow. When he did, I prompted Calix to give him more. After three more drinks, we both sat back on our heels, waiting.

The boy whimpered, his lip pouting. I released my breath. It was a sign he was coming around, at least. The tea would work.

It had to. Though I didn't understand how such things worked, Neirin and Calix had been certain in this.

"Stay with him," I said, taking a roll of bread from my bag and handing it to Calix. "When he comes around, encourage him to drink more. If he is hungry, he can eat, but he does so slowly. He will need his strength."

"What of the chains?" Calix asked.

"The Queen will have the key," Neirin said, using his torch to light another on the wall. Shadows hardened as more of the horror around us came into view.

I swallowed and placed my hand on Calix's shoulder. For a moment, he held my gaze, then he turned his attention back to Seros, speaking quiet encouragements and offering the water-skin once again.

Leaving them, I went to Neirin, bile in the back of my throat. Grateful, admittedly, to turn my back to the wall of death if only for a moment.

The small flame of Neirin's torch flickered. He knelt before a cage of rough iron bars. Crouching beside him, I balanced on my heels. The top of the enclosure came to eye level, and the width of it was no more than that of my forearm. Scarcely large enough to hold a dog.

"My cage," Neirin said under his breath. "The metal cuffs could not contain me, not when I shifted."

Bitterness rose in my throat, and I sucked my lips in. A hollow pain ached in my chest. Reaching out, I ran my fingers over the bars, which were rusted slightly and stained with blood.

"I bleed when I shift," Neirin explained. "Or at least I always used to. Before." He flexed his fist and stood. "It's in the past." His voice grated, hollow, like the ghost of a memory.

I stood. "What she's doing, Neirin, it's not in the past." I gestured to the back wall. "It may be over for you, but what is to stop the Queen from continuing this ..." I swallowed the lump in my throat, unable to finish the sentence.

Neirin started to respond, but his eyes caught something over my left shoulder. I turned to find a mirror propped against the stone wall. It spanned floor to ceiling, framed with elegantly carved filigree. I made a step toward it and felt the brush of Neirin's hand on my arm, but he retracted his touch, and I left his side.

A dusting of dirt coated the reflective surface, making my image appear faded. It had been some time since I'd seen my reflection, and for a moment I studied myself and tried to recall what Mother looked like. More like Aureus, I thought, but the memories were hazy. I was a mess, hair tangled and frizzed, skirts stained by dirt.

My gaze fell, and I drew my brows inward. Roughly three feet up from the ground, the mirror was shattered in several places: Each branching from a singular point of impact. Crimson stained the broken shards.

Neirin joined me before the mirror. In his black leather uniform, he was the same man I'd shared a tryst with the night of the festival. A man of power, of strength. He was a concept, the idea of a man I'd concocted in my mind to avoid closeness, to fashion a night of choices for myself, a night of obscurity and freedom.

Yet the way his jaw hardened and his fists tightened spoke of his pain, his depth. When I beheld him now, I no longer viewed him as that man but as the one I'd come to love. Complex, hurting, frustrating at times, but gods, perfect too, in every way. Even in his faults, in his weaknesses. In everything that made him who he was.

With a snarl, Neirin struck the mirror with a curled fist, and I sucked in a breath, shocked by his aggression and the suddenness of it. The glass broke and shattered with a sound of crinkling sharpness. Several shards fell to the ground, and when

Neirin withdrew his hand, my breath left me. The impact had left fresh blood from his knuckles. A single drip collected and sank through the dust on the surface of the mirror.

He twitched in a seemingly unnatural way. It sent a shiver of ice down my spine. Neirin gasped for breath, and eyes intent on his own reflection, he began to shift. It was nothing like what I'd seen before. Lacking was any fluidity, elegance, or air of awe. This was the fuel of nightmares, the whisper of demons speaking on the wind. A middle shift.

His form was entirely that of a man, close-fitted in his uniform. Yet from his tousled silver hair, the ears of a beast unfurled and pinned back. A horrid cracking echoed from him, bouncing off the walls of the stone room. Calix's whispering to his companion hushed, and the room took on a deadly silence.

Neirin wheezed, the sound a hushed exhalation of pain. The structure of his face elongated, no longer that of a man's, but not quite that of a creature's either. It was something in between, something broken and all wrong. Fur sprouted out in patches, a mottling of silver and dark gray. A sound came from him, nearly a whimper, restrained and laden with distress.

Despite the pounding in my heart, I stepped to him and placed a hand on his arm. He turned to me, eyes sharp, and snarled. This half-shifted form was even more terrifying face-to-face.

Gods, had the Queen made him stand before his reflection as a boy and witness this? Of course, he would believe her when she told him he was a monster. But this wasn't him. This was some forged fragmentation of his turmoil and inner anguish.

"Neirin." I raised my hand to cup his face, feeling the patches of fur and the disjointed bone structure beneath my touch. His eyes, though they bore distrust, were still those of the man I loved. Fear and pain trickled through our bond, and his distress poured over all else.

"Look at me," I urged, and coaxed him to turn from the

mirror. His body heaving with ragged breaths, Neirin locked his gaze on me. "You are not a monster."

A muscle twitched at his temple, the only response to my words. I drew a breath. "You are my defender, my protector. You are the clueless, hopeless fool of a romantic that says all the wrong things yet continues to try. And when you say the right things, they're perfect. You're the only man I've ever given my heart to or fallen asleep beside. And when I wake to your warmth, it fills me with peace and belonging."

Neirin let out a breath, and the panic through our bond tempered. I wrapped my arms around his neck, and the elongated half-snout he bore came nearly to my nose when he tilted his head down to me. But I wasn't afraid of him, even in this half-form.

"You're my heart and my soul, my home. I love you, Neirin. In all your forms, even in this one."

His body relaxed, and the mottling of fur withdrew. He lowered his snout to my neck with hesitant uncertainty and breathed in my scent. I held him and ran my fingers through his hair, stroking along one of his shifted ears, which was so incredibly soft to the touch. I comforted him with gentle words, and when he wrapped my waist and pulled me closer, breathing a sigh, the sting of threatening tears returned.

His body trembled, and he buried his face against me. The tip of his nose on my jawline felt familiar again, pointed and smooth. "I killed my brother." He swallowed. "The monster, the fox, he killed Thatcher."

It was what he'd feared to tell me before.

"Neirin, listen to me." I pulled back and held his gaze. "We all have monsters within us, the memories of unspeakable things we have done. But we cannot let these things control us forever. I am not afraid of your monsters. I know it was not done in malice. Your fox is good, I see it in his eyes. In your eyes."

Neirin let his forehead fall to mine. At the back wall, Seros rasped, then coughed, and Calix returned to his quiet speaking.

My thoughts returned to Ruairc. He'd died to protect me, and in that sense, his death was on my hands. But he would not want me to linger on that. He would want me to embrace the broken parts of myself and move forward. And that was what Neirin and I would do together. "If you are broken," I told him, "then I will be the piece that makes you whole. Together—" I took his hands in mine. "Together, we will put an end to what is happening here, and then together we will heal from our wounds. It is our brokenness that made us who we are, that formed us, and it will make us stronger too."

When Neirin spoke, his voice was low, heavy with the weight of my words, or perhaps the weight of what lay before us. "We will ask Nyana to have one of her girls set morning tea for Harlan in the gardens. I will confront him, make him see the truth for what it is, and hope that he holds some faith in me yet. He will be able to retrieve Astraea's key to free the boy from his chains. No more hiding. No more running or working in the shadows."

I nodded against his forehead and squeezed his hands to show my support.

"Calix," he said, "stay with your friend. Help him recover his strength. Evera and I will return with the key."

A blanket of what-ifs hung over us, but none of us addressed it. It was time to face things head-on and let fate guide us—or destroy us—together.

58

———

NEIRIN

TALL HEDGES CREATED pathways within the garden. I imagined from the upper balconies of the castle that the maze would be stunning, but I'd never seen it from that perspective. It was the same garden Thatcher and I had played in as boys, though we were not supposed to. It was from one of such balconies that Astraea had witnessed what happened that fateful day; the day she came to me, knelt calmly before my fox, and spoke gently to him until he shifted back, giving me control again. Then she'd comforted me, young and impressionable as I was. She'd told me it wasn't my fault but my fox's, my monster's, as I stared over her shoulder at my brother, his neck bent at an unnatural angle and crimson staining the ground.

All the things she'd told me, all the things I believed for so long.

"Be stronger than the monster, fight him down. These lessons are for your own benefit. Don't be ungrateful. Thank me. Plead for forgiveness for your belligerence and listen, learn. Push down the monster. He is a killer. He will kill everyone you love. No one must know about this. No one must know what happened to the boy. If you

573

tell Nyana, she will despise you. I will protect your secret. And you will protect mine."

I'd been such a fool. But now my eyes were open. Nyana may despise me for what happened to her son at my fox's jaws, but it was as Evera had said—no more running. I would take responsibility for my actions and set things right. End Astraea's lessons, end her commanding hand. No one else would get hurt because of her.

The trickle of the fountain caught my attention, and I slowed my steps, swallowing when I saw the stone centerpiece. It looked exactly as it had all those years before. The bench, however, had been replaced. Now there was a table and two chairs, one on each side. Steam rose from the spout of a brass teapot, and an assortment of small cakes, nuts, and fruits was arranged on a plate beside it. The prince—the King—added a cube of sugar to his cup and stirred it with a silver spoon, still unaware of me.

I cleared my throat, and he looked up, lips parted slightly as if he were sucking in a breath, as his eyes widened.

"Neirin." My name came out of him like an accusation. He stood, knocking over his chair. His eyes darted to two soldiers stationed opposite the fountain. They turned, hands going to their swords.

"Brother, wait," I pleaded, holding out my hands. "I've come home to explain."

"Mother has *explained*. Did you not receive my letter?" Though he was only a head taller than Calix, still a boy and twiggy at that, his voice had changed. As had the way he held himself. He was a King now. He'd grown up. Wasn't that what I'd wanted for him—to grow up? But I hadn't wanted it to happen like this. Not because he was forced into the position so soon. He was too young for the weight of rulership. A knot formed in my throat as I grieved for the Harlan that had only just over a moon ago sat atop a counter in the kitchens, eating berries and asking to be told stories of thieves and adventures.

"Your mother lied to you, Harlan." As soon as I spoke the words, I knew they were the wrong ones. Too forceful, too sudden. The soldiers grasped my arms, and I let them. "Please." I softened my tone. "Just let me speak."

"There's another." A third man spoke from behind me, and my blood chilled.

"Let me go, you brute," Evera hissed as she was dragged to my side.

I shot her a look filled with all my fear and frustration. I'd told her to stay with Nyana. But of course she hadn't.

"Who is this?" Harlan asked, authority in his voice.

"My mate," I answered, holding Evera's gaze. "My heart."

Harlan approached, stopping before her. "Mother told me about your kind, Neirin. She won't be pleased you've replaced her in your heart so quickly." A bitterness trailed off at the end of his statement, as if he were still displeased with the concept of his mother and I paired in any way.

"If Astraea told you about my kind, you would know my heart can only ever belong to my mate; my true mate. I've never held any affection for the Queen."

He turned his gaze on me, studying.

"I certainly never lay with her," I added, using all my restraint to keep my voice low and level, to not lash at the guards who held me and Evera.

Shaking his head, Harlan turned his back to me again. "I don't believe you."

"Harlan—"

He whipped around. "You killed Father." His voice broke. Composing himself, he raised his chin. "Why would I ever trust you again?"

"I didn't kill Father—"

"Did you not?" Venom laced his words now. "What of *your*

dagger we found in his chest? And if you did not kill him, why did I find you standing before him as he bled out while you did *nothing*—"

I gazed helplessly at my brother. I felt just as useless and lost as I'd felt standing over our father, watching the blood drain from his body. "Nothing could be done."

Harlan balled his fists. "Why did you run?"

My heart sank. Was this it? Would he never trust me? Would he not even listen, truly listen, and give me a chance? But how could I expect him to? I had run. But I'd done it because I'd believed it was the best way to keep him safe. Defeat laced my words. "I was wrong."

A crash sounded from the castle, and we turned toward its source—a balcony with doors open and curtains blowing in the breeze.

The guard on my right tightened his grip on my arm. "The Queen's quarters."

59

NEIRIN

"What have you done?" Harlan spun on me. Another clattering came from the Queen's chambers, accompanied by the shouts of guards within the castle. "Who else conspires with you?"

I stiffened. Calix.

Would he go after the Queen for what happened to his friends? I'd told the boy to stay put. Irritation tingled down my spine.

"Go," Evera said, her eyes locked on me. Worry seeped through the bond.

"No one's going anywhere," said one of the soldiers restraining me as he tightened his grip.

My fox tickled against my skin—a request, not a demand. But a request for what? He was only a daft animal; he had no interest in Calix's welfare. Did he?

"Go," Evera said again, firmer this time.

My brother wouldn't bring harm to her. Despite her association with me, she had not done anything wrong. I knew this, yet fear scraped at me nonetheless, my world divided. To leave Evera behind was unthinkable. Yet she could take care of herself. Her sharp mind alone would keep her one step ahead of the man holding her back, one step ahead of my brother, who was still learning to think in the ways of a man and not a boy.

My brother. Harlan.

He stood before me, eyes sharp with hatred. I'd seen this before. The fountain trickled. A breeze stirred the hedges.

If fate replayed itself—

Calix shouted, his voice recognizable even from this distance, but his words were impossible to make out. Heat warmed my body as the fox nudged at me, pleading. Releasing my breath, for I could not release my fears, I gave control over to him.

The shift happened fluidly, and as my arms slipped from the soldier's confines, warping, altering, the men stepped back, baffled. Their fear scent hung around them. The black of my uniform drowned my fox as he took form. In the next moment, Evera was beside him, freeing him.

Her guard reached to pull her back under his control, but Harlan spoke out, and the man halted.

"Go," Evera repeated, pressing her forehead to the fox's. "Protect Calix. I will be alright. You can come back for me. He needs you now."

Keening, my fox drew back, uncertainty rippling through him. His eyes found Harlan's— steady, distant, impossible to read. What storm brewed behind that calm? When had he learned to cage his emotions so entirely, to wear silence like armor?

Calix howled, and my fox's heart sped up. His paws itched, as if he could not make up his mind. And then he did.

The hedges moved by in a blur—the fountain, Evera, Harlan, the soldiers, all left behind. The grand doors that led from the main halls of the castle were open, and my fox did not hesitate as he ran past the two soldiers standing sentry. A commotion rose from the combined voices of men and women alike to see a wild animal within the castle, but none stood in his way. All stepped back with faces filled with shock.

Up a flight of stairs and down a long hall, my fox followed Calix's familiar scent until he came upon the Queen's chambers. A man standing guard pointed and hollered to those in the room, and another man came to join him. Whatever confrontation had happened was over now, already settled.

Where is Calix?

The men exchanged words as if unsure how to deal with the surprise appearance of a creature of the forest in their midst. Not waiting for an invitation, my fox ran between them and into the large chamber. Lilac curtains blew, dancing on the breeze, the only movement as everyone else fell still. The after-effects of a struggle cluttered the floor. A bookshelf, its contents strewn, lay half propped against the bedpost. Broken ceramic lay by the window.

"Neirin!"

Calix.

My fox spun until he saw the boy held back by a castle guard. Calix lashed out, but the guard held him firm. Evera appeared in the doorway, her chest heaving. Soldiers barricaded the door, but Harlan spoke up from the hallway. He instructed them to let her pass, warning that she would be restrained if she was not obedient, and to stand by Calix.

"Where is Mother?" Harlan demanded to anyone who might answer him as he passed through the doorway and strode into the room. His eyes lingered on my fox only a moment before scanning the chamber.

"Safe, in her study," one of the guards said, gesturing to Calix with a tilt of his chin. "We caught this one climbing in through the balcony with a dagger in hand."

"A dagger?" Harlan's soft features contorted as he snarled. The weight of rulership did not suit him. It was too much too soon. Father's death and Astraea's "illness," along with my framed accusations, would only have added to his stress.

The guard held out a small blade, its handle intricate, its metal of high quality. "We believe he picked it off one of the guards in the courtyard. It is one of ours."

Almost identical to mine, which had been taken the night of the festival.

A sickening feeling roiled my fox's stomach.

"Find out which man was dull-minded enough to let a child lift his weapon," Harlan commanded, running a hand through his hair, tousling it, his air of composure quickly wearing thin. "I wish to see Mother."

"What has happened here?" The Queen's voice came from the hall, and my fox snarled. Her tone betrayed her state, a disjointed combination of unease and formidable anger.

"Mother." Harlan went to the doorway just as she stepped into view.

When she saw my fox, she halted in place. The thin lines of her brows pulled in, then the corners of her lips turned up, and she laughed. The sound sent a shiver down my fox's spine. "I told you he would come back for me," she crooned, grabbing her son's chin before pushing past him to stand a few paces before my fox. She looked down at him with hatred pinching her features.

The way Harlan firmed his jaw and cast his gaze aside and to the floor—the way he submitted to her—led me to suspect that in her state of withdrawal, she'd become firm-handed with him.

"What did I tell you about giving in to your monster?" the Queen snarled at my fox. The ingrained memories of Astraea's lessons sent every instinct within both my fox and myself into hyper focus. *Submit,* they told us. My fox's eyes focused past the Queen, to where Evera and Calix stood a few steps back. No, we could not submit; we had to protect them. As if my fox had come to the same conclusion, he turned his attention back to Astraea and pinned his ears, holding his ground.

With a revolted snort, the Queen kicked at my fox's flank with the tip of her boot, sending him yelping and falling to the floor. His pain was my own, and for a moment he only lay still. The force of the impact had been enough to falter his resolve and left him battling with the horrors of our shared past.

"Mother—" Harlan's voice perked one of my fox's ears as he lay on the floor.

The Queen held up her hand, blatantly positioning herself as a higher command than her son in front of his men. "Mother is handling things, Harlan." Annoyance laced her words like venom. Again, her tone altered, a cool authority prevailing. "Shift back," she demanded. My fox's eyes met hers. Cold. Calculating. In her irises I caught the reflection of my fox, and somewhere deep within the fur that held my soul, I shuddered.

Panting, my fox got back to his feet. He swayed first, then bunched his haunches. For a moment, I was unsure if he would cower or lunge, but he held his position, teeth bared. The Queen hiked her dress and moved to kick at him again, and he recoiled, muscle memory anticipating the pain to come. She laughed. "Fucking pathetic." Shame flooded me.

A flash of movement caught my fox's attention as Evera stepped from the wall, the sounds of her boots echoing on the floor as she hastily moved to the Queen and shoved her from behind. Evera ground her teeth, as if she were unable to form words sharp enough for her emotions. Within the next heartbeat, two soldiers were at her sides, restraining her.

Bracing herself with a widened stance, the Queen whipped around to her unsuspected assailant. "You ..." A moment of quiet, and the Queen's voice lowered with suspicion. "You're from the festival."

"I'm his mate," Evera spat, her cinnamon waves falling in front of her face.

Those gathered fell silent, the soldiers and guard surely confused by the progression of events, by the Queen's belittlement of her son, by the way she spoke to an animal as if it were able to comprehend her, by her very state—the madness that she could no longer veil.

Again, the Queen laughed, then she slapped Evera across the face. "You bitch. He's *mine.*"

He's mine. Memories of the Queen's plays at control, of her possessiveness, sent a sickening swirl through my fox's gut.

"He was never yours," Evera bit back, arms still held behind her back.

A huff, and the Queen turned her wicked eyes back to my fox, dismissing Evera altogether. Through her teeth, she hissed, holding her hand out to the guard. "The dagger."

The guard looked to Harlan for approval, but the King kept his head down. Gone was his fight.

"Dagger," Astraea shouted.

The guard stiffened, then crossed the room to hand it to her.

When Astraea spoke again, her voice was low, tone calculated. "Now, Bastard, you will shift back and let me have what's *mine.*" My blood. My submission.

"Neirin, don't." Evera shook her head, eyes pleading. "She's mad—" She lashed at her restraints, but the soldiers held her firm. "Don't you see that, Your Majesty?" She addressed my brother. "Don't you see she's not sane? She's lied about everything."

Harlan only flinched.

"Harlan, you're just like Kaius was." Astraea's eyes rolled, and she huffed as she turned back on Evera and brought the dagger point to the dip between her ribs. My fox's flanks trembled, and a low snarl came from the back of his throat. A warning. Panic flooded my mind, barring me from making any reasonable deductions on a path to take. My fox, too, hesitated, as if locked in the same state of immobility.

In the Queen's profile, I detected a flash of bitter resentment as it flickered across her facade. "You're entirely lost to this magic, this false belief that you *love* that monster," she spat at my mate.

"I do love him." Evera raised her chin. "It is not only magic that has bound my soul to his."

Growling, Astraea pressed harder with the point of the blade, creasing the fabric of Evera's dress. The racing of my fox's heart pounded in his ears. Through the thickness of my fear, Evera's statement brought me strength, and I fought to control my thoughts.

Could I regain my other form if I tried? Would I be of any more use if I did, naked with no weapon? Helplessness tore at me. At least in this form, my fox could defend Evera. *If he could break from his fear of Astraea to do so.*

The Queen narrowed her hazel eyes, the same hazel eyes my brother shared with her. "I thought having his bitch killed would break my husband's curse," Astraea stated, the words drawn out with cruelty, "that he would fall in love with me again. But no." Her jaw firmed. "Died in childbirth," she laughed. "It was perfect. The bitch had given me a new source of blood, one that wouldn't *fuck my husband* and make threats to expose me for what I am."

A wall of black threatened to block me out, to push me down so far within my fox I'd never return. Astraea—she'd had my mother killed. My mother, whom I'd never had the chance to meet. Who could have raised me, taught me who I was? Who could have shown me love? Images of Nyana flashed before my mind, pulling me back. I was shown love. The betrayal and the hurt caused by what Astraea had done, would never fade. But I'd had a mother; I could not slight that.

"Just like you had Kaius killed?" Evera's cool tone brought me the rest of the way back, and I refocused on the scene before my fox's eyes.

The fox, not having suffered as deeply from the emotional impact of the Queen's admission, crept forward. A new resolve tingled down his flanks, raising the hair on his haunches. Death hung in the air. If it were to be the Queen or Evera, he would not let his mate fall.

"Mother, stop this." Harlan's voice came from near the windows, weak, pleading.

"Mind your place," the Queen barked. She turned her narrowed eyes back to my fox and twisted the dagger again at Evera's torso. "Make your choice, Neirin. Shift back, or you can watch her die knowing it's at your hand."

The soldiers exchanged uneasy glances. Within the fox's form, I was left to watch my life unravel before me. Yet I held faith in him to an extent that I could not put into words. He would protect her, would save her in a way I was incapable of in this moment.

"Stop this," Harlan spoke more boldly this time, having seemingly found his bravery. He came into my peripheral as he paced forward and reached for the Queen. She spun on him as if on a reflex, the dagger now pointed to his chest, her breasts heaving as she alternated between gasps for air and deranged laughter.

Astraea would never—could never—kill her son. He was her world. But she was crazed, beyond controlling her actions. My fox's paws itched as he stilled mid-step, eyes darting between Evera and Calix and my brother, who stood at the pinnacle of the Queen's delusions.

"Did you kill Father?" Harlan's voice shook.

Evera took the moment of distraction and stamped on the foot of the soldier who held her. She reached for her own dagger, but the soldier tugged her roughly back again before she could grab it. Calix snarled, spitting curses at the man for his rough handling of her. My fox growled low in his throat but remained still, sizing up the situation.

Astraea, with her arm still extended, dagger threatening the life of her only living son, turned her eyes back to Calix, and then to my fox. "That boy means something to you?" There was a wickedness in the chilled calm of her voice. "Calix, do they know what you did?" The corner of her lips twisted up, and she adjusted her hold on the dagger. "I didn't kill your father, my son," she crooned, her attention flitting back to Harlan. She drew back the weapon and pointed it at Calix. "He did."

The sinking feeling from before returned to my gut. It all fell together in a clarity I wished I could unsee.

Calix had killed Father. He'd taken a guard's blade in the gardens today to seek his revenge on Astraea. He could just as easily have taken mine the night of the festival. I'd always been keen on the boy's ability to pick things off others unsuspecting, but I never would have suspected—

"It's not true!" Evera cried. "All the Queen says are lies."

But Calix gave no defense. Lips a fine line, he looked down at his boots.

"Am I lying, Calix?" the Queen purred.

Swallowing, he raised his gaze to meet my fox's. "I thought coming here, killing the Queen … I thought I could right my wrong."

Astraea smirked. After all this, Kaius's murderer had been hiding in plain sight, had been falling asleep in Evera's arms, had been in my shadow and at my side. Had become my family.

No. If he did this, it was because he had no choice in the matter.

"Calix." Evera's voice was gentle, quiet. "Why?" A single word, yet it told me her thoughts had settled in the same place as my own. She'd asked the question I was unable to while in this form.

Calix sucked in a breath. "She told me it was the only way to save my friends." His voice came out as a whimper, a plea for understanding. "She told me you were leaving, Neirin, and that the only way to keep you here was to have you imprisoned. If you left the capital, my friends would all go mad. They would kill each other in their rage. They would have to be confined. But in the end …" He cast his gaze down again, and a tear ran down the length of his nose and fell to the floor.

"This is true?" Harlan asked. "You gave the order for that boy to kill Father?" He took a step back, and when his mother turned on him, he moved back again, falling into the protection of the soldiers. It wasn't a brave move, but it was the correct one. Harlan was not a fighter, not yet at least, and Astraea was acting unpredictably.

The Queen curled her lip and threw the dagger to the ground in her frustration. It skittered across the floor, metal clashing against stone. "You'll be twice the King he ever was," she reasoned, voice shifting in tone sporadically. "I've only ever wanted the world for you."

"Not like this." Harlan's eyes watered, but he sucked in a breath, holding the tears back. His hands flexed into fists at his sides, and his nose scrunched. "Guards, arrest her," he said, turning his eyes away and shielding his emotions from those in the room.

It was in that moment, as the soldiers moved on Astraea, that I detected the glow of light in her chest. It started small, then exploded into fragmented starlight, shooting out toward the soldiers advancing on her. Three men fell in an instant. A hum filled the air. Harlan covered his ears.

The castle guard, undeterred, grabbed the Queen's arms, restraining her. She hung her head, laughing under her breath, and raised her eyes to my fox. Words were not needed to decipher the expression she bore. She would make one final effort to destroy me. As she'd taken the life of my father's mate to control him, to bring an unfilled void to his life, she would do the same to me.

I would not be quick enough, even in this form, to reach

Astraea. To cut off her life before her magic took everything from me.

The words from Evera's book of lore came back to me. *The ability to perceive magic and to manipulate it.*

Gods, please let this work.

Searching within myself, I gave all my trust to the fox as the light within Astraea bloomed like the many tendrils of a ruined tapestry. Only my fox could save Evera now. I put my faith in him, in his magic, in his abilities.

Like a snake striking, one of the strands of light shot from Astraea in a sharp line toward Evera's heart. Time stilled.

My fox's growl reverberated through the room; Astraea's light trickled down like icicles melting. The drops of starlight shattered on the floor like glass and dissipated. A breath filled my fox's lungs, and then time moved forward at its own pace again. Everything happened at once.

Evera gasped. The soldier holding her back released her and joined the castle guard in restraining the Queen, his priority shifted, knowing Astraea was now the largest threat to the King.

Astraea screamed. It was not a sound of anger or even pain. It was the same cry I'd heard from her chambers so many times as a boy when she'd lost another of her unborn babes. It was a sound of complete and desolate devastation. Of loss.

Her light, her magic, remained confined within her chest, a spinning orb held under my fox's control. Its blinding white, however, had dulled. It broke and rumbled like lightning in a stormy sky, the visible form of a life marked by hurt, desperation, and heartache. For a moment, I held her eyes as Evera's words came back to me. *A part of me believes that in her mind, she sees herself as helping those children. In a way, I suspect 'helped' in a similar manner when she was young.*

With a howling moan, Astraea's light dissolved, and she fell to her knees. The two men holding her arms stumbled as her body went limp and she hung her head. The only sound was the Queen's choked sobs.

It was over. She couldn't control me anymore. She held nothing over me, would hurt no one else. Yet as I took her in, broken of soul and mind, I was humbled by the bitterness of the victory.

The Queen mumbled incoherent words. The light within her flickered once more and died, finally, as she fainted.

In the next moment, Evera's arms were wrapped around my fox's neck. Her scent soothed him, calmed his ridged muscles, and brought me back from my trail of thoughts. Evera was safe, Calix was safe. With his muzzle resting on Evera's shoulder, my fox caught Harlan's eyes. He nodded once, and his throat bobbed. He did not look at where his mother lay on the floor, as if he could not bring himself to do so. A part of me hoped that somehow he could save her from herself.

Released from the immediate threats, my fox offered control back to me. I took it, even as the shift left me naked on the floor of the Queen's chambers, holding my knees to my chest. Evera held to me, wetting my neck with her tears. In this form, her scent was less prevalent; I nuzzled into her hair to breathe her in deeper, to draw comfort from her.

Distantly, I was aware of Harlan instructing the remaining two living men to bring Astraea to the dungeon, to restrain her where no one would be near enough for her to harm them with her magic. Then, as an afterthought, he instructed one of the men to send for a healer. It was something I suspected he'd already attempted—finding a way to relieve her of her magic. The guard in me knew that a strong King would have the woman killed for her treason, executed in front of the people. But Harlan ... he was still just a boy wearing a crown atop his head that did not fit, bearing the burdens of responsibility that were much too heavy for someone his age to carry alone. I pushed the thoughts aside. Harlan would rule in his own way, taking a path of empathy where Kaius had taken a strategic. Perhaps it was what this kingdom needed. My eyes fell to the Queen. Perhaps it was what she needed.

I would help Harlan, offer guidance in matters of the kingdom if he wanted it, if he could find it in his heart to trust me again. He would need to find a balance. I had faith that in time, he would. At least he knew now that I had played no part in Father's death. Calix, I hoped, would receive forgiveness too. Regardless of what had happened, of what he'd done. He was a child, and he'd been manipulated, forced into a situation he'd felt he had no other option but to fall in line with.

"Calix," I said, my voice sounding unused, raspy.

He stood back in the corner, eyes downcast, though he was no longer restrained.

"We all have unforgivable truths," I told him, understanding the guilt and pain he bore. "I do not judge you for yours. You have a place in this family, should you still want it."

EPILOGUE: NEIRIN

Sunlight filtered through the glass windows at the back of our home that overlooked Evera's garden. It was spring, nearly a year after the confrontation with Queen Astraea. It was strange to think back on that time when everything had been so uncertain.

Warmth radiated from the mug I held, and I brought it to my lips, breathing in the hot steam and trying to detect what plants Evera had used to prepare it. It was a game we played, one I never won. A smile tugged at my lips as I took a sip. I could happily spend the rest of my life in this calm, in this contentedness.

A knock sounded on our front door, and I set my mug down and stood. A plush rug greeted my toes. It smelled slightly of soot for its proximity to the hearth, which had been lit the majority of the cold season—a sign our home was beginning to be broken into. A silly thing, but it warmed my heart.

Opening the door, I found a child standing outside—a girl. Younger than most of the children who came to us. A ball of light spun within her chest, flickering, as she fought to control her newfound magic. Through a breath, I called on my own abilities and pulled at the girl's magic, repressing it just enough to ease her panic, to give her a sense of control over her own body. The effects of my ability were temporary, but that was all the Alidian needed.

"It's alright," I said to the girl, "you're safe here."

Shuddering, she nodded, eyes wide. "Thank you, sir."

I gestured, inviting her in. "We'll get you help. It'll all be much less heavy soon."

Nodding again, she stepped over the threshold, and I closed the door behind her before making my way down the hall that led to Evera's study. A floorboard creaked beneath my weight, and again I smiled, remembering Evera's frustration when she'd found the stubborn board. A reminder, I'd told her, of the character of this place. Our home that we'd fixed up as a family, with our own hands and those of some hired shop workers from Elrune when it came to skills that we had no aptitude for. It would have been easier to pay a man in the capital to have the work all arranged and done for us, but Evera had wanted to repair our home together, so we had.

"Just through here," I told the girl as we neared the end of the hall. The door was made of wood with a glass window that let light through distorting the view of the other side into patches of color. "What is your name?"

"Myra," she replied.

I pushed open the door and was greeted by the warmth of the spring sun shining through the ceiling-to-floor windows. Shelves with countless bottles of tinctures and remedies lined what portions of the walls did not have windows, and dried plants hung from portions of the ceiling. Evera looked up from the round central table, and as it had when I first saw her and so many times since, my breath caught at her beauty—her cinnamon curls, longer now, and the dappling of freckles across her nose. The light in her eyes, the fire in her heart, the courage in her soul, the love she held for any who needed it—

for those who had it from no one else. A healer's trait. A mother's trait.

"Evera, love, this is Myra," I said. "Myra, this is my wife, Evera. She will help you."

Joining us, Evera crouched down to the girl's level, something that was becoming more difficult recently as her belly had begun to swell. Having a child of my own was both frightening, yet exciting as well. Something I'd never considered even wanting before I fell in love with Evera, before I grew so fond of Calix and the relationship we had developed.

Evera smiled and spoke softly to the child. She'd always been better with words, with comforting, than I was. The girl relaxed, and Evera called over her shoulder, "Calix, would you start the water boiling for some fresh tea?"

Calix appeared from the side pantry carrying a basket of plants, dried and tied in bundles. He grinned, his smile effortless now and beaming. "Another one? That's three this fortnight alone. I believe word is getting out." He set the basket on the table and went to rouse the fire back to life.

Standing, Evera encouraged the girl to join her at the table and pulled out a stool for her to sit on, chatting with her as she did. Already, the girl seemed more at ease, and a small smile tugged at the corner of her lips, accompanied by a giggle at whatever Evera had said to her.

I leaned back against the wall, taking in the moment. This life we'd built was nothing I could have ever fathomed, ever dreamed of, or hoped for. It was beyond what I deserved. It was everything to me, and I would cherish each day, each afternoon spent out in the garden, and each early morning walk to find local plant life. Each evening spent as a family sitting around the table sharing food and stories of our days, of the things Calix had learned from Aureus or Evera, or of mischief he'd gotten into with his friends. Some days, Soros would visit us for the evening meal as well. The boy was mild-mannered and kind, if not a bit shy, but his apprenticeship in the capital was slowly opening him up more.

Again, the girl laughed. The sound filled me with warmth. Calix, having set the water to heat, leaned against the table and picked up their conversation. He was no longer forced into a life of servitude for survival; he had grown healthy and bold. He followed Evera's training, taking to it adeptly.

Until the baby was born, I would not be visiting the capital again. The trip I'd taken a fortnight ago would be my last for some time. Harlan was doing fine without me. My guidance at this point was really more for the sake of conversation and a different perspective than anything else. He could rule the kingdom on his own. He had others, too, to take counsel from now that he had the wits and knowledge to listen to each person and consider their words, then make decisions for himself.

Once, I'd woken each morning in my guards' quarters, void of light or life, greeting each day with a cot, a chest, and a small table with a washing basin. Nothing more. Now, I had a home, a family, and friends I'd made in town. We were making a life where I could watch Evera shine, watch her use her skills, and fulfilling a purpose.

My mind flitted back to the evening we first met in the courtyard on the night of the festival. It was true what Evera had said about us all having monsters. At the time, I'd been too focused on the physical image of my fox to see the deeper meaning of her words, but now they rang clear.

Our monsters, our demons, were no more than the tribulations of our past. For Evera, they were the memory of her mother's death and of the man who hurt her. For Calix, his monsters were the lives of his family that he'd taken when his magic first came to him, when he'd lost control. And for myself, I released a breath, letting the pain come and flow through me, accepting it. Mine was the look in Thatcher's eyes in his last moments, and the knowledge that his death was my fox's doing. The horrors of that day had led me to believe Astraea's words, her lessons, when she told me to suppress the other half of myself.

I pushed off the wall to join my family. We would always bear our monsters, the broken pieces of ourselves. But together, with patience and care, we could embrace the broken, wounded, and fractured parts of ourselves and accept them for what they have made us. Accept that each unforgivable truth and each hardship shaped us.

Beyond the love and the connection we shared, that strength of acceptance would leave our souls forever bonded.